# *The*
# SOLDIER'S
# GIRL

ALSO BY SHARON MAAS

*Of Marriageable Age*
*The Lost Daughter of India*
*The Orphan of India*
*The Soldier's Girl*

THE QUINT CHRONICLES
*The Small Fortunate of Dorthea Q*
*The Secret Life of Winnie Cox*
*The Sugar Planter's Daughter*
*The Girl from the Sugar Plantation*

Sharon Maas

# SOLDIER'S
# GIRL

bookouture

Published by Bookouture in 2018

An imprint of StoryFire Ltd.

Carmelite House
50 Victoria Embankment
London EC4Y 0DZ

www.bookouture.com

ISBN: 978-1-78681-681-8
eBook ISBN: 978-1-78681-680-1

*In Memory of Trudel Elsässer (1909–2011)*

# Lili Marlene Lyrics

*Outside the barracks 'neath the lantern light*
*There you'll find me standing, I'll wait for you tonight*
*Under the lamp, that's where we'll meet,*
*I'll be there waiting on the street,*
*For you, Lili Marlene*
*For you, Lili Marlene*

*Our shadows join there, united in embrace*
*In the lantern light I gaze upon your face*
*Holding you close, we are as one*
*Remember this, when I am gone*
*From you, Lili Marlene*
*From you, Lili Marlene*

*There goes the bugle, it calls the last tattoo,*
*Leaving you here will break my heart in two*
*I'd rather stay here by the gate*
*Under the lantern, though it's late*
*With you Lili Marlene*
*With you, Lili Marlene*

*You'll be waiting for me, listening for my feet*
*I'll be longing for the day when next we'll meet*
*One last kiss, and we must part*
*But I will hold you in my heart*
*Just you, Lili Marlene*
*Just you, Lili Marlene*

*When I am marching in the freezing cold*
*Fighting as I'm ordered, and trying to be bold*
*Brave I am not, but love is strong*
*And if I die, you'll sing this song*
*For me, Lili Marlene*
*For me, Lili Marlene*

# Prologue

## June 1944

She jumped. Or rather, she let herself fall. Into the translucent night sky, silvery from the full moon's glow, inky and endless, empty. Beneath her, the dark shadow of earth. Above her, the universe.

The Lysander curled away above her, the whirr of its propellers humming into the night's vast silence. She was alone in the moonlit sky. For a moment she tumbled downwards, towards earth, but then the soft silk of the parachute unfurled and she hovered there in the in-between state of consciousness that lay between one identity and the next, one life and the next.

'Sibyl Lake must cease to exist,' Vera had said. And so she dropped not only from the plane but from all that had been before, that old self a mere skin. Yet: *here I am*. Here, and now. She slid out of the crust called me, that Sibyl-me, out of that persona with a name and a past, parted from it like an old skin, useless, defunct, a cast-off peel. *Here I am*. No longer in the old identity, not yet in the new, and yet more real, more present than ever, free of identity and the care and the fear that are identity's twin features – a new me, one without limits. The endless night sky, dominated by a great round shining moon, held her safe in its heart, in a sense of great purity, great fullness, great peace.

Downwards she floated, towards the unknown.

A thud, brief pain, the solid touch of earth. She collapsed into it, into her new self, new name, new future. The silk of the parachute flayed gracefully and floated down upon her, a soft white shroud. France.

# Part One

## Those Halcyon Days

*'Who says I am not under the special protection of God?'*

*Adolf Hitler*

# Chapter One

## September 1929

'Girls! We'll be there in five minutes! Put away your things, now, and tidy yourselves up!'

Obediently, silently, solemnly, Elena and Sibyl closed the books they were reading, packed them into the little canvas bags their mother had given them for the journey, bent over to find the shoes they had wriggled free of soon after leaving Paris, and buckled them into place on their feet. Without a word.

This wasn't right, Kathleen thought. They should be bouncing up and down in anticipation, squealing with excitement. Not once had one of them cried out, *Are we there yet?* Not once, in so many hours. Sibyl hadn't once complained, *Mama, I'm bored!* – screwing up her freckled pixie-face, tossing her auburn curls. As for Elena, her little chatterbox: she'd been as silent as... but no. Not that word.

Both girls had been perfect angels all the way from London; reading their books, playing card games, holding Mama's hand at station platforms, sitting quietly on the ferry instead of running to the rails to peer into the Channel's swirls, going to the lavatory when Mama told them to, eating their packed sandwiches without a grumble. This angelic docility was unnatural, disturbing; it might make life much easier for a parent, but Kathleen would have given anything for just one little squeal of impatience during the never-ending journey. Shellshocked. That was the word. All three of them. Still shellshocked. Though there had been no shells. The telephone call from Mervyn's secretary, Miss Hughes had been bombshell enough.

And now, this flight to France.

Through her numbness Kathleen remembered train journeys from when she was their age, back in British Guiana. She and her sisters Winnie and Yoyo had been squirming bundles of eagerness, even though they knew the Rosignol to Georgetown trip like the back of their little hands. And her girls, too, had until recently, behaved like children should on day excursions to the seaside. Train trips were inherently adventures, even from London to Brighton. And now, London to Colmar? The girls should be brimming over with the thrill of it all, unable to contain themselves. But then she herself was hardly bursting with exuberance. Hopefully Margaux wouldn't be too disappointed. For so many years they had planned and promised to meet again; and now that time had come and she was just a shadow of herself, of the bouncy schoolgirl Margaux would be expecting. Well, no wonder. Margaux would surely understand. That's why she was here. To recover from it all. Kathleen sighed, and helped Sibyl with her bag. That's why they were *all* here. Before they withered down to nothing from sheer sadness and broken hearts.

She stood up, straightened her clothes, removed a brush and comb from her travelling case and tidied her own hair in the compartment mirror, before attending to Sibyl's tangles and Emily's plaits, loosened considerably throughout the trip. They all put on their hats, edged themselves from their compartment into the narrow corridor and along it to the doors. They had left their three suitcases near the exit; now, Kathleen pulled them free as they waited for the train to chug into Colmar station. She leaned forward past the girls, pressed the handle, swung open the door and urged the them to jump down to the platform. She got out herself and reached back into the train for the suitcases.

'Kathleen! Kathleen! There you are! *C'est moi!* At last! You're here! Welcome, welcome; and these are your little girls! Elena,

Sibyl, I am your auntie Margaux! I am so happy to meet you at last! Let me look at you – Kathleen, you are so thin! And your girls, so tall! And so pretty! Little English roses! Come, give your auntie a hug and a kiss! You understand French? Shall I speak English? You understand me?'

It was Margaux, indeed, just as she remembered her, the words, bubbling from her lips, some English but mostly French. As ever, kisses and hugs everywhere, all the exuberance so lacking in herself spilling out all over them so that, in spite of herself, she smiled and flung her arms around her friend. And clung to her, not letting go. And shuddered, so that Margaux at last drew still and hugged her again, this time in silence, and in reverence, and in depth.

'I'm so sorry,' Margaux whispered into her ear. She only nodded. Yes, this was Margaux. The same Margaux who had coaxed her, Kathleen, out of her shell when she arrived at Château Montrouge, a shy eighteen-year-old shunted off to a Swiss finishing school by grandparents who, having failed to secure a suitable bridegroom, didn't know what to do with her. Her dormmate Margaux, brimming over with energy and conviviality, had opened doors to Kathleen's spirit; they'd giggled into the night, broken all the rules, and earned themselves the nickname *les jumeaux terribles*, the terrible twins. They had stormed the gates of adulthood together, only to be torn apart the following year when Margaux returned to her family vineyard in Alsace and Kathleen had been summoned back to Norfolk and staid British upper-class convention. Since then, the letters had flown back and forth; they had promised again and again to visit each other, but marriage and then childbirth had interfered. Until today: Kathleen precipitated into Margaux's arms by catastrophe.

Aware of the girls, who stood silently watching next to the suitcases, Kathleen pulled away. The two women gazed for a few seconds into each other's eyes. Kathleen's were moist with unshed tears. She was afraid a dam would break, and it was too soon for that, so she forced a smile, and, for the first time since alighting on the platform, spoke: briskly, calmly, as if she had not just been on the verge of a complete breakdown. She *had* to hold on…

'Come on girls, remember your manners: shake Auntie Margaux's hand!'

Which they did, solemnly and politely.

Fortunately, Margaux too quickly regained her own composure. With the help of a porter and a luggage trolley she whisked the newcomers through the station and to the carpark, bundled them and the cases into the battered Renault waiting there, tipped the porter and settled herself into the driver's seat. The flow of words continued the moment they turned into the road, and Kathleen was glad of it. Already she felt perked up. Hopefully the girls would feel the same, especially as Margaux was addressing them specifically.

'My children are so excited,' said Margaux. 'They can't wait to meet you. Elena, Marie-Claire is just about your age – you're ten, aren't you? Nine? Ten? She's ten-and-a-half, as she insists, and she can't wait to have some more girls her age around the place, because Victoire is only three – a baby. Leon and Lucien – well, they might be only boys but Leon's Sibyl's age and he is eager to show you around. He's a bit rough and tumble, a typical boy, but he's friendly enough. I hope you like animals, because Leon has two dogs of his own and he will share them with you – he raised them from puppies! And Jacques of course, like a third son to me… Is it the first time you have been to France? Your first time in wine country? Let me know if I am speaking too quickly – remind me to slow down and if you don't understand something, just shut me up and ask! But your maman said you have a French nanny? So you are almost bilingual? Is that right?'

'They *had* a French nanny,' Kathleen corrected, in French. 'We had to dismiss her, of course. After – after it happened.'

'Oh. Oh, yes of course, I'm sorry. So sorry. I keep forgetting. How you say it in English? I put my foot in it, didn't I? Me and my loose tongue. So terrible. I'm so sorry.'

'It's all right.'

'But you must tell me. What happened… You said you'd write a letter with the details but you never did. Just telegrams. I only know that…'

'I will tell you everything,' said Kathleen, softly, looking over her shoulder to the back seat, where the girls sat quietly; looking out the window, hopefully absorbed in the countryside fleeing past. 'Later.'

'Yes. Yes of course. Later. Later we will have a long chat, you and I, and you will tell me the whole story. So sad. Devastating. When your telegram came I immediately rushed to the phone, but no-one picked up. But of course, you could come! You have always been welcome. You can stay for the whole summer, all of you, in fact, stay as long as you like. There is plenty of room at Château Gauthier. You have come at exactly the right time, too! Golden September, and the grapes are just plump and bursting to be plucked, little jewels shining in the sunshine, heavy on the vines! The whole of Ribeauvillé is golden with sunlight and everybody will be out in the vineyards and you will love it – those succulent grapes! And the wine, Kathleen! It is all exquisite, like heavenly nectar – the best wine in all of France! And now – here we are!'

She turned into a driveway and had not even drawn to a halt before the mansion at the end of it before the front door opened and a horde of small people poured out of it and swarmed around the car, squealing and hopping, hugging and kissing in French exuberance. Normal happy children, children whose lives had not been blown apart from one moment to the next. *This will be the cure.* Kathleen breathed out a long sigh of relief. She could already feel the healing seeping into her. Ribeauvillé was the remedy.

# Chapter Two

Margaux popped the cork from the bottle and poured golden liquid into Kathleen's glass. The sun was about to slip behind the rolling foothills of the Vosges mountains, and shadows were growing long, but the terrace was still flooded with warm light. The children were off somewhere with the dogs, all of them, girls and boys, young and old together, Elena and Sibyl seamlessly assimilated into the flock. The transition had happened without a hairline break; gloom ignored and swept away like so much debris, smiles lured from long faces, sparkle returned to dull eyes. They had been first infected by Laroche effervescence and then whisked away on a joyful tide of *bienvenue*.

'There is so much to explore,' Margaux said. 'They will be fine. Don't worry about a thing. This is not London. It is safe. Let them run.'

And slowly her own tension was melting, slowly the tautness loosening; the cocoon of sheer desolation that had wrapped her in tight bonds over the last week releasing its grip.

'Now, tell me,' said Margaux. 'How did he die? *Raconte!'*

Margaux spoke French, but Kathleen replied in English. So had it ever been, ever since their Montrouge days: though both were fluent in both languages, and understood perfectly, Kathleen would speak English and Margaux French. Kathleen's letters were written in English, Margaux's in French. Communication this way was perfect.

'He hanged himself.'

Margaux's jaw dropped in shock. 'Oh no! *Chérie!* Oh, how terrible! Oh, you poor poor thing! How? Why? Did you find him? What happened?'

'I didn't find him like that, thank goodness. His secretary did. At the office. He tied a rope around the curtain rail and jumped from the window ledge, into the room. That's how she found him. At least he didn't do it at home. Imagine if one of the girls had found him!'

'Awful. Horrible! But why? Do you know the reason? Had you suspected? Did you know he was thinking of suicide? Had he ever tried before, hinted that he wanted to end his life?'

'Not a word, Margaux, not a single word! That's the very worst of it. He never let it show, never hinted that he had a problem. He was always the wonderful husband and father to me and the girls. It was out of the blue. The girls were devastated. And so was I. I never… I never…'

The tears came then, and she faltered. Margaux reached out and took her hand. She sipped at her wine. It was delicious. Liquid gold, Margaux had said, and indeed it was.

'I never imagined he could do such a thing to us. He loved us, loved us all. We were his whole life, I know it. He adored the girls. We had a good, strong marriage. And all the time he was pretending, pretending everything was fine and life could just go on the way it was. Living the good life in a lovely riverside house in Kingston, a perfect intact family. And it was all a lie.'

'But… but do you know why? Why would he do such a thing? Why would he ruin everything?'

'Because it was already ruined, Margaux. It was all a sham. We were in deep, deep trouble but he never let on. I still don't understand what exactly it was. You know he was in finance – investment and that sort of thing. And you know me and numbers. I never asked what he did because it was his world and I just don't get it. I let him get on with it. Signed things he told me to sign. He did things, Margaux; took some big risks. Our money, his clients' money. He re-mortgaged our lovely house – that was the thing I signed. I suppose he thought he would get it all back. I don't know what he thought; we never talked about his work or his investments because it all just bores me. Maybe I should have taken more interest, read the papers I signed. But I trusted him. And then, ten days ago, the London Stock Exchange crashed. We lost everything, Margaux, everything. The house, everything. I suppose he couldn't handle it.'

'So he just left you to deal with it! That makes me so angry!'

'It makes me angry too but in a way I understand. Apparently, so I'm told, there wasn't a solution. He was ruined. We were ruined. No way out. So he chose this way. Thankfully, apart from losing the house, I'm not compromised. He made sure of that.'

'Did he at least leave a note? Apologise? Explain?'

Kathleen took another sip and nodded. 'Yes. Yes, he did. He did say sorry, and that it was the only way out he could see. He told me to go and live with his mother. His mother! Ha!'

'I remember you told me you can't stand her!'

'But only because she hates me. She's a bitch.'

'How could anyone hate you? You're the nicest person I know!'

'It's not so much me she hates but my background. You know my mother's half-Jewish. She's Austrian, and she and my dad fell in love and he whisked her off to British Guiana to live on a sugar plantation. That's where I grew up. So those are two strikes against me. Bad blood, bad background. She wanted a different kind of girl for her precious son, her only child. An English thoroughbred, with a perfect English upbringing. I didn't have that. Growing up on a sugar plantation, in a distant colony – well, even my own grandparents found me too crude, too unpolished, for high society, unable to make a good marriage. That's why they packed me off to Montrouge. Thank goodness for that, at least. I couldn't stand living with them either, though I liked them well enough.'

'But how did you end up living with them anyway? Why did you come to England? Why weren't you with your parents?'

'When I was seventeen my mother fell ill. It wasn't a physical illness. I think she was depressed about some things. A baby died and her husband, my dad… well, it's a long story, I won't go into it now. And she was homesick for Austria, winter, snow, and didn't like the tropics. Anyway, she and everyone thought it best she return to Austria to get better. You heard of someone called Sigmund Freud?'

'The mind-doctor? Yes, of course.'

'Well, she went to him to be treated… but anyway she was out of reach for us girls for a few years, and then she went back to British Guiana. She did pass through England on her way back and we do write, but, well, she can't help. And my father. You know what happened to him. I wrote to you all about it.'

'Yes, convicted of manslaughter!'

'Yes, over in British Guiana. He got life imprisonment which he was supposed to serve in England but he died in prison. So for my dear mother-in-law, that was strike three against me, the last straw. And Mervyn wanted me to go and live with her! Imagine!'

'So where are you going to live then? And what about the financial mess Mervyn left behind? Who's taking care of that?'

'One of my uncles is a lawyer, Dad's youngest brother. I put everything in his hands. He's trustworthy. He's dealing with the whole chaos, making sure I have nothing to worry about. But also, nothing to go back to. No job. No income. If only I'd taken my education seriously, back then. Got a degree like my teachers encouraged me to!'

'It was just all fun and games, wasn't it, for us girls? Looking pretty to get a good husband!'

'And I did get a good husband and I was happy enough until it all tumbled down on me.'

'So what will you do? Go and live with your English grandparents?'

'I can't. They're old and frail and their eldest son and his family lives with them and they certainly don't want to take on responsibility for me and the girls.'

Margaux refilled both of their glasses. 'Well, what I think is this. First you've got to get yourself healed. Recover from the shock. Get back on your feet, emotionally. You shouldn't have to worry about your future while that is happening. You'll do that here. You'll stay with me, for as long as it takes.'

'But – what'll Jean-Pierre say about that?'

'Jean-Pierre will agree. He agrees with everything I decide. I'm that kind of a woman – very wise. He makes the decisions concerning the business, but domestic decisions? I make those, all of them. And he will agree. And anyway, this is my house and I get to say who can stay here.'

'Oh Margaux! If only! But I don't want to be a burden. And I'm not quite empty-handed. I do have some jewellery, quite a lot in fact, Mervyn loved buying me jewellery. I'm going to sell it. It's not enough to keep me and the girls in London forever, but…'

'You'll stay here. The girls will go to the local school. They will soon be perfect in French – children learn so easily, don't they?'

'They are both good. And they know German fairly well, too. They had a German governess for a while and I helped them learn. I'm fluent in three languages, you know. Languages are my one skill. And my mother always spoke to us in German.'

'Excellent! French and German are the languages of Alsace. And you will all learn *Alcasien*, as well, a fourth language! You must now speak more French, become more fluent. It's something to think about for the future because one day you will be strong and stand on your own two feet and it is good to know many languages. Languages are bridges to whole new worlds and you are fortunate. In the meantime, you'll stay here. You're most welcome.'

'I'm thinking, Margaux; maybe, later on, I could be a translator or something? With German, French and English. It's something to build on, isn't it?'

'Later. It's a thought, but a thought that must be saved for the future. In the meantime, you're here, with me, at long last. And I want to put a smile back on your face.'

Kathleen's lips twitched, and she raised her glass.

'I'll drink to that! *S'gilt!* Margaux raised her own glass; the very chink as their glasses touched seemed to be a harbinger of better days to come.

# Chapter Three

It all happened so quickly. One minute she was in the car with Elena and Mama and Auntie Margaux and the car had come to stop before a big ivy-covered house; the next minute somebody had grabbed her hand and pulled her out into the sunshine. The somebody was a tall girl with long dark hair that was not in neat plaits, like Elena's, but falling all over her shoulders and even across her face; and the girl was smiling – no, laughing – and once she had scrambled upright on the gravel in the sunshine, feeling a bit dazed, the girl was kissing her on both cheeks and chattering away in French. She understood every word, of course.

'You are Sibyl!' said the girl. 'I know it because you are the smaller one. I am Marie-Claire and I am so glad you have come! I'm ten and I've been dying to meet you. And you're Elena and you're about nine, and I'm so glad to have another girl my age because I am surrounded by boys and boys are so *méchant* aren't they! You are lucky to have a sister and not a brother. But they are not so bad, really. This is Leon, and Lucien. Boys, you must be kind to Sibyl because I think she is a little sad.'

*Un peu triste.* A *little* sad! What did this girl, this Marie-Claire, know about sadness, or what was in her, Sibyl's, heart! She had obviously never known a day of sadness in her life, whereas her own heart was nothing more than a red-hot bundle of pain, a little ball of agony, and she didn't know what to do about it. Somebody she adored had been ripped out of her life and the pain was devouring her from the inside; she couldn't even think a proper thought because of it. *Papa! Oh, Papa! Where are you? Come back!*

Marie-Claire was still chattering, looking from Elena to her and back again. Obviously, she had taken control of the entire situation, installed herself as leader. '… and this is Jacques. He is not our brother but he pretends to be. He is here all the time and he is the most *méchant* of them all, and the oldest and biggest so he thinks he is the boss but he isn't, because I am the very oldest. And my little sister Victoire, she is the very youngest. She is only three but she likes to be with us and I take care of her. And Elena! Let me welcome you too, I am so glad you are here! Welcome to Château Gauthier!'

Victoire had already flung her little arms around Sibyl's waist, and then the boys were grabbing her hands and grinning; three of them when she had been expecting two. Sibyl didn't know much about boys. She had encountered few of them in her short life; one or two cousins, Papa's nephews, but younger than herself. There were no boys at her school in Kingston. It was a girls' school. Boys were strange creatures, but they couldn't be all bad because Papa had once been a boy and Papa was the most wonderful man on earth. Had been! Had been! Papa was gone!

Boys were loud and boisterous; that much she knew and indeed, that was what these three boys were being, very loud and very boisterous, knocking into each other, cuffing each other, bending each other's limbs backwards (or so it seemed) and *loud!* Deafening! It sounded even as if they were arguing. What on earth were they speaking? It sounded familiar but she didn't understand a word of it. It sounded like German, but it definitely wasn't – Sibyl knew enough German to tell the difference – and were they arguing or not? It sounded like it, and they were almost fighting, it seemed, but laughing at the same time! Boisterous, indeed!

'Leon, Lucien, Jacques! You must speak French now, because we have visitors! Mama said we have to speak French! And you have not greeted Sibyl and Elena properly!'

Hands were grabbing at hers now, boy-hands, and boy-lips were kissing her cheek, and boy-voices, shrill and loud and incomprehensible, filled the air – it was pandemonium, so much so that she couldn't even feel that red-hot ball of fire that had replaced her heart.

Aunt Margaux was speaking now, telling Marie-Claire to take her inside, to their room, and then to show her around the place, and now Marie-Claire had taken her hand and Elena's and was pulling them away towards the house. The boys were still prancing around and speaking – no, shouting – in that bizarre language. Was it some kind of secret code, like you read about in books? Everyone in France spoke French. That was simply a fact. But these boys seemed to have a language of their own, a boisterous boy-language that nobody else could understand. It wasn't fair, and they were still hopping around and bouncing off each other and shouting so she could hardly hear Marie-Claire speak. Victoire had taken her other hand and so they entered through the huge heavy front door, into the cool darkness of the house, and then up a staircase – oh! She had forgotten her bag with the books and she needed it because she intended to do a lot of reading in France. Reading was the only thing that stopped the pain or at least kept it in abeyance, at least for a while. A parson had come to visit Mama several times in the last week and he had asked her if there was anything he could bring her and she had said books; and he had brought a whole box full. She had taken her pick, and brought as many as Mama had allowed to France, and she would read them all to dull the pain.

The boys tumbled backwards up the staircase, ahead of them, behind them, all around them, falling over the banister and still shouting in gobbledygook. Marie-Claire still held her hand but had let go of Elena's and they walked up together. She liked having that hand in hers. It felt steady and strong, sending a message that said, *it's all right. You are here, I am here; you are in good hands. Everything will be fine.* Thought it couldn't possibly be fine, ever again. Not without Papa.

'This is your room, and Elena's. Come in, Elena, see, this is your room. I wanted you both to stay in my room, it's big enough for three beds! But Mama said you would want to be together, at least at first, but later when we become best friends you can move in with me, Elena – and you too, Sibyl! And we will have such fun. I always wanted a sister – I mean, I do have a sister, but I mean a sister my age because those brothers… well! And two of them! And Jacques, who thinks he is a third brother and everyone thinks so too. I am buried in boys so you can't imagine how happy I am that you have come, you are like two new sisters. And we will go to school together, on Monday, and I will be able to show you off to all my friends and we will have such fun together! Do you like ponies? My friend Amelie who lives not far away, she has a pony of her own and I'm sure she will let you ride him, she let me! Look, I will show you Amelie's house. It's not far. Come.'

Marie-Claire pulled her over to the window and there they stood, all three of them –the boys had momentarily disappeared – gazing out over the valley. And she couldn't help it; she sighed at the sheer gloriousness of it. Gently rolling hills spread out before her, each one of them covered in the neat rows that she knew were vines, golden-and-green vines, bathed in golden sunshine, rolling away from her in wide undulating folds. Dotted here and there among the hills, a building, a rooftop; and in the distance, a village, a church tower. Clusters of trees, a field of cows. Not a road to be seen, not a car. After the piercing noisy grey streets of London, the stuffy claustrophobia of Grandma's place, this seemed like – well, like a piece of heaven. She could breathe again – a long, deep breath. And it seemed, though she couldn't be quite sure, that the searing ache at the centre of her being seemed to heave a huge sigh and release one of the bands that had held her so tightly in the terrible last ten days.

'That is Amelie's house,' Marie-Claire said, pointing, but Sibyl hardly heard her; she was too busy breathing in the splendour of the sight spread out before her. And for the first time since arriving, she spoke the one word, the only word, worthy of the vista spread out before her:

'*Magnifique!*'

# Chapter Four

The boy they called Jacques was rude. Maybe it was just because he wasn't a family member and so didn't feel obliged to greet her and Elena; but mostly because he was the one that insisted on speaking that strange language. While the others at least made an effort to speak French, Jacques spoke stubbornly in that strange tongue and all the others followed suit, except for Marie-Claire. Everything Jacques said or did seemed to cause disruption.

'Where shall we go first?' Marie-Claire said now. 'To see Gigi's puppies, or to the vines? Gigi's one of our dogs,' she explained, as if that wasn't obvious.

At the word 'puppies' Sibyl's head jerked up, and at 'dogs' she smiled fleetingly and a sparkle leapt into her eyes. As far back as she could remember she had begged for a dog, and just as far back Mama had said no. A dog had been the one thing missing in an otherwise perfect life; the one family member whose absence she had felt day and night. Now, of course, it was different.

*Papa!* The wail came from deep inside and once again she collapsed internally. Gigi and her pups evaporated, the sparkle in her eyes snuffed out. But Jacques, once again, was shouting something loud and brash in his gibberish, and Marie-Claire arguing back, the two of them in a violent verbal battle. Jacques stormed off, followed by the boys. One moment they were there, in the room with them, the next, Jacques was out the door with Leon and Lucien behind him, thundering down the stairs, while Marie-Claire was still in mid-speech.

Sibyl turned back to the window, to the view, so that no-one would see the tears gathering in her eyes. *Papa!* The boys came into view beneath her, racing out the door, across the driveway and disappearing around the corner of a building that looked like a huge stone barn.

'They have gone to see the puppies,' Marie-Claire said. 'They are four weeks old and so *mignon!* Jacques is besotted with them. He thinks he owns them. It is strange because Jacques is such a wild boy and he likes doing wild and naughty things but those puppies – *oh la la!* He thinks Gigi needs him to help take care of them but she doesn't. He's such a nuisance, that Jacques. I was going to take you to see them but now he is there, he's so bossy about those pups, so I don't want to go. I will take you to see them later when he's gone. We can go now to look at the vines. We also have a nanny goat. And two more dogs, but they like to go off to hunt rabbits. They are called Milou and Paris. Come, let's go. Come, Victoire, take my hand.'

'I want to hold Sibyl's hand,' said Victoire, doing just that. The four girls made their way back down the stairs into the kitchen; a big green square room where pans hung from the ceiling and pots of herbs lined a long windowsill. Mama was there with Auntie Margaux, who said,

'Hello girls; have you been up to your room yet? Did you like it? Isn't the view wonderful? Kathleen, I will take you up in a minute but I need to prepare the dough for the *tarte flambée* we are going to eat tonight. Run along, girls. Marie-Claire, you can take them to see the vines maybe?'

Marie-Claire was just like her mother, she never stopped talking. Sibyl knew it was polite to listen attentively, and that's what she did. Marie-Claire, leading them down a pathway that turned off from the main drive, was now explaining about the harvest, which, she said, was imminent.

'We have to find just the exact right time to start the harvest,' she was saying. 'When the grapes have achieved their maximum sweetness, when they are succulent and plump and just begging you to pick them. Monsieur Dolch is a genius, he always knows the exact day. Monsieur Dolch is the father of Jacques. He is our winemaker. He is very good. Jacques knows it too. Jacques can tell you exactly when it is time to begin the harvest. He thinks he knows everything about grapes already but he doesn't. His father knows more but is teaching him. Oh, here he is again. Jacques Dolch! Why did you bring those puppies? You should not separate them from their mother yet, they are too small! It is cruel! You think you know everything about grapes and puppies but you don't!'

Indeed, Jacques and the two Laroche boys had come running up, each with two puppies in their arms. Behind them ran a silky black dog, obviously concerned about her pups, looking up beseechingly at Jacques, who now held his two down for her to lick them.

'I just wanted to show *them*,' said Jacques, pointing at Elena and Sibyl with his chin, but not looking at them. Instead, he put one puppy in Sibyl's arms and one in Elena's.

These were the first French words he had spoken since their arrival. 'Gigi is right here. She doesn't mind,' he continued, in French, and then broke into a deluge of words in that strange tongue; his tone was quarrelsome, and so was Marie-Claire's when she replied.

Sibyl, busy stroking the squirming pup, couldn't help it. Irritated by this rudeness, she interrupted: 'What are you saying? Don't you know it is rude if you have guests to talk in a foreign language?'

Marie-Claire looked immediately apologetic, but Jacque's annoyance – with Marie-Claire, or with her, Sibyl couldn't tell – was palpable. He glared at her for a moment and then said, in perfect French, 'I am not speaking a foreign language. I am speaking *alsacien,* because I live in Alsace and I am *alcasien.*'

'In English, that is Alsatian,' said Marie-Claire, in English. 'But Jacques does not speak English. We should all speak English so he can see what it feels like.' She repeated what she'd said in French, for Jacques benefit, who, it seemed, did not understand English.

Jacques retort was in Alsatian, and there followed a stream of even more gibberish, but obviously wasn't, since Leon and Lucien laughed loudly and even Marie-Claire seemed to be holding back a chuckle, which to Sibyl seemed like betrayal. She needed to protest.

'But Alsatian is a dog – a breed of dog! It isn't a language!' Her favourite breed, besides. Her cousins in Norfolk had an Alsatian, and that was the kind of dog Sibyl wanted. Though any dog was better than none. And here there were *three!* And puppies! She cuddled the one she held, rubbing her cheek against its warm fur, and kissed it.

They laughed all the louder, though Marie-Claire stopped immediately, grew serious, and said, 'Did they not teach you history in your school? Did you not know that when you came to our place, to Alsace, you are coming to a country embedded in two countries, that we have our own culture, our own language, our own identity? If you want to understand us you must learn *alsacien.*'

Sibyl and Elena could only shake their heads. No, they knew nothing of all this. Sibyl felt ashamed of her outburst, ashamed of her ignorance, ashamed of putting that ignorance on display. Most especially, of doing so before Jacques, that most exasperating of boys. She stood there biting her lip, trying to come to terms with her ignorance and her embarrassment. But Jacques wasn't paying her awkwardness any attention. He had turned to the vine behind him, plucked one plump green grape and was inspecting it, shading his eyes as he held it up to the sun, before biting into it. A glazed, dreamy look came into his eyes; he seemed to be rolling that grape around in his mouth, savouring it with every cell of his body. *He is far away,* Sibyl thought, *on a planet of his own.*

'*Mercredi prochain,*' he said, in French, landing back on earth. He retrieved the puppies from Elena and Sibyl gently but firmly and without a further word in either French or Alsatian, clasped them to his chest, and gambolled off, Leon and Lucien scampering behind him, and Gigi prancing around them all, yapping.

'*Il est fou,*' said Marie-Claire, 'but he's probably right about the harvest. Next Wednesday! Let's just hope the good weather holds.'

# Chapter Five

The rich deep clang of a gong ripped into Kathleen's consciousness.

'*À table!*' called Margaux from the kitchen. Kathleen rubbed her eyes and sat up; she had lain down on the couch for a rest but drifted off into sleep, and right now she'd prefer to simply lie back down and disappear back into oblivion. Better yet, go up to her room, put on her nightie, and lie down for the night. Sleep! Delicious sleep! She had not slept properly for –well, not since her world had imploded, almost two weeks ago. She would have preferred to forgo dinner and lie back down and not wake up again until… until the world was back in order again. But that was not to be.

'*Je viens!*' she called back, standing up and walking to the downstairs lavatory. She splashed her face with cold water. That helped.

'Jean-Pierre is home!' said Margaux. 'He has been on business in Paris since Thursday but now he is back. He is just putting away his things in the office and then you will meet him. Where are those children?'

She walked to the bottom of the stairs and cried out, '*Enfants! À table!*'

The dining table was in a bay at the end of the kitchen, the windows on all sides overlooking the vines. The children appeared, one by one, and washed their hands at the sink, the Laroche children chattering away in Alsatian as usual, the Lake girls as silent as ever.

'Do not speak Alsatian here! We have guests!' admonished Margaux, and, mid-sentence it seemed, the chatter turned to French. Margaux smiled at Sibyl and Elena.

'Don't worry about it. You will soon pick it up, especially since you know German. Children are so good at picking up languages, aren't they?' This last was to Kathleen, who smiled and nodded but said nothing. She felt dulled from her rest and really wasn't in the mood for small talk, or any kind of talk, actually; and now she had to meet someone new, Jean-Pierre, and somehow be interested and polite. But no. None of that internal grumbling. It wouldn't help the situation. She was a guest; she had to behave. She pulled herself together just as Jean-Pierre walked in.

His physique was the exact opposite of his wife's. Margaux was short and soft and curvy; Jean-Pierre was tall and thin, with sharp edges everywhere. He had a long thin face, high forehead, a strong jaw and almost pointed chin. *Cold,* thought Kathleen spontaneously, *this man is cold.* Whyever did Margaux marry him? They are so unsuited... but there's no telling where love will fall, or on whom.

Introductions over, Jean-Pierre took his seat at the head of the table, facing the bay. Margaux placed a steaming hot *tarte flambée* in the centre of the table, returned to the oven and fetched another one. 'I'm sure you must all be starving,' laughed Margaux, and Kathleen discovered that she was, because as well as not sleeping she had eaten not a single full meal since Mervyn's death.

The conversation at table was polite. All mention of Mervyn was avoided. Marie-Claire helped by proclaiming that harvest would begin next Wednesday, according to Jacques.

'Is that so?' said Jean-Pierre. 'That boy is very astute and usually right, just like his father. I will go and see Maxence tomorrow. The Dolch men have wine running in their veins, not blood.'

Margaux looked at Kathleen. 'Monsieur Dolch is our wine-maker. He is Jacques' father. He is so clever when it comes to the growing of grapes and making wine.'

'Dolch – that's a German name! How strange; they both have French first names.'

'Yes; a lot of families here have German surnames and French first names – and there's a girl, too, Juliette. Madame Dolch, the

mother, died at Juliette's birth. Alsace is a hybrid nation. Back and
forth between France and Germany. Since the war we are French,
before the war we were German, and before that we were French.
Now we are French again; since the Great War. And we are going
to stay that way. That is just politics, though; the people just call
themselves *Alcasien* and have done with it. Let the politicians do
what they will. All we want is to raise our families in peace and
enjoy our wine. *N'est-ce pas,* Jean-Pierre?'

'That is so,' said Jean-Pierre, 'but in the end it's about the wine,
and Germany isn't happy to have lost that. Don't bury your head
in the sand, Margaux. Germany is unforgiving, a proud nation. It
does not accept defeat easily.'

'Pah! Let them suck it up. Now we are French and we will remain
French to the end of time. Germany lost the war and that is that.'

'Germany doesn't think so. They want Alsace back.'

'Let them try! Idiot Germans! We are French now.'

'Well, they have certainly left their mark. So many German
surnames, German place names – Turckheim, Kintzheim – even
Strasbourg is more a German name than French. And the Alsatian
language is based on German.'

'We are French! Don't even mention the word Germany to me!
We are French, are we not, children?'

*'Oui, Maman!'* came the chorus.

Jean-Pierre turned to Kathleen. 'Margaux is extremely anti-
German, because the Germans killed her beloved Papa.'

'The Battle of Mulhouse, 1914. The French army tried to get
back Alsace, which they had lost in the Franco-Prussian war. Papa
was in the first attack, when the army tried to recover Mulhouse.
But the Germans made a counter-attack and that's when Papa fell.
May he rest in peace.' She crossed herself.

'The wounds run deep, as you can see,' said Jean-Pierre.

Margaux rolled her eyes. 'Because the cut is deep. But in the
end we won and since the war Alsace has been French.'

'And Germany isn't happy. It's a proud nation – sooner or later it's going to want Alsace back.'

'Poof! Never!'

'Darling, you're so naïve. Germany is just across the Rhine. Do you think they are twiddling their thumbs?'

Margaux turned to Kathleen. 'My dear husband thinks there will be another war and Alsace will be German again. Over my dead body.'

'I would not advise you to say such things. Another war is a very real possibility.'

'Don't scare our guest. It's rude. Nothing is going to happen.'

'Nevertheless it is foolish to hide one's head in the sand. Everyone is tired of war, but…'

*'Exactement.* Germany is tired too. Alsace is French and will remain French. There's no need to be scared. Nothing will happen. Everyone is tired of war. Even the Germans –ordinary Germans I mean, mothers and fathers who only want to live their lives and raise their families in peace. People like us.'

'But there is danger of another attack, sooner or later. France knows this. Why do you think they are building the Maginot Line? Have you heard of the Maginot Line, Kathleen?'

She shook her head.

'Well, it does not even exist yet but it is planned over the next few years: it's a series of defence reinforcements all along the border, on the French side of the Rhine, mostly north of Strasbourg; battlements to defend us against a German attack. France would not go to such extremes if there were not a real danger of attack.'

'I said don't talk of a war that will never happen to our guest. I'm going to change the subject. Kathleen, how do you like our riesling? It is good, *n'est-ce pas?* Have another glass.'

# Chapter Six

'So, what do you think of Jean-Pierre?'

Startled, Kathleen looked up. She had been gazing into the darkness beyond the bay window, captured again by grief, and hadn't even noticed that Margaux, having gone up to say a last goodnight to the children, was back and had slid into the window seat opposite her. Elena and Sibyl had gone to bed an hour earlier, exhausted from the day of travel and adventure. Jean-Pierre had retired to his study. 'Work!' he had said. 'It follows me home – no respite for a winegrower!' And had left them to their own devices.

Now, Kathleen didn't know what to say.

'What an odd question!' she managed at last. 'I've only just met him – and besides, he's your husband, Margaux! Of course I – well, of course I accept him!'

Margaux wrinkled her nose. 'Accept is not the same as like! I would like your honest opinion. He is rather negative, rather cold, *n'est-ce pas?*'

'Well I… I mean, I don't think my opinion… ah…'

Margaux broke out in giggles; and once again she was that uninhibited schoolgirl from Montrouge, irreverent and seeing the funny side in all circumstances.

'Ah, your very English manners forbid you from telling the truth, I can see it! You don't like him but you won't say it out loud. But you can be honest with me, Kathleen; I won't hold it against you. I think we should be straight with each other from the start. No –what do you call it – beating around the trees.'

'Beating around the bush. Well, to be honest, I did find him a little, er, distant, maybe.'

'There you go, so polite! But maybe you are right, maybe distant is the correct word. He is certainly distant to me, his own wife, so I can imagine how he feels to a stranger. But you are my best friend, *chérie,* even though so many years have passed. And I do not want to have secrets from you, and I hope you can share your own secrets. You made a very good beginning this afternoon. Come, have some wine. This is our very own gewürztraminer, Domaine Laroche-Gauthier.' She filled Kathleen's glass and then her own, and set the bottle down. Kathleen reached out and took her hand.

'Margaux – I am so sorry. This afternoon I unburdened myself to you, poured everything onto your lap and I didn't even ask how you were doing. It just all seems so perfect here. Perfect home, perfect view, perfect children, perfect wine…'

'But not perfect husband, I'm afraid.'

'You never really told me, back then, I thought it was so strange. That you got married as soon as we left Montrouge. You didn't tell me anything about him, you'd never mentioned him when we were at school. But six months later, you were Mrs Laroche. I did wonder, but I was afraid to ask. It seemed so sudden. I just assumed it was a whirlwind romance; after all, I know you went to Paris immediately after school and I thought that was so romantic – but I wondered why you never mentioned falling in love so quickly, enough to marry. You never even described your fiancé and I didn't want to be nosy.'

'Ah, Kathleen. There's a story behind that. I will tell you. But first, let's drink to the future, and a new era. I just know that you have brought good fortune into my not so perfect life! *Santé!*'

Their glasses chinked, they smiled at each other, they sipped their wine.

'I don't know about bringing good fortune. But you have certainly already turned my life around. I feel so much better already!'

'Then *santé* once again! To a new beginning!'

They drank again, and then Kathleen said,

'So – you have a story you'd like to tell me?'

'Indeed. This marriage of mine. You thought it was a whirlwind romance? Ha! The opposite was the case. It was an arranged marriage, Kathleen. From the start. Even my attending Montrouge School was part of the arrangement.'

'What! How bizarre! How did that happen? Who arranged it?'

'Well, that's the story, you see. This vineyard has been in my family – the Gauthier family – for generations. But then my dad was killed in the Great War and I was the only child, no son to pass it on to. My grandfather was a very dominating man; he was in charge of everything but the vineyard had been doing badly for some time before that and he was worried about what would happen, seeing as I was only a young girl. So he thought it was better for me to marry a wealthy winegrower.'

'And your mother? What did she think?'

'Maman had no say in the matter.'

'Where is she now?'

'She is in Colmar, with her parents – her mother is infirm and she is looking after her. When they are gone she will move back in with me; we have a cottage waiting for her. Anyway – to get back to my marriage: I didn't really mind, at the time. It just made sense. So Grandpère cast his eyes around for a good match but there was no-one suitable in the Alsace. So he had to look further afield and he found the Laroche clan, from Burgundy. They had a handsome son of marriageable age, vineyards aplenty in Burgundy, and were looking to expand. At the time our vineyard was quite small, just twenty hectares. But next door there was another vineyard, and that was failing too. The Dolch vineyard.'

'Dolch – you mean…?'

'Exactly. Maxence Dolch, the father of Jacques. One of the best winemakers of the region, unfortunately not a good businessman. He knows about wine, not about money. He was forced to sell; the Laroches bought both vineyards and combined them to make one big Domaine, Domaine Laroche-Gauthier, and Max Dolch was employed as winemaker; that was his condition of sale. But I was part of the deal. The vineyard would be Jean-Pierre's Domaine, and I would marry Jean-Pierre.'

'Oh my goodness! Did you not have any say in the matter at all?'

'Remember, I was just a young girl. Grandpère was the head of the family – everyone did what he said, and it never even occurred to me to object. I sort of assumed that marriage automatically meant you fell in love with your husband and lived happily ever after. It was exciting! I let myself be swept up in the wedding preparations. I met Jean-Pierre of course, in Paris, and he treated me well. I saw no reason not to marry him, and if it would save the vineyard – well. Of course I was willing. All this was arranged when I was only sixteen.'

'But then – why did you even bother to attend a Swiss finishing school? If it was already planned that you should marry?'

'Ah, but you see, I was just a simple country girl. I grew up running around this place, mostly barefoot, at least in summer. Gorging myself on grapes. A little wild thing, very crude. And of course I spoke Alcasien, nineteen to the dozen! The Laroches were quite posh. Upper class wine people. They wanted me to be an acceptable bride, with good manners, speaking really excellent French. To be a suitable Laroche bride, a bride they could show around at Paris *soirées* and so on. You see, they were absentee winegrowers. They were never really involved. They'd never even picked grapes at harvest: imagine that!'

She shook her head and refilled both glasses.

'So finishing school it had to be. I had to be polished off. I had to learn manners, good French and English. A suitable Laroche bride. All my rough edges rubbed away to make me nice and shiny. But at least I met *you* there. My best friend ever, even though I had a secret I kept from you: that I was already engaged to be married. Frankly, I was a bit ashamed of it: you were such a softy, with all your dreams of falling in love one day and getting married, of meeting some Prince Charming who would sweep you off your feet! How could I tell you about my own very business-like marriage arrangement! So I left Montrouge all shiny and refined and all my rough edges removed and married Jean-Pierre in a fantastic, elegant wedding. After that they installed me in a mansion in Paris, and that's where I was supposed to live out my days. It was horrible!'

Margaux took a big gulp of wine, as if to cope with the very memory of that horror.

'Horrible!' she repeated as she refilled her glass, and tried to do the same to Kathleen's. Kathleen, unaccustomed to wine, her head already spinning, placed a hand over her glass and shook her head.

'I can imagine,' she said.

'Anyway. I soon found my spark. And my feet and my tongue. I refused to live in Paris. I insisted on moving back to Alsace, to this house, the house where I grew up. Luckily, Grandpère had made sure there were clauses in my marriage contract that said I could live here whenever I wanted and I dug in my heels. I knew I would raise my children here, and I did. So this is my home.'

'And Jean-Pierre? Does he mind? I mean, doesn't he prefer Paris?'

'Oh, Jean-Pierre! He doesn't matter. He takes care of the business, and he's good at it. He makes money. He lives here, in Paris, in Strasbourg. He comes and goes. He has his mistress in Paris and he's welcome to her. Marriage was a business arrangement for him and it remains that way.'

'That's so – sad!'

Margaux shrugged. 'Not really. I don't mind. I am very busy here and just being able to live in my own home, and watch my children grow, that is happiness enough for me. I am happy in my own skin, and Jean-Pierre – he can do as he pleases.'

'I cannot imagine being married to a man I did not love.'

'Ah – but you see, you are English. You dream of romance, of fairy tales and happy endings. We French are more practical.'

'I always thought it was the other way around – you know: Paris, the city of love, dashing Frenchmen, elegant Frenchwomen, romance, courtship…'

Margaux chuckled. 'And that is what we have done well! Sold you the fantasy, so that you English will keep coming to France! And now I have you here, I will keep you captive for as long as I can! As long as you want to stay! Come, have some more wine! No? Very well. I won't force you. Not tonight at least.'

'But, Margaux – I feel bad. I can't let Jean-Pierre support me. I mean, I will sell my jewellery and contribute to my maintenance, but there are three of us, and…'

'Pah! My husband will not be supporting you. *I* will. Grandpère's lawyer arranged the contract so that not only does the house remain solely in my name; I also get a good fair share of the profit from the vineyard. So I have my own income, and I can spend it however I want. I am queen of this house, and if I choose to embrace a homeless family of three, then Jean-Pierre cannot say a word! Didn't I tell you that what I say goes, inside this house and regarding domestic arrangements? Jean-Pierre does the business, but I am the heart and soul of this place and I want you here. *Compris?*'

Kathleen laughed. *'Compris.'*

# Chapter Seven

Kathleen awoke to sunlight pouring through her half-open window. The curtains fluttered in a cool breeze, and birds twittered in the trees outside. Margaux had given her an east-facing room and for the first time since Mervyn's death she had slept a whole night through, soundly, deeply, instead of tossing and turning the hours away. She stretched, got out of bed and walked over to the window and looked out. She could see activity among the vines and realised that everyone else must have been up for ages. She longed to crawl back into bed, enjoy more of that luxury sleep – but no, Elena and Sibyl were probably up as well, and she was a mother.

Washed and dressed, she made her way down to the kitchen. Margaux was clearing away the remains of breakfast, leaving one place setting.

'*Güete Morge!* I won't even ask if you slept well! The girls are up and out in the vines, helping out. I thought I'd take you out after breakfast, show you around?'

'That would be lovely! Thank you for taking care of the girls. I overslept – that never happens usually! I've been sleeping so badly, since…'

'It's a very good sign. Sleep is what you need. Sleep heals. Take as much of it as you need, for as long as you want. The girls are safe and happy. They were both smiling and even laughing at breakfast.'

'That's a miracle! They have been walking around with such long faces. I can't thank you enough, Margaux!'

'They are on the road to recovery. It is hard to lose a beloved Papa – I know it myself. You never really get over it and they are so young! I was fifteen and that was bad enough. So it is good that they are settling in. Come, have some tea – it's what you English like for breakfast, isn't it? And the jam is home-made with my own strawberries. I will show you my little garden first and then we will go into the vines. I grow almost all my own vegetables. And we have some fruit as well and lots of flowers. Gardening is what I do best, what I love. What do you call it: my hobby, but it is a useful hobby, and very healthy. It keeps me fit in every way – it is good to work with the earth, with plants! I will show you. We have all day. I am not going to do any housework today because a girl from the village is coming in to help, Leah. And you can tell me more about your life in England since Montrouge, and I will tell you all about growing wine.'

'Your story is much more interesting than mine,' said Kathleen, spreading a slice of bread with butter. 'I can tell you in one sentence: I met Mervyn, got married, had babies. But, you know, I was happy. I loved him. But it was a fool's paradise. I had no idea he was up to his neck in a financial mess and there was no way out, except – except the way he chose, which left a worse mess for me.'

Tears gathered in her eyes. Margaux said, 'Oh dear, I'm sorry. Maybe we should not speak of these things just yet if they make you cry. I am just going upstairs for a minute and I'll be back and then we'll go out and I will show you around and we will find the children.'


'We in Alsace produce the best wine in all of France,' said Margaux. She led the way along a long row of vines. 'It is because the location is truly exceptional, perfect for making wine. It is a blessed land; everything is perfect for producing the best grapes. Perfect soils, noble, wonderful climate – one of the driest in France, which means so much sunshine. These here are our riesling grapes; the leaves have been removed so that they can bask in our delicious sunlight and absorb it. See how plump they are! Go ahead, pick one and taste!'

The grapes indeed were plump, hanging in succulent bunches on the vines on either side of her. She picked one, put it in her mouth, bit into it. The grape burst open. Its flavour exploded into her mouth. Her eyes lit up.

'Oh! Oh Margaux, that was the most delicious grape I have ever tasted!'

Margaux giggled. 'Go on, have some more! But don't gorge too much because we have other grapes for you to try. Gewürztraminer, pinot gris, muscat, and also crémant d'Alsace which is a sparkling wine, and a basic blend. We only make white wine; most Alsace wine is white, but some wineries also make pinot noir, but we don't. Come along, don't devour all of our riesling otherwise there will be none left for the harvest! Come on, down the hill, this is where… oh!'

A man had suddenly popped up from behind a row of vines, and stood before them, grinning. Looking at Kathleen, he removed his beret with an exaggerated sweep and bow.

'*Bonjour, Mesdames! Bonjour,* Margaux! You have not yet introduced me to your beautiful guest!'

'Max! Max, you scared me, you could have been anyone hiding down there in the vines! What are you doing there?'

'Who did you think I was, a murderer escaped from prison? And since you are not going to introduce me, I will introduce myself. Maxence Dolch. Call me Max.'

He replaced his beret and held out a gnarled, weather-beaten hand to Kathleen, his grip firm but fleeting.

'Kathleen Lake,' she said.

'Ah! She is English. That girl you told me about, the one from that posh school?'

'Indeed. She is visiting for a while and I am showing her around.'

'I believe my son Jacques met your daughters yesterday? And they are all working in the vines this morning. Removing leaves from the pinot gris. And I – I am just inspecting. We expect to start the harvest on Wednesday. The weather is stable and everything is perfect. You will stay for the harvest, Madame Lake? Help with it, perhaps? We need all hands.'

'Yes, I'll be here and I'll be helping. I really look forward to it.'

'Then I will help show you around, and tell you something about our grapes, so you will know them when the time comes. You must talk to them when you are picking, you know. That is the secret of my excellent wines. My grapes are living beings and they understand every word, in any language. They want to be loved, and if you love them enough they will reward you with a wine that tastes like nectar of the gods. Is it not true, Margaux?'

'I'd say that's a good enough description.'

'Indeed. With every bunch you cut from the vine you must tell the vine *thank you*, and apologise for hurting it, and explain that the wound will heal and that it is going to give great joy to many people. You must be grateful and humble to the vine, understand that it is listening, that it is alive and quite willing to give you its best. See, I have revealed the great secret of the Domaine Laroche-Gauthier!'

'Max, you are *drôle*!'

'No, it is not funny. It is the truth. I know you are too practical to engage in such conversations with grapes, Margaux; I know you don't believe me and you refuse. But maybe your lovely guest will oblige. Will you, Madame?'

Kathleen couldn't help laughing. 'I certainly will, if you say so! I can't wait to start!'

'Then come along and let me introduce you to my grapes. They will be delighted to make your acquaintance. You have met my rieslings; now I shall take you to my gewürztraminers. This way, if you please.'

# Chapter Eight

And then the harvest was upon them. Jacques Dolch had been right; Wednesday was the perfect day to start, the grapes at maximum sweetness and just waiting to be plucked. Max gave the order. Grape pickers poured in, from Ribeauvillé and other villages and even further afield, including a group of young people from Paris who came every year because this was a time of celebration and great joy. They swarmed through the vines, armed with knives and other sharp tools and buckets, wearing bright head scarves (women) and floppy straw hats (men) against the still-hot late September sun. And as they worked they laughed and chatted and flirted, and in the evenings they sat around in the paddock next to the house and lit fires for cooking sausages and drank wine and sang and even danced.

And the Lakes were all a part of it; Kathleen out in the vines from early morning with Margaux, and Jacques taking charge of the girls. The moment they were home from school, their harvest began, Jacques collecting them at the kitchen door, waiting impatiently as they changed out of their school clothes, leading them off down the rows, standing by their sides to make sure they did it right. He was blunt and bossy but kind at the same time, the kindness swelling just below the surface of the blunt bossiness so that anyone with an ear for the subtleties of human interaction could feel it in the touch of his fingers, hear it in his voice, see it in his eyes.

'An extraordinary boy!' said Kathleen at the end of the first day. 'I am quite in awe of him! So mature for his age – not like a child at all.'

'He had to grow up quickly, not having a mother – she died in childbirth. Max did his best to be both mother and father to him, and he certainly succeeded. He can be a little rough around the edges but he has a good heart. He reminds me a little of myself as a girl – running barefoot all over the place, in love with the country, with the vines, with the grapes. But he is more mature than I was. If it is still warm after the harvest I'm sure he will take the girls camping. He has a little place in the Vosges mountains, a little cabin he built by himself next to a stream, and the children like to play there together.'

'You are not afraid, to let them go off on their own?'

'Me? Afraid? *Mais non.* For one, they are off my hands, and for another, they must learn to be independent and not afraid of the things of the countryside.'

'I could not let my girls go off on their own in London.'

'Well, that is why I did not want to live in Paris. One of the reasons, the other being that I am completely incompatible with big city life and I missed my home, this place, my beloved Alsace. The vines – oh, the vines! It is intoxicating, is it not? This is the best time of year. It is like the very air is filled with the spirit of wine; she floats invisible through it and whispers in our ears and fills out hearts with such joy. Do you feel it?'

'Yes – yes I do!'

'The patina of grief, that I saw in your eyes when you first arrived, it is slowly fading, Kathleen, and I am glad. You will always have good memories of your dear husband but he is gone and you must return to life. It is what he would have wanted. I am sure that he has found a happy place and you must too.'

Kathleen sighed. 'You're right. The sharp edge of grief has gone; it's still there, but it's no longer the black abyss it was when I first came. And I am not in any danger of falling into the abyss. I could even say that I am at peace now. In a way.'

'And your girls are recovering too. Did you see them laughing and dancing after supper, with those students from Paris? That girl, playing the guitar and singing?'

'I did! And Sibyl is delighted with the dogs, the puppies. It's what she always wanted, you know. It's like a dream come true, and Mervyn's death no longer haunts her. It's as though they have found the cure just by being here.'

'Children can bounce back quickly, under the right circumstances. And we have the right circumstances. Just us mothers; no Jean-Pierre to lecture us about politics and scare us about war.'

Jean-Pierre had returned to Paris; he had disappeared early one morning.

'I don't know why he does that. Every year it is the same. The moment harvest begins he is off like a hare, to the city. He is a winegrower with his cheque book, not with his hands. He does love to drink it, though, and he has an excellent palate – he knows his wines. People respect him for that.'

'Margaux, would you mind if I ask you something a little private?'

'Ask away! You can ask me anything you want. How often we sleep together, or even if we sleep together, and if he is a good lover!'

She chuckled, and so did Kathleen, who replied,

'No – nothing like that, but, well. I suppose it's none of my business, but I did wonder... you and Max... are you...?'

'Are we lovers? You mean, it shows?'

'Yes... I'm afraid it does. Your eyes light up when he appears. I noticed it the very first time we met.'

'Even though he was flirting with you!'

'Oh, I didn't take the flirting seriously. He was just being a typical Frenchman. But, the way you looked at each other; that was something beyond flirting. So – you are having an affair, right under Jean-Pierre's nose?'

'Well, Jean-Pierre has his mistress in Paris so why shouldn't I... but, Kathleen, you know, this is more than an affair, more than just a little *amour fou,* a little passion. Max and I were childhood friends, you know. We are deeply connected. And we are no longer lovers. That stopped with the birth of Victoire.'

'You mean… Victoire is…'

'Yes, she is. But then we realised we had to keep a physical distance. It is for the best. It is not a problem, for he lives here.' She clutched her heart.

'But… if you were childhood friends, why did you not marry?'

'We were childhood friends, not lovers. Marriage didn't occur to us. And we did not know we loved each other until we were both married with children and it was too late. Anyway I could not have married Max. We both had failing vineyards… it was not expedient. Max married a friend of mine and when she died, soon after Juliette's birth – well, I went to comfort Max and somehow love grew from that.'

'Juliette – I have not yet met her.'

'But you have surely seen her. She is that very pretty girl, always laughing. Today she wore a red dress and a yellow headscarf. I saw her playing with your girls, dancing with them.'

'Oh, that is Juliette! But – so you and Max just decided to love each other from a distance and pine for each other? And you say the French are not romantic!'

'Everyone has a bit of romance in their souls. But one cannot let romance rule one's life. One must be practical. Everything else is just sentimental, and sentiment is what ruins a good life. We should not take our sentiments and our dreams and secret desires too seriously, otherwise we are a little ridiculous, and weak. We must be stronger than our feelings. That is what Max and I have decided. It would be too complicated otherwise.'

'I suppose you're right.'

'I am right, no supposing about it. And now I am going to open a bottle of our muscat. You will love it. It will round off a most wonderful day and a most wonderful conversation. You are the only person in whom I have ever confided about Max.'

'But Margaux, you must learn to hide it better.'

'Then I will have to dig out my eyes. The eyes cannot hide the truth; they cannot hide love. And when I am with him, my eyes cannot help but speak. They speak to him; but you have read their language and discovered my secret. So we must drink to that.'

She filled the two glasses.

'It's so sad, though! People who love each other should be together!'

'Not at all. It's being apart that lends true depth to love. For if you cannot be together in body you are forced to dig deep inside to be together in the soul. All great love stories are built upon that premise. So you see, you need not feel sorry for Max and me. We are having a wonderful love story, the kind that would have you weeping in a motion picture. No, that is not a call for you to cry and go all sentimental. Drink up your wine.'

# Chapter Nine

## 1935

That was the first of five harvests the Lakes lived through in the Alsace. Wonderful years followed. Years in which Elena and Sibyl learned that grief can be managed; that it must not debilitate. That their father would live on deep within their souls, never forgotten, but that their lives would continue and their souls would flourish and this place, this Alsace, this château, would provide the nourishing soil out of which they would thrive and grow and blossom. It was the best of lives.

The girls attended the local school and made friends with the local boys and girls; with the Laroche children as their adopted brothers and sisters acceptance was immediate, and as for the language – well, what had seemed gibberish in those early days soon opened its secrets and, young minds being fresh and open and absorbent, in a matter of weeks both girls were chattering away in Alsatian as fluently as their friends.

Inevitably, there was a pairing off. Elena and Marie-Claire, being of similar age, became the best of friends. Leon and Lucien, of course, stuck together, as boys of that age do. And Sibyl: well, Jacques might be three years older than her, and a boy; but ever since he had thrust that puppy into her hands she adored him. And, indeed, he was adorable.

Yes, Jacques had a rough exterior. Having grown up without a mother, he was somewhat lacking in table manners – but then again, his favourite food was baguette and cheese, Munster cheese

from further south in the Alsace, which he ate by tearing off great
chunks of both, and never while sitting at a table. Jacques liked
to eat on the go; and he was always on the go. He disdained
schoolwork, preferring to help his father in the vineyards, and
had an innate knowledge of all growing things, of all things that
came from the soil. It was as if he had roots himself; that his feet,
so often barefoot in the summer, absorbed all the wisdom earth
could give, a wisdom far beyond the knowledge found in books.
Jacques simply *knew;* but he could never explain how he knew.

When he was not needed in the vines Jacques would disappear
into the cool shadowy forests of the Vosges foothills. Often he took
Sibyl with him. It was like being under a protective wing.

Sibi, he called her; or *ma petite soeur.* For although he had a
sister, only a year younger that Sibyl, Juliette was a daddy's girl, who
clung to her father and did not need the closeness or the guidance
of a big brother. That year's age difference also made Juliette just a
little too young for the adventures Jacques could offer, or to tune
into his depths. Sibyl was open to both. Her mother, trusting
Jacques, allowed her to follow him into the woods, and to learn.
She learned to fish and to hunt; he taught her the use of a slingshot,
though she would never, as he did, catch a rabbit with one, and
skin it, and roast it over an open fire. But she could watch him do
these things; and she learnt which berries and mushrooms were
edible and which not, and where to catch the best fish, and how.

It was possible to be silent with Jacques and never feel that
the silence had to be broken with words, because the silence was
complete; a heart-filling silence in which she felt such communion
with him it was as if they shared a soul; and from year to year as
she matured she began to understand that silence was Jacques'
method of communication, the way he learnt what the earth had
to teach him. The trees, the birds, the insects, the plants, the vines
and grapes, all these manifestations of nature had a common root,
a common source, a common wisdom, something that could be

known only by going there oneself; and going there meant learning a secret silent language. And slowly Sibyl learnt that language.

They were glorious years. All the more devastating when they came to an abrupt end. Sibyl was twelve, Jacques fifteen, when she was torn from him.


By 1934, Elena and Sibyl had become fully fledged *Alsaciennes*; Sibyl especially, could remember no other home, loved no other homeland; it was as if the previous years, the years as a happy English family with dear Papa at its head, were entirely wiped from her memory by their tragic climax and she could not remember England.

But sinister rumblings came from beyond the Rhine, as *Oncle* Jean-Pierre never ceased to remind them. Germany was a threat that loomed over them, cautioning them not to relax too deeply into their cradle of bucolic confidence. The now-complete fortifications along the Rhine, the Maginot Line, seemed to underscore, rather than relieve, the fear of every *Alsacien* that Germany lurked just over the river, eyeing their homeland with avarice and injured pride.

'Losing the war was bad enough,' said Jean-Pierre – the same litany he had sung at that first dinner, five years ago – 'but losing the Alsace, well, that was the final thorn in Germany's side. They want us back.'

'But we are French. How…?'

'French, German, French, German: mere labels. What the Germans want is our wine, our wealth. The Germans may be known for their expertise in building machines. But do not be deceived. The German soul is essentially more subtle than this skill in engineering might indicate. Remember, this is the land of poets and philosophers: the land of *Dichter und Denker,* as every German will remind you. It's the country of Bach and Beethoven and Goethe and Rilke, minds capable of soaring to the heights.

But such a mind can also descend to the depths; if such a mind is not tended, it can convert to its opposite, can become wild and murderous. The German mind longs for Truth and Beauty, and when it is denied those things, anything can happen. That is why the Germans are so admiring and so envious of the French: because we are so much more refined. But it is above all our wine that seduces them. And ours is the best. Mark my words, Margaux, Kathleen. The Germans will be back. They do not take defeat lightly.'

'Oh, you with your scare stories! Jean-Pierre, it is too much. I do not want to hear this nonsense and neither does Kathleen. Anyone would think you *want* the Germans to come, just to prove yourself right. Me, I do not believe in poisoning the present with fear of the future.'

'We must be realistic. Our government would not be going to the expense and trouble of creating fortifications from Switzerland to Luxembourg if there were not a present and real danger. Do not hide your head in the sand, Margaux. It is serious. It's not just about fear; it's about preparing ourselves just as France is preparing itself. The Maginot line is real and we too must do something real.'

'What are you talking about?' Margaux took a sip of her riesling and caught Kathleen's glance across the table. She rolled her eyes *(Jean-Pierre is such a scare-monger!);* but Kathleen could not grin back nor raise her glass. Once again, Margaux was dismissing Jean-Pierre on principle, not listening to his actual words. This had to do more with the state of their marriage than with logic, with the undercurrent of contention between the two that festered constantly in the atmosphere, a disturbance in the air that could not be precisely identified as it simply hung there, nebulous, a vibration that could only be picked up by an inner mental sensor; and only by a person who had such a sensor; and Kathleen did. And, unlike Margaux, Jean-Pierre's words sent a cold shiver down her spine. On this question of Germany she could only wonder: *what if it is true?*

'I am telling you not to hide your head in the sand.' Irritation trembled in Jean-Pierre's voice. Yet another fully fledged quarrel hovered on the periphery, ready to burst.

Once again, Kathleen found herself in the role of peacemaker. Could these two not see that sometimes it was just their choice of words, the tone in which they were relayed, that was the problem? That provoked? Why could one not have a sensible conversation, especially about a matter so serious? Why could Jean-Pierre not see that 'telling' Margaux not to 'hide her head in the sand' was guaranteed to ensure that she stuck that very same head still deeper in the metaphorical sand, precluding a sensible discussion? Why did marriage have to be so hard? Between her and Mervyn it had never been like this. They had *listened* to each other, even if there was disagreement, and chosen words that were respectful to the other. Now, it was her role to appease, as ever. The matter was too serious to allow it to descend into bickering.

'Jean-Pierre, if you are right, is there anything we could do? I mean, it's frightening to think of Germans at the gate but we are now in peace so surely we should…'

'Thank you, Kathleen. Margaux, your friend is again much more astute than you.'

Kathleen cringed. There it was again. An accusation that would only raise Margaux's hackles, an unwarranted belligerence which furthermore placed *her*, Kathleen, in the middle of a potential squabble. And suddenly, she was angry. For a woman who was basically mild-mannered, who never rose to any bait, who represented the best of English courtesy and equanimity in all circumstances, that was a sign, an indication that it was time to speak up, to let that anger out.

'Would you just *stop* it, you two!' she cried, and hammered her fist on the table.

Margaux and Jean-Pierre, shocked into silence, stared at her. She continued.

'Just *stop* it! This is not the time to fight or to live out whatever grievances the two of you have! This is serious! Margaux, I'm sorry but in this Jean-Pierre is right. Do you not read the newspapers? Listen to the radio? Are you not aware that there's a new leader in Germany, a chancellor who is full of rhetoric and aggression? Have you not heard the name Adolf Hitler?'

Margaux's jaw wobbled like that of a goldfish. Sounds came out of it, but none intelligible.

'Thank you, Kathleen! As I was saying…'

'You stop it too, you smug prig! This isn't the time to show how clever you are. You might be right but it's not enough. The question is, what will happen? And is there anything we can do? Any way we can prepare?'

Margaux sniffed. She wore an expression of boredom, but at least she seemed to be listening.

'If Germany attacks…' Jean-Pierre began.

'Germany is not going to attack,' said Margaux. 'If they do come they will just steal our wine. All I care about is the wine. We must hide it.'

And so it was Margaux, she who had adamantly and over years denied that there was any danger from across the Rhine, who not only won the argument but instigated the work that would occupy them over the following year.

Château Gauthier was built upon a huge cellar, one that extended far beyond the footprint of the house. It was Margaux who decided that part of the cellar should be sealed away, and their best and most valuable wines should be hidden behind a secret wall; Margaux who organised the building of that wall, and, in fact, built most of it herself, with the help of Kathleen, the children, Max and Jacques Dolch. And Jean-Pierre.

Somehow, Margaux's concession that the Germans were, after all, a present danger, and her decision to prepare for a possible invasion, was all that was needed to bring appeasement into her marriage. Jean-Pierre, he who never once had dirtied his hands with physical work before this marital ceasefire, and never would be seen in anything but an immaculate suit, astounded them all by rolling up his sleeves, changing into an old pair of dungarees that had belonged to Margaux's father, and plunging right in, carting bottles and crates back and forth across the cellar, mixing the mortar for the brickwork, and even driving the rickety old van to fetch bricks from the brickwork in Colmar.

But Kathleen was still not satisfied. 'It's one thing to hide the wine,' she said to Margaux one night while the cellar reconstruction was underway, 'but what about people? What about us? If Germany attacks…'

'Germany is not going to attack.'

'Then why all the work downstairs? Why hide your best wine, if you are so sure?'

Margaux only shrugged. 'Just in case.'

'So you concede there is a possibility of attack?'

'I do not concede anything!' Margaux raised her voice and emptied her riesling. 'But if – and it is a very remote if – Germany invades, and proves to be a threat, well, humans are more flexible than wine. Also, humans can adapt to circumstances, fight, or flee, as the situation demands. Wine – well, it would be totally exposed. We could not hide it overnight. Thus we must take precautions, where our precious wine is concerned.'

'But, Margaux, the Germans are said to be a brutal people. You have children. Are you not afraid for your children? If they attack…'

'I am saying they will not attack. The worst they will do is *invade* and reclaim the Alsace, just as they have done in the past. If – well, *if* they come, the worst that will happen is that we will all change nationality, become German instead of French, and life will go on. Grandpère changed nationality four times! That is why I am more concerned with them plundering our cellars than with actual danger to our lives. They will want the winegrowers to continue producing the best wine in the world, but for the German market, not the French. It is a politician's game. Why would they harm us? And anyway, remember, we have the Maginot line and we are safe behind it.'

'But, Margaux, Jean-Pierre said…'

'Oh, Jean-Pierre! He is such a big pussy with his fear of the Germans and he has infected you. This is because he is Parisian, and you are English, *une femme anglaise*. You hear the word *German* and immediately you are in panic, because the Great War is still haunting you. The past has you hobbled with fear of Germans. We Alsatians, we do not fear the Germans. They are just across the river; they are people like you and me, they grow wine too; we have that much in common. It is the politicians playing games that create such fears. I do not fear even Adolf Hitler himself – let him come! They say he does not drink wine; he is a teetotaller, and so he does not scare me, such people are rabbits. Me, I only fear soldiers coming here to my house waving their weapons about and raiding out cellar. But if you are really in fear you are free to go, back to England, with your children.'

Kathleen said nothing, because she was indeed fearful of the Germans, the great bogeyman of the last war. She wanted her children to be safe, and Jean-Pierre's warnings of war, substantiated by newspaper and radio reports, chilled her to the quick. The very voice of this Hitler person – well, if a voice alone could freeze blood, his was that voice. For all the love she held for Margaux and this idyllic place, she had to put the girls first. One could not be sentimental at a time like this.

But, the girls! They had made a home here. It was basically the only home they knew, England having receded far into the past. Could she take them away? Could she desert Margaux, who seemed to have her head stuck deeply in the sand? Could she truly return to England? After all, she was no longer the forsaken and devastated wreck she had been at first arrival. And a *situation* was developing… and six months later, a decision had got to be made.

\*

Kathleen had put her time in the Alsace to good use. Once her initial desolation had receded –a process that had taken a little more than six months – she had taken a course in shorthand and typing in Colmar. Soon after that, she had, through Jean-Pierre's contacts, secured a job as a bilingual secretary with a wine merchant in Strasbourg. She worked three days a week, rented a room in a boarding-house for working women two nights a week, and came home to Château Gauthier for long weekends. It was an ideal situation.

It was there that she met the Englishman Edward Clark. He was in his mid-forties, half-French, not particularly handsome but certainly not ugly, an accountant at the same company, practically her boss, but anything but bossy. He was courteous, engaging and slightly boring, which did not bother Kathleen, for boring seemed to her to preclude the dangerous venture that had destroyed her first marriage. She sought not new adventures but stability, solidity, calm, characteristics that practically defined Edward. She found she was developing feelings for him. Not exactly the romantic passion that had first drawn her to Mervyn but something quieter, perhaps deeper. Edward certainly had feelings for her, as he revealed on one of their after-work rendezvous in Colmar.

He came to Château Laroche one weekend, as a test. The girls liked him: test successful. A year later Edward was offered a job as the company's agent in London; a well-paid promotion, which it would be ridiculous to decline. Edward asked Kathleen to marry him, and to move back to England with him. She accepted his proposal. Secretly, and full of guilt, for fear of impending war was not the least of her motives.

'I feel terrible!' she confessed to Margaux. 'You have been so kind to me and now I am leaving you to – to whatever is to come, to the uncertainty of the future. How can you ever forgive me?'

But Margaux only hugged her and, philosophical as ever, encouraged her. 'Go!' she said. 'Go and build a life of your own. I will miss you, but I have felt your restlessness. Do not worry about us. We are strong, we are resilient. Alsace will stay Alsace, whoever is in power; wine remains wine, and even the Boche love wine and therefore will not destroy its source. Life goes on, through all the changes. So what if Alsace becomes German again? We will still make wine, won't we? But you, you are English and you will not be happy under Adolf Hitler.'

'But surely…'

'I loathe the man, and what I have heard of him. He is as un-French as is possible. My allegiance is to France, and always will be. But we are farmers, wine farmers. Kathleen, politics to me is a game men play, just like little boys playing with their guns. It is a power game. All I want is to be safe with my children. The British Foreign Office has advised your Edward to return, and return he must, and you must go with him. Though I will miss you desperately!'

'I will miss you too – and the girls! What will I tell the girls? This is their home; they will be devastated!'

'Yes – it will be hard for the girls to leave. But you know what, children are resilient, and adapt quickly, and as long as their Maman is with them they will be fine. They like Edward, and will accept him as a father. And, Kathleen, believe me, they need a father, a good father, even though they are no longer young children. Jean-Pierre can never be a father to them. He isn't even a father to his own children.'

'But I feel so guilty, deserting you at such a time!'

'Do not feel guilty, *chérie. C'est la vie;* circumstances change. We must adapt to the changes, even though they might not be to our liking. Make the best of things. I do not feel you are deserting me. I feel you are moving on with the flow of your life; it brought you here when you needed to be here, and it is taking you back to England because the time is ripe for such a move. You can go with an easy conscience because I want you to go, even though I will miss you.'

'I will miss you too! I will miss this place, your wonderful family, the house, the vineyards!'

'New and wonderful things will come your way. Look forward, not back. We will cope. The Boche is no match for Alsace!'

And she raised a fist, and shook it, in brazen defiance of anything the Germans could do, and laughed; but she laughed too soon, as time would show.

Elena and Sibyl were indeed devastated when told that they would all move back to England.

'But we belong here! It is our home!' wailed Sibyl.

'You will find a new home, in England. And you can come back to visit, every year. We are going, Sibyl. Please don't make a fuss. I know you don't want to but in life we cannot always get what we want and it is better you learn that now; it is a lesson that will make you strong.'

'My heart will always belong to Alsace!' said Sibyl as they drove away in the car, and Kathleen rolled her eyes. There was no such thing as *always,* and what did young people know? They had their dreams but dreams can easily fall apart, as her first dream, her first marriage, had done. Better to follow Margaux's advice, and be practical, and adapt to the circumstances of reality, the ones you cannot change.

Because, in her heart of hearts, Kathleen was terrified. The Germans were altogether too close, and too threatening; Jean-Pierre, whenever he came up from Paris, seemed to relish his accounts of just how precarious the peace was.

'Mark my words, the Boche will return, and Alsace will be the first to fall when they march in. The Maginot line will fall like a line of matchsticks stuck in the earth, and now that they have this Adolf Hitler…'

Unfortunately, it turned out that Jean-Pierre was right. In September 1939 Britain and France declared war on Germany following the invasion of Poland two days previously. The British deadline

for the withdrawal of German troops expired, and their worst fear
became their worst reality. War.

Jean-Pierre was also right in another matter. The Maginot
Line was useless. But it did not fall; it was simply ignored. When
Germany invaded France it was from the north, through Belgium
and the Low Countries. The Battle of France ended in a stinging
defeat. Paris fell. British forces were driven back to Dunkirk and had
to be rescued. Safe in her home in Sussex, Kathleen watched all this
with anguish, and yet more guilt and worry for her friend Margaux
and her children, from whom there was no news whatsoever.

Kathleen had encouraged both her daughters to train in skills
that would stand them in good stead through life by giving them
the means to support themselves, even if they were to marry and
have children. Her own life had taught her that it was not a good
thing to be entirely dependent on a husband. One never knew…

Elena went into training as a bilingual secretary, like her mother,
and soon after starting her first job met her husband. Sibyl had ideas
of her own. Through *Oncle* Jean-Pierre she had always known there
would be another war, and always known that she must prepare,
and always known she would become a nurse.

Sibyl began her nurse's training in 1938, in Guy's Hospital,
London. In September 1939, after war with Germany was declared,
a section of Guy's was evacuated out of London. Sibyl continued
her probation at the Kent and Sussex Hospital near Tunbridge
Wells, Kent, near her own home in Three Bridges. It was work
that cut deep into her consciousness. France! Her beloved France
was broken, wounded, dying. *She had to get back…*

In early June, 1940, the reality of war hit her for the first time.
Sibyl was ordered to report to Casualty, and there she was plunged
into the true horror of war: her patients, from now on, were the
wounded of Dunkirk.

They were brought in by running orderlies, some screaming,
some too wounded even to scream for they were unconscious.

Some with burns that covered their whole body, their skin black and blistering; some with limbs torn apart, their flesh in ribbons. Some had to have legs and arms amputated. She had to dress the remaining stumps; stumps on young men at the prime of life. Some were blinded. And those were just the physical wounds. All would carry invisible wounds; their nights evermore would be disturbed by horrendous nightmares. They would wake up screaming, howling, or never sleep at all but only howl. Their days would be distorted by memories; they had endured and seen horrors that no human should ever see. Things that would remain as memories never to be erased. They were maimed for life.

Some of them were French. As the only nurse, indeed the only employee, on the ward who spoke fluent French, Sibyl was indispensable, both as a translator and as a confidante to the wounded French.

Occasionally there were German prisoners of war; she translated for them too. Spoke to them. Some of them were no more than boys and they reminded her of her French adopted brothers Leon and Lucien. She wanted to hate them, but she couldn't. People were just people, she realised. All labels, all classifications, were just that: labels, classifications. Divisions. French, German – what did it matter? These were no more than *attributes,* labels; ideas, characteristics, descriptions superimposed over the foundation of one's basic *humanness,* one's true naked self. It was identification with labels that caused all the strife in the world. That divided people. All the messes, all the chaos, both internally and externally, came from people identifying with the label instead of their basic humanness.

Externally, such false identifying could, and had, led to war. The English now fought the Germans and sought to kill them and vice versa. One set of labelled people destroying another. These poor German boys: they were not evil. They were not the enemy, sinister and fear-inducing. They had only followed orders. They were only wounded boys. Their pain, their screams, were no different to the pain and the screams of the English or the French. Somewhere in Germany there were women whose hearts ached for them: their mothers. Every wounded and dead soldier was some mother's son, no matter what his nationality; because humanness, and the love that binds us, makes no distinctions and is free of labels.

So Sibyl tried to treat her German patients exactly as she treated her English ones. One could call it love; but maybe that was too strong a word. It certainly wasn't a word that could be spoken out loud. Because this was wartime, and she bore a label, and so did they, and the reality of these times demanded an adherence to those labels, a pretence.

As a nurse, a good nurse, her obligation was to care for all equally. At the same time, the reality of wartime meant that she must play the role she found herself in, and that was an English nurse, with an obligation, a duty, to take sides. With a hunger for the war to be over, the Allies to win, and France to be free.

It was a role that cut deep into her consciousness. France! Her beloved France was broken, wounded, dying. She had to get back.

Her training complete, Sibyl applied to join the Queen Alexandra's Imperial Military Nursing Service. She received her letter of acceptance. But then she met Mr Smith.

# Part Two

## 1943: Perspectives

*'The Victor will never be asked if he told the truth.'*

*Adolf Hitler*

# Chapter Ten

It was a most mysterious summons. Matron told her no more than that she should attend such-and-such a meeting at such-and-such an address in London; and that she would be given an afternoon off to do so. The ward was hopelessly short-staffed; Sibyl could not understand it, but she went anyway.

The address was at an inconspicuous terraced house in a dingy side street near Victoria station. She found herself outside a tall, grubby building, accessed via a door in an alleyway to the side, next to it a row of buttons with equally grubby name labels. She checked once more the slip of paper she had been given and pressed the bell next to the name 'Inter-Services Bureau' and waited. After a short wait the door was opened by a young woman smartly dressed in a grey suit. 'Hello, I…' The woman nodded curtly and took the letter out of Sibyl's hand, read it, and signalled for her to follow.

The woman led the way into a dimly lit hallway, then up a flight of stairs and down a second hallway, through a door that led to what seemed like a small, sparsely furnished waiting room with a small desk in the corner on which stood a telephone and a pile of ledgers. The woman knocked on a door at the far end and opened it without waiting for a reply.

'Miss Lake is here to see you, sir,' she said, and stood aside while waving Sibyl in.

This room was just as sparsely furnished as the waiting room, but the desk was large, too large for the room, really. The man behind it rose at her entry, stretching out his hand for her to shake. He smiled.

'Do sit down, Mademoiselle Lake,' he said, in French, and as she did so, continued: 'I do apologise for the mystery surrounding this meeting; I promise that it was necessary and you will understand why in due course. You may call me Mr Smith.'

Sibyl nodded, more mystified than ever.

'… but bear with me a little while longer. Before I come to the point, I'd like to know a little more about you. You were brought to our attention because of your ability with languages. Apparently you were a godsend on the Men's Casualty ward because of your ability to translate for the French patients as well as the German patients who were prisoners of war.'

'You were spying on me?'

He chuckled. 'One of my colleagues was a patient of yours. He heard you chatting with both French and German patients and was impressed – you are fluent in both languages, you speak like a native… and you were overheard telling a French patient that you spent some years in the Alsace. Is that right?'

Sibyl nodded again, and as he seemed to be waiting for an explanation, continued in perfect French, 'After my father died my mother moved there to stay with an old school friend. I was six at the time; but I was already fluent in French because we'd had a French nanny. We lived there for six years and returned to England when my mother re-married. My stepfather is half-French. We speak a lot of French at home. Mama insists.'

'Ah, I see. And do you also speak the local language, Alsatian?'

'Yes, of course. I went to the local school and mostly we children spoke Alsatian. Though we always had to speak French at home. My aunt's home.'

'Did you enjoy your time in France?'

'Oh, yes! I love France. My heart breaks at the thought of it in German hands. Especially the Alsace. We have had no news from our friends there since the war began, since the Occupation.'

'Well, unfortunately it is more than an Occupation. The Alsace has been annexed by Germany, who reclaimed it almost immediately. It is now officially part of Germany. The people of

Alsace are now German citizens. Probably the authorities do not allow letters to England. We are the enemy.'

Sibyl closed her eyes and took a deep breath. Of course. Of course that had happened. Obviously. But hearing it stated so bluntly: well, it hurt. It was one thing for the Alsace to fall within the boundaries known as Occupied France. But the maps she had seen had not been clear enough, they had included Alsace; France up to the Rhine. Perhaps the map-makers did not acknowledge the new German boundary. But for Germany, it would count – and for the people living within that border. It was exactly as *Oncle* Jean-Pierre had predicted. He, Aunt Margaux, the children, Jacques Dolch: they were all now, on paper at least, Germans. It was heart-shattering.

All of a sudden Mr Smith was speaking German. 'You also speak fluent German. Where did you learn that?'

Sibyl was certain he already knew the answer, but she replied anyway. 'From my grandmother. She's Austrian, from Salzburg. She lived with us for a while when we were children. She always spoke German with us, even though she could speak English. She said that was the way to learn, by immersion in the language. She said that another language is a bridge between two cultures, an important skill. In fact, she's staying with us right now; she fled Austria just before the war started.'

'She is, I believe, half-Jewish?'

'Yes. Her mother was Jewish.'

'You have a sister?'

'That's right. Elena.'

'And relatives in British Guiana?'

'Yes: two aunts, and several cousins. The Quints. Most of the cousins signed up; they're all in the BEF. Sometimes they come and visit us, when they have leave.'

'And they all speak fluent German.'

'Yes.'

The conversation came around to her training as a nurse. Here too, Mr Smith seemed to already know about her life. It was almost as if he had been spying on her. He knew details about her life that a complete stranger had no need to know.

'I understand, *Fräulein* Lake, that you have a – er – a male friend? An RAF pilot, Lieutenant Grant? Are you engaged to be married?'

Sibyl blushed. What should she say?

'Well, Lieutenant Grant and I have been – seeing each other for about a year now. But we are not engaged and have no plans to marry. If we are both alive when the war is over – if – you understand, it's impossible to make such plans at the moment.'

'I understand fully. Forgive my curiosity. You will understand later.'

*Let me understand now,* Sibyl yelled at him, but only in her mind. *What is this about? How do you know all this? Why are you interrogating me?*

But he had already moved on, and now he had switched back to French: 'I've heard that you were particularly commendable during the bombing of the Kent and Sussex hospital in 1940. Calm and efficient, your superiors say. Thoroughly trustworthy. We made further enquiries. In particular you have a reputation as being cool-headed in times of danger – such as after that bomb attack. Self-sacrificing, hard-working, compassionate, unshakeable under pressure. Is this how you see yourself?'

'Well – ah – I can't say, there are other nurses just as hard-working and self-sacrificing as I am. We are all like that. It's our training.'

'So I can add modesty and humility to the list of accolades.' He chuckled. 'Well, Mademoiselle, it might very well be that there are many other nurses just as capable as you. But we are looking at your special talent, and that is your languages. Fluent in French, German and Alsatian. That is rare, very rare for an English person. Particularly the last language, Alsatian. And this is why I wanted to have this informal talk with you. We are wondering if you would consider war work in France?'

'Of course! This is why I applied to the Queen Alexandra – I love France. I want to see her free again; I want to be a part of anything that will liberate her.'

He nodded. 'I'd like to speak about France again. Tell me more about your life in the Alsace, this family you lived with.'

Sibyl needed no further invitation; she spoke of her years in France with delight and yearning. She spoke of the vineyards and the harvests and the wine. She spoke of the people: Margaux and Jean-Pierre, her friends, Marie-Claire, Leon, Lucien, Victoire, Jacques.

'They are like my own family! The children, they are my brothers and sisters!'

'This boy, Jacques – he is not a member of the Laroche family?'

'No. His father is Maxence Dolch, the Laroche's winemaker. But they are all friends together. They do everything together. It breaks my heart to think that their home is in occupied France.'

'Annexed, not occupied. Strictly speaking, their home is now in Germany.'

'That is worse yet.'

'So, again – you became a nurse so you could return to France, if and when we invade.'

'Yes. I suppose that deep inside I was hoping I could be posted to the Alsace but I know that is an illusion. If Alsace is now German…'

He nodded. 'Work as a nurse in Alsace would be unlikely, impossible, in fact, even after an invasion. The field hospitals would be near to where the fighting is. The work you are being considered for is not in the field of nursing, unfortunately.'

'I see. Well, I would welcome any opportunity to use my skills, to help the war effort – please tell me more! I suppose it would be translation work?'

'Sort of. Perhaps a bit more than that. Unfortunately, I cannot reveal the details at this time – but I'm sure you'll be called for a second interview. Forgive the secrecy, any questions you may have you can ask at the next stage of the process. That is, if we both decide to take this further.'

'It's all so mysterious!'

'I'm afraid so. But if you can bear the mystery for a while, if you can be patient…'

'Yes. It sounds intriguing. I'd love to be of service.'

'I'm happy to hear that. It has been most interesting getting to know you. I think that's all for now. I'd be grateful if you had a word with Miss Eaglesham outside: there are papers to be signed, confidentiality documents – the Official Secrets Act and so on. You will be taking the train home, I presume?'

She nodded. 'I will take the train from Victoria.'

'I wish you well. We may meet again.' They shook hands, and the interview was over.

# Chapter Eleven

Sibyl was called for a second interview with Mr Smith, this time in a different location, in the north of London, again in a rather run-down district.

'So – we meet again! This time, Miss Lake, I'd like to tell you a little more about the work we have in mind for you.'

Sibyl took a deep breath. At last. He spoke in English again.

'The first thing you need to know, before we go any further, is this: the work is extremely risky. Dangerous, in fact. You will be putting your life at risk. If that puts you off, we can stop right now.'

'As a nurse I treated soldiers who had risked their lives. Some of them died. I felt so inadequate; so unworthy. As if I should be doing the same. So no, it does not put me off.'

He nodded, and a ghost of a smile played on his lips.

'Wonderful. You also need to know that it is absolutely secret. You may tell no one. Not your mother, nor your stepfather, nor your sister, nor your fiancé.'

'I do not have a fiancé. And I am good at keeping secrets.'

'Excellent. Now, if we send you to France we will keep in touch with your family from time to time. If anything should happen to you they will be informed. But on no account may they know the details of where you are and what you are doing.'

'You said that. I understand. But… what exactly are the risks?'

'I would say the survival rate is fifty-fifty.'

She gulped. Why, it was the toss of a coin whether she would return alive or not! But the soldiers – those soldiers. Their risk was as high, or even higher. They knew it, and still they had gone; whether following orders, or as volunteers, they had done it.

'I'll do it.'

'Not so hasty. I'd like you to take a few minutes now to consider what I have just explained before I continue. If you can say here and now that no, you have absolutely no interest in such work, that you would rather serve your country as a nurse – I understand you have been accepted into the Queen Alexandra outfit as a military nurse, congratulations – you can stand up right now and walk out of this room and you'll never hear another word from us. If, however, you are interested…'

'I'm interested,' said Sibyl without a second thought.

'… if you are interested I would like you to go home, back to your hospital, your ward, and think about it for another week. Don't rush into this. Take time to consider. Just as we, too, still have matters to consider where you are concerned.'

'I thought you had singled me out because you wanted me?'

'Indeed we do. However, there is one concern. The only reason why we have hesitated, Mademoiselle Lake, is that you do have one little flaw…'

'Oh Mr Smith, I have several flaws…'

'As far as we are concerned, just one. When I first listed your qualities, *compassion* was among them. Now, compassion in a nurse is a highly desired virtue. For a person assisting in secret work for the liberation of France, not so much: or at least, that compassion must be one-sided, biased and enormous. You must love your friends, your Allies, and be capable of dying for them, because this is war.

'Similarly you must hate your enemies and be capable of killing them. The person who was your patient noted that you were equally compassionate to your German patients, our prisoners of war, as you were to the English and French patients. While other nurses and orderlies shunned the Germans and treated them with contempt, you treated them with the very same kindness as you did your other patients. You chatted with them in German about their families. You attended to them and made sure they were comforted.

You held their hands, held water bottles to their lips, wiped their foreheads. Other nurses would ignore them when they were in pain; you eased that pain. Miss Lake, why is that? *Warum hassen Sie nicht die Deutschen? Es ist doch Ihre Pflicht, sie zu hassen?* Why do you not hate the Germans? Isn't it your duty, to hate them?'

And there it was, mid-sentence, back to German. Perfectly on cue, Sibyl replied in German.

'I am a nurse, Mr Smith. As a nurse I do not see nationalities, but only my patients and their needs. I would not be a good nurse if I did not care first for the basic humanity of my patients, if I did not treat them equally, regardless of race or religion or nationality. These men, these Germans who end up as my patients: many of them are hardly more than boys. They were conscripted into war. They are not Nazis. They are just doing their job. Somewhere they have mothers who are thinking of them and praying for them. I cannot help thinking of those mothers. I cannot help but see their pain. I do not think of them as Germans, but only as humans. As people in pain.'

'Could you kill a German? With your bare hands? Because the job we are considering you for might just require that. Or would you, in the moment of killing, remember his mother and let yourself be killed instead?'

Sibyl hesitated. She considered the question for several minutes. Mr Smith waited. At last, she spoke, slowly, deliberately.

'As a nurse, I learned to obey orders, to do things I did not like doing, things I disagreed with. Much as a soldier has to. It seems you are offering me a job as a sort of soldier?'

'You could call it that, yes. Do go on.'

"I have never been in a position where it is necessary to kill. My profession at the moment is to save life, not to end it. If I am to assume another profession, a profession that requires me to kill for the sake of freedom, for a higher cause, I assume that I would act –professionally. If you say I might need to kill professionally then I assume I would be trained to – to kill professionally. So that is your answer. If you train me to do it, I can. I would. I would not think of that man's mother. I would think of the freedom of France.'

Yet even as she spoke the words, doubt shivered through her. Was what she had just said with such confidence nothing but empty bravado? *Could I really kill? In self-defence, yes, of course. But in cold blood? As an assassin? Isn't that what he's suggesting? Could I?*

Mr Smith must have read her thoughts. 'We are not training you to be an assassin,' he said, 'but you must be prepared to kill if that is necessary. It is collateral damage in the grand scheme of subterfuge. It is inevitable. Sometimes it will happen at a distance, anonymously. Sometimes it will be close up, personal. That can be… upsetting.'

'As a nurse I have had to work in many upsetting circumstances. I have worked in operating theatres with horribly mutilated bodies. I have learned to be dispassionate in such situations.'

Mr Smith nodded, somewhat vaguely, as if he had not properly heard what she had said and observed her in silence for a full five minutes. When he replied, it was still in German, but it was a change of subject.

'I notice that you speak German with an Austrian accent?'

'*Ja* – as I told you last time, my grandmother is Austrian, and it was she who taught me. She simply spoke to us children in German, always.'

'I see. Now to return to your last reply: as you say, it is your professional duty to be compassionate. Does this mean that your compassion is not genuine, that it is only a professional act? That your kindness is false, a mask that you wear to observe your duty as a nurse?'

She shook her head. 'No, Herr Smith. I am a naturally kind and caring person. I like being that way; it makes me happy to help people, to relieve pain. But I think in a combat situation, in which I was face to face with an enemy eager to kill me or my colleagues, compassion would not be appropriate. I think you are confusing genuine *Mitgefühl* – just like its English counterpart, the word *Mitgefühl* says it all, *with-feeling*, com-passion – you are confusing it with sentimentality. Compassion is not sentimentality, which is a very weak distant cousin. Compassion is strong. But it is selective; it is granted only to those *deserving* of compassion. The Germans I would encounter would not, I think, be deserving of compassion. Their job is to kill.'

'Ah, but what if you are required to kill in cold blood. Do you have the guts for that?'

'Herr Smith I am a nurse. Do you think a nurse is gutless? Do you think she breaks down in tears when she is in theatre, assisting at an operation, when a surgeon has to saw through a man's bone, amputate a leg? Do you think she faints at the sight of a man whose entire skin has been ripped to ribbons, or burnt black and peeling off his whole body, or whose face has been blown off? Do you think that just because she does the dirty work in a hospital – cleaning up faeces and vomit and blood, bodily things that a normal person shrinks from in disgust, and does this without so much as a twitch of her nose – that she is somehow a weak person, unable to control her emotions? Do you think that the putrid smell of gangrene when a man's leg is rotting away is perfume to her, and this is why she can perform her job with good humour and sometimes even with grace and elegance?

'No, Herr Smith. Control of emotions is one of the first things a nurse has to learn, and perhaps this is why our training is so strict, our matrons such dragons: we must learn to control our natural inclinations of mutiny and disgust and sheer loathing, because that is required of us in our job. We cannot let ourselves be ruled by natural human reactions, which would scare away a normal person. We must ignore our moods and our own wishes. We are taught to do what is *right*, not what we want, and that is our strength.

'In my case, being a naturally kind person, I enjoy helping to ease another person's pain and it happens to coincide with the work I perform. It is a happy coincidence. In a military situation compassion is not required so I would shut off that compartment of my mind just as I have learnt to shut off the compartment of my mind that induces nausea when required to clean a man's backside of caked faeces or dress his genitals which are in a bloody mess because they have been shot away. I can slam shut the mental door on compassion just as I can shut it on the abhorrence and loneliness and sheer exhaustion that come with my job. So please do not dismiss us nurses as sweet, soft kind-hearted angels of light. We are tough, inside and out. And yes, if I were taught the methods of killing and my job required it of me these hands could kill as well as they can heal.'

She held out her hands to him, palms forward, and stopped for breath. Her next words were in English and spoken with far less passion than had been needed for her outburst.

'I am sorry. That was a rather impassioned speech which perhaps contradicts the message I was trying to convey. It does annoy me when nurses are dismissed as kind little saints.'

Mr Smith also reverted to English. 'I think that even saints have far more spunk than is generally recognised, *Fräulein* Lake. Being genuinely good is not for the fainthearted and I think you are wrong: we all admire and in fact revere nurses and the work you do and I only wish our gratitude towards you would be more apparent. You are heroines, and the fact that you are almost always invisible heroines does not detract from that fact.'

'Thank you.'

'And you would really rather be an agent in this work, with the risk of being killed, or killing, than be a nurse in the field, and save lives? Surely nursing is the more noble of those professions?'

'Noble? Who cares about nobility in war? I was a nurse during the Blitz. I nursed hundreds of war-wounded. I am at the moment all set to become a nurse at the Front, in a field hospital. I know what the work there is like, what I would have to do. The more damaged ones are evacuated and returned to England; but the bulk of them – we nurses and doctors just patch them up and send them right back into the field. Thousands, hundreds of thousands, of healthy young men, sent out to fight to the death! Where is the nobility in that, in enabling them to die! To die for their country – noble? Pah! My heart breaks for them, and they are indeed heroes, but what kind of a society are we, that we value the lives of our men so low? War is a politician's game, Mr Smith. There is nothing noble about war. There is nothing noble about fixing a broken body just so that it can go out and get broken again. It is despairing work. It does not lift the spirits. It breaks the heart. The job you are offering: it seems to make more sense to me.'

Mr Smith nodded. He looked pleased. He switched to French.

'Good. Then I can be more specific, tell you more about us and our work. It involves a bit of a history lesson. You like history?'

'It is interesting but I fear I did not pay much attention at school. And now – now, history just seems to be sweeping us all along. I would indeed like to know more about the background to this job you are considering me for.'

'Well, it is this: your languages skills are impressive, and your training as a nurse has given you a certain maturity. Most especially, though, it's your love for France, and specifically your allegiance to the Alsace, that attracted our interest. The Alsace is a headache for the Allies, and I'm afraid, rather neglected in the general scheme of things.

'The thing is: as I told you in our last interview, the Alsace was annexed by Germany as soon as the war began. That's far more serious than being occupied. It means that that the previous French citizens of the Alsace became automatically German citizens. Non-Alsatians were evacuated, and a Germanisation of the annexed area began; German taught in schools, French language banned and so on. Young men were called up to fight for the Wehrmacht. To refuse was to put their whole family into jeopardy; perhaps their parents would be sent to concentration camps. These men go with great resentment, calling themselves the *malgré-nous,* "in spite of us". It's an impossible situation for them. Some have nevertheless deserted, set up guerrilla units of their own.

'You have surely heard of the Resistance movement all over France. They are active in cities, in villages, in the countryside; the rural groups are known as *maquisards* throughout France. But the Alsatian Resistance could not in any way be a part of the greater movement, because the Alsace is now actually Germany, separated from Occupied France by an area called *Zone Interdite,* the Closed Zone. That Zone is swarming with Gestapo and impossible to pass through without special permission; the demarcation line is even tougher than the one into Vichy. Still, separated as they were, the Alsatian boys – for boys they were – did their best. They organised themselves.

'In September 1940 the first Alsatian Resistance movement was led by someone called Marcel Weinum; it was centred in Strasbourg and was composed of twenty-five very young men, all under the age of eighteen. Their activity was mainly the disruption and sabotage of German works wherever and whenever they could. The climax was an unsuccessful attack against the highest German commander, Gauleiter Robert Wagner. In the end Marcel Weinum was caught. He was sentenced to death by the Gestapo and executed in Stuttgart in 1942. He was eighteen at the time of his execution.

'I'm telling you this so that you know how very inexperienced the Alsatian Resistance was and still is, how young its members, how – shall we say – amateurish. Still, these men are heroes and on their shoulders rests so much if we are to win this terrible war. Their work is vital but extremely dangerous and requires the utmost in passion and dedication. Weinum's last words before his execution were: "If I die I shall die with a pure heart." Shall I continue, *Fräulein* Lake, or does that story dampen your enthusiasm?'

'Please continue.'

'This brings us actually right into the work we do. It was basically Winston Churchill's idea: that we, the British, should help these

Resistance fighters; send in agents with logistics help, training, hardware such as explosives and weapons, money. The aim is to disrupt and hinder the enemy by all possible means. Once they are trained, our agents are dropped behind enemy lines; they work in a clandestine network – in fact, in several networks – throughout Occupied France and Free France, in collaboration with the French Resistance network. Now hopefully we are nearing the end of this terrible war, but we are still constantly on the lookout for new agents.

'The final goal is to prepare for the invasion of Europe by Allied forces and for the liberation of France. The role is sabotage and subversion behind the enemy lines – basically a secret battle in the shadow of the official one.

'To return to the Alsace: at present another Resistance movement has developed, scattered throughout the Alsace. They have a strong and highly competent leader, with superior local knowledge and the maturity to lead his men properly and command their respect.

'However, because of the peculiar situation of Alsace this disorganised group is cut off from the regular Resistance networks in Occupied France and Vichy. Because of this isolation communication is extremely difficult if not impossible. We cannot support them as we do the other groups in France. They have hardly any equipment: no radio, few weapons, no explosives. They are basically on their own, doing good work but with primitive methods, slashing enemy tyres, felling trees across access roads, cutting telephone lines. They have absolutely no training in guerrilla tactics, and we cannot reach them through the usual channels.'

Without warning, almost mid-sentence, he switched language back to German.

'The trouble is that the French intelligence service in Occupied France and especially in the Alsace is in disarray. Essentially what has happened is that the Free French government-in-exile in London under General Charles de Gaulle had to create its own intelligence service – very difficult from abroad, as you can imagine. It's called the *Bureau central de renseignements et d'action.*

'Initially, it consisted of a single section, *Renseignement,* which works closely with the British intelligence agency MI6. Subsequently, other sections were added, including the *Action militaire* which works with us. The Alsatian *maquisards* leader was able to make contact with *Action militaire,* which in turn – reluctantly, for they are proud – contacted us. In a nutshell, they urgently need an agent for the Alsace to support and organise their work. And you can now guess where this is going. We would like to send you to the Alsace. Can you imagine yourself in such a role?'

Sibyl nodded. She had already come to this conclusion and saw no need to beat around the bush. It was hard to believe – they were sending her not only to France but to Alsace!

'I told you: yes and yes and yes, of course! But I'm curious. You refer to yourselves as 'we' – does this *we* actually have a name? Who are you? Who would I be working for?'

He smiled. 'We do, a rather unspecific name. We call ourselves Special Operations. Or Special Operations Executive, SOE. We select suitable agents, train them. I represent the division F – for France.'

'I am surprised that you would choose a woman, a young woman, for such work, and especially an amateur, someone with no experience in agent work. I always thought agents, spies, were men? With years of training behind them?'

'Indeed not. During the Great War there were several women spies, all heroines. Have you heard of Louise de Bettignies? A heroine of that war, and there were several others who helped us win. To date there have been thirty-nine SOE female agents active in France – you would be the fortieth. They come from all walks of life and our experience is that they are excellent in their role; in fact, being female often gives them an advantage a man would not have. They evoke less suspicion, particularly with the Germans. They have a rather exalted view of womankind.

'But there's actually a specific reason why we need a woman in this particular case. The thing is: in the Alsace, all men up to the age of thirty-five are being conscripted for the Wehrmacht. So we needed either an older man or a woman. But after the age of thirty-five, all SOE agents are retired. So, you see, it has to be a young woman.

'Previous experience in agent work is not a prerequisite. We are looking for fluency in French or better yet, French and German, and a knowledge of and love for France and a passion to set her free. And, of course, intrinsic qualities are required; courage, calmness under extreme pressure, level-headedness, the ability to think on one's feet. We know that you possess those qualities – reports say that during the bomb raid you had no thought for your own safety but in perfect calmness set about saving your patients and colleagues; you acted as a leader during the crisis. That's the kind of agent we want.'

Not knowing what to say to that, Sibyl said nothing. A chaos of emotions seized her heart and mind: patriotism, enthusiasm, fear, pride, courage, anxiety, all mixed up and grappling with each other all at once. She nodded slightly and held Mr Smith's gaze.

'How would I get there? And what would I be doing, specifically?'

'We would parachute you in, at night. Naturally you would be meticulously trained in advance. We would set up your contacts for you, give you a new identity, a cover name. You would join this Resistance group and instruct them in the use of weapons and sabotage. You would organise the drop locations and the delivery of supplies. You would be at the hub of a network of couriers. Planning the sabotage is the job we require of you.

'It is not an easy job. Usually we would place a new agent in the hands of a more experienced one in occupied France for further on-the-job training; our networks in Occupied France and in Vichy are by now quite widespread and interlocked with one another, supporting each other.

'This time we cannot do that. For one thing, there is no time. Secondly, we cannot spare any of our working agents, take them off for work in Alsace. This is not an ordinary peacetime job where you can simply transfer employees from one branch of a business to another. Thirdly, few of them speak German as well as French, and none of them speak Alsatian, and we regard this as an important aspect. Though most of the Alsatian Resistance fighters speak French and German, they do all speak Alsatian and so do the local people, and it is important for our agent there to be able to communicate with the locals. So we needed someone who speaks all three languages. You. So, once again: are you sure?'

She nodded. 'I would like to do this work. I would like to help free Alsace.'

'You understand that it is dangerous work. You could get killed.'

'You said so already. Fifty-fifty. The toss of a coin. I said yes. I could get killed as a field nurse in France, and still I volunteered.'

'You would be basically on your own, with no-one to help you if you get into trouble. If the Gestapo finds you – well. Their methods are not kind. They would torture you in order to get information out of you. We would however provide you with a suicide pill which you would swallow in such an event. Death would be instant.'

A wave of fear rose in Sibyl's gorge. She swallowed it and nodded. 'I understand.'

'You must not breathe a word of this to your family. Or your colleagues, your young man. What I have told you this far is highly confidential.'

'You said this already. I understand.'

'Then you should go home and sleep on it for a while before making a final decision.'

'I know my final decision, Mr Smith.'

'We will be in touch.'

A week later Sibyl had her third and final interview.

This was not with Mr Smith, and not in some run-down London district; it was in Baker Street, with a woman who introduced herself as Vera Atkins, which was, it appeared, not even a code name.

The neat black plaque outside the building at number sixty-four announced the offices of 'Inter-Services Research Bureau', an innocuous camouflage for the Special Operations Executive headquarters. Miss Atkins was entirely different to Mr Smith; she was warm, friendly and almost motherly towards Sibyl. It was almost as if she truly *cared* about Sibyl and was concerned on her behalf, like a parent whose child was to sit an important exam. Except, of course, this was not an exam. It was life or death. Vera made quite clear once again the danger involved in the Alsace mission; as if she assumed a certain responsibility and needed reassurance that Sibyl held no illusions that what she was being asked to do was not a matter of glamourous adventure but was seriously dirty work. But Sibyl had long ago made her final decision; she knew very well what war could do and held no prettified notion of the life of a secret agent.

Her training began. There was no time to lose; it was by definition a short training, considering the seriousness of the job, lasting only six months, but intensive and extremely thorough.

Sibyl was sent to Wanborough, near Guildford, for preliminary training in a mixed group of men and women, with the aim of improving physical fitness. It involved cross country runs, but also basic weapons training and unarmed combat. French was spoken all the time. Sibyl was aware of being watched and assessed constantly, as were all the students. One woman was removed from the group for speaking English in her sleep. A man was removed for speaking English while drunk. But Sibyl spoke only French, in her dreams and in her waking state.

The second phase of her training was guerrilla warfare. It took place in Arisaig, in the extreme north of Scotland, where the weather was wild and nature magnificent. Here she learnt the methods and tricks of sabotage: how to make and use explosives – for they were far enough away from civilisation to practice the setting off of bombs, the blowing up of bridges and buildings. She learnt the art of invisibility, of stalking, of picking locks, of seeing without being seen. She learnt navigation skills, and how to manage a small boat, and swim for great lengths underwater. She learnt how to live off the land, with little to sustain her.

She learnt about codes, about Morse and ciphers necessary for wireless operations. What was normally a very long and complex course had to be compressed as time was running short.

Sibyl was given a weekend's leave to return home to Three Bridges to say goodbye to her family.

Kathleen now lived a life of quiet domesticity, relatively safe from German bombs in the Sussex countryside; her son Eric was now five. Elena, married to an RAF pilot, had trained as a bilingual secretary, like her mother. She lived in London and had found work at the Foreign Office. Her two-year-old daughter was looked after by her mother-in-law while she worked.

The reunion with both was short but intense on Sibyl's part. It was hard, not being able to share the details of what she was really about to do. But utmost discretion was required, and straight out lies. Sibyl told her mother that she was enlisted in FANY, the First Aid Nursing Yeomanry, a British independent all-female registered charity active in France; her family accepted the confidentiality of her mission.

She returned to her training with a heavy heart, for perhaps she had seen her family for the very last time. In wartime, survival was never a guarantee.

*

She learnt to kill silently. She learnt to use a knife as delicately as an artist uses a paintbrush; here her nurse's training, her knowledge of anatomy and the uses of a scalpel came in extremely handy. She learned about the variety of knives at SOE agents' disposal: the dagger called in French a *cran d'arrêt*, whose two-sided blade fixed with a catch when opened; daggers that fitted into pipe stems, or tiny knives that fitted behind lapels, or inside fountain pens and lipstick cases and shoe heels. Then there were all kinds of guns: rifles, machine guns, lugers and revolvers. She learnt to differentiate between German, French, American and British weapons; how to handle them in the dark, or when they were slippery, by touch alone.

Yet killing was the one skill she could not actually put into practice during training. It was all simulation. *Could I do it, in real life?* she asked herself. *Could I? I am a woman; biologically programmed to give life, not take it. Added to that: I am a nurse, whose every reflex to date has been to save life, prevent death. Could I really kill? In cold blood, and not in self-defence? Kill for my country, for France, for freedom?* There was no answer.

For the next part of her training Sibyl was dispatched to Tatton Park, near Manchester, to Ringway Airfield where all the troops trained in parachuting. She was allowed only three practice jumps, all at night, before being sent off for her final polish at Beaulieu, in Hampshire's New Forest.

Here at Beaulieu, students were taught the true nature of their mission; final points of security and espionage. She learnt how to live in Occupied France – in her case, how to live in the Alsace, an area officially German but French through and through. She learnt how to communicate through silent signs and signals; a coloured headscarf, a shirt hung up to dry, a curtain drawn or opened, a flowerpot on a window ledge. Once she was roused in the middle of the night by men dressed in Gestapo uniforms, Nazi symbols on their sleeves; they were rough and loud and shone dazzling torches into her face and threw her out of bed screaming *'Raus, Du Schweinehund!'* They marched her along a corridor to an interrogation room where they threatened her with torture if she did not divulge her secrets. She didn't.

At Beaulieu, too, she met Maurice Buckmaster, head of the F Section of Special Operations; but Vera Atkins was undoubtedly the brains behind the business.

It was Vera who schooled her in her own specific cover. She was to become Jeanne Dauguet, a young woman of Alsatian heritage who had grown up partly in Alsace and partly in Paris (this to account for her slight Parisian accent) and had returned to Colmar for work.

The circuit's name was Acrobat, which also served as password for all agents in the circuit. There was, in fact, only one agent, herself. 'Normally our agents work in teams of three; the coordinator, the wireless operator, the courier. You will be alone. You will be your own wireless operator – we call them pianists – and your own courier. It cannot be helped. Alsace is different. We have not even been able to thoroughly investigate the situation there. We cannot give you much advice. You must work things out on your own. You are Acrobat One, and there is only one.

'Your supervisor in London is also Acrobat,' said Vera. 'That is all you need to know; he does not have a name or a number. You will report back to him through your wireless transmitter at pre-arranged times which you will learn by heart; you will diverge from those times only in emergencies. When meeting anyone new you must use the codeword. At all times. No real names are to be used. No surnames.'

'What happens if I am caught?' Sibyl asked, 'how will you know? What shall I do?'

'If you are ever contaminated – which is what we call an agent who has fallen into the hands of the Gestapo – you are on your own. We do not know you, you do not know us. You have your suicide pill: you must put it in your mouth and bite it. Death will be instant. If you cannot do that, and they torture you, there is one good thing as far as we are concerned: you know nothing of the wider network and what is going on there, and so you have no secrets to spill. The only people you will know are the *maquisards,* and only by their first names, which are not their real names.

'You will know their hideouts, their safe houses, and if you are tortured in the end you will be forced to reveal these. We only beg of you that you hold out for forty-eight hours, to give the others time to flee. But all in all you are not a high risk and I think the Gestapo also will not consider you of high importance. You are isolated from the other networks in France. They will know this. There is no communication. That makes everything much less complicated, for you and for us and for them. For everybody.

'In fact you are very fortunate. Your job is very specific: to prepare Alsace for the coming of the Allies who will drive out the Germans. Not easy, but nothing you cannot manage. The Resistance fighters you will supervise are already doing good work in sabotage and subterfuge; not one of them has been caught yet by the SS, not since the execution of Marcel Weinum in 1942. They have all matured through experience. All that is needed now is, first of all, someone to keep them supplied with weapons, ammunition, explosives, and, just as essentially, with money – these men have to eat. Secondly, someone to train them in the use of weapons and explosives. Finally, someone to organise and coordinate their work: to manage air drops – times and places, and keep in touch with us through wireless so that we know – and to coordinate attacks and acts of sabotage. That someone is you.

'You will possibly also help coordinate the passage of Jews to a safe house in Alsace, from where they will be sent on their way; it could be that all Jews have already left Alsace. This we do not know.'

'But you will find out the details once you are there. You can do it. You know how to keep a cool head in times of stress and you are extremely efficient and reliable. This is not advanced Intelligence work. We are not MI6. Although…'

She hesitated.

'Yes?'

'Although there is one Secret Intelligent Services agent working in the Nazi headquarters in Colmar and he will be in touch with you. As you know, the SIS doesn't hold Secret Operations in high regard – in fact there's been a small rivalry going on, as we are sort of a pet project for Mr Churchill. So traditional spies tend to look down their noses at us. Yet when they – the SIS – need us… well. But you'll find out more when you get there.'

'And these people I'll be working with, the Resistance? I suppose they are all men? How will they take to being led by a young woman with no experience whatsoever?'

Vera chuckled. 'Indeed – there might be some resentment there, but I think because of who you are, you will overcome that. There is something disarming about you which will work well on male vanity. I have every confidence that you will put them in their places with charm, diplomacy and dignity. Just be yourself. You will win them over – trust your intuition. And it's not true that you have no experience. You excel in the use of explosives, the laying of plastic bombs and the use of weapons. These are things young men are fascinated by and you will be giving them some very valuable tools and skills – they will respect you for that. They need you. You are putting guns into their hands! They will be overjoyed, and eternally grateful! So there's nothing to worry about. You'll be fine. One of the skills we selected you for is that you have a *way* with people. You can connect to others in a manner that is innate, that cannot be taught, and so is very valuable in this work. You emanate trust. That's a rare thing.'

Nevertheless, as Sibyl went to bed that night, the main impression she had gleaned from Vera's reassurance was that Alsace was more of an afterthought in Secret Operations' plans for France. An outlier, a place of lesser importance, to be considered only now when all the major networks were in place, and the invasion was in sight; and that she was a junior agent for a task not essential enough for a valuable seasoned agent.

This conclusion did not offend her. It filled her with determination and resolve; This mission in Alsace might be of minor strategic importance but they had chosen *her* for it because she was the best person; and she would give her all, throw herself into it, do everything she could to rescue it from Nazi claws.

# Chapter Twelve

The night was silver with moonshine. The Lysander stood ready and waiting on the airstrip at Tangmere, a camouflaged aerodrome in rural Bedfordshire. Sibyl had spent her last night on British soil at Hazell's Hall; she had been unable to sleep and now it was time to depart.

Unexpectedly, a jeep drove up and Vera stepped out. During their last preparatory meeting Vera had offered Sibyl suicide pills, capsules of cyanide which could be sewn into her clothing, to be taken in case of emergency. Sibyl had refused. 'I don't think I could ever commit suicide,' she said. But Vera had pressed them on her. 'You never know. Be prepared,' she said. So Sibyl took them; they were hidden in her backpack.

Now, Vera pressed a box into her hands. 'A gift from F Section.' Sibyl opened it; inside was a gold powder compact. On its underside were engraved the words *Fabriqué en France.*

It was shiny, new and feminine, in complete contrast to her camouflage jumpsuit. Sibyl was so touched she flung her arms around Vera. 'Thank you! Thank you for everything!' she said. Vera hugged her back. 'Thank *you,*' she said, 'for everything.'

Vera held both her hands; they were still for a moment; it was almost a moment of contemplation, of prayer. Then Vera spoke again.

'One last word. It is top secret, for the time being, but it might give you a further boost of courage. It is this: an invasion is immanent. It will happen, before long; it could be a matter of a week, or two, or of days. But it will happen. We will win this war. We are winning.'

The pilot's name was Dennis Beeks, and he was to be her permanent pilot for deliveries to the Alsace. The plane was already loaded: weapons, explosives, detonators, a radio. Sibyl's heart raced. She was sure Vera could hear it; if so, she didn't let it show, but signalled for her to climb into the plane. She turned and walked away.

The Lysander had a fixed metal ladder and the door at the top gaped open, jaws ready to swallow her into a new life. Dennis gave her a thumbs-up.

'Lizzie's ready, if you are. Let's go for it.'

She grinned weakly and nodded to reassure herself as much as Dennis. Grabbing hold of the ladder, she climbed in, settled herself and clicked her seatbelt into its lock. The plane began to purr, the propellers to rotate, slowly at first, and then whisking the dark air. It jerked into movement. Rolled down the airstrip. Lysanders were the chosen plane for this work as they needed very little room for take-offs and landings: a pocket-handkerchief of a field would do, and Sibyl knew that was where she would be dropped, along with the supplies.

The Lysander flew only to the north of France, as part of the Moon Squadron, so called because it could only fly on the moonlit nights of the month, and those when the moon was not covered by clouds. The harvest moon had been gaining strength for five days, and was at possibly its brightest; it would be their only light. Dennis would have to fly low, to avoid enemy radar, and also to find his destination by sight-reading his way across the north of France. They would detour over Belgium and Luxembourg, rather than travelling as the crow flies, to avoid the Vosges mountains to the east of Alsace. The Lysander carried no radar or instruments. It all came down to the pilot's expertise and knowledge of the land, how well he was able to find his way by picking out the shine of rivers and lakes, railway lines, church steeples, villages and towns. Sibyl trusted Dennis; but she also knew that this was his first mission to the Alsace, his first flight beyond the Vosges. The idea terrified her; but she reined in that terror, took a deep breath, and told herself it has to be done. He knows his job. Trust him.

Sibyl knew also that there had been elaborate plans laid for this, her arrival in France. She would be met and taken to Strasbourg and from there take a train to Colmar. Agents from the French *Action Militaire* as well as the American intelligence had liaised with one of the Resistance fighters to organise the landing near a village south-west of Strasbourg. A field had been chosen and Resistance fighters would be there waving torches as soon as they heard Lizzie's hum; she would land, and then the supplies would be landed. Yes, she had practised, but only three times. And yes, this particular location was safe. Yet still her heart pounded like a jackhammer as the plane made a first small circle. Below, lamps indicated the landing field, placed there by the *maquisards* receiving her. Dennis indicated it was time to put on her parachute and then – in just a few seconds – jump. Into France.

She jumped. Or rather, she let herself fall. Into her new life.


Hands pulled away the parachute shrouding. Someone was leaning over her. A light shone between their two faces. And then:

'Sibi!'

'Jacques!'

On French soil for not even a minute, and she had already broken the cardinal rule.

She had used a real name. And so had he.

# Chapter Thirteen

Later, she wondered how she had recognised him. She hadn't changed much over the last ten years; she had simply matured in looks. But Jacques!

Back in 1935, when she'd been torn away from Alsace, Sibyl had been twelve and Jacques fifteen: a fresh-faced youth bursting with *joie de vivre*, with an indefatigable, indestructible trust in life; a young man so in tune with nature he could feel grapes ripening in his blood and carried the phases of the moon in his rhythm of his heart. Jacques had taken her, taken then all, up into the Vosges mountains and they had slept on the bare ground and drunk from springs with water as clear as air and tasting of moss and earth. He had placed unknown sweet berries on her tongue, and warned her against others. He knew which mushrooms could be carefully picked and cooked them in a battered old saucepan, over a fire he'd made from flintstone, and the children had feasted on such meals and felt like royalty. Jacques knew all birds by their call and could hear their piping when no-one else could; his very soul seemed a mirror that reflected all the gifts of nature and his eyes had glowed with this love of life.

Now, ten years later, he was a haggard shadow of that youth, a spectre.

He was thin, so thin his cheekbones protruded like blunt blades, below which the straggles of a beard only barely concealed the edges of his chin. His hair was long, unkempt, almost to his shoulders, hanging in greasy strands pushed back behind his ears. On his head, the inevitable beret, but an ancient one, its grey wool matted. His clothes looked similarly ancient, unwashed and far too big for him, hanging listlessly on his emaciated frame.

Only his eyes had not changed. They were as fiery as ever, alight with a zeal that, though it may have changed course, burned as bright as it always had. Back then, that fire had been lit by a simple, unfettered passion for life itself, a perfect unity with nature that shone through every pore of his skin but mostly burned as loving kindness in his gaze; you felt it deep within when that gaze rested on you. At least, *she* had felt it deep within. His health, his youth and that inner light had made him glorious.

And somehow, it was still there, burning just as brightly but covered with another thing, a dark thing, a dangerous thing. It was an ember glowing beneath a veneer of darkness. The darkness veiled but could not extinguish the fire. It was the very same fire. She had recognised it instinctively; a spark leaping within their gaze as he bent down to help her up, and their eyes met that first moment, and those forbidden words, their names, the taboo words, had burst spontaneously, simultaneously, from their lips: 'Sibi!' 'Jacques!'

He was no longer glorious. But he was here, before her, in a different guise, a different form, but he was the same; that fire was the same. She had felt, known, in that moment. But she had been well trained, and pulled herself instantly together, and her second word was 'Acrobat.'

He nodded. 'Acrobat.' He tugged gently beneath her armpits so that in a trice she was standing, running with him into the dark shadow beyond the field which was the protection of trees, and they melted into that shadow while dark running shapes cut across the field to the parachute, balled it up and ran back with it to safety.

'Wait,' said Sibyl to Jacques, 'I am supposed to bury my parachute!'

'Leave them! They are salvaging the silk for their girlfriends to make precious things, lingerie and sheets and wedding dresses.'

'And what about you? Will they give you some for your girlfriend?'

'I do not have a girlfriend. Come, Sibyl. Do not fret about this. Let us go.'

He took her hand and led her, running, into the cover of the forest trees. She sighed and ran with him. And so, even before they had left the landing field, Sibyl had broken two cardinal rules from her handbook. If this was her example of leadership, then it was a bad beginning.

Later, when they were safe within the walls of a dilapidated wooden cabin hidden away in the woods – Jacques, Sibyl remembered, had always been good at finding dilapidated cabins, ruined stone huts hidden away in the woods – they talked. Nothing personal, at first, while the other men were with them; just instructions and tomorrow's plans and technical details of what was to happen. Then the others settled down for a few hours' sleep before dawn broke, on the bare earth, covering themselves with old ragged blankets for the night was more than chilly, it was cold. They seemed not to mind. And Jacques and Sibyl broke the rules again. They talked; of the past and of the present and of the predicament they all were in, every Frenchman and every Englishwoman, every person whom this cursed war had reached out to touch with its fingers of death and destruction.

Sibyl and Jacques leant against the wall of the cabin. They had eaten; some cheese and some old bread. He had offered her wine, which she drank from a cracked mug clasped in her hands. His eyes held hers through the darkness. His voice was low. He spoke French.

She wanted to know about the Laroches, and what had become of them.

'This war has torn that family apart,' said Jacques, in a whisper so soft she had to lean close to hear. 'When the Bosch invaded they tried to make us all German. Most of us resisted. Some didn't. Marie-Claire, she married a high-ranking German officer, a Nazi.

She thought it would help her family to have that connection. Instead it broke Margaux's heart. Made her more radical than ever. Marie-Claire is not allowed inside the home any more – she is banned. Collaborators are not liked in Alsace or anywhere in France.

'As for Leon and Lucien: all the young men in Alsace were conscripted by the Wehrmacht, Sibi! They were taken away against their will; they call themselves the *malgré-nous*, in-spite-of-ourselves. If they refuse to go their families are sent to concentration camps. I managed to escape in time. Leon didn't. He was sent to the Eastern Front and nobody has heard from him since the invasion. We don't know if he is dead or alive. Lucien was removed and made to join Hitler Youth. We don't know where he is either. Victoire – well, she is the only hope of that family! She's very young still but she's a fighter, a lover of Alsace. She will never give in, give up. She is like her mother.'

'And you? How did you escape the *Wehrmacht?*'

'I escaped over the Vosges. I know them like the back of my hand. I went over the Col du Donon mountain pass. There has been much fighting going on there between the Americans and the Germans but I knew a route more to the south and that is the way I went. I made my way to Metz by foot and then to Verdun and met up with a Resistance group and they hid me for a while and I learnt some of their tactics. But then I returned, the way I came. I was determined to build my own Resistance group here in Alsace. We are rather disorganised but we do not lack in passion and courage what we lack in weapons and ammunition and explosives and food and just about everything a man needs to defend his territory.'

'And your sister? Juliette?'

Jacques turned very still. He closed his eyes. Finally he said:

'My sister is dead. She went to university in Strasbourg and there she fell in love with a Jewish student. Jakob. A very fine young man. When they started to deport the Jews Juliette tried to run away with him. She followed one of my old trails over the Vosges into France. They were captured near the border and shot on the spot. Executed.'

Sibyl gasped in shock.

'Oh, Jacques!'

She wanted to say she was sorry, but sorry was inadequate and meaningless. Tears rushed to her eyes, spilled out. Jacques reached out, wiped them away with his fingers.

'It's awful I know but that is what we are living with these last few years. This horror. This nightmare. We must put an end to it, Sibi!'

'Well, that's where I come in, isn't it! But we must stop using our real names. We are professionals. You must call me Acrobat One; though since it is only me you can drop the One.'

'Welcome to Alsace, Acrobat! Or should I say, welcome back. It has been a long time.'

'And I must call you by your field name – what is it?,

'My men call me Dolch. Dagger.'

'No. That won't do. Nothing that can identify you.'

'Then – how about – David. He who killed Goliath. As I will destroy the Boche.'

'Yes – with your slingshot!'

Sibyl by now had finished her wine and her hand rested on her knee. Jacques took it and pressed it. It was not a romantic move. It was a move of deepest friendship and alliance, and it joined their hearts in an alloy stronger than anything Sibyl had ever felt before. It was as if a common spirit ran through them both, a common life. One life, two bodies. One passion, one goal. The moment felt so intimate she could hardly breathe; had to break that intimacy.

'And *Oncle* Jean-Pierre? What of him? He always warned this would happen.'

'Jean-Pierre went to Paris after the invasion. He had to, as a non-Alsatian, but he wanted to. The Bosch evacuated all non-Alsatians, Jean-Pierre among them. The whole of Strasbourg was evacuated. They took away the Jews. We don't know what happened to them. They were just thrown out and put on trains. Do you remember Leah?'

'The help? Yes, of course. I liked her.'

'Did you know she was Jewish? Margaux managed to hide her. The Gestapo came asking if they had any Jews and Margaux denied it. She could have been killed if they'd found her! They hid her in the cellar, in that room where they hid the good wine. Remember?'

'Yes – I remember. But how did they feed her? It was so dark in there!'

'Margaux built a hidden trapdoor into that part of the cellar. So she had access not only to Leah but also to the best wine.'

'Trust Margaux to think about the best wine, even in wartime!'

'Wine is important, Sibyl. It is a valuable commodity. The Boche is crazy about French wine. One of the first things they did when they annexed Alsace was to seize great stores of wine. They did this all over France. They sent tens of thousands of barrels to the Third Reich and ordered the conversion of thousands of hectares of vineyards into war production. Margaux's vineyard has been requisitioned; she still manages the vineyard but her wine must now go to Germany, not to France. She was clever to hide the best wine. As for my father, normally they would have sent him to a camp because his son – that's me – is a deserter from the German army. But he is winemaker; it is a protected profession. He has to work to produce wine for the Boche. Can you imagine how angry he is? But he has to do it. However, he too has his tricks to prevent them getting the best wine, just like Margaux. Good wine represents luxury to the Boche. They covet it; it represents fine living, superior living, to them. But they are so primitive, their palates so undeveloped, they cannot tell the difference. They are tricked into getting the second-class and third-class wine and we keep the best from them. Winemakers are doing this all over France. It is a question of national pride. The Boche have humiliated France but the French humiliate them in secret by fooling them with wine. It is a method of war. Unfortunately it has to be kept a secret but at least we know we are doing it and it restores a bit of self-respect to us. It is a war of wine, and it's a war the Boche will not win; not when it comes to French wine.'

'So Leah is still down there, with the best wine?'

'No. Margaux managed to get in touch with a Resistance group that helps Jews escape. They go over that same Col du Donon I first escaped by; I was able to show them the way. Once in occupied France there is a route down through the south into Vichy territory and then Spain. Leah got away. A few other Jews from Colmar and Strasbourg escaped this way as well. Margaux is part of the Resistance movement to help Jews. She has a safe house.'

'Oh! I was told that I might have to help get Jews to a safe house. So it's Margaux's home?'

'There are a few others in Strasbourg and Colmar but hers is the one they all end up at before they are escorted into France. She is wonderful. She'd love to see you, I'm sure.'

'I'd love to see her too but there is no time. When the war is over and this charade is behind me. For now, Jacques, there is work to do. I am supposed to train your people.'

'I know. We will discuss the logistics of that in the morning. But I have told you all about what has happened here in Alsace any you have told me nothing about yourself and how you ended up here. It is your turn to talk, Sibi. I mean, Acrobat. Oh, damn. I cannot call you Acrobat. You remain Sibi.'

'But only when we are alone. There's not much to tell. I trained as a nurse and then I was recruited for this job. It is my first mission. And I am a little nervous about it.'

'No need to be nervous. You will do well; of that I'm sure.'

They talked for a while about the work. Quietly, in barely more than whispers. The others were fast asleep, light snores and gentle breathing filled the cabin. Sibyl felt rested, comforted, her anxiety relieved; not a bit tired, but enlivened, alert, awake. But finally, Jacques said, 'Now, let us sleep. Here is an old blanket for you. I am afraid it is very old, and may stink a little, and does not offer much protection from the cold.'

'That's all right.'

They both lay down, facing the wall. Jacques gently drew her close, and whispered in her ear, 'I will keep you warm.'

They fell silent. Then Jacques stirred. Sibyl turned around to face him; in the dark she could just make out that he had raised himself up on his elbow, his head resting on his hand.

'Sibi,' he whispered, *je suis bien content.* It is a miracle that you are here. The past months, the past years – they have been terrible, hell. This war is hell. But you – I have been in despair lately but I prayed and then you fell from the sky as if in answer to my prayer, like a ray of light shining through the darkness. That sounds so sentimental and kitschy but that is exactly how it feels. It is marvellous. For so many years the only emotion I have known is hate. Hate for the Boche. Hatred has filled me, burned me up. But now you have fallen out of the sky and – and I feel the opposite of hate and it is like coming out of the winter to sit by a warm fireplace. I feel such peace, such healing. I know it's not a manly thing to say but emotionally I am full, satisfied, for the first time in so many years, and just because you have come, you are here. It is such a miracle. I have been praying for a miracle for so long and I thought it would be a miracle of war, a military victory. Instead it is you. You are the miracle. I have to tell you this. I cannot sleep; I have to tell you because I am so full, so overflowing, so content. Thank you.'

All she could see of him was a dark outline, a shadow darker than the darkness. And the whites of his eyes in the darkness.

'I feel the same,' she whispered. 'I didn't know, I never expected, that I would meet you here. Of course, I hoped to run into you when I came to Alsace and when the war is over and my job is done I would have looked for you and Margaux and the others. But to find you now, already – it is indeed a miracle.'

He squeezed her hand. But then he became urgent, perturbed. 'Sibi, sit up! *Je t'en prie!* We must talk about this seriously!'

She scrambled into sitting position; his urgency was infectious. He clasped both of her hands in his, firmly. His eyes shone white through the darkness. He whispered still, but the urgency came not from volume but from the words themselves, and their content.

'Sibi, chérie – we are not here for pleasure. In spite of this moment of joy we must be aware that we have a job to do. We will do it together and that is a wonderful miracle. We cannot jeopardise the miracle of our collaboration. We must be professional at all times. Yes, it is an emotional reunion but we are living in dangerous times and we cannot be ruled by emotion. We are up against Goliath and we must be as pure-hearted and single-minded as David if we are to win. The Boche has raped my country and that is why I am here now, why you are here now. I have given my life to this struggle and I will fight it to the death – my own life is of no account. I have before my eyes that poor boy, Marcel Weinum, who was executed by the Boche. I have met his parents and promised them he did not die in vain. He is a martyr to the cause and I will fight this cause to the death. Time is short, very short, and we must remain clear-headed. It is my duty, the duty of all of us who love France, to right the terrible wrong that has befallen our home. That must come first. I cannot jeopardise that goal with personal matters. You understand?'

She nodded in the darkness. 'Of course.'

'The goal of my life is to rid Alsace of the Boche. That has to happen. That must happen. I live from day to day, knowing that every dawn might be my last. I cannot think about the future. Once it has happened, *ma chère* Sibi, once the Boche is gone forever… then there will be a great celebration in Alsace and you and I – well, then is the time to celebrate. *Tu comprends?*'

She nodded, squeezed his hand because she knew he could not see her.

'We are one and we must fight as one. Let us now sleep. We must start before dawn tomorrow.'

They lay down again, then, and he held her close, and they slept.

# Chapter Fourteen

They woke before dawn. The others were not up yet. Jacques prepared a simple *petit déjeuner* of stale baguette with cheese. A ring of large stones containing ashes, charcoal and half-burned pieces of wood indicated their stove; a small pile of dried wood lay next to it. There was also a large canister half-full of water, a battered saucepan and an old tin can which, once opened, revealed a brown powdery substance which might be coffee or might be tea: Sibyl could not tell the difference but set about making a fire to boil the water. For the first time – for last night they were but shadows – Sibyl met the other men. Bearded like Jacques, they emitted a sort of jovial camaraderie, with laughter and back-slapping in what Sibyl conjectured was a show of masculine bravado put on for her benefit; they had not expected a woman, and a young (and pretty) one at that. They spoke a rapid Alsatian too quickly for Sibyl too fully understand; she found she had become rusty in the language through lack of use. Their glances in her direction confirmed her suspicion that she was the subject of their conversation and the reason for their odd behaviour.

Jacques returned from a visit behind the trees and held up a commanding hand. He, too, spoke Alsatian, but slowly, at a pace that Sibyl could follow, and she knew this was for her benefit, and was grateful.

'Comrades!' Jacques said. 'May I introduce our leader, who will be known to you only as Acrobat. I will tell you something about her you did not know: she understands our language and she understands what it means to be Alsatian, and what it means for Alsace to have fallen to the Boche. She is competent and passionate about her work, as passionate as we all are, and will do her best for us. She deserves your respect and I beg of you to treat her with the dignity she deserves. She is our leader and she has much to teach us. Last night you recovered the bounty she has brought with her; weapons and explosives. She knows how to use these things and she will teach us so please behave yourselves. You are not teenagers in the company of a woman for the first time. In fact she is not even a woman and you are not men: at this time we are all freedom fighters. Acrobat, these are the men I work with in the Colmar department: Alain, Gaston, Raoul…' He introduced seven men in all.

Alain, Gaston, Raoul and the others, immediately subdued, came forward, removed their berets, extended hands for her to shake, grinned at her, mumbled words of greeting, and Sibyl smiled back and shook their hands and knew they were all a step further. She had been accepted.

They sat down on the grass or on logs or stones and the Alsatian became rapid again and she strained to understand; but Jacques, next to her, waved a hand with a motion of dismissal and said, 'It's only small talk. Let me explain the important things.'

So, over the stale baguette and cheese and a non-descriptive beverage Sibyl learned more of the details of her mission.

Alsace, Jacques told her, was too large, the Resistance movement too scattered, to be organised as a single unit; and so it had been divided. The area known officially as Bas-Rhin, around Strasbourg, was called North Alsace and the *Maquis* leader there was a man called Henri.

'He will be here soon,' said Jacques. 'He is very competent, but a difficult man. *Très difficile.*'

He shook his head as if despairing of Henri, and continued.

'We are around Colmar and that is South Alsace for the purpose of the Resistance. Up to now I have been the leader down here, but I have been usurped by you, for a very good reason. The problem faced by *maquisards* both in the north and the south is that we have no weapons, no ammunition and no money. This is where you come in; you have brought all of these supplies and we are immensely grateful. Now our work can continue in earnest.'

'What have you done up to now?'

'Well – it is almost embarrassing to tell you. It is like child's play, but it has worked. Little acts of sabotage. Felling trees across roads used by the Boche. Slashing their tyres at night. Dropping large stones on their vehicles from bridges so that their windscreens are smashed. We wounded one of them by such an action. We interrupt their commercial activities. We halt their factories. We even use graffiti to annoy and irritate them! Anything to cause disruptions and slow them down. We use home-made bombs to blow up strategic buildings, bridges essential to them. But our bombs are not very effective as you can imagine. We want real bombs, hand grenades!'

'Plenty of those in the boxes that landed last night!'

'Yes. Our work will be more serious from now on, thanks to you. I understand you will give us a month of training?'

'That's right.'

'Well, we will begin today. There is a ruined castle not far from here and we will all go there and set up camp. It is hidden in the forest, in the Vosges – the Boche do not know of it. We can all stay there and learn. Henri is bringing six or seven of his men. Twenty of mine will do the training.'

'Why only six of Henri's men?'

'Because of the difficulty we have in being so spread apart. These men, they are all *deserteurs* the Boche tried to conscript into the Wehrmacht. They have all fled from their homes, from villages all over the Alsace. They have no way of communicating with each other except by going on foot to the next village, or maybe a farmer will take a man on his wagon or we can borrow a bicycle. But still everyone knows what he has to do. A few will learn with you in the

coming month and then go on to teach others, distribute supplies.
You brought a wireless?'

She nodded. 'Yes. A transceiver. It can receive and transmit
messages. I have brought two.'

*'Très bien.* Then they in the North can have one and communicate with us in the South – we badly need to co-ordinate. With
co-ordination we can achieve more, destroy more. We needed you
desperately, Sibi!'

'Well, I'm here now. And again: you must stop calling me Sibi!
And I may not call you Jacques. That is the very first rule. I am
Acrobat. You are David.'

Jacques snorted. 'I will never call you Acrobat, not even in
public. If I cannot call you Sibi I will call you something else. A
new code name.'

He was silent for a moment, then said, 'Lucie. You will be
Lucie, for me and my men. You have brought us not just weapons
but light.'

*'D'accord.* Lucie, and David. And your boys?'

He shook his head.

'We already know each other's names; it is too late for us. But
you: you are the agent. They must not know your real name or
your field name. It will remain our secret. To the Resistance, you
are Acrobat, known fondly as Lucie.'


Jacques announced it was time to move on. They all set about
clearing up the area, removing all traces of their stay as well as they
could. Most of the boxes of supplies they stored in a back room
of the building; the men would come back for these later, he said,
but now they had a meeting to attend.

He led the way out of the clearing uphill, followed by Sibyl and
the others. It was a well-hidden path, overgrown with brushwood,
through the forested hillside. They were properly in the Vosges

mountains now, Jacques explained, but a part unknown to the Boche, who never ventured this far; for the time being at least, they and the supplies were safe. Each of them carried a box of supplies. Sibyl carried the money herself – one hundred thousand Reichsmarks in cash. Each of the others heaved a box on to his head.

They marched steadily, single file. The trudge was strenuous and seemed never-ending; but eventually they arrived at the ruins of what looked like a small castle, the walls thick and tumbledown and covered in moss, the roof mostly collapsed in heaps of broken tiles. A rusty locked gate blocked a massive entry archway, but Jacques ignored it and walked around to the back of the building where a doorless opening led into the ruin. Through that, across a large overgrown space that might once have been a kitchen, and they found themselves in an open arena which had obviously been prepared, and perhaps even inhabited, for it was cleared of the ubiquitous weeds and bushes that had otherwise claimed the castle.

'Here we are,' said Jacques, carefully lowering the box of hand grenades he had been carrying. All the men followed suit. They lit cigarettes, flexed their arms and legs, some sat down on a low stone wall, others on the flagged moss-covered floor.

'I found this place many years ago,' said Jacques. 'It is a central meeting place for the Alsace South and North *maquisards*. And here is Henri!'

Henri was the largest man Sibyl had ever seen, not only tall, but burly, the thick muscles of arms and thighs straining against the fabric of trousers and his jacket. His face was square, heavy-jowled, a scowl, it seemed, his normal resting expression. At first glance Sibyl assessed his age at about thirty-five; but she could easily be wrong by ten years either way because the general aspect was one of a battle-bruised man made ageless through life-experience. He glared at her as he came forward.

'Who is this?' he asked in Alsatian, and aggression echoed in every word.

'This is our English agent. She is Acrobat, but since that is too impersonal a name we will call her simply Lucie. She is our leader. She will teach us the tricks of her trade.'

The scowl hardened.

'She is just a little girl. This must be a joke. Did she at least bring supplies?'

'Yes. As you can see.' Jacques gestured to the pile of wooden boxes set aside. 'There is more where those came from.'

'Well, let's open them and divide them up. My boys can go and fetch the rest. That's all we need.'

'Forget it,' said Jacques. 'The deal is that she trains us in the use of these weapons and explosives. You're not going anywhere without the training. A month. That's what we agreed.'

'You expect this child to train me? Look at her! Give her some pots and pans and let her cook for us, but don't expect me to take instructions from her.'

'Henri, that's exactly what you're going to do. You might be head of Alsace North but as far as SOE is concerned, and they are now our bosses because we are dependent on them for supplies, she is our chief from now on and you will bloody well accept and respect that or you will go back the way you came, empty-handed. And by the way, she also brought money. I thought you said your men were starving?'

Henri huffed and puffed and Sibyl decided it was time for her to intervene. She stepped forward, smiling, and held out her hand to him.

'*Bonjour,* Henri. I'm delighted to meet you and I'm sure we will work together very well. I have brought some supplies for you, but I cannot release them without first ensuring you are taught how to use them. I assure you that I am more competent than it appears at first sight.'

Henri snorted and seemed about to ignore the outstretched hand but finally took it in his own bear-like paw, and squeezed. Squeezed hard. Sibyl held her breath at the pain. But she did not flinch.

'I suggest we begin,' she said. 'Please, everyone, take a seat.'

Miraculously, they all obeyed, squatting down on their haunches, lowering themselves to the flagstones, or finding a semi-comfortable seat on a wall or stone, forming a loose circle around her. Sibyl, standing before them all, paused, letting her gaze drift from face to face. What a sorry lot of men! They looked like a ragtag gang of hobos, their clothes torn and ragged, shoes and boots scuffed and gaping open. The faces she saw were not eager ones. Not the faces of soldiers setting out to win a righteous war. As a nurse she had learnt to pick up silent cues from the faces of the people she was supposed to help; she had learned to read between the lines, to pick up hidden feelings. And what she read here was not good. She saw despair, anger, gloom, fear, resentment, distrust; resignation to a fate worse, almost, than death.

Their homeland was under siege, overpowered by a foreign power that had only its own dominance as goal. In particular, these men had no future if this war was not won, should Alsace remain German. They were renegades. They had evaded conscription. Should they be caught by the German police, or worse yet, by the Gestapo, their lives were over. They would be sent to concentration camps or executed. They were exiled from their homes, from their futures. There was no hope in those faces, no faith, no belief that they could actually win. They fought with sticks and stones against Panzer and Luftwaffe. They were completely cut off from all news of, perhaps, an imminent Allied invasion; German propaganda fed them a constant diet of German triumph, the certain victory of Third Reich, the swastika as grand finale.

Sibyl was not a natural speaker, nor a teacher. She had never had to stand before a class to impart whatever knowledge she had; and what knowledge *did* she have, in the present circumstances? Just theory, whereas these men had actually lived Resistance, some of them for years. What authority did she have to teach them? Book knowledge; practice in bomb-making, shooting a rifle. Yes, she could perhaps teach those things. But was it enough?

They were waiting for her to speak but no words came from her lips. She had always known she'd have to teach and she'd practised. Learnt some of the chapters from her SOE manual off by heart, so that she could reel out the words when the time came. But now trepidation seemed to have caught hold of her tongue and frozen her brain.

The men waited.

She cleared her throat.

*Speak!*

She took a deep breath and at last the words came.

'I'll start by giving you some of the basics behind SOE work,' she began. 'I welcome all of you and I'm sure we will all get along fine. The first thing I need to tell you, even though you know this already because this is what you have been doing, is that the purpose of our work is simply this: sabotage and subversion.'

So far so good. This was pure manual teaching, and she knew it by heart. Nothing new here; but the men were listening and no-one yet had yawned. The faces were still closed, but they had listened.

'Subversion, properly applied, is a vital weapon in our fight against the Boche, a vital arm in modern warfare. It has a fourfold objective: first of all, we must damage the enemy's material as much as we can, that is, his vehicles and buildings and also his means of communication and production. This is important because modern warfare is entirely dependent on production and communication. If those are destroyed, the war cannot be won. So we must destroy as many machines as possible and damage the means of production.

'The second objective is to strain their manpower resources to the maximum. We have now been at war for almost five years. They are running out of fighting men! They are getting desperate. You have seen this happening in the Alsace, all your best young men taken at their prime to fight for the Wehrmacht. All of you gathered here:

the Nazis would have recruited you too but you are here, resisting. That is good. Try to get as many young Alsatian men out of their hands as you can. And remember the first objective, destruction of property? Well, they are forced to divert manpower to protect their machines and buildings so there again we are weakening them.'

She took a deep breath. A sense of mission, of wave of energy, swept through her. She was getting into the swing of this, and she knew, now, what she must say:

'The third objective is to crack the morale of the enemy. This is already happening. In the first years of war the Boche were a proud and aggressive power, winning by brute force. They thought they were invincible. They are not. You may not know this yet but the Allies are going to win and slowly this fact is filtering though right down to the common German soldier. They have seen their comrades dying: that wasn't supposed to happen: Hitler had made them believe in the invincibility and indestructability of the German forces but that is clearly not true. They have eyes to see, ears to hear.

'And guess what, the common German soldier, who is as reluctant to fight as you are, who has been conscripted just as you have, is learning that he might die for nothing more than a myth. That Hitler has stolen his future. He is beginning to doubt. He is doubting the story fed to him that Germany will rule the world. He is doubting the invincibility of the Third Reich. He is beginning to understand that Hitler's system has cracked and is about to tumble. This undermines the will to fight in the common soldier. He is wondering why he should give his life to a losing war. This loss of morale and will to fight is vital. Part of this moral struggle is that you – every Alsatian man and woman – must show him that you disdain him and do not want him in your country. YOUR country. See, the Boche is an emotional creature and does not want to be disliked. Your hostility is a potent weapon against the aggression he likes to display. Know that it is only show! Behind every bully is a snivelling child! Stand up to his bullying by knowing you are the moral victors!

'Because, fourthly, that is your strength just as his doubt is his weakness. Every Alsatian must stand tall and believe in the moral victory. Inner conviction is half the battle. Know that we are in the right, and that from inner strength comes outer victory. Know this with every fibre of your body, with every figment of your soul. Feel that certainty rise up in your heart and fill you with power. You must feel this, know this, so that it becomes your very life. *Vive la victoire!*'

The last word was a shout, a battle cry of the heart with a fist shot high; and to her great satisfaction the *maquisards* caught the spark.

'*Vive la victoire!*' the shout went up. Fists raised, men jumped to their feet; they laughed and cheered and relief flooded through Sibyl. She had done it: caught the flagging hope in their beings, raised it up, elevated it into a force that would give them the passion and the strength for the weeks and months ahead. Something to build on. For it is not possible to build a movement with men who are dead inside, as these men had been up to this moment.

She had been terrified of this initial speech; she had never taught anyone before, much less a gaggle of battle-weary guerrillas, and she had balked at the idea of giving them a lecture. She had planned to keep to the words of the SOE manual, words she had learned by heart, but by the end of the hour she had found her own words, words that simply billowed from her, words filled with excitement and confidence and pride, and now, as she paused and let her glance travel from face to face, she saw that very passion reflected and she knew that she had won. She had disarmed them, and armed them anew with revived vigour and confidence; armed them with something even more valuable than the hardware concealed in the piled-up supply boxes behind her.

Henri came forward, his hand stretched out.

'*Merveilleux!*' he exclaimed. 'Lucie, I am glad that you have joined us.'


After that it was fairly plain sailing.

In fact, it was easy from now on because Sibyl was able to unpack what she called 'Churchill's Toybox', and she didn't need much more to hold the men's attention. They plainly enjoyed this. Their eyes lit up when the boxes were prised open and they finally saw the Sten guns that would be theirs, the bazookas, the hand grenades, the detonators. They touched the equipment with pure love, the way a young mother might touch her baby, their eyes soft with delight. The scowls that had seemed engraved on their faces melted into smiles as the magic of hope began to take hold.

Eyes literally bulged with delight as she unpacked one 'toy' after the other, lifted them out of their boxes one by one, held them up, described them and in some cases passed them around. Hand grenades. Pencil fuses. Plastic explosives. And guns, guns, guns.

She showed them tricks that were simple but so very effective. Lighting a cigarette, she waved it at them. 'A factory worker,' she said, 'can create havoc with this. Watch.'

She stuck the unlit end into a half-filled matchbox and closed the box so that the cigarette was jammed.

'All the worker has to do now,' she explained, 'is throw the box into a pile of rubbish – paper-rubbish, cardboard, anything that burns – just before he goes home. The cigarette acts as a slow fuse. The worker has left the building – but he has just committed arson. A crime in peacetime, a method of clandestine warfare in times like this. Now,' she said, letting her gaze move across the rapt faces, 'none of you are factory workers. You have gone underground. But there are hundreds of little tricks like that you can employ. You can drop a handful of sand into the axle of a railway waggon: if you get it into the correct part of the box, the axle will seize up. Bam. You have disabled a train the Boche is depending upon.

'And then this.' She held up a metal can. 'This is ordinary axle grease but it has finely ground carbondrum mixed into it. Replace the axles' lubricant with this doctored stuff and –*voilà!* You've ground the transporter to a stop. You've messed up the enemy's plan. He's delayed, he's angry, his whole military planning is in disarray.

'Smuggle yourselves into railway yards, into the siding offices. I've heard you're good at that sort of thing. Well, once you're there, jumble up the destination dockets and cards. The next day the Boche is going to connect engines with the wrong waggons. He'll send an urgently required tank track to Lyon instead of to Normandy. Anyone here know anything about machine tools? You, Gaston? Good. Slip the wrong-sized cog into a chain of gears – jam up the whole thing.

'This little toy here'– she held it up – 'is called the Clam. It's a limpit mine, packed with explosive, and it's magnetic. You attach it to magnetic enemy property and it will damage or even destroy, say, an electric motor.

'But my own favourite toy is this: plastic explosive, PE. It's like plasticine. You can use it anywhere, even under water. You can stuff it into dead rats and leave them lying around in a Boche factory and they will dispose of them by shovelling them into a furnace and –BOOM! Destruction, another waste of production time. You can leave the dead rats in the coal stocks of railway yards. You can stand on a bridge and drop them into the tenders of engines passing beneath you, for the fireman to shovel into his fire box.'

The *maquisards* listened and watched with rapt attention. *Men!* She thought. *Where does this fascination with blowing things up, destroying things come from?* Because this was not just about the war, not just about sabotaging the enemy. They enjoyed these lessons for their own sakes; as if the very act of destroying objects – or people – gave them satisfaction, and learning about the ways and means of destruction came as second nature. They listened, they asked questions, they were eager to learn: because the subject itself was fascinating.

By the second week it was plain to see that the *maquisards* had had enough of theory. They wanted practice. They moved on to the use of the various guns; target practice followed.

After a day of that Sibyl decided it was time for some real-life explosive practice. Jacques had told her about the Freiburg-Colmar railway line, of strategical importance to the Wehrmacht as it brought troop reinforcements across the Rhine bridge that separated Alsace from Germany proper.

'We will blow it up,' said Sibyl. 'We will destroy this line. Now, just this line. We will use *plastique.*'

'One day,' said Jacques, 'We will blow up the bridge itself.'

They exchanged a glance, and a grin. Sibyl nodded.

'Later. First the railway line, and the supply trains.'

It was a dangerous mission; it meant leaving their hideout at nightfall and making their way surreptitiously, by foot, to one safe house after another throughout the following three nights; it was too dangerous to travel by day.

'I can't take all of you,' Sibyl said. 'We will split the group. Jacques, you will come, and you, you, you and you.' She pointed out six men from the north and south divisions. 'Henri, you stay here and the rest of you can continue target practice while we are gone – it will be a few days. When we return we'll swap: I'll take Henri and the others – hopefully you will all have perfect aim by then – will go on another mission, blow up something else. Henri, you can choose the target.'

They set off down the hillside. She realised, now, how thoroughly Jacques knew his area. He led them through forests and vineyards, over fields and across rivers; he had friends everywhere, farmers who put them up in barns, farmer wives who fed them, places of refuge where they would be safe during the daytime. She realised, too, just how strong the support was for their work; Jacques had told her that ninety per cent of all Alsatians regarded themselves as French and wanted to see the backs of the Germans, and the other ten per cent collaborated only out of fear and self-interest.

'The Boche regard us as terrorists, and we will be worse terrorists once we are properly armed,' said Jacques, 'but for us, it is only self-defence. It is David against Goliath.'

Jacques impressed her with his knowledge of the exact timings of the troop-carrying trains. They aimed to blow up the six-thirty a.m. train on the third night, coming from Germany over the Rhine bridge and down to southern France via Colmar.

It was a moonlit night; Jacques led them all down an embankment to the railway line, and there Sibyl unpacked the PE – a soft, buttery substance that smelt faintly of almonds – and attached it to the cord, connecting it to the detonator. Detonating it would be Jacques' task.

They slunk back up the embankment and crouched beneath the trees and among the bushes. Jacques squatted behind a bush closer to the railway line, with the detonator. Sibyl was as animated as the rest of them; it was, after all, a first for her too. This was no longer practice, but a real-life bombing. The night was still and seemed to breathe with them. The moon was long gone; darkness enveloped them. They spoke only in whispers, or not at all. They waited. An owl hooted into the silence, as if announcing the imminent drama. Doubt flooded through Sibyl. What if the train was early? Then it would pass by undamaged. What if it was late? Then it would be stalled for a few hours while the line was repaired, but the dramatic impact of the bomb would be lost.

Had Jacques really got the timing right? The Germans were said to be perfectly precise, immaculate in their calculations – but still. They were human – or were they? – and subject to human error. She prayed that night, of all nights, for German meticulousness.

'Shhhh!' whispered Jacques. 'Here it comes.'

Sibyl heard nothing at first and then, from the distant east, she picked up the rumble of the approaching train. Every cell in her body tensed. Dawn had started its approach; the landscape was veiled in grey, through which the straight lines of the track could be seen. Then, to the east, movement. It looked like a toy, at first, moving steadily towards them through the half-light. There it was. A thing of menace, bringing death to Alsace. It was a long, long train, with an engine, two carriages, and then multiple open carriages carrying panzers. Heading for the South, into France, into the enemy's hands. It had to be stopped.

If everything went according to plan, then some of the soldiers in that train would die. And she would have killed for the first time. *Could she kill Germans,* they had asked her, and tonight, the answer was, categorically, resoundingly, *yes.* But it was a soulless kind of killing, impersonal. The thrill she felt, the anxiety, was not so much for these deaths but for the one tiny victory they would achieve that day.

It was time. She gave the signal. Jacques plunged down the detonator. There was a huge bang; the line heaved up, the engine and its carriages buckled and toppled and chaos lay before them. Some of the men let out a cheer; Sibyl shushed them, and signalled for them to run into the copse behind them; but once they were clear and certain of concealment they whooped and laughed and hugged each other.

They were now, officially, *plastiquers,* bombers.

It was only afterwards, on the way back, that Sibyl fully grasped the meticulous attention Jacques had invested in the planning of this attack, resting in the faith that one day he would have the means. Night after night in the preceding months he had gone to the embankment, lain in wait, timed the train, convincing himself of its punctuality.

'The Boche operate like machines,' he explained on the more lei-surely return march. 'Their confidence rests on precisely structured processes. They cannot abide chaos; they can't abide the slightest deviation from a plan. They love order. This might be just one train bombed, but it is a cog in a huge machine. Yes, the line will be repaired as soon as possible and the daily trains will recommence but think of the disruption to the machine further down the line!'

'We have created havoc in the machine today. We have removed one little cog that keeps the whole thing running. It is something to rejoice in.'

'My boys are rejoicing too much. They are angry, and angry men enjoy smashing things. It's not good to smash things in anger.'

'That's why we have the SOE. Why I'm here. To teach them the art of smashing things calmly, not angrily. Professional smashing. A matter of training.'

She had deliberately not included Jacques in the men who needed such training. It was Jacques who had first taught her the art of calmness. He needed no further training; when he smashed things it would be with studied deliberation. He'd proven it today.

But when they returned to the camp they saw that Jacques' worry was well-founded. Two of Henri's men had absconded, and they had taken twenty hand grenades with them, and two rifles. Henri himself was sleeping off a drunken night. The wine was finished.

*'Merde!'* said Jacques. 'But I will find them and they will be punished.'

# Chapter Fifteen

Sibyl had set up the transmitter soon after their arrival at the camp and sent a first coded message that she had arrived safely. The arrangement was that, at first, she would make contact once a week at prearranged times, different each week. In the third contact, the message from Acrobat contained a cryptic sentence: *The geese have flown south.*

Sibyl gave out an exhilarated yelp.

'They've done it! They've invaded France! It's happening!'

That night, the *maquisards* celebrated as never before: their regular gentil wine was just not good enough. Jacques opened five of his most prized bottles, Laroche-Gauthier riesling, 1938.

For the first time, the men laughed; they joked, and once they had downed a glass or two, raised their voices in rowdy songs; they teased Sibyl, flirted, asked her to dance (she refused) and the night ended with a rousing, if somewhat off-tune, rendering of 'La Marseillaise'.

That night, Jacques whispered into Sibyl's ear: 'Maybe, maybe there is a future for us.'

'We must believe in that future,' she whispered back.

The month was almost over, and the men were trained as well as they could be in the limited time. They had practised one further major bombing, this time a power station near Strasbourg, and this time Jacques had led the expedition, taking the men who had been left behind the last time, and leaving Sibyl to guard the supplies and supervise the others as they practised.

They had tamed their spirits considerably since that first day. With the money she had brought Jacques had slipped down to a nearby farm and purchased food: cheese, eggs, bread, potatoes. He shot and killed two rabbits and cooked a simple stew. The men now looked, if not exactly well-fed, at least not half-starved. The one thing they never ran out of was wine. Perhaps not the best quality, or even the second best, but an excellent blend from the Domaine Laroche-Gauthier.

And then Jacques was back, and there was just one week left, and it seemed to her a last week of freedom; a holiday, in fact, wrenched from the horrors of war, and though the living was rough and hunger gnawed at her belly every day, every night seemed precious, each moment a radiant jewel of time to be lived with the utmost of intensity.

Between Sibyl and Jacques had grown a communion that was almost mystical in its depths, nourished, no doubt, by the roots they shared, roots firmly planted in those halcyon bygone years. Now, that former youthful intimacy and joy returned, mellowed, matured, like good wine. They lived as one. A glance, a moment of silence, a slight gesture: they knew what the other was think-ing, feeling, living. The balled power that came with living on the edge, the knowledge that great danger and even death waited in the wings, that this was a respite torn from the hideous war machine and that soon, very soon, Sibyl would plunge deep into that very machine, vulnerable and alone, lent both sharpness and beauty to their communion. Theirs was a unity so deep, a beauty so pure, their souls so utterly fused that the word 'love' was never once mentioned; it was superfluous. They simply knew. At night they slept in each other's arms, their bodies two halves of a whole.

She had met him as a raggedy deserter who had neither washed not changed his clothes nor shaved in perhaps weeks, his face, more scraggly beard than skin, his hair long and greasy and hanging to his shoulder. His dishevelled appearance had gone a long way in preventing their relationship from taking a physical development, as might have happened in more propitious times; his wildness a barrier that she had, in secret, welcomed, even as she had embraced his being, explored every turning of his heart, an unspoken pact between them. A shower together under a waterfall of cold fresh water, a bar of soap she had packed in her luggage, went a long way in propelling their relationship to the next stage. That, and the knowledge that either or both of them might die before they'd meet again.

This last night they reached the very rim of the interlude granted them, the edge of the axe that would chop apart this war-stolen month and thrust Sibyl into the fray. Their bodies responded spontaneously. They made love, melting wordlessly, soundlessly into each other in the darkness, a consummation that simply completed all that had gone before.

And then it was time for her to go.


Vera had given her the clothes to pack, the clothes to wear. A simple tweed skirt, grey, not new, but obviously used and tired, fitting perfectly over Sibyl's slim hips. A cotton blouse, its floral pattern faded through many washes. Thick cotton stockings, and French-style boots with cork soles. More of the same, packed in her battered little suitcase, along with old cotton underwear. She had been checked and double-checked for anything English: bus tickets, coins, the flotsam and jetsam one collects without thinking about it. But the most important item in the suitcase was the MCR1 receiver, a miniature device which fit into a biscuit tin, as well as the transmitter. Together they weighed over ten pounds, which made the suitcase quite a bit heavier than if it had contained only clothes. Added to that: the Sten pistol. It had to be kept near the wireless devices, for once the latter were discovered the game was up and the gun was a necessity.

As her time approached, Sibyl had the persistent sense that caterpillars were crawling around in her belly. Just looking at the suitcase made her dizzy.

As Jeanne Dauguet she was to work as a cobbler's assistant in Colmar. The cobbler himself was an older man named Yves Girard who had his own shop; his previous assistant was a young man who had been conscripted to fight in the Wehrmacht, leaving a vacancy that had to be filled. By Jeanne. M Girard was an Alsatian through and through, detesting the Germans, supporting the Allies in any way he could. Recently he had taken on a more active role in the Resistance.

'You'll find out the details once you arrive,' Vera had said. 'You're to work at the front of the shop, taking orders for repairs, selling boots, shoes and shoe paraphernalia, while M Girard will do his cobbling in the workshop at the back. You'll have a small bedroom in his flat above the shop; you'll share a kitchen and bathroom with him.'

M Girard, Vera explained, was officially Jeanne's great-uncle. There really had been a Jeanne Dauguet, who had left Colmar for Paris as a child with her parents sixteen years previously; her father had been killed in a road accident soon afterwards. The real Jeanne had grown up in Paris; she had been an underground Resistance member but had been killed in a bomb a year ago. No body had been found so her mother, still active as an underground agent in the Paris Resistance, had offered up her deceased daughter's genuine birth certificate and other documents as a cover for a new agent: Sibyl. And so Sibyl was to step into Jeanne's shoes, and Jeanne would live on in Sibyl's body. Her great-uncle Yves was really that; Jeanne's grandmother's brother.

'If they search you, stand back and let it happen. Remember you are Jeanne. Wear your hair in a modest bun, away from the face,' Vera had instructed. 'Or in plaits, clipped down, circling your face. Not much make-up – you do not want to look provocative in any way. You do not want to stand out. If they ask where you got the powder compact, you must say it is a present from a fiancé who died and you still mourn him. Do not look men straight in the eyes, especially not Germans. You will have German customers; speak to them in their language and be always polite. If you know their name, use it. Herr so-and-so; if he's an officer, use his rank. They like that. Always be demure, soft-spoken. That is the character of Jeanne Dauguet. You must look the part. You are fairly pretty but unaware of it. You have the pure innocent look that German men like; use it, but use it discreetly. If they flirt, you may not flirt back. You do not want to appear forward. You will create an aura of modesty, untouchablility, around yourself. You are just a simple French girl, a girl from Alsace, returned from Paris to work in her uncle's shop. You are not political. You do not resist the German annexation of your country: you do not like it but you are co-operative. You do as you are told, observe the rules. You are not an elegant Parisienne, one of those superior classic women basking in self-assurance. You come from modest circumstances and you are modest. Your papers are in order; they show that you were born in Colmar. Your father is dead, your mother is a nurse in Paris. You have returned to the home you left as a small child. The German authorities might insist you are now German and need German papers. Go along with that – it is to your advantage to have authentic German identification papers. It will strengthen your credentials. Do it, but do not initiate that step yourself.'

Almost as an afterthought, she added, 'Of course, the most difficult part of the mission will be the journey to Colmar, carrying the suitcase. If they open that – well, it's the end.'

The most dangerous part of today's mission was the gap between the hideout and Strasbourg, for she had no cover story yet, only Jacques' instructions and company. At four-thirty, she and Jacques waited at the appointed meeting place, a junction where a footpath met a narrow road. They waited in silence, Jacques' arm around her, she leaning against his chest, eyes closed. It was still dark, but the greyness of early dawn was already creeping across the fields – gradually revealing a vineyard, and a meadow where a few cows grazed. Somewhere, a cock crowed.

Eventually, Jacques squeezed her shoulder and whispered, *'ça va?'*

*'Oui,'* she replied. But then, because she could not lie to him, she added, *'J'ai un peu peur, honnêtement.'*

'It's all right to feel fear. But fear will not win because you won't turn back.'

'No.'

'I too feel fear, on your behalf. But, well. Remember what we agreed the first night, Sibyl. We will go through this, come what may. I wish we could do it together but it's not to be. You have your role and I have mine and we will help win this thing.'

'Yes.'

'Here is the farmer. *Au revoir.*'

*'Au revoir,* Jacques.'

A horse-drawn carriage filled with farm produce plodded up beside them. The wagon had been specially modified so as to hide a human being between the cartwheels. Jacques and Sibyl lifted the suitcase into the back of the waggon, covered it with cabbages. Jacques helped her to crawl into the hideout space between the wheels. And then, without another word, he was gone.

The driver made several stops on the way, chatting with farmers as he picked up produce for the market; it took hours to reach Strasbourg and Sibyl could tell they had reached the city because of the traffic noises. Finally she heard him speak the words: *the apples are tasty this year.* That was the code. Sibyl scrambled from her hiding place, pulled out her suitcase, and slipped into the open door of a townhouse.

# Part Three

## A Question of Identity

*'What good fortune for governments that the people do not think.'*

*Adolf Hitler*

# Chapter Sixteen

From this moment, she had a cover story: the daughter of the house was an old school friend and she, Jeanne Dauguet, had spent the night, having travelled up from Paris the day before. She had a used train ticket, Paris-Strasbourg, to prove it. Her hosts were a middle-aged couple called the Schmidts; they ushered her into a small kitchen and served her breakfast, of which Sibyl could eat but little. From a secret pocket in her suitcase Sibyl removed a wad of paper money, which she slipped to Mr Schmidt. Those who supported the *maquisards* did so at great risk, and at some expense in these hard times, and had to be recompensed.

The daughter, Yvonne Schmidt, her supposed friend – her real name – played her part well, greeting her with a torrent of chatter, as if she really was her friend, and they kept up this charade until, at nine, Sibyl took her leave and, suitcase in hand, stepped out into the street. The Schmidts had given her walking directions to the station, now renamed the *Hauptbahnhof.* She arrived there without incident, bought her ticket to Colmar, and boarded the train. She was now Jeanne Dauguet, on her way to take up her new job as cobbler's assistant in Colmar. Only, deep inside, in a secret place that must never, ever see the light, lay Sibyl Lake, on her debut mission as Acrobat One; also known as Lucie.

A pair of uniformed men were making their way slowly down the train carriage. From their uniforms Sibyl identified them as local police. Just checking, no doubt. *Heart, slow down.*

They approached at a snail's pace; every passenger's documents were inspected. Some were accepted immediately. In other cases, the passenger was interrogated for what seemed an unhealthy length of time. Why? The passengers so questioned – as far as Sibyl could tell from further down the carriage – seemed innocuous enough. A middle-aged woman with a basket on her lap. A smartly dressed young man who looked as if he was off to work. An older man with a small girl on his lap, perhaps his granddaughter.

Finally it was her turn.

'Ihre Papiere, bitte.'

She rummaged in her handbag, found her identity card, handed it over.

'Where are you going to?'

'To Colmar.'

'Where from?'

'I came from Paris. I spent last night with a friend in Strasbourg.'

So far, so good; the first part was a lie; she had not come from Paris, but just in case, she had proof that she had. But it was true that she had spent the night with a friend in Strasbourg, and they could check it if they were suspicious. They weren't; they were more interested in her language. The incriminating suitcase was neatly stored in the luggage rack above her head. It took all of her willpower not to glance up. It took yet more strength to keep her attention focused on the questioning and not allow her mind to quiver at the thought of the deadly biscuit tin so innocently concealed above them. They remarked on her German; she explained how she had learned it.

'You speak excellent German.'

'Yes, my grandmother was Austrian and she always spoke German with me.'

That, too was true; her grandmother had indeed spoken German with her. *Sibyl's* grandmother; had Jeanne's? Perhaps. They would hardly be able to check.

Next they wanted to know why she was travelling to Colmar, what she was going to do there, how long she intended to stay, and if she could prove it. Indeed: she showed them a letter from the cobbler, her 'uncle' Yves Girard, explaining that his former assistant had been conscripted and sent to the Eastern Front, and that he urgently needed her help.

'It's a semi-permanent position, at least until the war is over and the assistant returns,' she added.

'If he returns!'

The officers both laughed, handed her back her papers, wished her a pleasant stay, and moved on. She took a deep breath. It was over. And, it seemed, the reason they had singled out other passengers for questioning was because, presumably, they had not been able to speak German – or not well enough. Jacques had explained to her that French was completely banned. In all the schools, now, German was the medium. Bookshops had been raided, all French books burned. No French newspapers were allowed; only German everywhere. She had already seen the swastika signs when walking through Strasbourg: on some of the cars, a huge one on the station building, more on the walls of the ticket office and waiting room and platform, portraits of Hitler everywhere. It sent chills down her spine.

There were no further incidents before the train chugged into Colmar's station – or Kolmar, the German version, as the station sign announced. She stood up, straightened her clothes and reached up for the suitcase. A fellow passenger, a man in his forties who had until now been buried in a newspaper and had spoken perfect fluent German with the two police officers, sidled up beside her.

'Erlauben Sie mir, gnädige Frau,' he said, and, before she could object, reached up for the suitcase.

'Meine Güte, that's quite heavy!' he remarked, which is exactly what Sibyl had dreaded. Yes, it was heavy. Too heavy for a normal innocuous suitcase, and chivalrous men everywhere would want to help. Another mistake she'd made as an agent: she should have arranged for a separate, clandestine, delivery of the radio. A man carrying a heavy suitcase would be left alone; a woman would be offered help everywhere. Too late to think of that now. She thanked the gentleman, refused his offer of further help, and lugged the case down the carriage and on to the platform, through the station and out into the streets.

There she stopped, placing the case on the pavement, to remove the sketched map from her leather shoulder bag. She found herself in a large square; this she had to cross to access the main street that would lead her to the cobbler's shop. In better days she would have taken a taxi, but none was to be seen.

She took a deep breath, picked up the suitcase, and marched across the square. Once again swastika flags, banners and posters adorned the buildings: hanging from windows, slung across the street like Christmas decorations, pasted onto lantern posts, on walls, everywhere. If you didn't already know that Colmar was now firmly German soil – according to the Germans – then you certainly would know now. Army Jeeps and trucks trundled through the town, swastikas flying from their hoods or pasted on their doors; Wehrmacht soldiers with apparently little work on their hands sat at small tables outside a café. A group of them stood at a fountain, washing their faces. Soldiers outnumbered civilians almost two to one; in fact, Sibyl saw few of the latter, and those she saw were invariably older women with children.

She soon learned the reason for the dearth of young women on the streets. Faces turned as she walked by, wolf-whistles and admiring grins followed her as she continued on her way. Some of the soldiers doffed their hats, or half-bowed towards her. No-one had ever called Sibyl beautiful, but today she might very well have been a film star. The attention was not only unwelcome but downright disconcerting. She wanted to be, needed to be, invisible. Why had Vera not warned her, advised her, that in a town overrun with German soldiers she would, simply by being female and young, turn heads?

But no: Vera *had* warned her, obliquely. *Wear this ring,* Vera had said. *It's an engagement ring; it might help establish that you're unavailable.* She had pushed a thin gold ring with what was probably a fake diamond on to her ring finger. *Not that a German intent on mischief will take much notice,* she'd added. She hadn't thought it necessary at the time, but had worn it anyway. But who, now, was looking at her hand, seeing the ring?

But it was too late, she could not blame Vera. She could not allow herself to show nervousness, and she must deal with it here and now. She straightened her shoulders and walked on, suitcase firmly in her right hand. At least, she thought, being an object of admiration is probably better than being an object of suspicion.

She was soon to change her mind on that reflection. She passed a café with several outdoor tables, at one of which sat a group of uniformed men enjoying, it seemed, a mid-morning cup of coffee. (Didn't they have a war to fight, she wondered? Or had the war not yet reached Colmar?) Again, every single head turned as she walked by, one man whistled – and one stood up. Her heart skipped a beat as he fell into step next to her. Giving a slight bow, removing his cap, he said,

'*Guten Morgen, gnädiges Fräulein! Darf ich behilflich sein?* May I be of help to you?'

He gestured towards the suitcase, and continued, '*Bitte, erlauben Sie mich, Ihren Koffer zu tragen.* Please allow me to carry your suitcase.'

She replied, in German, 'Oh, no thank you. It's quite all right. It's not heavy and I haven't got far to go.'

'But I insist! It wouldn't be right for me to allow you to continue so heavily burdened. Please, *gnädiges Fräulein.* You must let me help. It is a command, not a request. Oh, and may I introduce myself: Major Wolfgang von Haagen, Commandant of the Kolmar region, at your service.'

Did she detect a threat in those words, or was it only her own edginess, her guilt? *Let me carry your case, or I'll have you arrested? Searched?* She could not risk it. *It is a command, not a request.*

'Well, all right then. It's very kind of you. My name is Jeanne Dauguet.'

She stopped, set down the cases, stepped aside.

*'Ich freue mich, Sie kennenzulernen, Fräulein Dauguet.'*

He held out his right hand. She took it. His grip was firm, confident, a second too long. His eyes sought hers and though she had looked down, avoiding his gaze, something in it forced her to meet it. His eyes were dark blue, penetrating, questioning, admiring. He smiled, nodded slightly, bent his knees to take grasp the suitcase handle, lifted the case.

'My goodness, but it's indeed heavy! What have you got in there?'

She had, during the train journey, thought of an answer to that one.

'Books!' she said. It was the first thing that had occurred to her, and now she'd have to stick to the story, before he asked... 'I read a lot.'

'Indeed! So do I! What kind of books?'

A second's pause as her brain worked at top speed searching for a more elaborate answer, an explanation. *I'm a student and they are textbooks. A history student. No, literature.* No, she was a writer herself and the books were for research. No, they were antique books and she was a collector. All nonsense. She simply loved reading. *Keep your cover stories simple, as near to the truth as possible,* Vera had said. She was indeed an avid reader.

'Well – mostly novels. Literature. French literature and – and German literature, of course.'

Damn. She should not have mentioned French literature. What if he insisted on confiscating it, here and now? As for German literature: while she knew the names of some of classical German authors – Goethe, Mann, Hesse – she had not actually read any of them. She was more familiar with French and, of course, British literature, but whereas a love of French authors was plausible, Jeanne Dauguet being French, she could never mention Dickens, Elliot, Hardy, Bronte, Austen to a German officer. But what if he asked her, now, about Goethe or Mann? *Why had she lied?*

She was caught out. Not even an hour in Colmar and already knotted in a web of lies, contaminated, exposed. He was going to insist she open the case, show her the 'books'. She was finished. He'd blow a whistle and they'd come running to arrest her. The Gestapo. Lock her up. Interrogate her. Draw out her secrets. Forty-eight hours, her trainers at Beaulieu had said. Stay silent, or at least distract them, for forty-eight hours to give her team time to escape. Thank goodness she was new on the job and so had few secrets to be extracted if they tortured her. They already knew about Jacques. He was wanted anyway, for desertion from the German army. He was on the run, knew how to hide. He'd be safe.

But she'd have to talk about the ruined castle, try to indicate its location, the store of explosives, guns, grenades. Thank goodness she didn't actually know where they were. She had not seen the location on a map; all she knew was that it was hidden in the vast Vosges foothills, in a forest. It would take time for them to find it and by then, hopefully, the *maquisards* would have removed the supplies, the weapons and the explosives, and hidden them elsewhere. That was the first thing Jacques would do when he heard of her capture.

As for the *maquisards*: she had no idea of their real identities and that was a good thing, only first names. They were safe. But what about *Oncle* Yves? It would be obvious that he was an accomplice. He'd be arrested too. Perhaps he knew vital secrets and they'd torture him to extract them. He was contaminated, and she hadn't even met him yet. *Don't panic, Sibyl!* But she *was* panicking.

So much for her much-lauded calmness under pressure; the reason they'd recruited her in the first place. Gone with the wind! Calmness under pressure was easy as a nurse. Not so much as a spy, an agent in enemy territory. As a nurse she was a professional. As an agent she was a hopeless amateur, and right now she was exposed, and frantic. She had to control her body; it was trembling. No, it wasn't. That was just her mind, her imagination, trembling. Her thoughts. It wasn't real. Maybe, even, it didn't show. *Calm down! Breathe deep. It's all right. He's not a mind-reader. He's just a man trying to impress a woman. Just a man. That's all.*

That entire inner meltdown occurred in a fraction of a second. Now, in real life, von Haagen was speaking again.

'Indeed! I myself prefer poetry to fiction. Perhaps we can have a discussion on the relative merits of both forms of literature at a later date.'

'That would be – interesting.'

'Of course, for all my love of poetry, I readily admit that music is actually the highest of all the arts. "A higher revelation than all wisdom & philosophy," according to the incomparable Ludwig van Beethoven. And, of course, among all the composers, the Germanic ones are by far the best. Johann Sebastian Bach, the aforementioned Beethoven, my own namesake Wolfgang Amadeus Mozart. Speaking of Mozart, do I detect a slight Austrian accent? I must say, your German is excellent, unlike most of the citizens of this town, who speak it only falteringly. Where did you learn to speak so fluently?'

Damn it! She was supposed to have eliminated that telltale accent during her language refresher course at Beaulieu. Obviously, she had not succeeded.

'My grandmother taught me. She was Austrian.'

*Stick to the truth as much as possible.* It was unlikely that he would investigate Jeanne Dauguet's fictitious Austrian grandmother.

'Indeed! Where was she from in Austria?'

'From Salzburg.'

'Fascinating! Like the great Mozart! I myself am from Munich, in Bavaria just across the border from Salzburg. What a fortuitous coincidence! And where are you going to? I assume you are coming from the station – judging from the suitcase. Are you in Kolmar for the first time? Or are you returning after a visit elsewhere? I see you are wearing a ring on your engagement finger – yes, I admit I was curious enough to steal a look – perhaps you were visiting your fiancé?'

*Mind your own bloody business,* she wanted to say.

What she actually said was, 'I've come to stay with my uncle for a while.'

Jeanne Dauguet would never instigate a quarrel with a German officer, never be brash, never rude. Especially one who kept mentioning suitcases. *Keep your head down,* Vera had said. *Forget pride. Jeanne Dauguet is modest and compliant.*

He towered above her, which was in itself intimidating; his stride so long she had to quicken hers to keep up; although he noticed and slowed down. But the sense of intimidation persisted, emphasised not only by his physique but the entire military manifestation, in itself designed to evoke authority and respect. It worked.

He wore knee-high black boots, polished to a flawless shine, over wide-flapped jodhpurs of grey gabardine, topped by a single-breasted jacket (with its long sleeves, highly inappropriate for the warm June weather, but for that very reason asserting superiority) buttoned up to a high upright collar, smartly tailored with a wide belt at the waist. She scanned the jacket for Nazi symbols, swastikas or the double runes. At least there was that; he was *Wehrmacht,* not *Waffen SS.* Several medals decorated the jacket, and the oak leaves of merit adorned the collar.

Blond hair showed beneath the peaked cap, a wide-winged German eagle insignia on the soft grey fabric above the shiny black visor. As for his face: he was handsome, in a chiselled, cold, Germanic way: clean-shaven, square-jawed, narrow-nosed. His wide, thin-lipped smile did not reach the icy blue eyes.

He was also persistent.

'And your fiancé? Where is he?'

'He – he was in the French army. I'm afraid he was killed in 1940, soon after the invasion.'

A fictitious fiancé, it had been decided, would offer some protection against courtship attempts. It wasn't working.

'Ah. I see. My condolences. As you still wear his ring I assume you still have – feelings for him. But I think, after four years – well, life goes on after death and now you have come to Kolmar it's a good time to let go of the past. And… oh, may I help you?'

Sibyl had stopped to remove something from her shoulder bag. It was the sketch that had accompanied *Oncle* Yves' welcoming letter, showing her how to walk to his cobbler shop from the station. It would take a good ten minutes, he'd said.

Sibyl did not want to spend the ten minutes in the company of Major von Haagen, being grilled in a probing but outwardly informal interrogation. But how to get rid of him? He seemed bent on chivalry; now he had taken the sketch out of her hand, frowning as he inspected it.

'*Gerechtigkeitsgasse.* I don't know this street. But your uncle has indicated quite well the way you are to walk. We must turn right at the next corner, and then left again. It's in the centre of the *Altstadt,* the old town. A beautiful part of Kolmar, I have to say.'

He launched into an admiring description of Colmar's architecture, including several details about the history of the town and its changing status from German to French and back again, and how this had affected its character. He insisted that it was the prettiest town in Alsace, if not the whole of France, but not quite as pretty as the picturesque villages of Bavaria and Austria.

They walked on, Major von Haagen still loquacious, Sibyl still reticent, only half-listening as her mind worked strenuously trying to figure out how to get rid of him once she arrived at the cobbler's. What if he insisted on delivering her safely into the hands of *Oncle* Yves? How well would *Oncle* Yves play his part? She had to get rid of him at the door – but how? How to shake him off?

But it was too late anyway. They turned a corner and a sign in spiky German script indicated they had arrived at *Gerechtigkeitsgasse,* Justice Lane. It was hardly more than a passageway, so narrow only a single vehicle, if it were not too wide, could pass through. It was a pretty cobbled street lined by narrow half-timbered houses on both sides, many of them with pots of flowers in full bloom flanking the doorstep or brilliantly red geranium boxes hanging from the windows. All of this leant a quaint, fairytale character to the road that belied the stiff and pompous name the conquering force had bestowed upon it. She wondered what the original name was; she knew that all French street names in Alsace had been abolished and replaced with German ones. She might have asked the Major, if it were not for the fact that she simply had to get rid of him. They walked on.

Some of the buildings had shops on the ground floor, large picture windows cut into the thick stone walls. A bakery – *Bäckerei,* the sign outside declared – with an empty shop-window. A charcuterie, *Metzger,* with two or three limp sausages on display. A haberdashery: *Kurzwarenhändler.* One sign read *Geigenbauer,* violin-maker, but the window was roughly boarded up and the word *Jude* scrawled crudely in huge red letters across the wooden panels. And, finally, at number fifteen, a large sign announced, in jagged German script, *Schuster.* Cobbler.

Sibyl stopped and held out her hand for her suitcase.

'Thank you for your help, sir,' she said. 'Here is where my uncle works and lives. *Auf Wiedersehen.'*

Perhaps now, at least, he would deposit the case on the pavement. Her hand remained outstretched, empty.

'But I won't hear of it! I would be less than chivalrous if I did not deliver you safely into the hands of your uncle. I will put this suitcase into his hands, and his alone. Now, do you want to enter first, or shall I? The shop seems to be open.'

Indeed, a sign hanging inside the window read *Ouvert.*

'Also, I need to have a word with your uncle. That sign must be changed to a German one.'

Sibyl shrugged; there was nothing to be done. She took a deep breath and pushed open the door. A bell jangled. She entered the shop; to find a narrow space no more than four meters in width, divided down the length by a counter, with standing space for customers on one side and shelves along the wall on the other. On the shelves rested the odd pair of shoes or boots, as well as shoe paraphernalia: a few boxes of shoe polish, packets of shoe laces, brushes and leathers and soft cloths for cleaning shoes, random heels, and a few leather pouches and bags.

Von Haagen was right behind her. Breathing down her neck, in fact, in the narrow confines of the shop. She had no idea how to get rid of him.

A door at the back of the shop opened. A man in his late seventies or early eighties, white-haired, bent, bespectacled, and wearing a rather soiled full-length apron, peered out from what was apparently a work-room at the back; he came in wiping his hands on a rag. His eyes lit up when he saw her, but, as his gaze wandered further, and he took in the tall uniformed man standing behind her, they widened. It was the moment Sibyl had been dreading. But the next moment *Oncle* Yves, after his initial inner leap of shock, landed on his feet.

*'Jeanne?'* he whispered, *'C'est toi?'*

*'Bien sûr, Oncle Yves, c'est moi.'*

He opened his arms. Sibyl rushed into his embrace. He hugged her as if she were, indeed, his long-lost niece. Further words of endearment followed: *How you have grown! Let me look at you! You are so pretty! It's good to see you, Uncle! Maman sends her love!*

Von Haagen coughed, interrupting the welcome love-feast. He had, at least, set the suitcase down on the wooden floor.

'May I remind you to always speak German? I intend to oversee this error in view of the situation but from now on I expect you to speak German. Remember there is a fine of five *Reichmarks* for speaking French.'

His voice, so solicitous and obliging while speaking to her, had turned harsh and demanding.

*Oncle* Yves adopted a humble mien and replied,

'My apologies, *Herr Major*; you must forgive an old man. It is true that I spoke German in my youth, before the Great War, but I am afraid since then my brain has grown somewhat rusty and I am not as fluent as I might be. Again, my sincerest apologies and I will of course comply with the rules.'

He spoke in perfect, if excruciatingly slow, German, and Sibyl detected an undercurrent of satire behind the words. Von Haagen, though, seemed not to notice; obviously satisfied with the simpering apology, he nodded smartly and said,

'Major Wolfgang von Haagen. I found your niece struggling along the street with her suitcase and assisted her in transporting it to this address. I find it very interesting that you are a cobbler, Herr Girard. I am sure you have already noticed with your professional eye that my own marching boots are in a deplorable condition.'

'I have not inspected your boots as yet, Herr Major. But yes, I can see that they could do with a complete resoling. Unfortunately, though, leather is very expensive at this time due to scarcity. Many of my customers therefore elect to resole their footwear in wood.'

'Wood! Do you think I am going to march in clogs, like a Dutch peasant?'

'I certainly did not intend to suggest that, Herr Major. I merely indicated the realities of war. Unfortunate but true: many Colmar residents have resoled their shoes in wood. My former leather supplier in Paris is no longer accessible to me since the annexation, and I have not yet been able to find a supplier in Germany, unfortunately.'

'If your only problem is to find a German leather supplier than that can be quickly solved. I and many of my fellow officers have had great problems with our boots. As you can see, mine are the original knee-high marching boots issued at the beginning of the war; now unfortunately the *Wehrmacht* issues shorter boots due to the scarcity of leather which you have mentioned. I take good care of these boots: a man's character is after all reflected in the condition of his footwear, which must be immaculate at all times – excluding, of course, on the battlefield. I polish them black myself. But there is nothing I can do about the soles, which would require studs and steel caps to prevent wear and tear. Can you do this?'

As he spoke he lifted his left foot so that *Oncle* Yves could inspect the boot soles. He bent over to have a good look, before replying,

'Yes, I can see they need work. Do you have a second pair as *Ersatz?* If you can indeed find me a good German supplier and have him send me the required material I would be happy to replace the soles, and of course I can add studs and toecaps, but you will need to have another pair to wear in the meantime.'

'I have four pairs of boots altogether: two old-style tall pairs, which of course are my preferred boots, and two of the modern-style shorter ones. Only the tall ones – both pairs – need resoling. I can have them done one pair at a time. It would as well give me the opportunity to make the further acquaintance of your charming niece, who, I understand, is to take up work in your shop. In the meantime I will now take my leave as my fellow-officers are no doubt wondering where I have absconded to. *Leben Sie wohl, Herr Schustermeister;* we will meet again. *Leben Sie wohl, gnädiges Fräulein Dauguet.* Until we meet again.'

'*Auf Wiedersehen,* Herr Major!'

Sibyl was so glad to see the back of him she almost stuttered over the words of farewell. She had placed herself protectively in front of the incriminating suitcase, pushing it slight back into a corner. She had feared that von Haagen would insist on opening it right there searching for forbidden French books, or to instigate the threatened conversation on German classical literature. Thankfully, that was not to be.

*Oncle* Yves did not return the farewell. Once von Haagen had left the shop amidst a tinkling of bells, he glared at Sibyl and then, in fierce staccato German, faster than he had spoken before, said:

'*Das war aber eine schöne Bescherung!* That was a nice present you brought along! Whatever occurred to you to pick up a German officer on the way? Are you off your head?'

'I'm sorry! I didn't pick him up – he forced himself on me and I couldn't get rid of him.'

'I think we can speak French again now that he's swaggered off. Let me just check.'

He walked to the door, peered out onto the pavement and down the road, and then spat, loudly and ferociously, onto the cobbles on the street. Re-entering the shop, he slammed the door shut and locked it. His voice, as he continued to speak, was belligerent.

'This is what comes when they employ young girls as agents. Whatever were they thinking? Colmar is swarming with single male officers. You're actually lucky you picked up one who seems at least moderately polite and benevolent! Some of them are brutal!'

'I didn't…'

'Never mind for now. That's past. You need to think about the future. You can't allow him to ride roughshod over you as you allowed today, and I mean that in a literal sense. You need to learn to act professionally. You have not seen the last of that man, I can tell you now. I saw the glint in his eye. Better figure out now what you are going to do about him. In the meantime follow me. This is my workshop…'

He led Sibyl through the door at the back of the shop. The room they entered was dark, lit only by a dusty bulb hanging from a rafter in the ceiling. The walls were lined with wooden shelves, on which lay tools and gadgets of all sorts: scissors, knives, measuring tapes, inner soles, lasts, rotary cutters, pliers, saws, and several gadgets

Sibyl did not know the names for. On another shelf sat shoes in half-finished condition, shoes that seemed to have gone through the wars themselves. A basket in a corner contained shoes that, presumably, had been thrown away, judging by the condition they were in and the layer of dust that covered them. A box contained blocks of wood. Racks along the back of unshelved walls were filled with more shoes, and boots. In the middle of the room was a small, low table, also covered with tools, and a workbench, with a stool next to it, and on the other side an industrial-sized sewing machine with a foot-pedal. The smell was pleasant: a blend of rawhide, and ageing leather, linseed oil, and, yes, wood. At the back of the workshop was another door.

*Oncle* Yves sat on a stool at his workbench and took up where he had no doubt left off; indeed, filing a wooden sole down to size, fitting it against its designated shoe.

'… though I might as well call it my play-shop judging by the amount of work I have to do in these hard times. Nobody is buying new shoes and resoling old shoes with wood or cork doesn't buy even a week's worth of potatoes. Times are hard, Jeanne. And I can't pay you a salary, you know that. Don't just stand there. Have a seat. You must be weary after all that walking. There's a jug of water if you're thirsty.'

He indicated a cracked porcelain jug, its opening covered with a small cloth, next to it a glass.

'The SOE is paying my salary. And I have brought money for you too.'

She poured herself a glass and looked around for a chair or a stool. There was none. *Oncle* Yves seemed not to notice, or to care. He went on working.

'Well, thank goodness for that. And I suppose the one good thing that will come out of this major mess is that he seems serious about fixing me up with a German leather supplier. I suppose that will count in the eyes of some of my neighbours as collaboration with the enemy but frankly I don't care. I have a job and I want to do it. I need leather and I need work. I don't care if the shoes belong to French people or German people. They all wear down the same. And if I can get good leather – well. There are still some rich people around who will want new shoes of good leather, German or not. He was right in that you can tell a person's character by the quality of their shoes. Why are you still standing?'

She shrugged, and swept her hands around to indicate the lack of seats.

'Oh, I see, no chair. I don't have many visitors. Use this.'

He upended a wooden box and offered it to her as a seat. She perched on it. He went on talking as he moved about the shop, putting things away, tidying he shelves.

'Anyway, let's get you settled in. Are you hungry? I can't offer you much. A potato and a turnip in yesterday's soup and a bit of cheese. And some chicory coffee. Though if you say you have brought money you can run off and do some shopping. I will need to get ration cards for you. And you must register yourself at the town hall. You'll have to change your name. It's overrun by Nazis, of course. First thing they did when they rolled into Colmar with their tanks: occupy the *Mairie,* roll out their huge Swastika banners from the windows. *C'est la vie.* We have to move forward. Would you like to go upstairs and rest? You must be tired after your long walk from the station though I am glad you did not have to carry your valise. What to do. *C'est la vie.*'

'Actually, I need to get my luggage out of the shop, take it upstairs, hide the wireless. As soon as possible. If he were to come back or send someone to search…'

'I assume in that case is a radio?'

'Yes.'

'Madness, to bring it here openly like that. What were you thinking? That you look like an innocent woman making an innocent train journey with a suitcase? Do you not know that a woman carrying a suitcase is always going to attract the attention of some chivalrous gentleman? And you might not consider the Boche as gentlemen but they do have this fantasy about women and you saw the result today: they think you are frail little flowers who cannot carry a suitcase down a street. It could have been downright perilous for you. Silly girl!'

'I know. I know it now. It was reckless of me. I know better now.'

'You cannot afford to learn as you go along. There is too much risk involved. And you would have involved me as well if you had been caught.'

'But I wasn't caught, was I! *Oncle* Yves, I'm not going to waste time berating myself for my mistake. I know better now and I just want to move on. I need to set the radio up. Where will it go?'

*Oncle* Yves jabbed the air with a finger pointed upwards. 'Up there. In the attic. You can take it up now, or later. Through that door.' He pointed to the door at the far end of the shop. 'Up the stairs, right up to the top, to the attic, for anything incriminating – you have the wireless, weapons? Hide it up there. Your personal things, two flights up. You'll find it. Forgive me if I don't help. Arthritis.' He rubbed his hip.

'That's fine. I've had enough with men helping me today. It's not that heavy.'

'Heavy enough for you to drag the damned Boche into my shop.'

Ignoring the last jibe Sibyl fetched the case, lugged it into the shop and straight through to the back door. She emerged into a dark hallway which seemed a storeroom for odds and ends – a broom and other cleaning materials, an old desk, piles of firewood. A door at the other end indicated a back exit to the building – always a bonus. Two very old bicycles were leaning against one of the walls. A narrow flight of wooden stairs, so well used that the treads were worn down at the centre, led up into yet more gloom. Holding the precious suitcase in both hands, Sibyl walked up.

On the first floor was a very narrow hallway with a door at the end. Curious, she set down the case and walked to the end, opened the door; it led into a long and narrow sitting room with windows facing the street. The room was the length of the shop and the workshop together. Two more doors along the corridor led into a small bathroom with a claw-footed tub and a sink, and a very long and narrow lavatory. The stairwell itself encompassed a doorless kitchen, with a dirty-paned sash window at the far end. She walked over and peered out, noting that the back of the house opened onto a large closed courtyard shared with several other houses on the street. On the other side was what looked like a large barn and, perhaps, storerooms. As she watched, a man emerged from the back door of one of the neighbouring houses and opened one of the double doors into the barn and entered, closing the door behind him. It appeared not to be locked. At least not in daytime. Interesting…

She climbed the stairs to the next floor. Another corridor, this time leading to a medium-sized bedroom at the end, overlooking the street, and, along its length, two more rooms, one furnished as a tiny bedroom – with a single bed, a table, and a small wardrobe – and the other, unfurnished, a storeroom cluttered with boxes, suitcases, more odds and ends. The bedroom, no doubt, would be hers. She took note that everything was immaculately clean, and wondered who did the cleaning, and how often.

She went on up, to the attic. This final flight of stairs was narrower than the other and led into the eaves, ending in a door, locked, but with the key in the lock. She turned it and entered. The eaves steepled up above her head; there was room to stand upright only in the very centre of the room, but in any case, various items were packed under the lower slopes of the eaves – mostly old furniture; a baby's cot, a desk, a dining table and several broken chairs, and, again, the ubiquitous boxes and trunks and suitcases, filled no doubt with the paraphernalia all families collect over the decades and store for the generations to come, which never come, or, if they do, have no use for what is now just sentimental detritus.

She wondered about *Oncle* Yves. Had he always lived here? Raised a family? The baby cot implied that yes, there had been at least one child, and so a mother, a family. No doubt she'd soon find out the details. As Jeanne Dauguet, Acrobat had informed her, she did not need to know. She had left Colmar as a baby, had never returned until now, had never asked her mother about *Oncle* Yves' background. *Oncle* Yves was anyway from the paternal side of her family. She would get acquainted over the next few days and weeks.

Now, though, she was Acrobat One and had precious cargo to hide. This attic would become her transmission room. She opened a dusty wooden sideboard and found it packed with moth-eaten blankets. She removed the blankets – surely *Oncle* Yves would be happy for them to be thrown out – and inserted the biscuit tin in their stead, shut the door to the sideboard, turned the key. Similarly, she hid the pistol.

Blankets under her arm, she returned down the stairs. She deposited the old blankets in the stairwell at the bottom, and in so doing noticed a wooden trapdoor. So, there was a cellar as well. She'd inspect that later. Now, it was back to *Oncle* Yves.

'Back already?' he asked. 'If you're hungry, as I said there's some leftover soup you can have. Just warm it up.'

'I'm not hungry,' said Sibyl. 'I'd rather discuss the actual work with you. I understand you already have several important contacts.'

'Yes. There is one of us working in the *Mairie*; a German working for de Gaulle right slap-bang in the middle of the Nazi setup. We get a lot of military information from him. Information about possible targets. It will be your job to identify those targets and get your *maquisards* to blow them up. He sends information through – well, through shoes. Have a look.'

He removed a shoe that had obviously seen better days from the shelf. Its sole, was, as usual, worn away. *Oncle* Yves picked up one of his instruments, poked around at the heel of the shoe and part of it fell away. He held out the shoe to Sibyl. The heel was hollowed out, leaving space for – well, any small thing an agent wished to hide in there.

'I have several such shoes. I get information from this fellow and pass it on.'

'How do you pass it on, and to whom?'

'The cleaner, Madame Guyon. She takes it in her brassiere. A simple but effective hiding place when it comes to older women. Trust me, the Boche is not interested in searching a middle-aged woman's brassiere. They are not interested in middle-aged women. They do not think such women can be spies. They do not think such women even have a brain. They do not exist for the Boche. They are invisible, all the better for us. Your handlers would have done better to send a middle-aged woman instead of you. Nobody would have offered to carry her suitcase.

'The trouble is that your employers seem to have overlooked the dangers of placing a young pretty female in this situation. Overlooked the basic animal nature of men. And of women, may I add. Many a French woman has indulged in what we called *collaboration horizontale* with the enemy. I would hope you are not one of them.'

Sibyl flushed. She wanted to fling back an angry retort, but decided against it.

'Let's not bring that up again, *Oncle* Yves. I know you don't approve of me for being too young and a woman but sadly I'm what you've got and you just have to deal with it.'

He scrutinised her for a silent moment, eyes narrow. Finally he nodded.

'*Bien.* Let's continue. The thing is, I am getting a bit too old for all this spying business so you will be taking over as liaison. We work for the *Bureau central de renseignements et d'action.* Gathering information, passing it on. A little out of your work description but we are all working together on this. So that is two of our agents: Herr X is directly responsible to the chief of staff of the *Sturmabteilung* in the main office, which is situated in the *Mairie*. His information is gold, and will win the war for us. For the Allies. We are only waiting for the final battle, the battle for Alsace. I don't know what is taking the Allies so long. When is this damned invasion going to come? What are you British doing, twiddling your thumbs?'

'*Oncle* Yves! You don't know? You haven't heard? The invasion has already taken place! Weeks ago – early June, in Normandy! The Allies are in France! It's only a matter of time. A few months!'

For once, *Oncle* Yves smiled: the first time since she had arrived, excluding the initial exuberant welcome show put on for the sake of von Haagen. He smiled, and then he chuckled, and then he laughed.

'*C'est vrai! Mais c'est merveilleuse!*'

'How come you haven't heard yet?'

'But how are we to hear these things? The Boche is feeding us only the information it wants us to have. It feeds us the propaganda dictated by dear Mr Goebbels. Germany is winning! Germany will rule the world! The enemy has fallen at our feet! That is the news we get. No wireless, only newspapers all saying the same thing. We are cut off from the world, cut off from the real news, cut off from your precious BBC. We are fed a constant diet of fake news.'

'But we must tell the people! They have to know! It will be such a boost to the morale of Colmar citizens, the French! Think of it: if they only knew, what a positive spirit could be derived from that! A positive spirit is half the battle! We must spread the word!'

'Indeed we must. And I know how. *Écoute*, ma *chère* Jeanne.'

He lowered his voice, took on a conspirational tone and expression, and continued. 'One of our friends is the forger, I will call him Pierre though that is not his real name. You too have access to him, by the way, if you need documents for your *maquisards*. He is very good. He has contacts within the Colmar newspaper

*Colmar Quotidien* which the blasted Boche has renamed *Kolmar Heute.* Now see if you can figure it out yourself.'

Sibyl grinned. 'Yes! I understand! We will do it ourselves, inform the people, write a flyer, print it, distribute it. We'll do it. Although…'

She hesitated. Her face fell.

'What's the matter?'

'I just remembered Sophie Scholl.'

'Who's that?'

'You never heard of Sophie? No, of course you haven't. You don't get the news. Sophie was a German Resistance fighter. She and her brother did exactly what we are planning: produced an anti-war, anti-Nazi leaflet, and distributed it. She was caught, hauled before a sham military court and sentenced to death. She and her brother were executed by guillotine.'

'Well, we'll do the same but we won't be caught. Let's both think about it, and how we will execute the distribution. I am sorry for the bad joke. I am sorry I was rude to you. Can we be friends now?'

She nodded. Their eyes met. Finally *Oncle* Yves shrugged, and clapped her on the shoulder.

'Yes, I am just a grumpy old man. I have lived alone for so long. It is good to have a young woman in my life again. You will wake me up. It is good, to have a new niece at my age. I welcome you into the family. And now, yes, I really am hungry. It is time to warm up that delicious potato and turnip soup, I think. I am afraid I am not a very good cook, especially not with the meagre portions we are allowed. I hope you are able to feed yourself adequately. You have good meat on your bones. A few months in Colmar, and you'll be skin and bones. What a tragedy. What a horror is this war.'

'I can cook. I will prepare something, even if it is only a gruel. I will go upstairs and see what I can do. And I will unpack and make myself at home upstairs, and maybe have a rest. It has been an exhausting day.'

# Chapter Seventeen

They abandoned completely the idea of distributing leaflets themselves, but not the general concept. It was, in the end, quite simple.

On her second day in Colmar Sibyl set up the wireless and, on the assigned date, made her first transmission. Vera had warned her frankly that the average SOE radio operator, known among agents as pianists, lasted only six weeks before being intercepted by the Gestapo, arrested, interrogated and either sent to a prison camp or executed.

'But don't fear. We think it's far less risky in Colmar than in, for instance, Paris. They're not on high alert there.'

The truth was, German interception would depend on the frequency and regularity of calls. Sibyl did not need to make contact with her superiors frequently; she was, basically, running the Alsace show on her own, coordinating, supporting and supervising sabotage attacks to be organised and led by Jacques in the south and Henri in the north. She was to make contact with Acrobat in London once a week, but on a different day and at a different time each week; coded messages that would make no sense to a German interceptor. She had memorised this schedule; nothing was to be written down. And this was the day for her third scheduled message.

*Aunt Noreen has finished sewing the curtains.* That was her message for this week, and it meant that everything was going to plan, no problems. But Sibyl remembered the opening address of her SOE training course. Sabotage was not the only aim.

*You can raise the morale of the population of the occupied countries by various forms of propaganda… to unify the*

*population in a common hatred of the Boche... there should*
*come the sort of non-cooperation with him which is so*
*important to us... implant in them a conviction amounting*
*to a certainty that the Allies will win.*

Informing the Alsatian population of the Normandy invasion, of the fact that Germany was suffering terrible losses and that the Allies now had the upper hand, progressing northwards through France – well, what could be more morale-boosting than that? They had to know.

Sibyl realised that she really was living, along with the Alsatians, in an information blackout. No wonder almost every French person she had met to date, starting with the *maquisards* and ending with *Oncle* Yves, seemed to be stuck in an abyss of despair, surrendered to the enemy in practical terms as a survival tactic, but inwardly cowed, beaten. Jacques had managed to keep alight a spark of hope, and so had Henri, the Schmidts, and, presumably, Madame Guyon and the few individuals who worked with *Oncle* Yves. But the rest? They had to be told!

Sophie Scholl had been caught while trying to distribute the sixth leaflet produced by the Resistance group, the White Rose. But on the back of that failure, the leaflet was smuggled out of the country and scattered over Germany by Allied planes. Surely that could be done again, now?

But Sibyl faced a dilemma. She was only on her second day in Colmar, her second day on her official job, not counting the training of the *maquisards*. Would it be out of place for her to suggest an air distribution of flyers? Would it be considered overstepping her role? But if she didn't, if she simply stated the situation – that truth of the invasion and an almost certain Allied win was being withheld from the Alsatians – would her supervisors make the decision on their own?

As a nurse, Sibyl was naturally respectful of an established order of command, shy of putting herself forward in a situation where her role was clearly defined; a hierarchy served the simple purpose of getting things done without the chaos of human egos colliding with each other, slowing down the process. But this was serious. She alone of all the SOE high command had first-hand knowledge of the present situation in Alsace, and she alone could assess the problem and the solution. The solution was simple: inform the people. It was her job to make sure this was done. It was not her job to do it. It was her job to request help. It was her job to request an airborne distribution of the vital news.

The decision made, Sibyl radioed her message. She sent the coded message requesting aerial distribution of news of the Allied invasion and further military success in France. At the worst, she would be reprimanded. At best…

At best, just two days later, Allied aircraft flew over Alsace, over Strasbourg and Colmar and several villages. Hundreds of thousands of leaflets floated down from the sky like oversized snowflakes. People gazed upwards, caught them as they fell, picked them up from the ground, read the words.

> *Citizens of Alsace! Awake! Allied forces stormed the beaches of Normandy on June 6th 1944 and in the following weeks have started the work of recapturing France. France is for the French! Alsace is for the French! Alsace belongs in France! Germany has kept this information from you but it is the truth. Soon you shall be liberated! Take heart, Alsatians, for the end of German occupation and oppression is just around the corner.*

Sibyl was jubilant. Yes, the wording was crude and not much better than German propaganda newsprint. But it was the truth, and best of all, it gave hope to the people. Change was to come, and she was a part of it.

That night, she and *Oncle* Yves celebrated by opening a bottle of Château Laroche-Gauthier crémant. It had been hand-delivered to them by Jacques, also known as David, himself, and, for Sibyl, that was the best news of all.

# Chapter Eighteen

Special Operations agents worked in teams of three: the organiser, the radio operator, known as the pianist, and the courier. But as in so many other aspects, the Acrobat Circuit was different. It was so very small, so very limited in staff. As a result Sibyl held down two of those roles, that of organiser as well as pianist. As courier, the choices had been limited. There was, basically, only Jacques, who also played a double role: that of leader of the *Maquis*, and head saboteur.

The shop bell's jangle announced the entry of a young man, limping in with the aid of a crutch. Sibyl, sitting on a stool behind the counter, jumped to her feet.

'*Bonj… Guten Tag…* oh!' It was better to address all customers in German, *Oncle* Yves had said, since one never knew who was plain-clothed Gestapo, or a spy for such a one. But the stumbling greeting soon turned into a cry of joy. She would know those eyes, the eloquence of that gaze, anywhere.

Now, she almost didn't recognise him. The beard was gone. The hair, cut in a conservative, almost military style was side-parted, sleek, neat. He wore a dark grey suit which, though it had seen better days, was clean and fitted the gangly body beneath it well. A blue shirt, a blue-and-white striped tie, and well-worn but well-polished shoes completed the outfit. Over his shoulder was a leather pouch, in his free hand a burlap bag containing some very bulky objects. The bell jangled as he opened the door and in the same movement placed the bag on the counter.

He placed the crutch aside and put a finger on his lips.

'*Bonjour, Mademoiselle*,' he said, his eyes twinkling. 'I have emerged from the underground, a little the worse for wear, bringing boots that need resoling... and a few other things. Perhaps you can help? Please excuse me if I do not speak German. I am out of practice.'

He unpacked a pair of well-trodden men's boots – she recognised them as a pair he had worn in the hideout.

'*Mais bien sûr!* Why don't you come into the workshop and speak to the cobbler yourself.'

The moment the door to the outer shop closed behind them she was in his arms.

'Jacques. Oh Jacques!'

'Ssshhh!' Again, a finger on his lips. 'My name is David Laforêt. *Voila!* With a flourish, he swept an identity card out of the front pocket of his jacket. Sibyl inspected it; to all appearances it was genuine. But it wasn't: it bore Jacques' photo.

'Where did you...?'

'Our forger. He's good.'

'And this?'

'Medical reports, and an exemption from military service. History of congenital dislocation of the hip. The crutch is a nuisance, but it helps. I've already been stopped twice by the Boche.'

'Isn't it risky, though? What if...?'

'Riskier to wander around Colmar as an able-bodied young man. This way, they see the crutch and assume I'm exempted.'

'But I thought you're on the wanted list?'

'Jacques Dolch is wanted by the Gestapo. David Laforêt is not. There is no way they can connect the two. They do not even have a photo of Jacques Dolch. He is invisible to them – just a name.'

'Well, be careful.'

'Of course. But enough of me. Tell me about yourself. The journey went all right?'

'Yes – but – oh, it was terrifying!'

'The young lady has had her first encounter with a German *charmeur*,' said *Oncle* Yves, who had remained seated at his workbench, filing at a block of wood. 'She escaped with her life and her virginity intact. I don't know about her heart, though. Be careful, young man; he was very attentive and very determined.'

'*Oncle* Yves! How ridiculous! And how dare you…'

'Just teasing, my dear. In fact as I said before, you were lucky. He could have been of quite a different nature and then you would have been in deep stew.'

Jacques, looking from one to the other, frowned. 'What…'

'Oh, Jacques, don't listen to him. It was an – an incident on my first day. And yes, it was scary but in the end nothing at all.' She told him about Major von Haagen. He frowned again.

'Be careful, chérie. He'll be back, I guarantee, and you need to be quite strong, and yet polite and above all, tactful. He sounds of a certain type – they don't take rebuffs lying down.'

'No man does,' put in *Oncle* Yves, 'but especially not a tall, good-looking officer of the Boche.'

'Do we have to discuss this now? Jacques, isn't there business to discuss?'

'Don't call me that. *Mon Dieu,* you're supposed to be the group leader – I shouldn't have to remind you! I'm David.'

'Sorry. David. Isn't there business to discuss?'

'There is. But not here. Sorry, *Oncle* Yves, but it's confidential. Where can we go?'

'Let's go up to my bedroom.'

*Oncle* Yves whistled. '*Oh la la.* But she's a fast one!'

Sibyl ignored him. She led the way out of the back door, making sure the door was locked, and up the back stairs.

'I'm assuming no-one followed you down the lane.'

'Of course not. I don't know if anyone was watching me from a window, though. This is a residential area and some of the women in the houses – well, they are watchers.'

'But probably not Nazi spies?'

'Hopefully not.'

'You scare me!'

'The thing is, we are never safe in Nazi Germany and like it or not, Alsace is Nazi Germany now. You never know who is friend or foe. But if anyone asks I have my cover story and so do you. If anyone asks why I was so long in the building, well, I will just say I was making love to the beautiful new assistant to M Girard.'

'And if they ask how you got to know me so quickly, what will you say? Considering I only arrived the day before yesterday, and I have only left the house once, to register at the *Mairie* and to get my ration card and buy a turnip and two beetroots…'

'I will say I met you in Paris before the war and you have returned. To Colmar to be with your one true love.'

'But, officially, I have a fiancé! He died on the East Front and I am still mourning him!'

'Your mourning is only a front. In truth it is me that you love. Come, give me a kiss. I am clean now. Do I not smell of soap? Madame Schmidt helped me to clean up and I am fresh enough for a kiss from you. Come here.'

A few seconds later, Sibyl said,

'We need to work.'

'Yes. Let's work.'

# Chapter Nineteen

Jacques had not brought a map. Agents should never carry maps. He did bring, however, an old notebook, half of its pages still blank, and on this he sketched out for her the area beyond Colmar and marked the targets planned for sabotage in the coming days and weeks, both in the North, Henri's domain, and in the South. The targets were: two electric power stations, a tyre depot, a spare-parts factory (formerly for civilian, now for military vehicles), a military vehicle maintenance garage – and, of course, the usual telephone lines, railway lines and storerooms. The old tactics of blocking roads and slashing tyres would continue: the men were practiced at this, and experts. But now, with equipment, their targets were more sophisticated, their methods more complex, their tools more technically advanced. Plastic explosive, after the success of both trial targets during training, evoked, apparently, almost reverence in the minds of the *maquisards*.

'They are like boys with new toys,' said Jacques. 'I need to cool down their passion –Henri or I will lead all attacks involving PE.'

Sibyl nodded. 'And what happened to the men who stole the guns?' she asked. 'Were they ever found?'

Jacques shook his head. 'Not yet. They are in hiding. But we will find them.'

They talked strategy for several hours. They exchanged news. Sibyl told Jacques about the aerial leaflet drop. Jacques told Sibyl of his investigations along the western bank of the Rhine; his grandest plan was to blow up two bridges at Brisach and Chalampé, for it was over these two bridges that the Germans replenished their supplies towards the South.

'We will have to wait for that,' said Sibyl, 'and plan carefully. Blowing up a big bridge is not the same as blowing up a railway line – that was just practice. The bridges are bound to be heavily guarded. Be careful.'

'I am,' said Jacques. 'I wait and I watch. We will do it.'

They discussed the next delivery of supplies, what would be needed, the time and place of the next drop; they discussed the budget. They would need more money soon.

As they made their way back down the stairs Sibyl gave a satisfied sigh. 'That was a good meeting, I feel as if I'm finally doing the task I've been sent for. I'm an agent. I'm going be a good one. As good an agent as I was a good nurse.'

'You've been a good agent from the start. My men are totally in awe. Even Henri. They call you *Lucie la Terrible*. But I don't see you as terrible. Quite the opposite.'

They had reached the bottom of the stairs. He pulled her close, kissed her, then released her.

'Not here and now. There is a time for everything. But when the war is over…'

'When the war is over…' She pushed open the door into the workroom. They walked through.

'In the meantime, *voilà. Un petit cadeau.*'

He opened his leather shoulder bag and removed a bottle of gewürztraminer.

'It's good, to be the son of a winemaker. Because the wine never runs out. Find an occasion to celebrate and celebrate. *Au revoir, ma chère.*'

He slung his pouch over his shoulder, picked up his crutch. 'I will collect the repaired boots next week, *d'accord?*'

The bell jangled as he opened it and limped out into the gathering dusk.

# Chapter Twenty

Several days had passed before von Haagen returned. Sibyl had even started to hope that he had forgotten her, forgotten the shop, forgotten the resoling of his boots. It was not to be.

The door swung open, the bell jangled, and there he stood, on the customer's side of the counter, smirking down at her in thin-lipped cold-eyed greeting.

*'Guten Tag, Fräulein Dauguet.* You see, I am back.'

'I see.'

'And I have brought boots for your uncle to repair, and a book of poetry for you to read. Rainer Maria Rilke. I wasn't sure which of his books to bring. I chose this one: *Das Stunden Book, Volume One. Das Buch vom mönchischen Leben.* "The Book of Monastic Life." I hope you enjoy it.'

He slapped a book down on the counter. Sibyl glanced at it, touched it, withdrew her hand as if scorched.

'Go on, open it. Read it. Read it aloud.'

Hesitantly she opened the book, glanced through the pages. Closing it again, she pushed it across the counter to him.

'I – I don't know. Perhaps you should read.'

'Very well. It is hard to choose a single poem, though. But what about this one… one of my favourites.' Opening the book, holding it up, he read, in a dramatic voice and every now and then glancing up at her: '*"Immer wieder, ob wir der Liebe Landschaft auch kennen…"* Shall I continue?'

Without waiting for a reply, he continued:

*"Again and again, however we know the landscape of love*

*and the little churchyard there, with its sorrowing names,*
*and the frighteningly silent abyss into which the others*
*fall: again and again the two of us walk out together*
*under the ancient trees, lie down again and again*
*among the flowers, face to face with the sky."*

'Is that not beautiful?'

'Indeed, very beautiful… but I'm sorry, Herr Major, I don't think…'

'It is too intense for your liking? You don't think it is appropriate, that a man and a woman of only slight acquaintance, should recite love poems to one another? I quite understand. You may think it forward of me. Let me explain my motive. I am aware of the fact that many of my co-soldiers have behaved despicably toward the French women in our care – yes, the French, and especially the women, are indeed in our care during these troubling times. We have a duty of protection towards you and you may have heard some distressing rumours that belie the implications of that responsibility.

'But I wanted you to know that I am not of that ilk. I am not of such primitive calibre. I have the refined intellect for which we Germans are historically renowned. I am a man of culture, of good taste and civility and I abhor vulgarity in all its forms. I categorically reject all behaviour in which women are disrespected. And I wanted to make my intentions quite clear right from the beginning. I have been impressed with you, *Fräulein* Dauguet, from the first moment I saw you, struggling with that heavy suitcase. I was distressed by the comments expressed by the men at my table – extremely crude, vulgar even, quite inappropriate for German officers, and I felt embarrassment on your behalf. I leapt to your rescue as a demonstration of chivalry, of the correct behaviour of a man towards a woman. This is the way of refined culture. This is the true German way. The true German is not an uncouth brute but a man of polished sensibilities, a man of culture. We must constantly prove our superiority, the refinement of our intellect, not through words but through behaviour, through little acts of humble benevolence and gallantry such as I displayed towards you on that memorable day. And I want to make it clear to you, right from the start, so that there is no doubt whatsoever, that my intentions are absolutely honourable. Let there be no doubt whatsoever on that subject.'

He stopped for breath and tried to catch her gaze, which was wandering somewhere along the rafters that held up the ceiling, following the movement of a spider, as she tried with all her might to suppress a giggle.

'*Fräulein* Dauguet?'

There was nothing for it. She had to look at him. And remove the twinkle from her eyes. His every word had been spoken in earnest and somehow, inexplicably, she felt pity for him. Every word he has spoken – he was actually serious. It was unfair to laugh, perhaps dangerous. She had often met men who liked the sound of their own voices more than was good for them. But a man who liked the sound of his own voice, all the while believing he and his entire nation was of a superior calibre to all others, and at the same time so blind to his own haughtiness as to actually use the word *humble*… well. Words failed her, and so did the latent laughter.

'It's a beautiful poem,' she mumbled, 'and I will certainly read more of Rilke. But, Herr Major, your boots…'

The attempt to change the subject backfired horribly. He exploded.

'We are discussing love poetry, emotions, not boots! My goodness, how *shallow* can one get!' But in the next breath, he had brought his tone back under control.

'Excuse my outburst, *Fräulein* Dauguet but I did hope we could extend our conversation a while longer, before turning to more mundane matters. Really, women are supposed to be the more sensitive sex but in reality, they are often so immersed in domestic thoughts it acts as a veil between them and the subtleties of higher thought. The only remedy is education, and self-education. I do implore you to read this book in all earnestness and with your full attention, and perhaps you will then be capable of carrying on a conversation of more depth. In the meantime, perhaps you would so kind as to summon Herr Girard so that we might indeed discuss the condition of my boots.'

Sibyl flushed in the effort to contain a fitting retort. 'Very well,' she said. 'Just a minute.' She walked to the door to the workshop, opened it, and peered in.

'*Oncle* Yves,' she said, 'Herr Major von Haagen is here to speak to you about the resoling of his boots.'

She turned back, her agitation now under control.

'He'll be right here. Thank you for the book. I will indeed read it.'

'It is my own personal copy. A gift for you.'

'Thank you. I appreciate it.'

'Perhaps you would do me the honour of accompanying me to a small event at the officer's club next Saturday. I would be proud to be your escort.'

'Oh! Well, I don't know – I am flattered, but…'

'You need not be shy. It is in fact a rather exclusive event. There will be other ladies there of course, other French ladies even – but cultivated ladies. No-one of ill repute, I assure you.'

'May I – may I think about it?'

'What is there to think about? It is a high honour – why should you hesitate? I have already declared myself as having nothing but honourable intentions, why would you even *think* of declining such an offer? Really, I do not understand this. It could not possibly be that you, like some of your female compatriots, refuse to fraternise with Germans? Even after I have gone to considerable effort to explain our culture…'

'What is it? Can I help?'

Thank goodness, *Oncle* Yves had arrived. He looked from one of them to the other.

'What's going on?'

'Herr Girard, I have requested the honour of your niece's company at an event at the officer's club this coming Saturday. She is hesitating to accept my proposal, I would be grateful if you would encourage her to accept. Of course, there are advantages for both of you.'

'Well, of course she cannot give an answer before discussing the matter with me! The girl is only twenty-two. She got engaged at the age of nineteen, to a man who went off to fight a war and was instantly killed, by Germans, as it happens. Her wariness is only natural. She is like a daughter to me; since the death of her father, in fact, even though I have not seen her for many years, I do regard her as the daughter I regrettably do not have myself. Obviously, she is inexperienced and reticent when it comes to men and courtship. Obviously, she must discuss such matters with me and then, and only then, can she agree to a rendezvous. As a man of chivalry, you must understand this. And I would be grateful if in future you would direct all such invitations to me. It is exceedingly impolite to go over my head. This is not the way the French do things. It is not considered *comme il faut.*'

In tone as well as content it was a severe reprimand, and von Haagen seemed to hang in the balance between accepting the reprimand as a man who had offended etiquette, or as a German officer insulted by a lowly civilian. His head jerked backwards; literally taken aback, and once more Sibyl suppressed a giggle.

And then the decision was made; reprimand accepted. Von Haagen, firmly put in his place, finally changed the subject. It so happened that von Haagen, through family connections, had found out the address of a leather wholesaler in Munich. He had brought a list, with prices. He and *Oncle* Yves discussed the placing of orders; the financing of such orders, and the fact that *Oncle* Yves was quite, to put it bluntly, *pleite* – broke – so further negotiations took place. It seemed that, since the footwear of German officers stationed in Colmar was generally in a terrible condition, it would be possible to conduct business between them, the wholesaler and *Oncle* Yves. *Oncle* Yves, in fact, was to become the unofficial *Staatsschuster,* State Cobbler, for the officers.

Before he left, von Haagen turned back to Sibyl.

*'Fräulein*, my invitation for next Saturday still stands. You will enjoy it I am sure. Would you at least consider it favourably when you discuss it with your uncle?'

She hesitated. 'I'll – think about it. Perhaps you can drop in on Wednesday, and I will give you my answer.'

He beamed and gave a little bow, a brief nod of the head. 'That is most gratifying. I shall come by then, and hopefully the response will be positive.'

He replaced his cap, bowed again, and walked out the door to a jangle of bells.

'I'm not sure that was a very clever move,' *Oncle* Yves said as von Haagen was finally back out in the street.

'You really had little choice, *Oncle*,' said Sibyl. 'And thank you: quick thinking, about the rendezvous. In future I will always ask your permission in matters of love and courtship.'

'Pah! I can see that happening.'

Yet the levity was not long-lived.

'I'll have to report all of these developments to Acrobat,' she told *Oncle* Yves, 'and I doubt they'll be happy. And one thing is for sure: I can never meet David here again.'

# Chapter Twenty-One

In fact, Acrobat insisted that Sibyl accept Major von Haagen's invitation. The instructions were to watch and listen; to let the Boche get drunk but not to drink herself. Drunk German officers were likely to spill secrets, secrets that might help the Special Operations mission of sabotage and subterfuge. As for von Haagen: she was to go along, within reason, with his efforts at courtship.

'Do you think you can handle him?' *Oncle* Yves asked.

'Yes,' Sibyl replied. 'As far as I can tell, he truly does have honourable intentions; he seems to get a thrill out of talking about himself and discussing German poetry. That's something I can handle. He seems to be yearning for something beyond the reality of war: music and poetry and art. He's only human. My guess is that it's his way of staying sane throughout Hitler's madness.'

'Pah! Germans are not human. Do you know what happened on this very street? There was a Jew down the road. A violin maker. A good friend of mine, Joseph Meyer. Before the war we used to meet some evenings, enjoy a glass or two of wine, talk into the night. Joseph of course played the violin; his wife played the flute. He had five daughters. They all lived in that house down the road, the one with the red shutters and the boarded-up shop. They would have musical evenings at the cultural centre; but also singing and dancing, laughter and just good community. They were proper Alsatians, proper Colmar citizens. Not rich but minding their own business. Do you know what happened to them?'

'I'm listening.'

'Well. Let me go back a little. Before the war there were about twenty thousand Jews living in Alsace and Lorraine. These Jews were well aware of what was going on in Germany, of the pogroms – after all, we are right beside Germany and we were hearing those terrible broadcasts of that crazy fellow Hitler and his plans for the Jews. And how they were to be persecuted and exterminated. We heard of that horrendous *Kristallnacht*. So Jews here were better prepared for what was to come than Jews in the rest of France. They knew. They had no illusions. So they organised themselves, protected their businesses and assets and of course their families.

'Joseph had close friends and when things got threatening he distributed his most valuable violins among us. He had five or six very valuable ones. I myself still have one in the attic. It's easier to hide a violin than a human. I would have hidden a human, one of his daughters, but he didn't think it necessary. Not yet. He wasn't a practising Jew, wasn't active in the Jewish community in Colmar. So he thought he could get away with it. With staying in Colmar.

'The Boche marched into Colmar in June 1940. On June 16th all the Jews still in the town were told to come to the police station. They were allowed to bring along a suitcase each, two thousand Francs, food for four days. They were all packed into trucks and transported to France. They weren't allowed to take gold or jewellery. They weren't sent to the German camps. It was all relatively civil, compared to some of the stories we've heard since – transports to concentration camps and such. No, the Colmar Jews went south. But Joseph, stubborn fool, refused to go. He had a German name; he thought he could get away with it. We lived on this quiet out-of-the-way street. *My life is here. I was born in this house. Why should I go?* He said. His workshop was here. His violins, his tools, his livelihood. *What'll I do without my tools? I'm not going. We're staying. They won't know I'm Jewish. We'll take the risk.*

'All went well for a year or two. But then – well, someone must have ratted on him. It was already 1942. The Gestapo began interviewing us, neighbours, asking about Joseph. If he was Jewish, if he went to the synagogue, and so on. Well, he didn't go to the synagogue so when they came I answered that truthfully. I said we never spoke of religion which was only half true but they weren't to know. Joseph got scared. He decided to leave voluntarily, but now it was too late to be evacuated. Colmar was supposed to be *Judenrein*, free of Jews. Joseph was suddenly terrified. He had to get his family out! One by one, first the daughters. He had ambitious plans: he'd get his family to Vichy and then to America. He had a brother in New York and that was where he was headed, or so he thought.

'We had it all planned. This was how I actually began to work for the Resistance. He had to get his family out secretly, through safe houses and so on. There was a route for rescuing Jews. We heard of a family-run vineyard near Ribeauvillé which was helping to hide Jews. Sarah was eighteen, a big girl who could look after herself. So she went alone first of all. In 1942 the rest of the family was to go there and they would hide them and get them down to the south through a planned route of safe houses. We got Sarah and two more daughters out.

'But we were too late. One night, actually it was early in the morning, we heard shouting in the street, the shattering of glass. I looked out of the window and saw those German thugs; Gestapo, in uniform. They had smashed the glass of his shop and broken down the door. They dragged the family out into the street. The youngest was five, Rebecca. She was terrified and began screaming. They yelled at her to stop screaming but that made it worse of course. They began to beat her with a club. Joseph and his wife tried to stop them beating her but they were just clubbed down themselves.

'I ran out to try to help, I yelled at them to stop but they had surrounded the family and beat everyone away. I got a few blows of the baton. In fact, they broke my arm but that was nothing. They beat Rebecca to death, right here in the street, in front of her parents. What had that child ever done to hurt them, the cowards! Joseph and his wife were frantic, yelling and crying for them to stop, to beat them instead. But they did not afford them such mercy. A truck came and took them away. We never heard from them again. You can still see Rebecca's blood between the cobbles. It's stained dark and we can't get the stain out.

'We had heard by now of trains taking Jews to concentration camps in Germany but we do not know if that's where they went and if so, what happens to them there. We will find out once this terrible war is over. After that of course they raided the house and took away all the other violins and other items of value. The house is still empty, waiting no doubt for a German family to move in when the war is over. If Germany wins, which of course it won't. But the Boche did not know that at the time. Now, where was I going with this story? Why did I tell you it in the first place?'

'You were trying to convince me that Germans are not human.'

'Ah yes. Well, there you have it. What human behaves in this way? To kill an innocent child in front of her parents? Simply for being of a certain race? Tell me, is that human? Animals behave better than that. I know of a female dog who had puppies and she adopted a motherless kitten and suckled it like one of her own. It is a human instinct to care for our young. If you lack that instinct so far as to actually destroy a young one then you are not human. That is my final word. And anyway, at some point the Germans declared Alsace to be *Judenrein,* and we have been that ever since. The Boche are not people to be toyed with and I do not at all like this new instruction, for you to start fraternising with them to extract information. That is not the work of an SOE agent, as far as I understand their mission. I thought they were just here in France to blow things up.'

'They are in France to win the war. By whatever means available.'

Sibyl, agitated by *Oncle* Yves' story, hardly slept a wink that night. Her claim that the Germans were only human; that von Haagen was only human, now seemed nothing but naïve wishful thinking. *Trust no-one,* Vera had said. She had laughed to herself at von Haagen's pompous and condescending lecture, believing she could see right through him; but had she any idea what went on behind those cool blue eyes? Obviously not: but now, her duties entailed trying to find out. Accepting his courtship and helping the greater cause by pretending he was human; but was it all a sham because he was not, could not be, human? What did it even mean, to be human? Did humanness by default imply inherent goodness?

No, she concluded; no matter what, Germans were human, even the evil ones. She had no right to strip von Haagen of his right to be human, to make of him a beast. Whether she trusted him or not, he was human. There is a living spark in all of us, she reminded herself, something beyond good and evil, an essence of life that is, indeed, inherently good – even if buried deep in a morass of evil.

Could it work? Was she up to it? In the darkness she shivered, but not from cold; and the thumping of her heart echoed through the silence. This was war, and she was caught in the middle of it. She had chosen this route, and there was no way through but forwards.

# Chapter Twenty-Two

Sibyl removed a pair of heavy boots from the cobbler-shop window and replaced them with a pair of delicate ladies shoes, with high heels. *Oncle* Yves hadn't made such shoes for years, but that was irrelevant. The exchange of shoes was a pre-arranged signal for Jacques. It meant: do not enter the shop. Back-up meeting place.

The back-up meeting place was the back room of a carpenter's shop. *Oncle* Yves drew a sketch of the way there and shook his head in sadness.

'He used to be Jean Carpentier. Overnight, he became Hans Zimmerman. I'm only lucky they have not yet forced me to become Karl Schuster or some such thing. It seems that after the age of seventy they are less strict. And you: you will be renamed Dagmar Müller. Give them time.'

The Germanification of Alsace, *Oncle* Yves had told her, entailed not only the renaming of streets and shop names but surnames and the most mundane details of daily life. Taps in bathrooms could no longer be *chaud* and *froid* but had to be *heis* and *kalt*. *Sel* and *poivre* became *Salz* and *Pfeffer*. *Le pain* was now *das Brot*.

'They have banned the wearing of berets: too French. Everything French has to go. Our culture, our language. Overnight, they removed all Alsatian teachers, sent them to Germany for retraining and replaced them with German teachers. The poor schoolchildren, especially those who do not speak Alsatian! We're not allowed to use the Larousse dictionary. We had to remove all certificates and diplomas from our walls. It was so petty! They banned Binda thermometers because the alcohol in them is red against a white and blue background. The Lycée Bartholdi was Germanised and Nazified

and renamed the Mattias-Grünewald-Schule. Schoolchildren had
to learn to write in the Sütterlin script, that ugly jagged calligraphy
resembling the teeth of a saw. Everything has to be German.

'But the worst of it is that not all Alsatians are against the Boche.
There has been so much collaboration, even support; even some
men voluntarily joining the German army, even the SS army! They
think it's best to know what side your bread is buttered; but one
day they will pay the price. I am sure of it. The Germans must go.
Anyway – enough of that. Complaining won't change anything.
Here's how you get to Jean Carpentier.'

She found the shop with ease, not least because of the sign on
the window proclaiming Zimmerman in large black letters. The
teeth of a saw, Sibyl reflected. That's exactly how those letters looked.

Just as at *Oncle* Yves' shop, a bell jangled as she opened the door.
But unlike the cobbler's shop, this was a cosy, friendly place; just as
narrow, but with beautiful wooden articles displayed on the shelves
and on the floor: toys and household items; candle-holders, chairs,
stools and tables. A beautiful full-length mirror, in which Sibyl saw
herself for the first time in months. How thin she had become!
Her cheekbones stood out, her eyes seemed sunken in her face,
and her clothes, drab and worn anyway, hung loose on her body.

'I'm looking for a birthday present for my aunt,' she said, which
was the password.

'I have a beautiful set of cooking spoons,' was the correct reply.
'Go on through to the back and up the stairs. He's waiting.'


He was on the first-floor landing. He must have heard her footsteps
on the stairs. Without a word he gathered her into his arms, held
her there, silently, for a while as they absorbed one another. And
then, again without a word, he led her into the front room – as at
*Oncle* Yves' house, a small sitting room at the front of the house,
overlooking the street.

They parted, each taking a seat across from a central dining table, made of solid oak as were the four chairs around it.

'So,' he said finally, 'what's happened, that we have to meet here?'

Sibyl gave him a quick summary of her last conversation with von Haagen, and Acrobat's order that she should accept his invitation, his courtship.

'So now they've promoted you to proper spying? Intelligence work? I thought that wasn't the domain on Special Operations?'

'Sabotage and subterfuge. Subterfuge covers a multitude of areas. In this case, it's about – access.'

'You mean – you could…'

'Exactly.'

*'Mon Dieu.* Sibyl – Lucie – I don't like it. I don't like you going in there! It's too dangerous.'

'And what you're doing isn't dangerous?'

'Yes, but…'

'But what?'

'But – I love you.'

She did not reply. She reached out her hands across the table. He took them, held them, squeezed them.

'Remember what we said – what you told me – that first night, after I landed? It's better for us to stay – disengaged. To not get distracted, personal. To do our jobs without emotional attachment. That's what we swore.'

'But it *is* personal, now…'

'I took on this mission knowing of the risks and consequences. It is my professional duty to do whatever is required, and I will do so. If I do my job well, which I will, then it will speed up the end of the war and then you can love me as much as you want and I can love you back. But for the time being we must do what we have to do. For the sake of the bigger goal. You know that. Wait. Be patient.'

'And this – this von Haagen. He sounds odd. A German Wehrmacht officer who recites love poetry?'

'Why not? Despite everything, these people are human. We think of them as monsters because they are German but they are not. I treated many of them when I was a nurse and that's what I found out. I knew they very likely had done atrocious things that it would fill me with loathing to know about but still, as a nurse, it was my duty not to see that but to see the spark of humanity that we carry inside us and treat that with the dignity it deserves. Before they were soldiers, they were normal people. They were babies whose mothers loved them and then they were children and went so school and learnt normal things. Just as I learned Shakespeare and Milton and you learned Racine and Molière, von Haagen learned Goethe and Rilke. So now he recites poetry to me.'

'Except that I did not learn Racine and Molière. You know I had no interest in school! I am not an academic. Would you prefer an academic? Someone you can discuss poetry and books with?'

'Don't be silly, Jacques! You're sounding jealous. Jealous of a German officer? It's ridiculous! This is the enemy. I'm just doing a job. You know that.'

'This is more than blowing things up. It means you have to lead him on, to lie and deceive him. I do not see you as a deceptive person. It is contrary to your very nature. Gain his trust and then – a knife in his back. Not literally, necessarily, but…'

'My nature is to do my job well, whether as a nurse or as an agent.'

'Do you not feel conflicted?'

Again, she paused. 'To be quite honest, there is definitely a conflict. I do have a conscience, Jacques, and it is not in my nature to lie and deceive and break someone's trust. And it is not in my nature to kill. When they asked me, at my interviews, if I could kill someone, I said yes, if I am taught how. And so I have learned to overcome my nature, for the sake of a greater good.'

He nodded. 'This is war and other rules apply. I have killed; in many of my attacks, people have died. I know this and I ask God for forgiveness, because I know that killing is a sin. Yet still I have done it and will do it again, because the means justifies the end, and the end is something great and good – the freedom of my people. But these were anonymous deaths, the deaths of strangers. What you are about to do, to lead someone on, earn his trust, only to – it doesn't feel right.'

She squeezed his hand. 'I know what you mean and I agree. I have thought about this a lot, Jacques. Deep into the night, to be honest. It keeps me awake. But I have negotiated a method with my conscience. This is it: just as an actor in a film or play can be a villain, do things he never would in real life, so too I must learn to separate a part of myself, play a part which is separate from the real me. As if I were acting a part; throw myself into the part, and yet a spark of the real me stays awake and aware and knows that one day, the play will be over, the film will be over, the war will be over. And then I will discard that role and be myself once again.'

'It sounds wonderful in theory. Can you really do it?'

'I believe so. I am determined to do it. When I was a nurse I was able to see beyond the evil a man might have done, see beyond what a terrible person he is – and some of them were terrible still as patients – and still treat them with the care and consideration a nurse is taught to give.'

'Promise me you'll be careful.'

'Of course. But you must promise me the same.'

'I do.'

'Well, then, let's talk about you and your work which is every bit as dangerous as mine. What are your next plans?'

Jacques described to her the various targets they would be hitting over the coming days and weeks. 'But to be honest, all this is child's play. We need to get the bridge, the Brisach bridge. I am obsessed with it. I want to take a few days to properly reconnoitre the site and see how best we can explode it. It is particularly well guarded on this side of the Rhine.'

'Well, there we go. You talk of my dangerous work; yours is just as bad, if not worse. And I will not let you do this alone. I will be with you.'

He ignored her words. 'And we will need more explosives. More powerful stuff. PE isn't going to do it.'

'I'll arrange for a delivery – in maybe two weeks' time. The same landing place? Where I came down?'

'Yes. That's the best place.'

'Anything else you need? Weapons? Hand grenades?'

'Hand grenades, always. My boys love them. Weapons, no. But – well, money.'

'Always money.'

'Always.'

# Chapter Twenty-Three

Major von Haagen came to the shop on Wednesday, as arranged, to confirm the invitation for the following Saturday.

'I would come but I do not have anything suitable to wear. This is all I have.' She brushed her hands downwards to indicate her clothes.

It would be wrong to appear too eager; and anyway, it was true. She could hardly go out wearing her everyday skirt and blouse and thick stockings and clumpy shoes.

'It is no problem. I will see to that. I personally do not care what you are wearing but I know you ladies like pretty clothes. You will have pretty clothes.'

She shrugged. 'In that case, I will come.'

'I am overjoyed, *Fräulein* Dauguet. I will pick you up here at eight o'clock.'

'Very well.'

He came on the dot; she had not expected less. Smarter than ever, medals and boots gleaming, he swept into the shop, and, as Sibyl was still upstairs, went right through to the workshop without knocking, bowing his head as he passed under the low lintel. *Oncle* Yves, having expected his appearance at this time, was appropriately reading a German newspaper at his desk. He looked up.

'*Guten Abend,* Herr Major. I believe she will be right down. Do have a seat.'

He indicated the upturned box.

'I prefer to stand,' said von Haagen.

'As you please.'

'I see you are following the news. It is good to be informed.'

'Indeed. It is all very interesting.'

'That is a *Freiburg* newspaper, I see.'

'Yes. They come with the morning train. I try to keep up to date.'

'And the news is good?'

'According to this newspaper yes. But I wonder.'

'What do you wonder, Herr Girard?'

'I wonder if it is all the news. There has been gossip that the war is not going too well for Germany. That the Allied forces are making swift progress through France. Why am I not reading this in a German newspaper?'

'Do you listen to gossip? Are you doubting that Germany will win the war, Herr Girard?'

'Indeed I am.'

'It is not possible. There is such a thing as a higher destiny. It is an absolute truth that Germany will be victorious in the end even if there are at present temporary setbacks.'

'Ah – so you too have heard of the setbacks.'

'It would interest me intensely, Herr Girard, to know where you have received information about alleged setbacks?'

'Oh, I don't know. It is just gossip, as I said. Just gossip. And – ah, here she is. My dear, you are looking beautiful – beautiful. Your beau is here for you, waiting impatiently. I am sure you will have a splendid evening.'

He kissed Sibyl on both cheeks and passed her on to von Haagen with a light hand on the small of her back. She walked forward, hand stretched out. Von Haagen took it, shook it and did not let go, in fact, clasped it in both hands while gazing at her in admiration.

'You look delightful! The dress is a perfect fit. It suits you so well!'

He'd brought her a dress the day before. It was simple and glamourous all at once; a satin floral print with a sweetheart neck and full skirt that emphasized the slimness of her waist and the flare of her hips; the bodice skimmed her figure, the skirt ended just below the knee. He said it was of Mulhouse silk. Through friends, *Oncle* Yves had managed to get hold of a pair of silk stockings, also from Mulhouse. Sibyl had not worn anything so pretty in years. Having spent the last few weeks in the drabbest of worn-out garments too big for her and the month before that in camouflage trousers and jacket in the forest, she felt almost guilty – it was astonishing, how a change of clothes could lift one's spirits. While she did not exactly look forward to an evening in a German officer's club, she could not deny a sense of positive expectation as to what the night would bring. It was, at least, a change from the humdrum routine of the last few weeks. Because even her agenting work had grown into routine.

Outside the shop von Haagen had parked a motorcycle with sidecar. He helped Sibyl into the sidecar, mounted the motorcycle, put on his helmet and goggles, gave her a wave and a smile and rode off. Sibyl reached behind her head to clasp her hair; not that it had been styled in any particular way, but she had loosened it from the inevitable plaits circling her face and for the first time her natural auburn curls bounced free, with only a grip on each side to keep them behind her ears and, as they gathered speed, spread out behind her, in need of taming. She wore no make-up except for a bit of powder from her compact; but she had managed to buy some beetroots in the market that morning, extracted a little juice and coloured her lips with it. Again, a tinge of guilt. Dressing up for an evening out with a German officer! It was disgraceful. No. It was work.

The officers' club was housed in the ground floor of a stately house on the outskirts of Colmar. Sibyl stomach turned. She recognised this house. The sign on the iron gate, back then, had read Château Bellevue, and had been changed to Haus Schönblick, but the house itself was distinctive with its beautiful gardens and bright blue shutters. She had been there with Aunt Margaux before they had left France. Margaux's mother had lived in Colmar with her own ageing parents, and they had been friends with the family who lived here. Sibyl couldn't remember their name, but one thing she did remember: they had been Jewish, and she had often played here with their children. Where were they now? She didn't ask. She wasn't supposed to know.

Now, von Haagen explained, as he released her from the sidecar, it housed the Wehrmacht officers in the upper stories while the downstairs rooms contained a kitchen and dining-room in one side, and the officers' club on the other as well as a conference room.

*'Meine Dame – ich bitte!'* said von Haagen, reaching out his elbow to her. She took it. They entered the building; the spacious, richly carpeted main hallway was unchanged from the pre-war days, a wide staircase leading to the upper stories to one side of it. The oversized, ugly garderobe was obviously new, and overflowing with bits and pieces of uniform – jackets, coats, helmets, caps, and, on the bottom shelves, an untidy array of boots.

'This way,' he said, placing a hand on her elbow and leading her to a door on the left side of the hall, from behind which came a muffled sound of raised male voices. He opened it, led her over the threshold, and stopped as a cloud of noise, the blur of voices trying to be heard above each other, enveloped them.

*'Heil Hitler!'* cried von Haagen, thrusting his right arm forward, and immediately all the faces in the room turned to him and the echo of *Heil Hitler!* went up and a hundred male arms shot upwards. It shocked Sibyl deeply; but she kept a neutral face and her arm down and waited it out, surveying the scene. There was a slight hush as some faces continued to stare, but then the noise resumed as people returned to their interrupted conversations, their card games, their beer glasses, their back-slapping raucous laughter.

From several small tables grouped around the room, uniformed men and a small number of women, drank away the evening in swirls of cigarette smoke, smoke so dense she could not breathe.

Her lungs rebelled at first and only reluctantly and hesitantly nipped at the stinking air.

One or two men stood up, waved to von Haagen. Cries of 'Wolfgang! Wolf! Over here!' reverberated above the hubbub. Faces burst into beams of admiration as glances moved from him to her, curiosity merging into appreciation. A wolf-whistle or two. More men stood up, bowed towards Sibyl, beckoning arms indicating their way to a table at the back.

Scattered here and there around the tables were women; Sibyl's glance took in women in elegant dresses displaying deep décolleté necklines and abundant sequins; women wearing flamboyant hairstyles, red sulky-sultry lips, heavily outlined long-lashed eyes; women watching her, silently, appraisingly, and, ultimately, dismissively.

Von Haagen led her between such groups to the table he had been called to. Five men sat around it, and one woman in a slinky green dress, blonde hair piled in an untidy bouffant. All except the woman leapt to their feet at their approach, bowing and grinning in sycophantic greeting. All of them spoke at once.

'Wolf, so this is the girl you've been keeping to yourself!'

'Charming!'

'Lovely!'

'You lucky fellow, Wolf!'

Von Haagen said nothing at first but only smiled secretly and allowed them all to have their say. Only then did he deign to introduce Sibyl.

'Gentlemen – and lady – may I introduce: *Fräulein* Jeanne Dauguet.'

He introduced the men by their first names and rank: Heinrich, Major; Karl, Major; and so on; one by one, Sibyl, highly alert, committed faces and names to memory. The woman he introduced simply as 'Ilse, Heinrich's girl.' She nodded her head as if infinitely bored and accepted Sibyl's handshake with a grip as limp as a wet flannel. Immediately she turned back to Heinrich, languidly placed a new cigarette in a silver holder, and pointed it at him. He lit it with his own. The two fell back into conversation, loud, but indecipherable above the general clamour. Indeed, one had to shout here. Von Haagen pulled back an empty chair, gestured, and Sibyl sat down. He looked around and found an empty chair at another table. Everyone moved their chairs together and he squeezed in, next to her.

All the other men immediately showered Sibyl with unbridled and unmistakably admiring attention. Where did she live, what did she do, how did she meet Wolf? One of them remembered that first day, when Wolf had leapt from their table at a Colmar street café and run after Sibyl, grabbing her suitcase.

'He was simply the fastest, *Fräulein* Dauguet. We all would have done it but he shot off before we could catch our breath.'

'The early bird catches the worm,' said von Haagen. His arm lay languidly across the back of Sibyl's chair. An expression of infinite smugness and possessiveness was plastered over his face. Had she not been on the job Sibyl would have been tempted to slap him. She merely smiled vaguely.

'But your girl is certainly no worm!'

'A good catch nevertheless!'

Someone waved for a waiter.

Sibyl was offered beer, wine, sherry, cocktails. She refused it all and asked for water. The empty banter went on for another hour. The others ordered another round of beer. The waiter removed their empty *steins*. They were all incredibly picky about their beer. They ordered Weizen, Pilsener; a Helles and a Dunkel and a Doppelbock. They laughed and joked while ordering, teasing Sibyl.

'But you must drink beer now; Alsace is Germany and Germany is beer country! Your French wine is like syrup!'

'I don't drink wine or beer,' said Sibyl.

*'Anti-alkoholiker, ja?'* said someone.

'Not really. Alcohol just doesn't agree with me.'

'Ah, but it takes practice! What joy is there in life without alcohol?'

They all laughed.

'Actually, she is a good example for us all. After all, our beloved *Führer* also does not consume alcohol.'

It was von Haagen, leaping to her defence. Up to now he had not participated in the banter and the teasing, and Sibyl could see why; the conversation had been so far below his usual pompous standard. She had to wonder what he had in common with these men, who all seemed, well, to use a word her mother would, incredibly common. It all seemed so very much – beneath him. Why had he brought her here? To show off?

It had become clear to her that German women were in very short supply in Colmar –the Germanisation of Alsace had not yet led to any great female influx across the Rhine. And French women were notoriously reluctant to hobnob with Germans, which is why they seemed to spend much of their time indoors, out of sight: to prevent being accosted on the streets, just as Sibyl had been. She was well aware that romance between a German soldier of any rank and a Frenchwoman would be not only frowned upon but bring down the wrath of her compatriots, who would judge it as collaboration with the enemy. It was a risk she had to take: it was her job.

Her job was also, she realised with a start, not only to gain access but to get these men talking.

Get them drunk, and let drink do the rest, she had been instructed. And now, with von Haagen's mention of Hitler – for the first time this evening, apart from the initial Hitler greeting – she had her opening.

'But why do you not follow your *Führer's* example? Surely that would please him?' There was a short silence as the men contemplated the question and their by now rather befuddled heads thought of a reply. Finally the man introduced as Karl spoke.

'No! Our *Führer* is *erhaben* – exalted – above the vices. He must remain pure to ensure his vision remains pure. That is the secret of his magnetism – purity of vision. But we lesser men: we are red-blooded. We are his arms, his feet. Our spirits are fired by his vision, but it is our lower nature that carries out his work. It has to be so.'

'We are brutes in comparison!'

'Long may he live! I raise my glass to the *Führer!*'

Karl jumped to his feet and indeed, raised his *stein* as he cried the rallying words. It was a call to action: all the men at the table followed suit, and those at the neighbouring table turned their heads and noticed, and officers jumped to their feet and raised their mugs and glasses, and soon all the men were standing with drinks held aloft and the room echoed with the cry: 'Long live the *Führer!*'

Sibyl felt sick. She actually felt the vomit rising, physically, in her gorge, but she could not let it show; she watched and waited – as did Ilse – until everyone was seated again and the conversation moved on to anecdotes. These stories of what they had done that day, which citizens they had harassed and how, made her sicker yet, and still she sat through it with an interested mien, eyes fixed on each speaker as if fascinated by his words; and all the time she said to herself: *I am just playing a part. It is my job. I am an actor in a film. Playing a part. This is not me.*

'I need to go to the Ladies',' she whispered to von Haagen. 'Where is it?'

'You're best off going to the one down in the basement,' he whispered back. 'It's a bit cleaner.'

She stood up, excused herself, picked up her handbag, and left the room. A staircase in a corner of the large hallway led up to the bedrooms; and another led down. She took the down staircase, and found herself in a large, bleak area. Lockers occupied one corner of the basement and there was a storeroom, which she remembered from the days when she used to play here with the other children and they would come in through the back door, covered in mud. There was also a lavatory.

When she came out again she found a woman waiting outside; she had been sitting at the next table; Sibyl had noticed her looking across several times. 'Sorry I took so long,' said Sibyl.

'It's all right,' said the women. And then, in a furtive whisper, 'Can we speak French?'

'*Bien sûr!*'

'Excuse me talking to you like this: I really need to speak to someone! Someone in the same position! My name is Grete, what's your name?'

'Jeanne. Pleased to meet you.'

'It's just that – you seem like a lady. And you have a German friend. Like me. I was wondering – perhaps we could be friends? I am so lonely. All my neighbours, all my former friends, they detest me for being a collaborator. But what can I do? I have a child to support, a child to feed! I cannot let my child starve! But I do need a friend. Perhaps?'

'Of course. I work in the cobbler's shop in *Gerechtigkeitsgasse*.'

'Where is that? I do not know all these new names in Colmar!'

Sibyl described the way to her, and returned to her table. She knew what Grete was speaking of; she too had noticed that the French women she ran into shunned her, looked down at her. But it had not bothered her; she was not looking for friends. But Grete was welcome to come for a chat, if that was what she needed.


And so the minutes passed, and the hours; and then the men began looking at their watches, or up to the clock on the wall, above the door. The atmosphere seemed to buzz with nervous anticipation and the raucous half-drunken bellowing most definitely lowered several notches as the clock's hands moved towards ten, and men began to whisper: 'Sssh! It's coming! Nearly time!' and then it *was*

there: complete silence, but just for a moment because little darts
of radio static pierced the silence and then a voice: *Soldatensender
Belgrad.* Solider transmitter Belgrade. *'Lili Marlene'.*

Several beats of military march music punctuated the silence,
melting into a sultry female voice. Plaintive, yearning: a song about
a young German soldier waiting for his love beneath a lantern,
outside his barracks, before going off to war.

The effect on the men around the table was electric. These men,
these soldiers who had just a minute earlier had been extolling their
brutish acts, boasting of their ability to browbeat little old ladies for
speaking French or raiding a house suspected of hoarding French
books in the cellar – they became, right before Sibyl's eyes, little
boys. Beefy faces flushed with too much alcohol fell forward; eyes
hard and flat as stones melted and leaked. Handkerchiefs flew out of
pockets, to wipe away stray tears and blow runny noses. Shoulders
slumped, elbows rested on the tables as heads fell into receptive
hands. Sibyl looked around: it was happening everywhere, at every
table. She turned to look at von Haagen, in the chair beside her. He
sat far back from the table and, his head tilted slightly back, gazed
into space, arms crossed at his chest, legs wrapped around the legs
of the chair. His face seemed etched in stone, but then he turned to
look at her and she saw that he was struggling with some powerful
emotion; struggling, and losing, for now he closed his eyes and
yes, those were tears stealing out from beneath those closed lashes.

One of the men – Gottfried, was his name, Sibyl remembered
– leaned forward, throwing his upper body onto the table, and
wept openly, loudly. Behind her, a man was blubbering. Some
were stroking other men's backs, or even, she saw, holding another
man as his shoulders heaved in silent sobs. It was extraordinary,
unbelievable. How could a song produce such an overwhelming
effect?

The song came to an end, men came to their senses. They blew their noses, wiped their faces, exchanged awkward glances and embarrassed comments: *So, that was it for today – she really hits the soft spot – every time, damned tears – home, my shining star.*

Von Haagen looked the most embarrassed of all; a mortified smile, a self-conscious removal of his cap and stroking the back of his hair, revealed a discomfort Sibyl knew too well; it was the expression male patients bore when as a nurse she washed their intimate body parts. It had to be done and she did it, and now she knew it was the same: von Haagen had brought her here for this very reason, to hear this very song, and for nothing else. She gave him a slight smile, encouraging. He had opened a totally new area of exposure to her. It had to be encouraged; and indeed, the smile finally brought forth words.

'Were you able to follow the lyrics?'

'Yes, mostly: a soldier saying goodbye to his beloved, under a lamp-post.'

'It is wonderful, isn't it? We listen to it as often as we can. Radio Belgrade plays it every night for German soldiers everywhere, by popular demand. It unites us all: wherever we are, whatever we are suffering, we remember the one we love. This song brings us together, for we all listen to it. We listen, and we weep. Whatever loneliness we are suffering, being away from our families, it touches the heart. You see, German soldiers are not the soulless brutes the French dismiss us as. We are all at depth sentimental fools, dreaming of our beloved, of our homes, our *Heimat*.'

'Is this why you brought me here? To see this, to understand this?'

'Exactly. Because I can feel, I can sense, your prejudice against us, against me, against the German race, and it is painful to me. Only by exposing you to the romantic over-enthusiasm you have just witnessed can you comprehend the complexity of the German soul, the profundity of its depths.'

'I see. But why do you want me to understand this?'

'But surely, *Fräulein* Dauguet, you are sensitive enough to feel what I have no words to express?'

'I cannot read minds, *Herr* Major. If you want to tell me something, just tell me.'

*And don't be an arrogant jackass about it. No amount of maudlin songs can correct* that *side of your pompous complex soul,* was what she wanted to add, but didn't.

'If this is what you wanted me to hear – can we go home now? It's an interesting conversation, but maybe another time. I'm tired, it's past my bedtime.'

'Yes, yes. Of course. Let's go.'

They said their farewells. Sibyl shook everyone's hand, and Ilse's was even limper than before. Many of the officers squeezed hers so tightly it hurt, or held on to it so long she had to pull away.

'I apologise for their behaviour. They are all drunk,' said von Haagen as he helped her into the sidecar. 'So *primitiv.*'

He helped her out again when they reached the cobbler shop.

'*Fräulein* Dauguet, you hinted that we could meet another time. May I be so presumptuous as to assume that means you would allow me to escort you out on another occasion? The next time, perhaps, a slightly more intimate engagement? Perhaps at a nice restaurant – *Der Rote Löwe* comes to mind – or even a ride out into the country? For the latter I would of course borrow a sturdier vehicle than this old thing' – he patted the motorcycle –'and we could make a day of it, on my next day off.'

'That… that sounds pleasant,' she tried not to stutter, straightened her back. 'I have Sundays off. That is the only day I could take time off during the daytime.'

'Well then, let's say next Sunday,' he said. '*Auf Wiedersehen, gnädiges Fräulein.* It was a pleasure spending the evening with you. I do hope you enjoyed it.'

'Indeed,' she said. 'Thank you.'

She hunted for the door key in her clutch purse, threw him a smile, turned the key in the lock, and entered the shop. Once inside she threw herself against the closed door and took a deep breath. It was over – for tonight.

'There you are,' said a voice in the darkness. 'I was beginning to get worried.'

'*Oncle* Yves!' she leaped away from the door, reached in the darkness for the cord that would switch on the shop's single ceiling bulb. Light flooded the shop. At the back, next to the door leading to the workshop, puffing at a cigarette, he sat.

'Where did you get the cigarette from?'

'Don't be so nosy! You agents are supposed to understand the principle of never ask, so that you don't know! A man has to have his secrets. What took you so long? And – pooh! You ask about my smoking – what about yours? You stink, my dear. That lovely dress. You will never get the smell out of it.'

'I'm going to give it back to him anyway. I'm not accepting presents from him just yet.'

'He probably got it from one of his whores.'

'Whores! Really! *Oncle*, you are terrible!'

'But of course he has his whores. There are two whorehouses in Colmar, one with French whores and one with German ones. The soldiers can take their pick. But I believe the German ones are reserved for officers.'

'How do you know all this?'

'Again, too many questions. Now tell me about your evening.'

She drew up a stool from behind the counter and she told him.

'Ah, yes. The lovely Lili Marlene. She is quite a famous lady. Beloved by soldiers everywhere, not just the Germans. Did you know there is also an English version? I heard it on the BBC.'

'Since when do you listen to the BBC?'

'Too many questions again. What is this, an interrogation? You don't need to know. Yes, Marlene Dietrich sings it in English and all the Allied soldiers listen to it. Whereever they might be, Africa, Asia. Europe…'

'You know this about some silly sentimental soldier song, yet you did not know about the Normandy invasion. Very strange.'

'I am picky about the news I hear. And anyway, my BBC connection is only recent. And that is all I am going to tell you about it. So tell me more. Did your Herr Major declare his undying love for you?'

She sighed. 'No, it didn't come to that. But I fear it he was hinting at it. Or something like it. He wants to meet again. Next Sunday. A picnic in the country or something. The Wehrmacht in Colmar really are a lazy bunch, going off with girls on Sunday. I thought they were fighting a war.'

'In Colmar there is no war to fight. They only have to harass the citizens into following the rules and making us all into good respectable Germans. Over my dead body.'

'Don't say that, *Oncle* Yves. It gives me the creeps.'

'The day I become a German is the day they take me out of this house feet first. Speaking of which, let me tell you a joke about dead Alsatians, *oui*?'

'One should not joke about the dead.'

'But this joke is really funny, and all the more funny because it is true. See, there was this family, the Kaltenmeiers, they lived in a big house over that way.' He gestured vaguely. 'A good old Alsatian family, but they were half German and the lady of the house went to visit her relatives in Cologne, in Rhineland. And she had an accident there and died. And because returning the body here – not to mention buying a coffin and burial – would be so expensive, the family here requested that she be cremated over in Cologne. So they did that. The family that side put the ashes in an empty soup jar, with a screw top, and sent it back. So the family here cooked the soup which tasted a little bland so they added cabbage and beetroot and enjoyed it. A week later the death documents arrived. What a commotion! They had eaten their own mother. And serve them right, for collaboration with the Boche.'

'*Oncle* Yves, I don't believe a word of that story.'

'Suit yourself, but it is true. Everyone in Colmar laughs about it. About the family that ate corpse soup. And did you hear the one about the family that had their grandfather's ashes in a tin on the shelf and a child was playing with it and it fell and spilled on the floor and the maid…'

'*Oncle* Yves! That's enough. I'm off to bed. I'm exhausted.'

'Good night, my dear. You know, I'm starting to feel you really are my niece.'

'Thank you, *Oncle. Bonne nuit.* You are coming too?'

She planted a kiss on his forehead and helped him to his feet. Arm in arm they made their way through the shop, then single file up the stairs.

# Chapter Twenty-Four

There would not be a chance to see Jacques before the next meeting with von Haagen, and certainly no wireless contact with Acrobat. She was on her own with this.

Midweek she received post from Colmar's town administration; her new papers were ready, she should come and collect them. Her case-worker was a portly sergeant, the buttons of whose uniform strained to remain closed, the seams of his sleeves slightly overstretched. He sat at an oversized desk, files piled up on one side of it, the other side empty but for a single framed photo of the Führer; the same photo hung on the wall behind him, along with swastika banners on either side.

He beamed as she approached.

'So, now you are officially a German citizen! I congratulate you, *Fräulein* Schuster. So take a seat.'

'*Fräulein* – Schuster? I think maybe you have the wrong person?'

'Indeed not. As you know, the Germanisation of the Alsace region involves the renaming of all those who still have French names. Your former name was undeniably French. We have taken it upon ourselves to give you an appropriate new name. The name chosen for you is, as you can see, Marlene Schuster.' He pushed a brand new German identity card over to her. It bore her photograph, and indeed, the name Marlene Schuster.

'Now all you need to do is sign these other documents, showing that you have received your new identity. You may apply for a passport if you so wish, but you will need another photograph and, of course, to pay the fee. So – please sign these documents.'

She trembled with outrage; but she could not let it show.

'Who – who chose this name for me? And why?'

'Naturally, it was not just picked out of a hat. The surname was chosen due to your relationship with the cobbler Yann Schuster.'

'Yann Schuster? But…'

'I believe he still clings to his French name, your uncle – there is a dispensation for citizens over the age of seventy, as they will not be procreating and will soon die out. But that is his official name.'

'And why – why Marlene? Why not at least something similar to my old name? Johanna, for instance?'

'Sadly there is already a Johanna Schuster on file in Colmar. We wanted to avoid duplications.'

'But then – surely…'

'The issuing of new documents and new names is a process that usually takes months. It can be speeded up under special application. In your case, there was some intervention through the Wehrmacht. The name Marlene was chosen for you and your case prioritised. You must have friends in high places – it helps.'

By now, Sibyl's outrage had subsided and she was beginning to see the positive aspects of this new development; and to smile at that very initial reaction of indignation. It showed how much she had identified with the name Jeanne Dauguet, how much she had actually *become* Jeanne Dauguet; that was a good thing. She had truly shed one personality and taken on another. Marlene Schuster was nothing more than a label, and it helped to solidify her presence in Colmar. An official German citizen, approved by the powers that be, issued with genuine documents by the enemy – what more could an amateur agent want? What better cover? *Friends in high places* – that could only be one person. So, von Haagen was behind the name Marlene; her camouflage was complete. The label was irrelevant. A German citizen, with authentic German papers! She smiled to herself. SOE headquarters would be pleased.

'You may now have your original documents back: your birth certificate and lycée certificate from Paris. They are no longer needed. Just a signature, now, *Fräulein* Schuster.'

She signed the dotted line – a strange new signature, foreign, unfamiliar, but now hers, her very own stamp of authenticity, handed to her on a plate by the enemy. She tucked the new ID card into her purse and stood up.

'Thank you.'

*Oncle* Yves was not impressed. 'Marlene Schuster! What a farce! How ridiculous! To me you remain Jeanne, my beloved niece.'

'But as you know, *Oncle*, even Jeanne is not…'

'Ssshh! *Tais-toi!* I don't want to know. For you it might be a thing of ease, to slip out of one identity and in to another, just like a lizard changes its skin. To me and to the people of Colmar it is an abomination. So you now see it?'

She nodded. 'Of course. And my first reaction was indeed infuriation – how dare they? But don't you see, *Oncle*, this is the very reason I am here. Changing names, identities: it's the bread and butter of an agent, not to be taken personally. To speed up the end of the oppression, to chase the Boche out of Colmar. It is going to happen, *Oncle*. I promise you it will happen.'

'Pah! When you told me of this Normandy invasion back in June I was at first excited, thinking the end of the war was near. But what has happened since then? Nothing! When are your troops coming to Alsace? What are they doing to liberate us? I believe in fact they have forgotten us.'

'It takes time, *Oncle*. The main thing is the invasion has happened and Germany is slowly losing the war, being pushed back bit by bit.'

'And who is to guarantee that these wonderful glorious Allied troops will ever reach Alsace and push back the Boche over the

Rhine? It is my fear that even if the Allies win the war, Alsace will remain in German hands. That the Germanification process has gone too far to reverse. That it is too much trouble to clean this province of the Boche; that the new border will be the Vosges mountains and not the Rhine. Because nothing is happening here. Nothing! Just a load of uniforms strutting around harassing the people.'

'You are forgetting that I was sent to do just that: to help your own Resistance. And that is what I am doing. Exactly that. It is what Jacques and Henri are risking their lives for.'

'Humph! Well, they better get on with it.'

# Chapter Twenty-Five

'It is a car fit for a lady,' said von Haagen as Sibyl stepped out of the shop. 'A Mercedes Benz; one of our staff cars I managed to borrow for the day. Isn't she a beauty?'

He held open the passenger door for her to step in. 'But not as beautiful as my passenger.'

He settled in, pulled on a pair of black leather gloves, and smiled over at her. 'And…' he paused as he switched on the ignition. The car slowly moved forward. It only just fit in the street; had Sibyl reached out, she could have touched the buildings as they crept along.

'This is the very car Adolf Hitler drove in when he came to Strasbourg in 1940,' von Haagen informed her. 'As such it is a historical vehicle. Ah, here we are, out of the unbearably narrow alleyway.'

He accelerated and the car swept into a main street. There was little traffic; it was Sunday morning, after all, and many people had gone to church or were enjoying a family day. Sibyl, who also usually attended the ten o'clock Mass, had gone to early Mass today. Jeanne Dauguet had been Catholic, and so, now, was Marlene Schuster. The car was a convertible, and because it was a lovely sunny day the leather hood was down. So, again, was Sibyl's hair, but today she wore a turban to keep it reasonably tamed; and a light floral shirtwaist dress, with a cardigan over her shoulders. No stockings though; she could not bear to wear those thick monstrosities, and she had no others.

'I am taking you to a very special place,' said von Haagen as he drove out of town. 'Up near the vineyards. It is almost harvest time, the most beautiful time of year in the Alsace. You really must see it.'

She saw a road sign pointing towards Ribeauvillé and when von Haagen steered the car in that direction her heart began an involuntary racing, a violent thudding which she feared he could hear. Apparently, though, he couldn't.

'Here we are. A delightful spot further up this lane.' He had turned off the main road, on to a dirt track that led towards a copse, tucked into a hillside that rose up between two vineyards. The car came to a halt in the shade of a spreading oak tree. He removed his gloves, opened the door for her, offered her a hand and led her from the car to a spot beyond the tree.

'Wait a minute, please!'

He strode back to the car and returned with a picnic blanket and a wicker basket, filled with various articles wrapped in newspaper. He spread the blanket, bid her take a seat. She did so. He sat down beside her, waved his hands to embrace the landscape. The vineyards spread out around them in gently undulating rows, the vines a brilliant green; beyond the vineyards, hills of a different shade of green rolled out to a brilliantly blue horizon. To their right, the purple mountains of the Vosges rose in the distance. Best of all, the gurgling of a small stream that flowed from the copse and lost itself among the rows of vines lent a voice to the scenery; a gurgling, cheerful voice, eons away from the hideous clamour of war. After so many weeks almost constantly cooped up in the narrow cobbler shop, Sibyl felt, against her will, liberated. Happy, almost.

Between the hills they could see the spires and roofs of villages. Von Haagen pointed them out.

'Riquewihr. Ribeauvillé. I will take you there for a stroll afterwards. They are like villages out of a Grimms' fairytale. And the vineyards…' He swept his arms wide. 'In a few weeks they will be golden-brown, and the grapes bursting with succulent goodness. I am a wine man rather than a beer man, even though I like to adapt to company – that's why I drank beer the other night. But wine! There is a vineyard here, the Château Laroche-Gauthier. Their wines are exquisite. Maybe we can drop in and I will purchase a bottle for you. You can share it with your *Oncle*, I'm sure he will be pleased.'

Her heart skipped a beat. Quickly, too quickly, perhaps, she said, 'Please don't, *Herr Major*... I really don't drink wine – ever. I don't like any alcohol. And my uncle – yes, he enjoys it but he shouldn't. It's not good for his health and he would only have to drink alone.'

As she spoke he unpacked the basket. In it were treats she had not seen since the start of the war. A side of ham, pink and fresh. Cheese: the local Munster. A baguette, of course, and cake and – wonder of wonders – a jar of fresh strawberries. A slab of chocolate! A bottle of wine – indeed, it was Château Laroche-Gauthier. He replaced that in the basket at her words, and laughed.

'I won't drink if you won't. But a woman who grew up in Paris, who does not like wine! I never heard of such a thing! But now you are German, aren't you; and we also have some excellent wine. But what am I saying? If you do not like wine I will no longer discuss it. For me, though, it is the ultimate symbol of sophistication and good taste. There is also excellent grape juice and apple juice to be had at this time of year in this region. I can get some cheaply for you. Anyway – what were we talking about? Oh yes. You are German now. How does that feel?'

'To be honest, *Herr Major*...'

'*Fräulein* Schuster – how happy it makes me to use that name! – I would be delighted if you would no longer address me as *Herr Major*. I think we know each other well enough now; you may call me Wolfgang. Or, to be a little more intimate, Wolf.'

It was a delicate moment, an invitation to a higher level of familiarity; she knew the etiquette involved. As a woman, etiquette gave her the prerogative of inviting him into a more familiar form of address, denoting a more intimate relationship. It was up to her to offer him *her* first name first, and suggest they move from the formal *Sie* to the familiar *Du*. But now he had taken the unusual step of offering his Christian name first, suggesting intimacy from her to him; it would be vice versa only if she reciprocated. It would be awkward if she did not do so; the unbalanced forms of address now gave her the advantage. Politeness demanded that she offer him the *Du* and her first name.

As a woman, she could not.

As an agent, she should. Intimacy was to be encouraged. The more, the better.

For a brief moment she wavered. In the next moment she knew what to do. 'It was you, wasn't it, who suggested my new name: Marlene.'

'I confess, indeed it was. I hope you like it.'

'Well, I don't. I was not ready. I was happy with my name Jeanne. I don't care about Schuster but my Christian name, my baptismal name – well. It was the name my parents chose for me. I should honour it.'

She spoke with more confidence than she felt. How far could she go in crtitisising his actions? But it was a thing that needed to be discussed. It would lead the conversation in a direction she wanted it to take, needed it to take.

'But you have no choice; it is the law that the name be changed. By suggesting the name Marlene I speeded up the process, which normally would take months. So now you are already German.'

'I was quite happy being French.'

'Alsatian-born French. It meant you are automatically German, whether you like it or not. When the war is over…'

'When the war is over, Germany will have lost. Surely you know that! Surely every German citizen, much less every German military man, knows this! Germany cannot win; that was clear after the Stalingrad affair. What good will German citizenship do me in a vanquished country?'

He flushed and for a moment she depicted a note of anger in his expression. Had she gone too far? *Be bland, boring. Neutral. You have no opinion on anything, political or otherwise. You must blend into*

*the background. Without emotion, without personality. That is how an*
*agent in France survives. You are an observer, a witness, not a player.*

Now this. She had broken the rules, spectacularly so. Expressed
opinions: an opinion on her new name, and now, worse yet, a
political opinion. Worse than ever, the opinion that Germany
might just not be the victors. That was just not opinionated, it
was downright antagonistic.

But she had to, surely. She needed to get him talking. The
role she now played went beyond sabotage and subterfuge; it was
about access. Prising out opinions, and thus facts and details,
was the whole point of access. Access to him, his thoughts, his
feelings; access, hopefully, to secrets he might share. Access,
possibly, to buildings she might bomb. Access to worlds cur-
rently closed to her. Access, possibly, to military plans. But she
had to tread carefully. Antagonism was not the way. She had to
open the vault of those worlds carefully, cleverly, cunningly. She
needed to take a step back. She had to be warm, accommodating,
friendly, attractive.

She laid a placating hand on his arm. It was time to pedal back.

'I'm sorry. I should not have said that about Germany being
vanquished. It is not my place.'

He said nothing. And then: 'How do you know all this? Who
told you? There was a ridiculous leaflet circulating a few weeks
ago – did you read it? Did you believe it?'

'I didn't need to. I was in France at the time of the invasion. In
Paris, where we had access to the news. We heard all about Stalingrad
and the carpet bombing of Hamburg and the flattening of Dresden.
We know about the Normandy invasion. Everyone in the world
knows, except maybe the people of Germany, because you are
keeping this information from them. Germany cannot win this war.'

She spoke softly, almost tenderly. She knew instinctively that
with this particular man, antagonism would not work. The simple
truth, delivered calmly and without passion, not as an attack but as

a statement of fact, just might. She had to play her cards carefully, utilising the strategies she had learnt as a nurse. Delve past the layers of ideology and dogma and party line and propaganda in which he was cloaked and poke her finger into the veracities he denied. Stir him into revelation. Yes: it was against the official SOE rulebook. But so was this particular situation. *You are on your own,* they had told her. *There is no script. If you are forced to interact with the enemy, you will have to write the script as you go along. Use your intelligence, your wiles, your intuition.*

And so she recounted, for him, the reality of certain German defeat, one incident after the other. As she spoke his entire demeanour went through a process of metamorphosis. He no longer gazed at her with those puppy-dog eyes, so incongruous in an otherwise stiff and formal disposition, the very caricature of a haughty German officer. He looked away, into the distance, so that all she saw was his chiselled profile. His jaw tightened; she could see blood vessels pulsing in his neck, the clenching of muscles. Now it was time to pedal back. Soften the blow. Relate everything to him.

'Wolfgang,' she said, 'look at me.'

That word, that name, did it. He turned back to her and now she could read his eyes. There lay not the heat of fury she might have provoked, nor the coldness of loathing. There lay, raw and blistered, anguish. It was time to poke further.

'Does it cause you pain, to hear these things?'

'Whose side are you on?'

'It's not a question of taking *sides* any more. It's a question of facing reality. You know these things but you have refused to accept them. But you must.'

He shook his head, slowly, as if refusing to accept her words, but knowing he was defeated. As defeated as the Third Reich. Before her eyes, he collapsed.

'What am I to do? What will become of me! What is the way forward? *Ich bin komplett am Ende!* I am completely finished!'

It was a cry of anguish, of absolute torment and utter self-pity. She remained unmoved, unpitying.

'Those are questions millions of people have had to ask themselves and for millions the answer was quite clear, for only death awaited them. War is a terrible, terrible thing. Germany wanted this war and must accept the consequences.'

'I don't give a damn about Germany! What about *me?*'

She smiled to herself. Isn't that what it invariably boiled down to, with the exception of a few genuine heroes? *What about me.*

'Well, what about you? Assuming you survive till the end – it's not quite over yet; there are still battles to be fought. But if you survive, then what?'

He took time to respond.

'All I want, all I ever wanted, right from the start of this horrible war, was to lead a good life. It was a life I wanted for all of us. A beautiful home, a loving wife, a family; a garden to grow vegetables in, sweet children to hug me every evening. And of course culture. This is the dream of every German soldier, all they are longing for when the war is over. This is what we all yearn for. Family. Home. *Heimat.*'

'We all want to be happy, that's what it boils down to, doesn't it. But we cannot be happy if we trample on the happiness of others. War has brought devastation and misery and death to millions.'

'The *Führer* had a great dream and it is now shattered. It was a dream of happiness for all.'

'How could that dream be achieved through killing? Through war?'

'Sometimes, the means justifies the end.'

'Even atrocities? How can you ever justify – I won't even mention them by name. You know what I am talking about. Are you religious, *Herr Major?*'

The conversation had taken too serious a turn for first names. It seemed – well, inappropriate. She had only used it as a wedge into the inner workings of his mind. Now she was there, she preferred to revert to formalities.

'Wolfgang – please, call me Wolfgang. Yes, I am profoundly religious. I am a devout Bavarian Catholic.'

'Then how on earth can you justify the persecution of Jews? The *elimination* of Jews, as proscribed by your *Führer?* Is that Christian?'

'*Fräulein* Schuster, your questions demand complex responses. Why don't we just enjoy the picnic and engage in appropriate light conversation?'

Their eyes were still locked: she held his gaze. But then it was as if a curtain drew across his, a blankness, an opaque glaze and she knew she had lost him. As if relieved to have regained the fervour that energized him, he took a deep and audible breath.

'You see, I cannot, I must not give up hope! There is still hope. We must keep the faith. I cannot let the message of defeat infiltrate the ranks. I must motivate my men, give them the feeling they are fighting for their dream and it will come true. We all believe that Germany is destined to be the perfect society. I believe this destiny is divinely ordained, and will come about even though the future, at the moment, looks grim for Germany. But miracles are always possible: last minute miracles, if the end is God's Will. We must lead the way and I cannot allow this conversation to destroy my morale! We will fight to the end!'

She shrugged. 'As you wish. Let us change the subject.'

'And let us eat! The food is waiting!'

'Where on earth did you get all these things? I have not seen such a feast since, well, since long before the war.'

'We have our sources. You needn't worry your pretty little head about that!'

They spent the following hour eating and discussing the poetry of Rilke, which Sibyl by now had read, and the writing of Goethe, whom she had not. It was as if the initial exchange had never taken place; as if he had wiped his mind free of it, free of truth, free of reality, and all that now mattered was the dream, the vision, the poetry and the beauty and the glorious achievements of culture, German culture. Sibyl participated. It was her job.

# Chapter Twenty-Six

'As I mentioned earlier, I would be delighted to show you one of the charming villages of the Alsace wine region, Ribeauvillé perhaps, or Riquewihr, both of which are only a few minutes away.'

'I really should be getting back home.'

She could not take that risk. She had gone to school in Ribeauvillé. As a young girl she had known many of the merchants. Yes, she was now a young woman, grown up, changed, but still, someone might recognise her. All that was needed for her world to collapse was for one dear soul to call out, 'Sibyl! But you are back! How are you – how you have grown!'

'But it is early yet. We still have many hours before it grows dark. Let us make the most of them.'

'Well then, let it be Riquewihr. I think that's where one of my aunts used to live – a great aunt, in fact, an old lady but very kind to me. I remember well, visiting as a small child, sitting on her lap as she fed me peeled grapes. I would like to refresh my memory, I remember how beautiful the village was.'

It was all she could think of in the frightening spur of the moment – an inadequate story and impossible to confirm since there was no aunt, then or now. Once again she would have to play it by ear.

'Riquewihr it is!' They packed the basket with the remains of the feast, loaded it and the blanket into the car, and von Haagen drove off.

A few minutes later they were in Riquewihr. 'This is the Dolder gate,' he said as they passed through an imposing rampart, 'a thirteenth-century defensive gate. Riquewihr itself, of course, is a magnificent example of German medieval architecture. Notice the picturesque half-timbered style, similar of course to that of Colmar but, in my opinion, far more appealing due to the almost enchanted nature of the village as a whole, tucked as it is among the vineyards and rolling hills. As I said before, it's like stepping into a fairytale. It really is the jewel of the Alsace. I am glad we came here and not to Ribeauvillé, thanks to your aunt!'

He parked at the edge of the market square and once more took her hand as she stepped out. Always the gallant *charmeur*, he never missed an opportunity to be the epitome of German chivalry; a knight, thought Sibyl, smiling to herself, in shining armour. Were she not a spy she might have fallen for it. Now, his attentiveness took the form of offering her a guided tour of the village. The thieves' tower, the church, the medieval fountain: everything was described to her in meticulous detail. She listened attentively, nodding appropriately, commenting now and then, and all in all doing her best to conceal her exasperation.

She saw other things. Yes, she remembered Riquewihr well. But she remembered it without those gaudy oversized banners displaying the black swastika against a white circle and a red background, hanging, it seemed, from every second building. The charming wrought-iron shop signs had all been crudely painted over. The bakery was now the *Bäcker*. The butcher was now the *Metzger*. The candlestick maker – well, there wasn't one of those, but there an *Antiquitätenhändler* had morphed out of the quaint little antique shop where her mother had sometimes liked to pick up ornaments to add to her collection, all of which were shipped over to England and now adorned her home in Three Bridges.

'Interesting,' Sibyl said. *Ghastly,* she thought. Not only the banners and flags and German signs distorted her memory of the town, but the soldiers; soldiers, standing in groups near the fountain, two of them walking slowly down the middle of the road, three of them in a parked jeep near the church. They were everywhere.

'Why do you need so much military in the village?' she asked. 'It's such a quiet, peaceful place, why?'

'To supervise. The moment we turn our backs they revert to French. We are here to ensure the complete Germanification of every Alsatian town and village. And as you know, we Germans are particularly thorough.'

'I noticed that.'

Sibyl noticed something else, something not as obvious as the inescapable military presence. It was an atmosphere. A sense of menace, a feeling of fear, a mood of sullenness that soaked the very air of Riquewihr. She remembered this place; she remembered the freshness, the friendliness, the good humour of the Riquewihr citizens. Aunt Margaux had known practically every shopowner, and walking down the street had been a relay of handshakes and greetings and smiles: *Buschur! Güata Tàg! Göte Tàij!* Little chats along the way, invitations to drop in, inquiries as to health and children and old parents and the farm and the harvest and the grapes and the weather. Now there was only silence and glum faces. Nobody looked anyone else in the eye; and they avoided von Haagen and Sibyl altogether, sidling out of the way for them, and at least once, even crossing the street to avoid them. Though von Haagen was not in uniform, his aura was quintessential Wehrmacht; he reeked of it and the Riquewihrans caught whiff of it and skulked away; and as for Sibyl, she was guilty by association.

That guilt permeated her. She wanted to scream: *I'm not! Not really his girl! I'm on your side! I grew up here! I'm only doing a job! I'm helping to free you, for God's sake!* But the scream remained silent and her mien remained bland, the way she had trained it to be, and only her eyes could speak, if someone would take the trouble to look into then; but no-one did, and she remained a stranger in those cobbled streets, an alien, an enemy.

Her eyes took in another thing; at first, only in her peripheral vision, but then she began to look closer, and the closer she looked the more concerned she became. A poster, pasted on a few lantern posts, on random walls, even on shop windows. A face. Big black lettering: WANTED! She would have stopped to read the writing more carefully, but didn't dare; what interest would Marlene Schuster have in a wanted man? But she recognised the faces, for there were two, side by side. She had seen those men.

They were *maquisards*. Jacques' boys, or Henri's.

Yet she had to know, and so she asked. 'Who are those wanted men? What have they done?'

'Oh, they are terrorists. They tried to bomb one of our outposts up in the Bas-Rhin area. Luckily they were extremely incompetent. We initiated a hunt for them and we were successful. We caught them yesterday. The posters will come down next week.'

'Oh! And what will become of them?'

'They will be sent to prison, probably at Natzweiler-Struthof in Alsace, or else sent to Germany for trial and conviction.'

She had heard of Natzweiler-Struthof. Halfway between Strasbourg and Colmar, it was more, far more, than a prison. It was a concentration camp, the only German concentration camp in France, a name that evoked horror in the minds of *maquisards* for, if caught, that was where they ended up, sentenced to hard labour, starved, and, quite often, executed. It held tens of thousands of prisoners, all former Resistance fighters from all over France. And now, her fighters were behind its walls? Why had she not been told? Why had Jacques not immediately informed her? What was going on? Now she had no option but to keep questioning von Haagen. Wolfgang. The name tasted bitter in her mouth. She had still not offered Marlene in reciprocation; she still could not bear it, and probably it was a good thing. Marlene was hard to get, which only improved her chances.

'Do you have many terrorists in Alsace?'

'Unfortunately, it's a plague that has worsened in the last few months. At first it was just a few isolated and amateur incidents, which the police could easily deal with. But now, well, there is evidence they are receiving outside help from enemy sources. Their weapons are more sophisticated, their methods more – shall we say, more proficient. We have had to employ Gestapo agents to deal with them. But never fear, they will all be caught, one by one. The Gestapo, the Secret State Police, will make short shrift of them.'

Sibyl could actually feel the hairs on the back of her neck standing on end. She shivered, but only internally. Outwardly, she continued in the manner of a naïve but inquisitive girl making small talk with her boyfriend.

'Really! So the Gestapo is here, among us, in Alsace?'

'Indeed! They have been here since the beginning of the war but in the last few weeks they have increased their presence. They are among us, but you can't tell. See, even that man over there might be Gestapo: who knows!' He chuckled, and indicated a man reading a newspaper on a bench near the fountain.

'Oooh! I hope he doesn't arrest me!'

She giggled. He chuckled, laid a protective arm around her. She let it be.

'I will not let that happen, my dear! I will protect you with my life; even the Gestapo will find a formidable enemy in me!'

'I have to say, it is all quite scary. It was even worse in Paris; that's why I was happy to come here, to Alsace. I thought it would be quieter. I wish the war was over and we did not have things like terrorists and Gestapo agents crawling about the place.'

'The war will be over, sooner or later. As we discussed earlier. And if all goes well –well, I have my cherished dreams. As I suppose you do.'

'I suppose we all have dreams. But in times of war we must all be realistic. Even in times of peace few dreams can be realised.'

'Still, we can work towards their fulfilment, and as long as we are not too demanding, not dreaming the impossible, then why not? Now, I told you my dream, earlier; you did not tell me yours. May I ask?'

'Of course, and I will tell you that it is all very vague. How can it be other than vague, since we do not know how it will all end? But one hopes for the best, and the best is a quick end to the war.'

'And when the war is over, then what? Have you dreamed further?'

'As I said, very vaguely. A husband, I suppose; a home, children. The usual things.'

'Then our dreams are very similar. Perhaps…'

'*Herr Major* – Wolfgang – please. I think that is enough of dreaming. Maybe it's time to go home.'

# Chapter Twenty-Seven

Just as von Haagen was reversing the car on to the street for the return journey, Sibyl caught a glimpse of another car, a battered green pick-up, one that she immediately recognised. And she recognised the driver. Had she been Sibyl Lake, and not Marlene Schuster, she would have cried out, *Aunt Margaux!* and leaped from the Mercedes. As it was, she was condemned to watch as her beloved aunt, the person she would most like to see in all the world, if given the choice, parked, opened the driver's door, descended into the street and walked away.

How she had changed! Sibyl remembered her as a soft, round, maternal figure, with a face that smiled constantly, a large and bouncy bosom, and solid legs. The woman who now walked away towards the town centre wore threadbare dungarees that hung on her frame as on a wire effigy. She must be half her size now – reduced, like so many, by the war. But it was her face that had gone through the most alarming transformation. It was haggard. The bones, once nicely packed in the flesh of softly rounded cheeks, were now sharp promontories above hollow valleys. The lips were stiff, unsmiling; in fact, the entire face seemed carved and contoured by an underlying anguish, a blend of despair, capitulation and sheer exhaustion. She wore a headscarf tied behind her neck, out of which fell lank tendrils of grey, greasy hair. So forlorn, she looked, shoulders rounded, gait slow as if in considerable pain, as she walked away from Sibyl. No comparison to the bundle of energy that Aunt Margaux had been.

Yet she was unmistakeable; in the split second as Aunt Margaux turned her face while parking to look behind, Sibyl had known. No recognition had flashed in the older woman's eyes; not surprising, as she was obviously preoccupied with pressing burdens, and Sibyl was not only the last person she'd expect to see, but was now a grown woman instead of a twelve-year-old girl.

It cost Sibyl all her strength not to fly out the door, run after Aunt Margaux, fling her arms around her, and beg for sanctuary. Beg for refuge, refuge from all this. Beg for a return to home, to normality, to the place where she belonged, the only place on earth she had ever felt happy, and the people who had helped that happiness to flourish.

As ever, the demands of reality restrained her. But she was thankful that, on the return journey to Colmar von Haagen remained silent, deep in thought himself. She kept her head slightly turned from him, her gaze fixed on the vineyards flashing past, because she feared the tears that might moisten her eyes; that he might see beyond the mask.

This excursion back into the past had agitated her more than she had expected. The vineyards, so brilliant green in the summer sun – the memories they evoked! Of halcyon days with Jacques, in the fields and in the forest and in the vines. Aunt Margaux, the good spirit and pulsing heart in the warm brick walls of Château Laroche. Marie-Claire, Leon, Lucien, Victoire, the laughter that echoed in every corner of that home! Yes, it was home, home in a way the house in Three Bridges had never been and never would be.

Her mother had torn her away from that home just as she was blossoming into womanhood, and deep inside Sibyl had never forgiven her. Not that she had gone through life resenting Kathleen for making that crucial move – even at the time, she had been mature enough to recognise that her mother needed to build a life of her own, find a love of her own, return to her own roots, which were in England. The threat that Germany had posed even then leant an even more compelling argument to the decision. But with Kathleen returning to her own roots Sibyl had lost hers, and had had to build a new life from scratch with only wonderful memories as a foundation. Nursing had provided an escape from that life, a reason to give herself to something bigger, grander; to align herself with France, with Alsace, with home.

And now here she was. In an Alsace that was not Alsace, but an Alsace owned by Germany. Living a false life under a false name, the false girl of a false German major. Because yes, everything about von Haagen was false. He had shown his true face today. Which meant she was doing her job well.

As a nurse, Sibyl had learnt how to handle men. All men, in all shapes and sizes, in all varieties. She had learnt what made them tick, what lay beneath the so-tough exteriors; the little boys that hid behind the arrogance and the bluster and, as was so often the case, the bullying. She had seen it all; men screaming with agony with half of their skin ripped away by burns, or limbs hanging on by mere ribbons of flesh and skin. Men who took their rage and their despair out on her, because she happened to be there, caring for them, touching them. She had sometimes wrestled with men as they resisted treatment; men who kicked and fought and hit and spat and called her all manner of hateful names. But most of, she listened. Listened as they talked. When the bluster left them, how they talked! She knew what moved men. She knew that at the moment when death is hovering as a shadow in the wings, all façades drop, all masks, all pretence, and they become vulnerable and small and needy. Putty in her hands, both as a nurse and, now as an agent. And that was why she had never been deceived by von Haagen, and would never be deceived by any man. She knew the truth of their being. In the end they all grovelled for love.

Von Haagen lay in the palm of her hand. Marlene Schuster was no more than a shadow, a superimposition; all of Sibyl Lake's skills were at her disposal, and all she had to do was to play her cards cleverly. But now, at the very moment of most promise, had come the moment of most danger.

The arrest of two men from the *Maquis*. Who were they? How much did Jacques know? How much did they, the men, know, and might reveal under Gestapo interrogation –which, in the end, meant torture?

The orders were clear. The moment one of them was caught, contaminated, the network had to dissolve. Go into the underground.

If that was what she had to do, she knew exactly where she would flee to. She had seen and recognised her refuge, just minutes ago, and longed for it. But stronger yet than that longing was the need to fight.

She had to report back to Acrobat. This was an emergency. But first, she had to contact Jacques.

# Chapter Twenty-Eight

'Why didn't you tell me? It's been a whole week since it happened and not a word from you. Jacques, that's not how it's done! You know that! Who are these men?'

It was the first time she had ever rebuked him, but it had to be done. The capture of a *saboteur* was a serious matter, especially an amateur *saboteur* who had not been trained, as she had, in the methods of interrogation and was not prepared for torture and did not carry an L-pill.

'They are idiots. Remember the fools who ran off with rifles and hand grenades? Henri's men? That's them. Raoul and Gaston. They broke into a sausage factory, imagine! It was all about food. And a factory near to where they are originally from, in the Bas-Rhin, so the guard they tried to shoot – and missed – recognised them and snitched to the Boche. They got away. There was a huge police action with posters all over the place and eventually they were caught by the local *gendarmes* – Alsace police, born and bred Alsatians – to be held until the Germans could talk to them. By that I mean the SS. But you know how it is. The Gestapo had to come from Strasbourg and by then news had spread that local boys were in the local prison. Henri bribed one of the guards and they organised a staged break-in. The boys are free again and in the underground, like the rest of us.'

'Still, you should have told me right away. I need to be informed…'

'Told you, how? I only heard myself three days ago when I saw the posters. I thought it was more important to call a meeting with Henri and that was the right thing to do because that was how we got them out of jail.'

'Von Haagen said they were sent to Natzweiler.'

'He lied to you. It's just the usual German bluster, showing off. That's where they would have been sent once the Gestapo got to them but they never got that far. Your German boyfriend would never admit to you that they actually escaped from custody! He would never admit any Boche failure, would he?'

'Actually…'

'So how are things going with your boyfriend?'

'Please don't call him that. You know very well that it's just a job.'

'I hope so. But these German officers – I don't know.'

'Jacques, jealousy doesn't suit you. Don't worry about me, worry about yourself. Because the bigger message is that the Gestapo have increased their presence in Alsace and are suspecting British involvement. SOE involvement. That means we need to lay low for a while. No more attacks for four weeks. They're all over Colmar. They wear black uniforms and just the sight of them gives me the creeps. And not all of them are in uniform. They could be anyone. So, my instructions are that. Keep to the hills in the next few weeks.'

'I'll tell my boys that. But for me, it's different. I am still investigating the bridge situation. There are two supply bridges in the Alsace, at Chalampé and Brisach. The Brisach one is the more important – it's a railway bridge that connects Colmar with Freiburg and the southern state of Baden. I need to get that bridge. Once I have destroyed that, I will bomb the Chalampé bridge.'

'You cannot do it alone, Jacques. I would do it with you but even I have never blown up a bridge of that size before. I think it's better I request an expert from headquarters. You cannot risk it. Especially with reinforced SS activity all over the place.'

'You're telling me to back off? Sibi, this has been my dream for months, if not years! The main ambition of my life!'

'All your dreams and ambitions are of no account here. Do not place your personal fulfilment at the centre of this because it is bound to go wrong! Why do men like to measure themselves by their achievements? "I need to blow up this bridge to prove myself." That's what I'm hearing and it's nonsense. You're not to do it, Jacques. I'm going to get in an explosives expert to figure it out and do the deed. It's not your place.'

'You mean – you're giving me the order to withdraw? You're not letting me blow it up?'

She sighed. 'Please don't make it into a power game, Jacques! Please don't be upset. Just don't do it. *D'accord?*'

*'D'accord. À bientôt.'*

He walked out the door. Sibyl sighed. Jacques, too. The old Jacques, the real Jacques, the man of the forest who could listen to grapes ripening and feel the heartbeat of a bird –wiped out by the exigencies of war, this quintessentially male need to demonstrate power and triumph by making huge explosions and big bangs, all, finally, to validate themselves. Wasn't that what it was all about? Where was the real Jacques in all of this? Buried, somewhere beneath it all. When the war was over he would have to be unburied.

That night she made an emergency radio call to HQ. She gave a short summary of the capture and eventual escape of the men, explained that she had stopped all sabotage action for the next few weeks, and requested an expert to blow up the bridge.

They would consider that request, said Acrobat.

She also told Acrobat about her conversation with von Haagen.

'I see,' was the guarded response.

# Chapter Twenty-Nine

In the days following the Riquewihr episode Sibyl fell into a sort of slump, a mental apathy in which she no longer *cared;* not about anything. Not about Margaux and Jacques and the Château and the vineyards; not about winning the war and spying and easing secrets out of von Haagen and leading him on and winning back Alsace. Not about Marlene Schuster or Jeanne Dauguet or Sibyl Lake. She just wanted to *be.* To do her work as a cobbler's assistant, answer to whatever name others called her, eat to survive, dress to cover her body, wash to keep clean.

She discovered the lady's bicycle under the stairwell in the back hallway; that is, she had seen it before but never connected with it. Now she dug it out and dusted it off. *Oncle* Yves, the only person she actually conversed with at this time, dug out the tools necessary to repair the flat inner tubes, pump them up. It seemed otherwise fine.

'Used to be my wife's,' said *Oncle* Yves. He sometimes mentioned this elusive woman but never went into detail. He hinted that she was dead, and also hinted that he wanted no questions, and would not answer any. She respected that desire and did not ask. Let people have their secrets. She had enough of her own.

Once the bicycle was repaired, she rode it around town. She avoided the main streets. It seemed to her that military presence was more dominant than ever; and it chilled her to see that more and more of these military men wore black uniforms – SS uniforms, signifying Hitler's own army: the Schutzstaffel. She remembered from her training how very different these soldiers were from the Wehrmacht. The Waffen SS had started out as a bodyguard unit for Hitler, with the function of protecting him at political speeches and rallies; basically the armed wing of the Nazi Party. It was headed by Heinrich Himmler, Hitler's right-hand man, who, it was said, was one of the most powerful men in Nazi Germany, responsible for the execution of the most heinous policies. Under Himmler the SS had grown to one of the most powerful organisations in Nazi Germany, the foremost agency of security, surveillance, and terror within Germany and German-occupied territories, existing alongside the regular Wehrmacht but under Himmler's direct authority.

Now they strutted around town as if they owned the place, or simply stood, watching. Their red swastika armbands screamed danger. The very sight of them turned her stomach to lead, their very presence strangled her; she felt watched, followed, stalked wherever she went. Over the weeks of her relationship with von Haagen she had become familiar to the regular Wehrmacht officers: von Haagen's girl, they called her and they waved to her, smiled at her, the leering of her first walk through the town completely obliterated. These new SS soldiers did not leer. They simply watched; with not lust but evil in their eyes.

But they were not here, in this part of Colmar. Not in these cobbled streets of charming medieval timber-framed houses, similar to the ones of Riquewihr. Here and there she sailed among the alleyways, finally finding herself in the enchanting world of Little Venice, where slim medieval houses slept beside the river Lauch and there was no indication whatsoever that, not even a mile away, the ugly world of Nazi Germany began. Not a swastika, not a banner, not a flag. The few people on the streets seemed more relaxed than those of Riquewihr; all seemed to share her state of spiritual suspension. She dared to believe that this, this beauty, this wonderland, was the reality; that it was not just a bubble of goodwill and peace but it was real and true and lasting, that here her soul would mutate and come to rest and all burdens drop from her; and they did, as she pedalled along the riverbank, to the fishmonger's district and the market gardens.

She had been here often before, as a child, for here was a rural community of wine-producers, where Aunt Margaux had friends who had children. They all used to play and bathe in the river and love life. And more memories came flooding back, bringing delight; and she ventured further afield, into the countryside, and slowly, gradually, she found herself again, that inner being trapped beneath all the identities she had worn, and there at last she felt anchored, strong once more and not pulled apart from the roles she had to play, the job she had to do.

She cycled, too, to all the churches of Colmar and leant her bike against their walls and entered and sat on pews and prayed. She prayed for peace to come to this fractured land, the peace it cried out for; and she cried too, with the land and with its disenfranchised people. And she knew she had to fight on. There was no escape.

Work in the shop was slow. Nobody needed new shoes or boots these days; it was all repairs, but nobody had money for repairs. *Oncle* Yves repaired their shoes nevertheless; they would give him whatever they could in return. A pot of soup. An egg. A pair of old but undarned socks. A book. Whatever they could.

Grete, the woman she'd met at the officer's club, came to visit several times. She would come and just sit there, and talk; sometimes she brought her little girl. She had a need to talk, and talk, and talk. Sibyl listened; her heart went out to Grete, whose situation was sad indeed. The Germans passed her from man to man; that way, at least she and her daughter could eat.

Von Haagen took her out on two more occasions; once to a restaurant called the Rote Löwe, which seemed to be a meeting point for German officers and their girlfriends, and once to the cinema, to see a German film called *Die Feuerzangenbowle,* with

Heinz Rühmann as star. In the middle of the film von Haagen reached out and touched her hand. She tensed, and looked at him; his eyes glowed bright through the darkness.

'May I?' he whispered. She considered, and then nodded. He squeezed her hand, and lifted it over to rest on his own knee, where he continued to lightly stroke the back of it with his thumb.

The following day he was there again, in the shop; to pick up his boots – now repaired to his satisfaction – and to say goodbye.

'Goodbye? You are leaving?'

'Do I detect as hint of sadness in your voice, in your eyes? Yes, I am leaving. But not for long, hopefully. I have been called to Berlin. There are – things to discuss. The Führer wishes to lay forth his plans to his officers. It seems the Alsace is coming into focus at long last. And I am pleased. It has been quite boring, sitting here in this dead town doing nothing more than ensuring that people speak the right language and read the right books and wear the right names. It is time for some action!'

'Action! Do you mean the Allies are going to invade the Alsace?'

'They would be foolish to do so. But it is a possibility. We must be on the alert. Whatever happens, Alsace belongs to Germany and we will defend it with our lives. More than that I cannot say, regarding the war.'

'But…'

'But one good thing Colmar has brought to me. And that is you. You must have felt it too, Marlene – I may call you that now, I hope – that you and I have a strong and subtle connection, one that goes deep into the soul. The very thought of you fills my heart with such joy, such hope; it gives me something to live for. A soldier needs something, someone to live for and for me, it is only you.'

She stood there, stunned, before him; at one point she realised her jaw was hanging open, so she closed it and stuttered a few words, not knowing what to say.

'No – no, you need not speak now. I only wanted you to know in no uncertain terms. I told you right from the beginning that my intentions were honourable. They have always been so. I have no time for a dalliance with a girl such as you – it would be a waste of my time. Well. That said, I am not going to make a formal proposition now. There is time enough for that, and I do not want to rush you. But I hope, I pray, that you give earnest thought to this and upon my return you will be ready to make me the happiest man on earth.'

'How – how long will you be away?'

'I cannot say. Certainly, a few weeks, as I shall visit my parents on the way back – a few days leave is due to me – and clarify a few matters with them as well. I am not sure how much of my time the Führer will need.'

'I shall look forward to your return.'

'And so shall I. And now, dearest Marlene, would you find it very forward of me if I were to take you in my arms and kiss those lovely lips of yours? Yes? May I?'

'Well – I suppose so.'

'Then come out here from behind that counter – it separates us so! And allow me to take leave from you properly.'

She raised the flap and emerged from behind the protective counter. She stood before him; she could not have felt more exposed if she were naked. But it had to be. And she had to relax. He drew her to him, placed his hand under her chin, raised it, and planted his lips on hers – lips that were as dry and cold as the sense of dread now filling her heart. The sense of falling into a well that was too deep, too dark; bottomless. Where would this lead? There was no way of knowing, except to wait and see. And play along.

He tipped his cap. '*Auf Wiedersehen,* my beloved!'

'*Auf Wiedersehen,* Wolfgang. Good luck in Berlin.'

'It's not luck. It's strategy!'

# Chapter Thirty

'You've got him by the balls,' was Acrobat's reaction to Sibyl's report.

'Yes, but…'

'It's a good thing. Lust is one thing. Love is another. Play along as well as you can.'

'I can't. He's gone to Berlin.'

'He'll be back. Play along.'

And it was done; a new role, a new challenge, one so much harder than the one she had signed up for. Managing a group of Resistance fighters was one thing; to deliberately deceive and betray von Haagen on a personal level quite another. She felt sick as she put away the wireless equipment and returned to her room. Yes, he was the enemy, a German, a representative of the Nazi regime, even if, as he had assured her, he was not a party member. Did that justify stringing him along? He was human, too; and that human spark was, unfortunately, Sibyl's Achilles' heel. Mr Smith had rightly diagnosed it. She recalled his words, at the second interview: *Compassion in a nurse is a highly desired virtue. For a person assisting in secret work for the liberation of France, not so much.*

She had reassured him that she was capable of restraining that compassion if her job called for it. She had spoken with confidence and determination; she had meant it.

But actual betrayal of a person's love?

During training there had been discussions, advice. The honey trap, it was called. Pillow talk. An important tool in an agent's arsenal, especially for a female agent. Lure a man into bed, get him to talk. It wasn't a method she'd find easy, but if called upon she'd do it, with clenched teeth. She'd actually been thankful that von

Haagen had made no such demands on her; it had been so easy, up to now. He was such a pretentious prig that conversations with him amounted almost to entertainment; she enjoyed sparring with him, taking him down a few pegs, sticking fingers into the holes in his bluster, reducing him, at times, even to tears. Buried in him was tremendous guilt. Exposing that guilt, digging it to the surface with the delicacy of a scalpel had been a challenge she'd been happy to rise to. Playing a role, she'd thought; it had both surprised and delighted her how easy it was to strip bare that guilt.

But now, her next moves, if she were to play along as Acrobat requested, this would not be exposure of guilt. It would be betrayal of trust. And the guilt, in that case, would be on her side.

But she had to do it; right up to the final consequences.

*You are an actor on a stage,* she told herself sternly. *Just do it.* This is the job.

Nevertheless, she was glad he had gone to Berlin. With luck, he would never return. Yes, it would be unfinished business, an opportunity lost, but that was the loss of Special Operations, not hers. What she had now amounted to a holiday. There was only one thing for it. Enjoy the respite, however long it would last, and prepare for his return.

Meanwhile, there was Jacques to deal with. He sent, via their secret mailbox system, a message to say he would not be at the next programmed meeting. Was he sulking? Because she had given him strict instructions, forbidden him from carrying out the bridge demolition himself? Was he insulted, because she had cast doubt on his prowess? Men could be so sensitive; questioning their ability to achieve any goal could be seen as an attack on their masculinity. But not Jacques, surely. Not the real Jacques, so well established within himself, so in touch with his own fundamental sense of self that he could commune with, it seemed, all of nature, all of life; who had no need of external applause or confirmation or validation; who radiated wholeness and well-being. But that was then. The war had stripped him of so much of his essence she could not help but doubt: did she really know him, now?

She loved him; that she knew. She was not sure if she still knew him. Whatever the case, she had ordered a pause in all *Maquis* activity, and he was definitely holding to that. Perhaps that was why he had cancelled the meeting: because no action was planned for the next few weeks. But still, wasn't it worth it, to meet, just to see each other? She shrugged these doubts aside. For the moment, she had space. It was time for a little holiday.

# Chapter Thirty-One

She dreamt of Château Gauthier; that she was there again, running through the vines. Jacques appeared before her, holding up a bunch of grapes. He plucked one and held it in his hand and it grew to the size of an apple; pale green, translucent, bursting with juice. 'Harvest will be in four weeks' time!' said Jacques. 'Until then we must lay low. No action.'

'But.., but they are ripe!' said Aunt Margaux.

'Let me try the riesling,' said dream Sybil, and suddenly they were in the kitchen, around the table, and her mother was there, and Elena, and Aunt Margaux was pouring the wine but it was red, and it was not wine, it was blood; and then someone knocked on the door.

'I'll get it,' said Aunt Margaux and got up. The banging grew louder and louder.

It woke her up. Had it been in the dream? Had it been real? Because it had stopped; there was only silence. But, then, through the silence: a crash like the splintering of glass followed by *Oncle* Yves bursting through her bedroom door and she was on her feet and grasping for a gun which wasn't there because, of course, the gun was up in the attic with the radio.

'You are all right? What is it?' cried *Oncle* Yves.

'I don't know! Someone broke in!

'Mon Dieu! Gestapo!' And her heart galloped as she pulled on the dress she had worn the day before.

And then there were feet, footsteps running up the wooden stairs, and someone crying,

'Acrobat! Acrobat!'

'Acrobat!' she yelled back as she lurched into the corridor and then a body leapt up the final flight and, panting, flung itself at her, grasping her arms.

'*Mademoiselle! Vite! Vite!* You must come with me! Immediately!'

It was Pierre, one of Jacques *maquisards*, a boy of about eighteen.

'What is it, Pierre? What's the matter? Did you break the window?'

'Yves, I'm sorry, I had to because you did not answer the back door – you must come, *mademoiselle* Lucie, Jacques is in danger and so are you! He has been caught! You must flee right away!'

'*Oncle* Yves. You too,' cried Sibyl. 'If I am in danger so are you. Let's go.'

'The wireless? Upstairs?' *Oncle* Yves, in white longjohns and a vest, was struggling to pull on his trousers.

'You must leave it, Mademoiselle. No time.'

'No. I cannot. It is the most compromising thing in this house. It won't take a second. *Oncle* Yves, you go down with Pierre. I'll be right there.'

She dashed up to the attic and grabbed the suitcase containing the tranceiver; kept packed away for just such an emergency. And the Sten gun. She flew down the stairs and met up with Pierre and *Oncle* Yves at the back door.

'*Vite, vite;* follow me,' said Pierre once they were in the back courtyard, and now he was whispering. The neighbouring houses were all shrouded in blackness; it seemed no-one had heard the racket.

Pierre ran, but too fast; *Oncle* Yves could not keep up. He doubled back and slowed his gait but his impatience was palpable.

'Where are we going?' Sibyl, lugging the suitcase, was caught between the two; hurrying to keep up with Pierre, slowing her feet so *Oncle* Yves could keep up. *Oncle* Yves, clearly out of breath already, panted as he kept up at a limping run. Pierre was leading them through cobbled back streets, a labyrinth of lanes and alleyways, none of which Sibyl had seen before.

Eventually they reached the river Lauch. Pierre slowed his gait. 'I think they won't find us here,' he said.

'Who are they? What has happened?'

'Jacques tried to blow up the Brisach bridge. He failed but they saw him and gave chase. I was with him. We drove out towards Ribeauvillé and Jacques told her to stop and let him out; he would hide himself. He didn't want to get her into trouble, you see. She was in so much danger already.'

'I'm not following. Who is she? What trouble?'

'That's her.' Pierre pointed, and there, at the corner, parked in the shadow of an enormous oak tree, was a van; a van as familiar to her as the pick-up she'd seen so recently; and standing beside the van was Aunt Margaux.

'*Tante!*' cried Sibyl and propelled herself into the arms of the woman who had once mothered her so well, had mothered her even in her dreams.

'Sibyl. My little girl. But come, come, there is no time to waste. You must get in the back. You and the old man.'

She opened the double back doors of the van. Sibyl helped *Oncle* Yves in and then climbed in herself. Aunt Margaux climbed into the driver's seat, Pierre entered the cabin through the passenger's door; the van drove off.

Sibyl leaned on the back of the driver's seat.

'Aunt Margaux. You must explain now what has happened. Jacques tried to blow up the bridge? Is he mad? How are you mixed up in all of this?'

'I helped him,' she said. 'I was fool enough to help him. I drove him there and waited for him – for him and Pierre, who kept watch but the yellow sentries saw them and gave chase. Jacques was shot.'

'Oh my God! Is he…?'

'No, not dead – Pierre stopped to help him. He had a leg wound, bleeding badly, couldn't run any more. Jacques told Pierre to run away and he did. Jacques tried to get up but he stumbled. He was bleeding.

The yellow picked him up. Pierre saw them take him away. They must have taken him to hospital, I think. But he is in custody. The network is shot. I had to let you know immediately. It's what Jacques told me. If anything happened, warn you. Rescue you. Just in case.'

'In case – Jacques talks?'

'Jacques won't talk, Sibyl. He loves you. He won't talk. But…'

'But in the end everyone talks. Nobody can withstand the Gestapo interrogation. They… their methods… they use torture and everybody talks. Does he have his L-pill? Do you know?'

'He doesn't. He has always rejected it.'

'How do you know all this, *Tante?*'

'Jacques is like a son to me. He tells me everything.'

'He should not, you know. He should not be telling anybody. That is a serious security breach.'

'Oh, Sibyl, do not talk like a bureaucrat. Jacques is family. He is carrying a heavy burden. Sometimes he needs to unburden himself. Everybody needs that. Don't you?'

'I may not, *Tante*. It is forbidden.'

'Then one day the burden will make you crazy, like it is making Jacques crazy. Anyway it is too late for recriminations. That is the situation. Now we must decide how to proceed.'

'You say they have taken him to hospital?'

'Yes. I'm pretty sure. What else can they do? They can't let him bleed to death. He is too valuable for them.'

'So, not yet the Gestapo…'

'No. But the Gestapo will come, once he is patched up.'

'I know. They are already on the alert for terrorist activities. They call us terrorists.'

'Pff. It's the yellow who are the terrorists, they have terrorised Alsace for years.'

'Where are we going now?'

'To Château Gauthier. The main thing was to inform you, and to get you out of the way.'

'But if they have to patch him up first, there is still time.'

'Yes. Time to think. I am already hatching a plan. While I was waiting for you, I was thinking.'

'You have a plan?'

'Maybe. It all depends.'

'So?'

'No, first I take you home and give you breakfast and then I will tell you my plan.'

'*Tante* – we still have a problem. *Oncle* Yves' shop window has been shattered. Pierre broke in. We cannot leave it like that all day. For one thing, thieves might really break in. For another thing, the neighbours will see and alert the police and search the house and it will look suspicious – the same night that someone tried to bomb the bridge. Maybe even the *Sicherheitsdienst,* the SD, will come to investigate. If they connect me to the bombing…'

'Do you have anything incriminating in the house?'

'No. I brought the radio with me. There is nothing else.'

'Good. Then we will organise that as well.'

'Yes. Actually, I have an idea. But we have to go back. Or someone has to go back –maybe Pierre.'

'Later. Not now. It is not yet even dawn – nobody will go there yet.'

Aunt Margaux, all this time, was driving through a complex network of back roads and lanes through vineyards. 'I know this area like the back of my hand,' she said. 'If they are looking for anyone, they won't find me. We'll soon be home, safe and sound.'

Indeed; half an hour later Sibyl and Yves were safely tucked into Margaux's kitchen at the Château Gauthier, hugging warm cups of a delicious concoction Margaux had made for them. 'It's a special herb,' she said, 'and with milk added – well, it's better than coffee.'

'You have milk?'

'*Mais oui!* You forget our goats? They are still thriving. And the hens. And rabbits. I even have bacon – the farmers around here, we share produce. I shall make you a lovely breakfast.'

Before breakfast, though, Sibyl asked for a sheet of paper and Margaux tore a page from a child's old exercise book.

'Pen?' asked Sibyl, and Margaux produced a black crayon.

'Better yet!' said Sibyl as she took it. Across the blank page, in big black letters, she wrote:

**'COLLOBARATEUR!!!!!'**

'See! Now, we'll wrap this around a large stone and Pierre will go back to the house and place it in the window. If they come to question me I will say that I have enemies in the town because of my friendship with the German major. That it was only an act of hatred; that when we heard the window break *Oncle* and I fled the house because we were afraid of robbers. We will go back later today and board up the broken window. *D'accord, Oncle?*'

'Yes. We must return as soon as possible, if there is no more danger to my niece. We cannot leave the shop exposed in that way. I too have my secrets.'

'Ah, but yours are really well secreted, *Oncle*! I think there is no danger.'

'I will wake Victoire. She will drive Pierre back to Colmar to deposit the stone and the note.'

Margaux left the kitchen and a few minutes later returned with a young girl, still buttoning up a long man's shirt which she wore over loose farmer trousers. She had long black hair, tousled still from sleep, around a face, that in spite of the heavily sleep-laden eyes still bore the promise of extraordinary beauty.

Sibyl jumped to her feet.

'Victoire! It's you, and all grown up! My word! Do you remember me?'

'*Certainement!* It is wonderful to see you again, Sibi.'

'But after this morning you do not know each other, *bien?* It is an emergency. Victoire, you must drive Pierre to Colmar. Pierre will tell you what happened to Jacques on the way.'

'Something has happened to Jacques? What? Is he in danger?'

'Pierre will tell you. Go. *Vas t'en.*'

She gave Victoire instructions.

'I will go with you,' said *Oncle* Yves. 'I cannot leave my house empty with a huge hole in the window,' he insisted. 'If the Boche come I will say it is vandals, people trying to persecute my niece because she is the girlfriend of a Boche. It is quite simple.'

'I cannot let you go without offering you hospitality! Let me give you something.'

Margaux quickly packed up a side of ham in some newspaper, and then two eggs. 'These are already hard-boiled,' she said. 'Take them. You need them for strength.'

'I'll see you later, *Oncle* Yves!' said Sibyl.

Victoire hooked her arm into his and led him out to the van. She turned to cry out as she left: 'You must bring back Jacques! If you don't, I will!'

'She has turned into a lovely young lady,' said Sibyl.

'Yes, and she adores her big brother,' said Margaux as she and Sibyl took their seats again, 'just like you used to adore him.'

'Her brother? Jacques? But…'

'Half-brother, yes. You were too young to know back then but it is no secret now, that Jacques' father is also Victoire's father, and my lover or ex-lover, as the case may be. You remember Maxence?'

'Of course! Does he know about Jacques? About the *maquisards?* Will you tell him what happened last night?'

'No. He knows nothing – only that Jacques has defected, did not let the Boche conscript him. It is for his own protection that he does not know. It is bad enough having a son who is a defector from the German army. To have a son who is also in the Resistance – it would not be good for Maxence. He is only free because he is so valuable to the Boche as a winemaker. And so am I, as the owner of Château Gauthier and of the magnificent label Laroche-Gauthier. You see, the one thing the Germans appreciate about the French is our wine. My wine has given me many advantages. For one, I refused to change my name to a German one and also my wine label stays French. Wine is my trump card.'

It was the Margaux of old, chattering away as she prepared breakfast for her guests. Sibyl could hardly get a word in, but a question burned on her lips and she simply interrupted as she had to know; as much as she was eager to hear the gossip, one thing was more important.

'*Tante* Margaux, you said you had a plan to free Jacques? Shouldn't we be discussing that?'

'I was coming to that. There is nothing to discuss. What I am telling you, it is all relevant information, it is why I am explaining about the wine. Don't be impatient, girl, let me tell you. Listen. What was I saying before your interruption? Ah yes. The wine. My trump card. Do you remember, when you were a little girl, how we built a wall in the cellar to hide our best wine from the Boche, because my husband, your *Oncle* Jean-Pierre, was so terrified the Boche would attack and requisition it? Ah, we were so clever, building that wall, hiding wine, and indeed, all over France the yellow did steal the wine. Good wine is like the crown jewels of France, and here too, we had to hide our best and our second best, so that only the lower quality wine was visible in the cellars. It was a lot of work. Even the children helped. You may remember.'

Sibyl nodded. Margaux set a plate of bacon and eggs in front of her. There was bread, too, on the table, and butter, and cheese, all luxuries she had not seen for years. Ravenous, now, she began to eat.

'Well, as it turned out, it was all a waste of time, though not really as we used the secret cellar for something else – I'll tell you that story later. Where was I? Ah, yes. The wine and Les Boches. Well after they annexed Alsace we knew they would come and come they did. They inspected our low quality wine, which we had disguised as high quality wine by relabelling it and throwing carpet-dust all over the bottles so they looked old. We got carpet dust from the *aspirateur,* the vacuum cleaner. The bottles looked very impressive, very old, and the Boche were deceived and very impressed. But you know, we had a tolerable sort of Boche Commander and they did not create any destruction and did not go on a rampage in the wine cellar. No: the yellow made deals with us and bought our wines for export to Germany. Of course, now all the wine in France goes to Germany instead of to England. I suppose you could call us *collabarateurs* in that sense but really we had no choice and anyway we had to accept their prices, which were much lower than previously. Still we cannot complain. On the whole, with a few exceptions, winegrowers did quite well after the Boche took over. Where was I again? Ah yes, the best wine we still had hidden away. It turned out to be quite a treasure chest because any time we needed something done by the Boche, or when we wanted them not to do something, all we had to do was hand over a bottle or a crate of our best wine. See, the Boche are as much susceptible to bribery as any other human being! And so our wine remains our strength, and with our wine we will free France and free Jacques!'

'Free Jacques?'

'Yes my dear; that was what I was coming to. We will find out where he is, find him in that hospital, and bribe the guards with our very best Château Laroche-Gauthier 1919. That is the year the last war ended and you know the saying. So you see, your *Tante* Margaux still lets her mouth run as ever she did but always she has something useful to add to the discussion, isn't it so?'

'You really think…?'

'*Mais oui*. I do it all the time. In fact, I am now an expert in the fine art of bribery and corruption, and believe me there is not a Boche on earth who can resist the lure of a good bottle of Château Laroche-Gauthier 1919. It is better even than sex. Next time you come or at the latest when Alsace is free and you come to celebrate we will open a bottle together. I promise you, it is the nectar of the gods!'

'Oh, *Tante!* It's so wonderful to be here again, if only for an hour or two! To hear you talk – I have been so lonely in Colmar, all on my own.'

'Then you must come. Come more often, whenever you want. You have left it much too late. Why didn't you come before?'

'Because, because I am an agent and I was not supposed to tell anybody…'

'Pah! I can keep secrets as well as anyone despite my big mouth. I can talk nonsense at a hundred kilometres an hour but the real secrets are locked in my heart. You must come. If anyone asks, you can say you met me somewhere, maybe at the Colmar farmer's market, and we became friends and that's how you know me. Nobody will care. The Boche will not think, ah, maybe she is an English girl who lived here when she was seven years old. Why would they? You must come. Especially, you must come and help with the harvest. It is soon. You always loved the harvest.'

'Oh, *Tante!* That would be…'

'*Magnifique.* I know!'

'You know, I saw you once, a while ago…'

'In Riquewihr. I know. I saw you too. With your German *Majeur.*'

'You recognised me? But…'

'Of course I did. But as I said, I know how to keep a secret. Do you think I would jump into your arms crying out "Sibyl! Sibyl! You are back from *Angleterre!*" No, I am very discreet. But you were surprised, no? You looked very surprised. Shocked, even.'

'You seemed so – changed. But you aren't really.'

'That was the day after I got the news. About Leon. Leon is dead, Sibyl. Killed in action on the Eastern Front.'

'Oh, no! *Tante*, I'm so sorry!'

She jumped to her feet and flung her arms around Margaux. Margaux allowed it without reacting, and then shook her off. Sibyl returned to her seat.

'It is nothing. I am just one Alsace mother with boys over there. Sooner or later I will hear the same thing about my Lucien. I am resigned to it. Don't cry, *chérie*. I have accepted it. It is all part of life. Millions of mothers have lost their precious sons in this damned war; I am not the only one. Here, here's a napkin. Dry your eyes.'

Sibyl dabbed at her eyes and sniffed.

'Sometimes the tragedy of it all is just so… So overwhelming. And Marie-Claire? How is she? I heard…'

'Do not mention that name to me. She is no longer my daughter. She is another price I had to pay when the Boche invaded us. I do not even want to hear her name. This war has taken three of my four children from me. All I have left is Victoire. That is why I look like the living death. It has eaten into my flesh. I am surrounded by death and I myself am almost a skeleton – look at me! The horror of living under the thumb of the Boche has left its mark on my face and on my body. It is true – in a way I am a broken woman. But it is not true because deep inside there is a spirit that cannot be broken! I will not allow it! I must fight on another day! Now there is hope that the war will soon be at an end – do you know, we get the BBC here? We have a secret radio, though it is forbidden. The Allies are advancing quickly across France. It is just a matter of time till they free us from our horrible yoke. It has been years of being strangled at the neck, and good riddance. But tell me about this *Majeur*. I heard he has gone to Berlin. For how long? Does he love you? Do you love him?'

'He is not my major, *Tante*. He is my job. Did Jacques not tell you that?'

She chuckled. 'Jacques is a man. He does not see it that way. You must comfort him, Sibyl, and forgive him this foolish action. It is the action of a man who doubts himself and so thinks he must prove himself to the woman he loves by some grand action, some big show of power. It is the way of men, to prove themselves to us women. Men think they have to win wars to show they are strong, and they only demonstrate how weak they really are. Because otherwise, why? Why does this fool Hitler think he has to rule the world? It is only weakness. This war has weakened Jacques and your affair with the major… well, it is hard for him, as a man. You must reassure him.'

'But first you must free him. Do you really think…?

'We will free him. Later on I will drive you back and then I will go to the hospital with my best wine. I will take a whole crate – I might have to bribe a few guards but I will do it, Sibyl. Never fear.'

'I will come with you.'

'No! You cannot be seen together with me! I am known to be an old friend of his but you – you must never be seen with him. It is a security risk.'

'I need to see him, Margaux. I need to know.'

'You will take such a risk, at such a time? The SD will be on high alert, Sibyl, after this attack. You cannot be seen anywhere near him – he is a terrorist in their eyes.'

'I will wait in the van. I cannot let you do this alone.'

Margaux shrugged. 'If you insist then I cannot stop you. But we must think this through, do it properly. You are a nurse, Jacques told me, and he is wounded. What do you think will happen?'

'Well, first they will take him to theatre to remove the bullet, if there is one in his leg. I do not know – how bad is the wound? Did Pierre say where it is, where he was hit?'

'It is in his thigh.'

'They will operate to remove the bullet and then they will put him in a ward to recover.'

'No. He is a prisoner. The yellows will put him in a private room with a sentry. That was my experience, the last time I did this.'

'You have done this before?'

'Yes, in the first year of the war, that is how I know it can be done. It was not a resistance fighter, it was a boy they arrested because he is a Jew. You know I used to help the Jews escape?'

'Yes, Jacques told me.'

'The Château was a safe house; they would stay here and then Jacques or someone would escort them over the Vosges into occupied France to another safe house. But in the last years there have been no more Jews. They were all evacuated to Vichy. Thank goodness, not to Germany: we have heard terrible things about Jews sent to Germany! But I once got a Jewish boy out of custody this way; he too was wounded, though not from a shot. But I got him out. That is how I know it can be done. Good wine opens doors. But anyway, according to you, he will be having an operation.'

'That's what I assume, yes.'

'And then?'

Yes. As soon as possible after that, we don't know when, they'll take him to Gestapo HQ for interrogation.'

'I'll find that out.'

'How?'

'I told you: wine. My second-best, Château Laroche-Gautier 2014. It will open doors; it's like gold. Listen: they will take him to the Louis Pasteur. I know people who work there, doctors, nurses, administrators. They all buy their wine from me; they know me and want to keep in my good books. Everybody appreciates discounts. I will make a few phone calls to the hospital. Find out if he is there at all, and if so, how he is doing and how well he is being guarded. The administration is still French. They will help. If possible we will go in tonight.'

'That sounds good. But now we must make plans. I think I should go back home as soon as possible. The main thing is that the transmitter is no longer there; that was the most incriminating thing. But first I would like to use it, if I may; I need to report back to headquarters. And hopefully you will allow me to keep it here for the time being? Until the danger is over, I mean.'

'You can keep it here as long as you want. This is my suggestion: I will return you to Colmar to your house; if someone from the yellow comes you just plead innocence. It was some horrible vandal who hates you because you are friendly with a German officer. You must hide behind your major. You must insist that he is your sweetheart and you are engaged to him, and that is why your home was attacked. You have nothing to do with the terrorists. You must use that word and be offended that you are under suspicion. But in my view that is all just a precaution. In my view they will leave you alone.'

'That's a good plan. And now, if I may, I will help you clear up and then I will go off to use the transmitter. I will go up to the attic; that room we used to play in as children? It would make a good hiding place for the equipment.'

'It is all fine – run along. Don't bother about the kitchen, I will do it.'

'Then I will go.'

Sibyl grabbed the suitcase and made her way up to the top of the house. The door to the playroom creaked as she opened it. She entered and switched on the light. A wave of nostalgia swept through her. This was where they had all played, mostly on winter evenings when it was too cold and dark to play outside. All of them: she and Elena and the four Laroche children and Jacques and Juliette. Now of the eight of them, two were dead, one was fighting in Russia, one was estranged from the family, one was wounded in the hands of the Boche, and one, Elena, was no longer in France and could not return before the war was over. She sighed and walked over to the mansard window where the old wooden table on which they had played multiple card and board games still stood. Jacques and Marie-Claire had been such rivals! Marie-Claire always was so triumphant when she won against Jacques; annoyingly so, whereas Jacques had merely shrugged it off. Jacques had never cared much about winning. Until the war. And now, winning was all he could think about, all they could all think about; and they would win. The Allies would win. And she and Jacques would be a part of that victory. But now Jacques had made a terrible mistake and somehow she had to explain that to her superiors.

She set up the radio and found the frequency. 'Acrobat!' she said.

'Acrobat. What is the matter?' Came the reply. This was not a scheduled call, and thus was immediately recognised as an emergency call.

'I'm afraid there's bad news.'

She succinctly described the events of the night. Acrobat was, predictably, not pleased.

'You had asked us to send over an explosives expert for that bridge. We were in the midst of arranging that. Why this ridiculous solo action?'

'I can't explain it, Acrobat. He had thoroughly reconnoitred the area and he thought it could be done.'

'Did you give him permission?'

'No. I told him I had requested an expert.'

'So he acted against orders. And in so doing endangered everyone. That is, in particular, you, since you are the network.'

'I suppose so, yes.'

'There is no supposing about it. We cannot afford renegade actions. He has jeopardised you and the entire operation as now we will no longer be able to send our explosion for the bridge. It is quite serious. He could have set us back months. Apart from that he has now put you in jeopardy. The circuit is contaminated. Fortunately it's a small one, consisting of only you. He'll squeal under torture.'

'I was getting to that. Actually we've planned a rescue – he is in hospital now, we think, and if so we hope to get him out.'

'When?'

'Tonight.'

'Good luck with that. But, Acrobat One, you're on your own in this. We cannot help you. You need to hide as best you can.'

'I understand.'

'Well, nothing to be done now. Even if you pull off the rescue attempt successfully, I want no more action at all for the next few months; probably not ever. Lie low. It could very well be that the war is coming to Alsace and the *maquisards* have outlived their usefulness. It would have been good to get that bridge down, as it would have destroyed their supply flow to the Alsace. Very annoying.'

'So – what am I to do? I mean, if all goes well tonight?'

'Wait there. I will let you know at the next scheduled call. Over and out.'

She was trembling as she put away the transmitter. Acrobat's anger had been palpable through the waves. Sibyl, as a nurse, had almost always followed instructions, except in those few instances when she had truly known better than the attending doctor: because she knew the patient better, because she had more actual experience in a particular treatment; or because the doctor had not given the case more time and attention. In the few cases she had acted against a doctor's orders it was because her instinctive and innate knowledge of the situation had directed her. It had never been out of bravado or overconfidence, never an attempt to prove herself right, the doctor wrong. And she had always been right, in every case, as had been proven by the recovery or improvement of the patient. So a reprimand from her superior dug deep; a thorn in her flesh. But there was nothing to be done.

His last words, though, were both enigmatic and exciting. *The war is coming to Alsace. The maquisards have outlived their usefulness.* What did it mean? Did it mean that she, too, had outlived her usefulness? Would she be recalled? Sent back to England with her tail between her legs? To return home in ignominy would be unbearable; because if the war was truly coming to Alsace, that was exactly the time to do her bit. Up to now, it seemed, she had been but treading water.

And so she was quite glum as she returned to Margaux, who by now had cleared away the kitchen and was out in the yard letting out and feeding the chickens because dawn was breaking.

'Just help me a bit with the animals, will you,' she said, 'and then we'll drive back to Colmar. Pierre and Victoire, by the way, are back. Everything went without incident; however, the main streets around Colmar are crawling with the yellow. They were stopped and questioned twice! Once on the way there, once on the way back.'

'What did they say?'

'The usual: delivery of wine. As ever, wine is the magic word. I suspect they gave away a bottle or two.'

'It's all rather frightening.'

'We are used to it. We have lived with this terror for four years.'

'It might soon be over. I think the Allies are moving in!'

'Is that what your boss told you?'

'Not in so many words. It would be confidential if that was the case. But he hinted at it. It might be the end, Margaux. Think of it! I believe it is true. Major von Haagen also hinted at something like that; he was called back because of Allied activity in the region, he said. Maybe it is true! Maybe it is the end!'

'Well, if the Allies are coming, it means it is not the end but the beginning.'

'The beginning?'

'The beginning of the end. It means the war is coming to Alsace. Don't you understand, Sibyl? The Boche have dug themselves in. They can only be driven away through war. And it will be terrible.'

# Chapter Thirty-Two

She returned home to find that *Oncle* Yves had already boarded up the broken window. Now it was the second boarded-up shop on *Gerectigkeitsgasse,* along with the violin-maker's.

'I will replace the glass when Alsace is free again,' he said. 'Until then, let the boards be a testimony to the yoke we are living under. My customers know I am here. They can find me.'

Sibyl went up to her room to freshen up, and returned to the shop for a late start at her job: it was now almost midday. Because of the boarded-up window, the shop was dark. *Oncle* Yves did not want to waste electricity and so he provided candles, which gave the area an almost romantic atmosphere: cosy, glowing, and with the pleasant scent of melting wax.

There were few customers that day; even fewer than before the break-in. And then, shortly before two, the Boche came. They came in the form of two black-uniformed officers; one rake-thin and stern-faced, the other heavy-set, the kind of thuggish figure one would not like to meet in a dark alley. They entered to the usual jangle of bells.

'*Sicherheitsdienst.* Good afternoon, *Fräulein.* We would like to question you regarding an incident that occurred last night,' said the thin one.

'I will fetch my uncle. He is the owner of the shop,' said Sibyl. She opened the door to the workshop. '*Oncle* Yves, there are some officers here to see you.'

*Oncle* Yves came through, removing a pair of goggles.

'How can I help?'

'You name and ID card, please.'

The thin one did all the speaking while the burly one cast beady eyes slowly over the shelves at the back of the shop. Having done that, his gaze rested on Sibyl, sitting quietly on a stool behind the counter. She had the distinct feeling of being mentally stripped naked. She shuddered.

'It has come to our attention that there was a break-in here,' he said. 'In fact, we can see that the window was broken. When did this happen?'

'Last night when we were asleep.'

'At what time?'

'It must have been about two in the morning, *n'est-ce pas*, Jeanne? We both woke up and came downstairs.'

'Have you reported the crime to the Kripo, the criminal police?'

'No, I did not. I simply cleared up the mess and boarded up the window. I do not have time to report it. I may do so later in the week.'

'Did you see anyone? Did anyone come upstairs?'

'No. We saw no-one.'

'A terrorist act was committed last night. At least two terrorists were involved. One was later apprehended. The other one escaped. We are concerned that he was aided by members of the population. Did anyone associated with terrorists seek refuge in this shop?'

'No, indeed not.'

'Why then was your shop broken into?'

'That itself was an act of terrorism. This is what we found.'

He produced a large stone and a sheet of paper ripped from an exercise book, with the word 'COLLABORATEUR!!!' scrawled across it.

'What does this refer to?'

*Oncle* Yves shrugged. 'We do not know. Perhaps to my niece's friendship with a German officer?'

The thin officer turned his attention to Sibyl.

'Your name, *Fräulein*?'

'Jeanne – Marlene Schuster.'

'Show me your papers.'

She produced her identity card. He inspected it and handed it back.

'What is this about a German officer?'

'He is just a friend. We go out occasionally. He is a major in the Wehrmacht.'

'His name?' She told him.

'Can this officer vouch for you, that you are positively inclined to the National Socialist government of Colmar and have no sympathies towards terrorists?'

'I am sure he would vouch for me. Unfortunately, he is in Berlin at the moment.'

The two officers exchanged looks.

'Having a German officer as a friend is not necessarily an alibi. Any whore can have an officer friend.'

'Are you suggesting…'

'Save your outrage. I am just suggesting that it is easy for a woman to have an officer *friend*, especially if that woman is seeking a cover for clandestine activities. It is easy to hide behind an officer, but we are not fooled. It is also easy to stage a break-in. It is rather coincidental that this break-in occurred less than half an hour after the terrorist act. Someone escaped, sought refuge, perhaps came here? I think we will need to search the building, Herr Schuster.'

*Oncle* Yves seemed not to have heard; he had been fiddling with the shoe in his hand and, apparently, not listening. He did not look up.

'Herr Schuster?'

'What? You mean…? Ah yes, Schuster. That's me. I forgot. *D'accord.* What were you saying?'

Sibyl said: 'They want to search the house. They are looking for terrorists. They think we are hiding them.'

'Oh. Well, let them search. They will find no terrorists here. I do not know any terrorists.'

'You go, Kurt,' said the thin one. 'I will stay here with the two of then.'

The burly one nodded and went through the workshop, leaving both that door and the door to the stairwell open. A moment later his heavy footsteps could be heard thudding up the stairs. And then, clumping around on the ceiling above their heads.

He took his time. But half an hour later he was back, shaking his head.

'Nobody is upstairs, sir.'

'Did you look in all the cupboards? Under the beds?'

'Of course. There is nobody.'

'Well, then we will move on. But we will keep an eye on you two.'

'Good luck finding your terrorists,' said *Oncle* Yves.

The thin one nodded curtly. The officers exited the shop. Sibyl and *Oncle* Yves, once certain they had gone, hugged each other.

'Well, my dear, you have managed this far without arousing suspicion. Now, I fear, it will be a bit different. These people – they can actually smell spies. It's a sixth sense in the brain of the Gestapo.'

'These were SD officers. *Sicherheitsdienst.* That's what they said when they came in. That is actually above Gestapo.'

# Chapter Thirty-Three

Margaux came later that evening, with news.

'I called the hospital, someone I know. Jacques is fine. He is recovering well. The bullet was removed and he is in a private room on the first floor of the hospital. I have arranged everything. I have already handed out several hundred Reichsmarks worth of wine to hospital staff and they will turn a blind eye to what is to happen tonight. He has a guard from the SS with him in the room twenty-four hours a day. Tonight, that guard, after being fed his supper by the hospital staff, will feel very sleepy and in fact he will fall asleep. A friend will enter the room and inform Jacques of the plan. He will be helped through the window. There is a drainpipe outside that room he can climb down.'

'That is – wonderful – well done! And there was no problem, bribing the staff?'

'If you ask me I almost did not need to bribe them. They are French – Alsatians. They hate the Boche as much as anyone. They are Resistance fighters as much as anyone. They know Jacques is not a terrorist. Jacques' father was operated on here a few years ago. Some of them even know Jacques. We Alsatians stick together!'

'It's just odd that the Germans would put him in such a low-security hospital.'

'It is the only hospital. Though it was officially Germanised, it is still run by Alsatian staff. They do have a small military hospital but it is for the military, not for prisoners.'

'And the prison?'

'The prison does not have its own hospital. When a prisoner needs treatment he is sent to the local hospital with a personal guard.'

'Well – anyway. It sounds like a good plan if we can make it work.'

'We can. Pierre is willing to be the one to go in to Jacques and help him escape. It will be easy. And in the morning the guard will awake after a deep sleep and wonder what happened. Never mind. He, too, will have a glass of Château Laroche-Gauthier with his supper. I'm sure it will be much appreciated. But you: you cannot come. It is too dangerous. They do not suspect you yet. You must stay out of it.'

'Too late for that.' Sibyl told her about the visit of the SD officers.

'They came to Château Laroche-Gauthier too and searched but did not find the radio; they were looking for Jacques, not an object. And of course Maxence's place. We are now all under suspicion. You cannot take that risk. You must stay out of it. For you, the stakes are too high. They will execute you if you are caught.'

Sibyl shook her head. 'They'll execute you, too, and anyone else they catch.'

'But you: as an agent…'

'It's dangerous work, we all know that and still we take the risk. I'm coming tonight. We must be all the more careful.'

'If you insist.'

'And when we have freed him, where will he go?'

'I will be waiting in the van nearby, with you. Pierre will bring him to us.'

'I mean, where will he stay afterwards? He cannot go to your place. That is the first house they will search and you are already under suspicion, as his friend.'

'He must go to a safe house. He will know of someone who will put him up.'

'But I've been thinking. There's an alternative. I know where he could stay, without putting anyone in danger at all.'

'Where?'

'You'll see. Let's get him out first.'

Sibyl crept down the stairs and out the back door at one that night. The moon was still new; the surrounding buildings were dull black, the sky luminous black, and Sibyl herself a black shadow from head to toe. She sidled along the buildings, turned into the cobbled road outside the courtyard, and kept going at a quiet jog until she had reached the appointed place where Margaux and her van were waiting.

'If the SS stops us now, we're done for!' said Margaux, but so carelessly she might have been telling a joke. 'Nobody with honest intentions drives around at this time of night. Not in a battered old wine van.'

'It feels odd, not having a cover story. But I suppose they won't be on the prowl any more now they've caught him. Not at night, at least.'

'Once out of town we'll be safe. I'll park in the same place as last night. Pierre parked a bicycle near the hospital and will bring Jacques.'

She took a turn down a quiet lane that seemed to lead to a farm, then down another lane into a wooded area.

'The hospital is about two kilometres away. If all goes to plan they should be here in about an hour. Now it's just a matter of waiting. Have some wine.'

She pulled the cork out of a bottle and handed it to Sibyl. She pushed it away.

'How can you drink at a time like this?'

'How can you *not* drink?' Margaux took a slug from the bottle, wiped her mouth on her sleeve. 'Just don't let me overdo it. I can't afford to have an accident, tonight of all nights.'

'You can't afford to have an accident at all, Margaux. You really should…'

'Now don't you start lecturing me about my drinking. Yes, I know I drink too much. Yes, I know I need to slow down. But on a night like this? I need it, Sibyl, I need it. I'll give up wine tomorrow.'

'Yes, yes, I'm sure you will.'

'Are you doubting me?'

The banter, sometimes light-hearted, sometimes serious, continued as the minutes crept past. Why is it, Sibyl asked herself, that when you were on edge and desperately nervous, that was when time slowed down to an impossible crawl? And when you were happy and enjoying yourself, it flashed by in a wink? The repartee was distracting but it did not speed up time nor lessen her nerves, which were sharpened to the point of fraying. Margaux, meanwhile, had finished the bottle and Sibyl was seriously worried about her ability to drive afterwards. Yes, she herself could drive instead, but only back to Colmar. After that it would have to be Pierre at the wheel. Though Margaux did not appear drunk; the only evidence of the emptied bottle was a slightly slurred voice.

An owl hooted. An animal squealed in the undergrowth. Margaux jumped.

'What was that?'

'Just an animal.'

'I thought…'

'We're both jumpy. You're sure Pierre knows where to find us?'

'Yes, yes. Of course. He found me yesterday, didn't he?'

'It's just that…'

'Shhh! Listen!'

It was unmistakeable. A sort of vague whirring noise, and growing louder. They both jumped from the van, one on each side, and peered into the lane leading through the forest. A dark lump could be seen approaching, the whir of the bicycle wheel growing louder.

And then they were there, Pierre, slowly sailing up with a squeak of brakes; braking further with his feet and dismounting cautiously, supporting the bicycle as Jacques carefully slid off the crossbar and stood on one leg.

'Jacques! Jacques!' Sibyl's arms were around him as she whispered his name.

'I made it, Sibi. I made it!'

'Come on, you lovebirds, get in the van. Pierre, put away the bike and get in the back. And now, Sibyl, you kindly tell us which way to go. Where is this wonderful hiding place of yours?'

'Back to Colmar.'

'Back to… are you out of your mind?'

'Maybe a bit. But we can risk it. Nobody's about yet – or still. They're not looking for Jacques. It's not like last night. They don't know he's gone.'

'Yet.'

'Just drive, Margaux. Trust me.'

Margaux trusted her, and drove; following directions.

'Nearly there! Turn left here.'

'But Sibyl, this road drives right past…'

'I know. *Gerechtigkeitsgasse*.'

'Sibyl, you must be mad. You can't put him up in your own home!'

'I'm not. I won't. This is better. Stop here. Pierre, I'll need your help – Jacques, get down carefully… that's right… arms around our shoulders. Margaux, you can come too, to unlock the door. The key's in my pocket.'

They drove into the cobbled courtyard at the back of *Gerechtig-keitsgasse*.

'Sibyl – this is insane. You can't…'

'I'm not, Margaux. I said, trust me, and get that damned key.'

Margaux fished in her pocket as they walked, Jacques hobbling between Pierre and Sibyl, arms around their shoulders. They walked right past the back of the cobbler's shop.

'Where…?'

'Right here. Open that door.'

They had stopped in front of the back door of a house four doors down from Uncle Yves.

'Whose house is this?'

'It's no-one's. Though I suppose the Germans think it's theirs. It used to belong to a Jewish violin-maker. Now it's empty. *Oncle* Yves was his friend and had a key. It's the safest place he could possibly be. And best of all: I'm four doors down. I can dress his wounds, bring him food and drink…'

'*Bien*, I get it. It is brilliant, Sibyl. Now let's get him upstairs. I think we will have to carry him.'

'I'm not an invalid, and I'm not dead yet! Stop talking about me in the third person; I'm right here and I can get upstairs – ouch – with just a little help.'

Jacques tried his damaged leg but stumbled; he caught himself and, holding the banisters, managed to lever himself up one step.

'We'll carry you. What you need are crutches. I'm sure *Oncle* Yves can make them for you. He's got enough wood.'

# Chapter Thirty-Four

'I'm sorry. I was a fool.'

Jacques, from the double bed in what was once the main bedroom in the violin-maker's home, watched her as she dressed his wound, changed the bandage. Sibyl had requested various supplies from Margaux who, as usual, was able to get her hands on almost everything she needed. The bandages were strips of cotton cut from a clean sheet. Margaux had even disinfected them all by ironing them. There was alcohol and iodine and even a sterile packet of cotton wool, left over from happier days, and rubber gloves of obscure provenance.

'Yes, you were. Foolhardy. Why, Jacques, why? I told you not to.'

'I've been thinking about it. I think I needed to – to prove myself. To stand tall, to pull off something spectacular. Everything in the last month has been so, well, small. Ever since that first train bombing. That was the best attack and actually it was your attack, not mine.'

'You wanted heroics.'

'I suppose so.'

'This is a war, Jacques, it's not a time for personal aggrandisement. I'm very disappointed in you, and Acrobat – well, Acrobat is seething. I got a good telling-off.'

'But it wasn't your fault! You told me not to! I went against orders!'

'I was – am – responsible for your actions.'

'How can you do that? You can't watch me day and night. You did what you had to, you warned me not to do it. I disobeyed your orders: it's all my fault.'

'Acrobat doesn't see it like that.'

'Well, I'm sorry. I apologise.'

'Well, what's done is done. Now it's a case of what we do in future, and that is: precisely nothing. It's over, Jacques.'

'What do you mean?'

'Precisely that. No more action, ever. Acrobat's orders. There is no more Acrobat network. No more drops. No more *Maquis* action, at least, not under my charge; they can do what they like with the leftover supplies. He hinted that the Allies are going to move into Alsace soon. Our job was to prepare the way, weaken the province. We did that, and now we can disband.'

'But what about you? Does it mean you have to go back to England? Will they recall you?'

'I don't know, Jacques. He didn't say. Seems he wants me to stay here a while.'

'I'm glad about that.' He reached out and touched her arm.

Sibyl finished wrapping the wound. She tied the bandage firmly, removed her gloves and took his hand, and only then looked up to meet his eyes.

'Jacques – you don't need to be a hero; not for me. You should know that.'

'Maybe I wanted to be a hero for myself.'

'But you don't need that either – you shouldn't need that. You are by your very nature the strongest, finest, man I know; you don't need to blow up bridges to prove your worth. Your worth is…' she searched for the elusive word. '… intrinsic. Inherent. Innate. None of these really sums it up. It's something that shines out of you, when you are really yourself.'

'I haven't been myself for so long. This damned war…'

'But it sounds as if it will soon be over.'

'Did he really say the Allies were coming in?'

'He didn't say it. He hinted at it. It's what I gathered from his words.'

'But that means the war is coming to Alsace. I don't think the Germans are just going to turn tail and flee. They will defend it!'

'You think so?'

'I know it, Sibi. There is going to be fighting, for sure.'

Sibyl felt a sudden leadenness in her stomach, a tightness at her throat. It was true; isn't that what von Haagen had hinted at, as well? That the Allies were about to attack? What did that mean? How soon? What kind of an attack? Would there be Panzers creeping through the streets of Colmar? Would, God forbid, Colmar be bombed, as German cities had been? Not that the Allies would bomb Colmar; for them it was in France. But what if Hitler, forced to retreat, ordered it to be flattened, as a leaving present? As in, what I can't have, nobody should have?

'I wonder why I wasn't recalled, if the operation Acrobat has been called off.'

'I think I know, Sibi. I think it's about von Haagen. You told them he went to Berlin to discuss strategy?'

'Yes, I did.'

'Well, then. There you have it. They expect he'll be back and the two of you lovebirds will carry on the way you began, and he'll tell you all about these strategies, which you will dutifully report back to Acrobat.'

'You think so?'

'What other reason could they have for leaving you here, if the war for Alsace is about to begin? Why endanger you that much, unless they still have use for you?'

'But…'

'Take it from me, Sibi. I am sure. They want you to be his lover. That is the only thing that makes sense.'

The constriction around her throat tightened; she could hardly breathe. She could actually feel the pounding of her heart, a quick-march pounding in her chest. And a rushing in her ears as the implication of Jacques' words opened their true meaning to her. He caught her eye.

'Don't look away, Sibi. Look at me. Look at me and tell me you love me. The way I love you. Because I do. You know I do.'

'I love you, Jacques. I always have. You know it. Nothing can ever change that.'

'This damned, damned war. Come here.'

He reached out, clasped her upper arms, drew her down towards him. She gave a little gasp and let herself be pulled. She buried her face in the pillow beside his, and a sob burst from her.

'I can't, Jacques, I can't.'

'You can. It's for France. For Alsace. For us.'

# Chapter Thirty-Five

A week later, Jacques was limping about the house and chafing at the bit.

'I can't stay here any longer. I mean, it's wonderful being near to you and seeing you every day, every night – but I need to get out. Do something. I'm wasting time. Why aren't the Allies here yet?'

She shrugged. 'They'll be here in their own time. Where will you go? I won't let you go to Margaux.'

'I'll find a place. Don't worry. I just need someone to drive me out of Colmar and set me down in the countryside. Perhaps around Türckheim. I know people there – a farmer – it'll be safe.'

'If you insist. I still think you're safest here.'

'My safety – what about the safety of Alsace? I need to be with my men. I need to know what's going on. You can't keep me for yourself all the time, you know!'

His eyes twinkled; he drew her close. She laughed, ran her fingers through his hair, nuzzled into his chin. It had been a wonderful week, a week of much needed respite: no plans for bombings or dangerous drops, for Jacques, no hiding from the Gestapo. For him, just rest and recovery. For her, just looking after him and his wound, and being with him at night. Sneaking down the back stairs and into the courtyard and up his backstairs, like a student nurse with a secret boyfriend, courting behind Matron's back, climbing through the downstairs window after curfew. You could even forget there was a war on; that the war was slowly creeping towards Alsace. You could almost forget it. But not quite. Again, weeks passed; for Sibyl, weeks of stifling uncertainty. Her next scheduled call with Acrobat brought no relief, no news and no instructions. She gathered that the Allies would, at some point, arrive to take back Alsace; but no details and no date were forthcoming. It could take forever, and here she was, in Colmar, with nothing to do but polish shoes and take orders for the resoling of German boots or – more and more – orders for cloglike footwear for the locals. Food shortages grew more severe; and everyone, it seemed, looked forward to the wine harvest. So did she.

And then the wine harvest, the *vendange*, was upon them. Margaux paid her a surprise visit, inviting her to come and help. 'You must, my dear, you must. It will cheer you up. It will cheer us all up. Regardless of the war, we must have wine. The harvest is the one bright spot in the Alsace year in these dark times. You will stay at my place.'

'But, you know, your association with Jacques? It is known. I shouldn't risk it.'

'Pfft! Do you really think the Boche care about Jacques any more? About some possible British agent? Darling, they have bigger problems. Did you know that the Americans are right now in the Vosges, fighting for the freedom of Alsace? And the Free French Forces up north, fighting for the liberation of Strasbourg? This is a harvest of celebration. It is the last harvest of the war. Everyone knows it. Alsace will the very last corner of France to be liberated, but we will be liberated. It's a matter of weeks. *Les Américains* will sweep through and drive away the Boche as if they were swatting away flies. And our own army is motivated as never before and there will be triumph and rejoicing.'

'How do you know all this?'

'The grapevine, the radio, the BBC. It is common knowledge.'

'I can hardly believe it. It's so quiet here in Colmar…'

'They are pissed afraid in Colmar. Hitler is pissed afraid. They are all terrified of *les Américains*. They are all hiding in Colmar. And what about your *majeur*? No news of him?'

She shook her head. 'Not a word. I believe that episode is over.'

'Your people in London, this Acrobat fellow, will be disappointed. I think he was expecting great things from your liaison.'

'We all thought that. It's not to be. What happened to Jacques?'

'Jacques? Oh la la, Jacques. My golden boy Jacques – well, as you know, he was hiding out in Türckheim and then he came home. You cannot keep Jacques hidden away for long. Especially when there is a harvest on the horizon. Yes, my dear, Jacques is home and it is he who is organising our *vendange*. He has grown a beard and dyed his hair jet black but otherwise – well, Jacques is Jacques. The Boche have more serious problems than to come looking for him. So, I take it you will come to help?'

'I will have to ask *Oncle* Yves to give me some days off. But if he does – yes, of course!'

That harvest, the harvest of 1944 at the Château Gauthier, was the most glorious of them all. For the locals, the Alsatians, there was, at last, hope. Yes, the war had come to Alsace and soon there would be freedom. Margaux's words – *they will be swept away like flies* – was repeated and passed on and improved upon: the Boche will be sucked up like ants by the American vacuum cleaner! They will be devoured by the American fire-breathing dragon! They will be crushed underfoot like under the boots of a giant! And so the people rejoiced and passed through the vines plucking and laughing and cracking jokes; bursting with hope as the grapes were bursting with juice and goodness; and Sibyl and Jacques worked together, laughed together, hoped together, planned together. It was just a matter of weeks. Alsace was on the brink of freedom. It would be French again. The Boche would slink off like a defeated beast with its tail between its legs. Sibyl believed it all.

Before the war, the vineyards, including Château Gauthier, had employed itinerant workers who came from far afield to pick the grapes. Since the war, this was no longer possible; and so people came from the villages and towns to help: women and children and older men, as all the young men had been conscripted. The *vendange* must go on! Sibyl worked side by side with Jacques. Around her people laughed and joked; they spoke French, they wore berets, they sang French songs of freedom and revolution, and she sang with them.

And then, out of the blue, it was there: an ugly grey army truck embellished with swastikas, and a swastika-embellished soldier standing on the back with a megaphone, and the strident announcement, in German, of course: 'All wine-pickers to leave the vineyard. All wine-pickers to come to the road and stand with your hands behind your heads. There is to be an inspection of identity documents. Once you have been inspected you are free to continue picking. All wine-pickers to leave the field. All wine-pickers must immediately come to the road.'

'*Merde!*' cried Jacques, and he ran. In the opposite direction to the truck, away from the road, towards the forested hills where the vineyard ended. At first the man on the truck did not notice, but from his vantage point he did no doubt notice a turbulence in the steady line of people walking towards him; and he raised a pair of binoculars to his eyes, and let out a shout. Soldiers jumped from the truck's cabin and rushed into the vines, pushing their way past the pickers, shoving them aside.

Sibyl looked behind her, in the direction that Jacques had run. She could see his head, bobbing above the vines, speeding towards the forest. A shot rang out; the head ducked and Jacques was no longer visible, just neat green rows of golden vines. Her heart throbbed violently; a soldier bumped into her, threw her aside. Pickers blocked his path.

'*Geh weg! Aus dem Weg! Aus dem Weg!*' he cried, but it seemed that the pickers were doing the opposite; they crowded together to create obstacles. They bent down as if to tie their shoelaces. They blocked his way as best they could. This was happening in all the rows. The soldiers cursed and shouted; a few shots rang out. But their pursuit was hampered and by the time they reached the forest Jacques would be well on his way; and Jacques knew these forests like the proverbial back of his hand. He was gone. He would be safe, God willing, but only for today. They had all been far too optimistic, underestimating the determination of the Gestapo to catch their escaped terrorist.

Sibyl reached the road along with the other pickers. She did as she was told; stood with hands behind her head, as did the others, a row of them along the road. Officers with swastika bands on their arms walked down the row, stopping at each picker, asking questions, inspecting their ID cards, sending them back to the vines. The *vendange* must go on.

When it was Sibyl's turn the inspecting officer looked at her ID and then at her face.

'You! I know you! You are the cobbler's girl!'

Indeed: it was the Gestapo officer who had come after the break-in.

'That is right.'

'What are you doing here? This Château Gauthier is well known as a hideout for terrorists. Do you know Madame Laroche?'

'I know of her. She owns this vineyard, does she not?'

'Don't be cheeky. Why are you working for her?'

'For the same reason as all the other pickers here: because she pays well.'

'It's a long way to come from Colmar. Why did you come here?'

'I told you: because she pays well. Better than my uncle the cobbler, so I took a day off. Many people here are from Colmar. Madame Laroche sent a vehicle for us.'

He snorted and handed back her ID. 'I will be keeping a closer eye on you. Something is not right. You may go and continue picking.'

Sibyl tucked her ID back into her pocket and returned to the vines. But the joy had been sucked from the *vendange*. It was not over yet, she realised. *The war is still with us, and Alsace is still under the German thumb. It is too early to celebrate.*


When she returned to Colmar this was confirmed. There was no sign of defeat on the part of the Germans stationed there. If anything, their presence seemed even more permanent, and more sinister. She avoided as a matter of course the centre of town, where they stood around and sat around and stared; but now she spotted them even in the quieter streets, strolling along the cobbled lanes, incongruous in their grey-green uniforms. She saw them knocking at doors, no doubt checking that Germanisation was satisfactory. She was stopped once, cycling home from a visit to the market, and asked for papers. An aura of suspicion and fear hung in the air – it gave her goosebumps. Something was wrong.


And then von Haagen was back, standing across from her in the shop, in his hand a somewhat bedraggled bunch of roses. He held them out to her.

'They are from the climbing roses at the Villa Schönblick,' he said. 'I thought of you right away. *Fräulein* Schuster, here I am again, at your service.'

He gave a little bow and Sibyl had to swallow and take a deep breath before she could reply and take them from him.

'Oh – they're lovely! Thank you so much!'

'Now tell me, beautiful woman – did you miss me as much as I missed you?'

'I missed you, yes, of course!'

'There's that English saying, "absence makes the heart grow fonder".'

It was a shock, hearing the English words, and she looked up. 'That's certainly the case with me! Do you understand?'

She shook her head and he translated the idiom into German. 'I didn't know you spoke English,' she said.

'Oh yes, of course. English was a main subject on our curriculum – it's useful to know a second language. It is an important part of the higher German education system. Didn't you learn it in France?'

'A little, just for a few years. I've forgotten most of it, though.'

An awkward silence fell between them, unusual for him. She decided to break it.

'You've been away quite a long time. Did you have a good time in Berlin?'

Was that a shadow passing over his face? But it was just that: a passing shadow.

'Yes, yes indeed, and I have some excellent news! I have been promoted to colonel! And after Berlin I went down to Munich as I have some leave due, so I went to see my parents; there was a small matter I needed to discuss. But now I'm here. But unfortunately I must be going – I just dropped in to let you know I'm back, and to ask you to meet me this evening for dinner. Is that possible?'

The hesitation was less than a moment.

'Of course! I'd love to!'


He took her to the Rote Löwe. Von Haagen had reserved a table, a cubicle in a far corner, separate and somewhat private. A few tables were occupied: two with uniformed officers with Nazi armbands, one with a well-dressed couple. Sycophantic waiters hovered around them, shoving the table slightly so that Sibyl could slide in, and shoving it back again once she was seated, laying a serviette on her lap.

Von Haagen ordered lamb cutlets for them both, with potatoes and beans. It was the first full meal she had had since his departure to Berlin, and she told him so. It was necessary to make conversation.

She couldn't just sit there in silence, letting him do all the talking, which was her inclination. But how? Her own body refused to relax and just be natural, a young woman being courted by a handsome young man. She felt stiff and formal, and no conversation came readily to her lips. The rules of etiquette never told you what to do when the young man courting you represented the enemy, and you were the agent employed to betray and defeat that enemy; and your job was to be nice. She had told Acrobat that her agent role would be much like acting; it was playing a role. She had never expected the role to be that of leading lady in a romance; she had not studied for this part, she had not rehearsed. It was all playing by ear, and all with the knowledge that the romance was destined to be a tragedy.

'It's good, isn't it? The lamb? So tender. It's straight from a farm. We have a deal with the farmer. He keeps his best lambs for us. Though of course they're not so young – it's a summer lamb.'

'Delicious. I haven't eaten this well for weeks. Not since you left.'

'Haha. That's why I had to return, to feed you up! Can't have you starving away! Now, my dear, you must tell me what you've been up to in the last few weeks.'

Under other circumstances she would have giggled at the irony. She would have said, *oh, nothing much. Just helped a captured Resistance fighter to escape from German hands, hidden him in the empty house of a deported Jew, nursed him back to health, discussed the coming war in which the Allies will wipe out the Germans, picked grapes alongside him and watched him run from the Gestapo!*

Instead, she played into the irony of the situation and, in all innocence, looked up at him and said, 'Oh, nothing much. It was quite boring, actually.'

'I'm glad to hear that. I wouldn't have wanted to hear that you'd been living it up with my *Kammeraden* in uniform! I know any one of them would love to get their hands on you…'

She choked on her food and coughed; a piece of meat lodged itself in her windpipe. She coughed and coughed.

'… are you all right? *Herr Ober! Wasser, bitte!*' He held up a hand and snapped his fingers. The waiter ran up with a glass of water. Sibyl took several sips and a deep breath and at last she regained her composure. This would never do. Coolness under pressure. That was her strength, Mr Smith had said. Praise indeed; but entertaining a German officer required a far greater supply of coolness than did rescuing the wounded in the rubble of a Blitz bomb site.

Conversation continued; he told her about his parents, his home, his family. He spoke about the beauty of Bavaria, the mountain chalet where the family often went for weekends *–before the war; we have not been for years –* the wonderful castles and lakes in the vicinity. He made Germany sound like a holiday paradise, instead of a war-ravaged country on the verge, as Sibyl now knew, of defeat.

Dessert was served: *Apfelstrudel.* Not a bad effort, but Sibyl had tasted better. The pastry was soggy, and there was no cream. Cream, perhaps, was beyond even the influence of the German occupation forces.

'Excuse me. I must… I'll be right back.'

He stood up suddenly and strode off towards the toilets. When he returned he grinned at her and slid back into his seat.

'Where was I? Oh yes. I'm a lucky man, *Fräulein* Schuster – did we agree that I could call you Marlene? *Ja? Wunderbar.* And I've been thinking so much about you when I was in Berlin that I knew, yes, I knew beyond a doubt, that you are the woman I have been yearning for. The woman to fill my heart. The woman I want to spend the rest of my life with. And so –I brought you this.'

And before she could take another breath, say another word, he had whipped a little box from his uniform pocket – she had seen a little bulge there beforehand, and wondered –and was down on one knee before her.

'*Fräulein* Schuster – I mean, my dear Marlene – would you do me the honour of becoming my wife?'

# Chapter Thirty-Six

Her jaw dropped open. She almost cried out, spontaneously, *'What! No! Are you mad!'* but managed to suppress the words and close her mouth. She only stared, speechless.

He waited, gazed fixed on her. In her peripheral vision she became aware of a stillness in the room; waiters gathering near the door to the kitchen. Watching, waiting. Time, suspended.

The world held its breath and waited. Her own breath was trapped inside her, unable to escape.

And then, from some deep place within her, Jacques' voice, his impassioned cry: *'For Alsace! For France! For me!'*

Her breath broke, it rushed from her, carrying the word of release: 'Yes!'

And the silence split open, and the tension, and the room erupted: the waiters clapped, the other guests cheered and raised glasses. Von Haagen sprang to his feet, reached for her hands, pulled her up and clasped her to himself, his face alight with unmitigated joy. Then he let her go, clapped, and cried: 'She said yes! Champagne! Bring the champagne!'

The next few minutes brought a flurry of activity as Sibyl and von Haagen sat down again and a beaming waiter ran up with the champagne and glass flutes. Von Haagen released the cork which flew across the room and the golden liquid quelled up and spilled to the floor and everyone laughed as he filled the two flutes and he and Sibyl raised their glasses, clinked them, and von Haagen cried: 'To us! To Victory! To Peace!'

Around the room other uniformed Germans raised their glasses and cried out in echo but the cry that went up was not *To Victory!*

*To Peace!* but *Sieg, Heil!* And Sibyl, behind the smile she offered her brand-new fiancé, collected all her strength to not break down with the secret lament rising to her throat and struggling to be heard above the clamour: *Oh Lord, what have I done?*

They drank, and von Haagen's smile melted in a second. Though his gaze still clung to her; it was an oddly altered gaze, the unalloyed delight of pre-toast changed into something doubtful, questioning, insecure. He said nothing but she could tell he wanted to speak.

'What is it, Wolfgang?'

'Marlene. You have made me the happiest man in the world. You must know that.'

Yet the doubt that clouded his words was palpable. She smiled to reassure him.

'I'm glad to hear that.'

'I know – I do know – that my love is not yet reciprocated. I can feel that you don't love me yet. That perhaps, even, you are marrying me for convenience. I don't mind. Love can grow if there is mutual respect and, and the *will* to love, and I have every faith that you will learn to love me. I am not a bad man, Marlene. I am not a bad man.'

And then, before she could formulate an appropriate reply, his eyes turned moist as tears gathered, and he closed them and still the tears spilled out and his face crunched with the vain effort of holding them back. But he couldn't.

'Oh Christ!' the cry escaped his lips and he buried his face in his hands.

Sibyl reached out, touched his hand.

'Wolfgang! What is it? Tell, me, please!'

Words burst from him. 'I'm ruined. I'm ruined. Everything is ruined. It could have been perfect. You, me, our home, our family. All ruined. It's all over. Finished. It's a catastrophe.'

'What do you mean, Wolfgang? Tell me, please!'

He dabbed his eyes with his napkin and looked around the room. People had lost interest in them, continuing with their own meals. The well-dressed couple had left. Waiters were gliding here and there, serving wine and dessert. Nobody was watching. Yet still he lowered his voice.

'Marlene – let's slide down a bit further. Into the corner. I want to tell you something.'

He slid further back into the cubicle; she did the same. They ended up sitting side by side at the deepest end, out of sight of all the other diners. He took her hand, and when he spoke his voice was low.

'Marlene, I'm going to tell you something only you can hear. It is a secret, you understand. But you are now my fiancée, the confidante of my heart. I know I can trust you.'

She nodded. 'Of course, Wolfgang.'

'It's true, what I just said. We're finished, Marlene. Germany is going to lose the war. The Allies have already reached the Ardennes. Most of France has been cleared of our forces, Belgium too. Paris has fallen! Paris! The very symbol of our domination! It is all a farce! We are near the end. We have been told falsehoods regarding Germany's inevitable victory. It is all a myth, a terrible myth. We have been deceived!

'Marlene, in Berlin I learned the truth. I spoke with generals who told me the reality of our situation. They are trying to tell Hitler but he won't listen; when they tell him the truth he shouts them down. He is an ugly man, Marlene, an ugly man. And mad! Off his head, some of the generals are saying!

'Marlene, my beloved, do you realise what all this means? So much death, Marlene, so much devastation. Europe in ruins. And it's not over yet. Marlene, my dearest: the war is coming to Alsace. Alsace is now part of Germany and Hitler is determined to keep it that way, whatever the cost. Even if France has fallen, even if Paris has fallen: Hitler needs to keep Alsace. That was why he called this catastrophic meeting in Berlin. It is to let us know that Alsace is to be the fiercest battle of all. We must never surrender Alsace, he said.

We must fight to the death! Never retreat! He lambasted the rest of his army, called them cowards, because they retreated. *That must not happen in Alsace*, he said. He sacked some of his most loyal generals. And he told us how we can keep Alsace. He's stripped away badly needed units from the Eastern Front, he's combed the Reich for all the manpower he can find to bring his battered formations in the West up to strength. He's also hoarded precious fuel and Panzers. And it's all top, top secret so as to surprise the enemy. Alsace, he says, will be the last stand and it must be a glorious victory.

'He's already assembled a strike force of unbelievable strength; the enemy hasn't seen such powerful German forces for years! It's already started in the Ardennes with the Operation *Wacht am Rhein* but it will proceed into the Vosges and then to Strasbourg and Colmar. We're going to send the finest and fiercest troops into the Vosges. That's what he's done. Kept the best for the last. Alsace is a matter of pride for him; even if all else is lost, Alsace must remain German. And I will tell you something else. This is top secret, Marlene. You understand.'

'Of course.'

'I met Heinrich Himmler. You know who Himmler is?'

'I've heard the name. I'm not quite sure…'

'Hitler's right-hand man; he's head of the SS, the *Sicherheitsdienst,* the Gestapo. A man of extraordinary power and so – so *dangerous,* so *evil* – beyond words evil. I've only now found out the extent. Marlene, I don't – I can't – the things he said – I am devastated. A broken man. I'm so ashamed – so ashamed – to be a German – to know these things – what he has done – it's happening right now – those people!'

He was close to collapsing in tears. Sibyl reached out and took his hand. He clasped it, kissed it, squeezed it.

'I am so grateful that I have you, that you said yes, that you are mine, the other half of my heart. I have kept all this deep in my soul and it has almost killed me. I needed to tell someone, and I am so grateful that you listened, that you are listening. To things too dreadful to even believe. I heard rumours before but I did not believe them. Who could believe such terrible things, that Germany could do such terrible things? But it is not Germany. It's Himmler. It is his idea, his plan. He calls it the final solution. But it is no solution, Marlene! It is a catastrophe! It is, it is – I can't find the words even to describe the horror of it. And it has been confirmed. It is happening. It is real.'

'I don't understand… what's happening? What's real? What do you mean with final solution? Solution to what?'

'To the Jewish problem.'

'Oh… I see… and what is the solution, according to Himmler? I know that Hitler sends them to labour camps.'

Of course, she knew about Hitler's obsession with Jews; the stories horrified her. Jacques' sister and her Jewish sweetheart. Margaux's maid Leah, having to escape, and Margaux's work in harbouring Jews to be secretly sent to France. And, of course, on her own street: the violin-maker's story. The *Reichskristallnacht,* the Night of Broken Glass, had made international headlines. Hitler's rants, broadcasted around the world, in which he blamed Jews for all the world's problems.

'Labour camps? Labour camps? Do you know what those camps really are? They are death camps! They are systematically murdered! In their thousands!'

She listened, stunned, as von Haagen described Himmler's plan for the clean and final eradication of all Jews from Germany, from Europe. His voice trembled as he spoke; he reached for her hand and clasped it as if it were a lifeline. He cried tears, he snorted into the serviette. Her shock turned her blood to ice. She could not believe it. It couldn't be true.

'It is true, Marlene. It is true. He showed us photos – with pride, bragging! He is proud of this solution! And I – I am devastated. As every honourable German should be. To think that…'

The room began to crackle. Someone had switched the radio on. 'Here is *Soldatensender Belgrad...*'

Followed by the the yearning, nostalgic, melancholic crooning of Lale Andersen, singing the heartbreaking ballad of Lili Marlene.

'I can't stand it. I can't. Come, let's go.' Von Haagen pushed away the table, edging himself free of it, held out his hand to help Sibyl slide out. He threw a wedge of Reichmarks on to the table, and practically pulled her to the door; outside, the motorcycle and sidecar were parked. She refused to get into the sidecar.

'Wolfgang, stop, stop; let's talk some more. I need to know... tell me... is it true? Are you sure?'

'Yes, I am sure, absolutely sure. And I am devastated, ashamed; I am sorry I asked you to be my wife... now you know. How can I take you to live in a country that has done such things? How can you bear to accept me, a German?'

'Wolfgang, please. It is not you who has done these things.'

'But I am responsible. Every German is responsible. We gave this party, these people, that man, power. I am serving in the army. I am fighting to preserve such an evil regime. And there is nothing I can do about it. Marlene: I have been conscripted for field duty. Next week I am to join Army Group G under General Balck. Most of all, we are to ensure that Strasbourg stays in German hands. But, Marlene, the enemy forces there are so mighty. We must fight not only against the USA Seventh Army but against the French First army and the Free French Army. And they are strong. Marlene, I fear too strong. I do not know if we can hold Strasbourg. But it is what Hitler wants. He says we must fight unto death! Marlene, my precious: I must go and I do not know if I will survive this. It is perhaps a suicide mission. Morale is low among the Germans – I know mine is – and strong among the French. Marlene, I want you to promise one thing: pray for me!'

'I will, Wolfgang. I will. I promise.'

# Chapter Thirty-Seven

Sibyl and Margaux had a code, by which Sibyl could request a pick-up. She was to go to a public phone booth and dial Margaux's number. With that in mind, the next morning she dialled Margaux' number, and when Margaux picked up, she said, 'Bonjour, Madame. Do not forget it is Aunt Blanche's birthday on Tuesday. We are expecting a delivery of pinot gris.'

'*Bien sûr,*' was the answer. 'We have the order in writing and the crate will be delivered at four.'

That afternoon, at four, Sibyl waited at the usual meeting place. Margaux was five minutes late, by which time Sibyl's insides were a hive of bees. They packed her bicycle into the van, Sibyl joined the bicycle in the back, and Margaux drove off. They had decided that it was not safe for Sibyl to be on the passenger's seat in the cabin; Margaux had been stopped three times in the last month, asked for ID. The back of the van had never been searched.

Once at the château, Sibyl made an emergency call to Acrobat; she managed to give a concise account of von Haagen's news.

'Apparently they are using their very strongest forces and will fight to the death,' she reported. 'Army Group G, under General Balck.'

'Very good. Excellent. This is the kind of report we've been hoping for. We expect more of the same and have made a contingency plan: you are to be given a pianist of your own, Acrobat One. We will be dropping the agent in as soon as possible; please arrange a place and date. It's all arranged from this side.'

'A pianist?'

'Yes. You'll have a pianist. You are to be concerned only with gathering information. The MI6 is in on this. They know about you and von Haagen. You need back-up. Do you have a courier?'

'I suppose, well, Marg…'

'No names, please. We get it. Over and out.'

'Wait… wait… there's more…'

She wanted to tell Acrobat about Himmler, about the supposed death camps for Jews, but it was too late. Acrobat had signed off. She sighed and returned downstairs to Margaux.

'It seems, Margaux, that Acrobat Circuit is finally taking shape. I'm to get a pianist – a wireless operator – and it seems you are to be the courier.'

She gave Margaux a summary of the conversation with von Haagen, more detailed than the one she had given Acrobat. She described his tears, his breakdown, his belief that he might be killed. 'He asked me to pray for him, Margaux, and I promised to do so!'

'Well, it's a promise you'll have to keep. One does not promise such a thing in vain.'

'But, but how? How can I pray for Germany to win?'

'That's not what he asked you to do. He asked you to pray for him. For his eternal soul. For his salvation. So, even if he is killed, his sins will be forgiven, hopefully. That you can do. You must do it.'

'I will.'

'But you must also pray for Jacques. We heard from Jacques yesterday. You will never believe where he is – he is in Strasbourg!'

'In Strasbourg! What is he doing there?'

'Jacques has joined the General de Gaulle's *France Libre* Army; they have been conscripting volunteer Resistance fighters. All of Jacques *maquisards* have also joined up. What's more, France Free has joined forces with the regular army, the French 2nd Armoured Division under General Leclerc. And both these armies have joined with the

Americans Seventh Army to defend Alsace and free Strasbourg. Sibyl, it looks as if your two lovers will be fighting against each other for the liberation of Alsace! Now, what do you say to that!'

# Chapter Thirty-Eight

Well, what was there to say? She was thrilled at the news. Beyond thrilled; Jacques, no longer a renegade, Jacques doing what he had to do, fighting for France, but now legitimately, protected by de Gaulle's army, no longer on the run.

On the other hand, knowing what she now knew, knowing the strength of the forces he'd be facing, knowing that this was Hitler's last stand, the fiercest battle with the strongest forces: it terrified her. We must fight to the death, von Haagen had said. To the very last man! That would mean, surely, to that last man on both sides?

If that was true, then Jacques was finished. Alsace was finished. France might have been cleaned of the Boche but Alsace was still well and truly in German hands. *Fight to the death* meant that Hitler would not surrender this last bastion. It would have to be wrested from him after the war as a whole was won; and who knew when that would be? And in the meantime, it was *fight to the death.* And there was nothing she could do but sit in her cobbler's shop and wait for news: the fate of women in times of war since time began. Women, holding the world together while men slaughtered themselves, women, doing their best to maintain a world worth living in; women, their hearts ripped out as their menfolk fought like wild beasts, their own courage and stalwartness overlooked in the stories of bravery and valour.

She thought, now, of von Haagen. His breakdown had astonished her, but more important was the vital news he had passed on which she, in her turn, had passed on to her superiors. That was her contribution to the war effort, and hopefully it would be of use. Acrobat had been palpably delighted, as if, at last, her appointment was showing results. This was a matter for MI6, he'd said; it would be passed on to military intelligence, as that information went beyond the scope of Special Operations. She had passed it on and never once looked back; she had lived up to her promise that she would do her job no matter what. That she was not just a soft-hearted nurse too weak to make tough decisions. It had been no decision at all; and yet her concern towards von Haagen had been genuine. She had been touched by his confession, moved by his heartfelt cry for help. And yet, in the very next breath, she had betrayed him. Perhaps that was what it meant to be an agent.

But there was no time now for reflection. She had new orders: she was to be given a pianist, and had to arrange the parachute drop. And she had no-one to help arrange it, since, according to Margaux, all of the *maquisards,* except Pierre, had joined the Free French forces. She'd have to think of alternatives and, inevitably, that meant Margaux and Pierre. Together, they would receive the pianist, welcome him to the team. It would be done on the first of the three next moonlit nights – if the weather allowed.

It was, thankfully, a lucidly clear November night. The swollen moon was one night away from fullness, a yellow floating ball that seemed to be sailing, due to a few puffed clouds drifting past, blown by the cool night breeze. It was a chilly night, and the three of them were dressed for the cold in sheepskin jackets, woolly caps and gloves. The lanterns were filled and waiting to be lit; no need to waste fuel. As ever, the wait seemed endless; they had chosen exactly the landing place at which Sibyl herself had come down so many months ago. Only months. It seemed like years. They waited.

At last, Sibyl discerned the hum of a distant plane. 'Here they come,' she whispered, and the three of them sprang into action, lighting the lanterns, placing them at strategic positions around the perimeter of the field.

The Lysander was above them; it circled once, and then, like a huge white umbrella, there was the parachute, the pianist a black shape dangling below, suspended in space. This time there were no supplies to be delivered. This time, the only delivery would be human.

The pianist fell to earth, shrouded in the billowing silk of the parachute. The Lysander disappeared back into the night. The three of them rushed to help the figure struggling with falling folds of fabric, trying to be free. Sibyl pulled away the material from the pianist's head and gave a cry of shock.

'Elena!'

'Sibyl!'

It was an almost comic repeat of her own landing, when Jacques had pulled away the parachute from her face and they had recognised each other. But now, Elena!

Later, in Margaux's kitchen, Elena explained.

'I was recruited just three months ago; I'm here as your pianist.'

'But, Elena – how? To be a wireless operator – well, it takes a huge amount of training. You must only have had a couple of weeks! How can you be a pianist in that short a time?'

Elena chuckled. 'You think you're the only one with secrets? I had my secrets too. I told you I worked at the Foreign Office didn't I? Do you know what I was actually doing, for the four years of the war? I was a wireless operator! Fully trained! I'm an expert in codes and ciphers – better than you. I am one of the people who received the messages of SOE agents, decoded them, passed them on!'

'That is – that is…' Sibyl was lost for words, but finally found her tongue. 'But of course. You have the same languages that I do.

Why wouldn't they recruit you! But that's marvellous! And now we can work together!'

'That's right. But, you know, I didn't know where you were either, that you were an agent in Alsace. I didn't know they were sending me to you, and to Margaux. It's all so secretive!'

'I didn't know either, that I'd be coming to Margaux.'

'Why Margaux, I wonder? They know she has links to Jacques?'

'They also know I'm the safest person around. My wine keeps me safe.'

'But, Elena – what about your husband? Your little girl? How could you leave her? Who did you leave her with? Or was she evacuated?'

Elena's face froze into a mask.

'My husband – his plane was torpedoed. By Germans. He is dead. My daughter, my little girl… no, she wasn't evacuated. I couldn't bear to send her away. But I should have.' The muscles in her face twitched in the effort to retain the mask.

'My little girl is dead too. Her grandmother was looking after her at home, in London. A doodlebug hit the house. It was flattened.'

'Oh my God! Oh Elena! I'm sorry!'

She took her sister in her arms. They cried together, then Elena pulled away.

'And that's why I here. To kill Germans. Those damned doodlebugs!'

'I'm a bit confused… what's a doodlebug?'

Elena chuckled, but it was a dry, humourless chuckle.

'A toy of Hitler. A pilotless missile. They are aimed at London and attack randomly. Radar can't find them. They come hissing through the air and then silence and when they go silent that's when you have to run for shelter but you don't know where, you don't know…'

Elena swiped fiercely at her eyes with the back of her hand. Margaux handed her a serviette and placed a comforting hand on her shoulder.

'Now all I want to do is kill Germans. Every last one of them.'

'Oh, Elena! I – I don't know what to say.'

'There's nothing to say, is there. I'm here now. I'll be staying here, Margaux, with you. If I may. Acrobat's orders.'

'Of course.'

'My cover story is that I'm a second cousin, from Strasbourg, come to stay with you and help out in the vineyard; I knew the war was coming to Strasbourg, so I fled. My name is Nicole Arnaut. I am by profession a seamstress. You know I was always good at sewing!'

Sibyl remembered. All during the early war years Elena had kept them clothed; she had a gift for reassembling pieces of material into dresses and blouses that could even be deemed fashionable.

'You can begin with that parachute!' said Margaux. 'My underwear is in rags.'

'Well, that of course has to be secret – but I'm to be looking for work in the villages, patching up clothes and so on.'

'As if the villagers can't do that themselves! Really, these cover stories are too ridiculous. We don't need a seamstress down here. People know how to use a needle.'

'Well, the main thing is I'm a coward fleeing the war. But my impression is – what I read between the lines – is that it won't be long now. A few months at the most. But apparently you, Sibyl, are going to help shorten that time.'

'So – I'm the agent, you're the pianist – who's the courier?'

'We haven't been given a courier.'

Sibyl and Elena both turned to Margaux.

'Don't look at me! I'm not your damned courier!'

Sibyl and Elena said nothing. They waited. Margaux sighed.

'I'm guess you aren't giving me a choice.'

# Chapter Thirty-Nine

Sibyl introduced Elena to the wireless transmitter and together they made their first call to Acrobat.

'Acrobat Two.'

'Acrobat. Good. So all went well with the landing?'

'It did. Here's Acrobat One with a message.'

'Acrobat One. I didn't get to finish my message last time. There's more important information.'

'Go ahead, Acrobat One.'

Sibyl took the mike from Elena and as succinctly as possible related von Haagen's story: that Heinrich Himmler himself had revealed that the final solution to the 'Jew Problem' was not labour camps, as she and others had believed, but death camps; camps so horrific in their concept and execution it made the pogroms seem like mild foreplay.

'We have heard such rumours, Acrobat One. They have yet to be confirmed.'

'Percy said…'

Percy was their code name for von Haagen.

'What Percy said is not evidence, Acrobat One. And anyway, there's nothing we can do until we have won the war and invaded Germany. If this is true, we'll find out in due course. Your job is not to repeat rumours. It's to aid the war effort by extracting German military intelligence from Percy. You've done well so far; you were right that their forces were tougher than expected. Continue in that vein.'

'But Percy himself is now on the battlefield! He may not survive.'

'Oh, he will. Don't worry about that. Over and out.'

*

Weeks passed, quiet weeks in which Sibyl wondered if she had imagined it all; if Elena had been sent for nothing, for there was no war, no bombs, no artillery anywhere near Colmar. If not for Margaux, she would never have known…

But there was Margaux, on November 23rd, shaking with excitement. 'Sibyl – you've got to come to the château. You've got to hear this yourself… You too, Yves; come on, both of you.'

She shooed them both out of the building to the street where the van was parked and drove them to the château; obviously bursting with good news but refusing to reveal it.

'No, no, it is not for me to tell you. You must hear it first-hand. From the BBC,' she insisted.

Sibyl found the château in a state of joyous uproar. French flags hung everywhere, and both Victoire and Elena, laughing and more than a little tipsy, grabbed her as she entered the kitchen and swung her around in a dance of triumph.

'We're free! We're free!' cried Victoire, grinning, and she moved on to Yves, kissed him, danced with him; Yves, bemused, let it all happen all the time muttering,

'What's happening? What's going on?'

'Strasbourg has fallen! The Germans have been defeated in Strasbourg!' cried Victoire, breaking the secret.

'Sssh!' ordered Margaux. 'It's the six o'clock news… here we go…'

Silence descended. They sat around the radio as Margaux turned up the volume.

First the BBC's famous five pips, followed by one long pip. Then, a cut-glass female announcer:

*You're tuned to the General Broadcasting Service of the BBC World Service. This is the British Broadcasting Service. Here is the news.*

*Strasbourg is free! The German army today was defeated and driven out of the city or captured. The 2ⁿᵈ French Armoured Division of General Leclerc, supported by the 7ᵗʰ US Army of General Patch, entered Strasbourg this morning. Strasbourg, the capital of the north-eastern French province of Alsace, was annexed by Germany in 1940 and has since been part of the regime of the Third Reich resulting in forced Germanisation of Alsatian citizens. The Allied forced were guided into Strasbourg by the local Free French forces of General de Gaulle's Government-in-exile, who captured alone 4500 German soldiers, 50 policemen and 4 Gestapo agents along with a variety of guns and ammunition.*

*'This afternoon at 2 p.m. the French national flag, the Tricolore, was raised on the cathedral of Strasbourg and the city's inhabitants poured out of their homes amid great rejoicing. The sound of cheering and singing of 'La Marseillaise', the French national anthem, broke out on the streets as citizens celebrated their freedom after four long years. The Marseillaise was, coincidentally, written in Strasbourg in 1792 by Claude Joseph Rouget de Lisle after the declaration of war by France against Austria and was originally titled 'Chant de guerre pour l'Armée du Rhi', 'War Song for the Rhine Army'. Here today at the Rhine the anthem was very appropriately sung again as Strasbourg rids herself of the German yoke.*

*'The rapid Liberation of Strasbourg has produced a torrent of joy in the newly liberated French nation and was a hugely symbolic victory for the French people and the Western Allies in general. The Liberation and Tricolore raised over the cathedral is considered to be the last major objective in the Liberation of France; Strasbourg was the last bastion of German domination.*

Tears of unalloyed joy gathered in Sibyl's eyes as she listened to the report, and as the first verse of the Marseillaise poured from the radio so did the tears stream down her cheeks and her heart swelled and she rose to her feet and let herself be gathered into the generous embrace of Margaux.

'We're free! We're free!' sobbed Margaux, and it was hard to tell who cried the most, Margaux, Victoire, Pierre, Yves, Sibyl, or even Elena, the late arrival to the trials of Alsace.

It was only later, much later, after nightfall, because nobody was sober enough to drive them home, that Sibyl dared to put into words the question that had gnawed at the back of her mind ever since that first *'Strasbourg is free!'* cry went up. Tentatively, hesitantly, at last she spoke the words:

'I wonder what happened to Colonel von Haagen?'

'Oh, I expect he's dead,' said Margaux. 'Or else taken prisoner. You're rid of that creature at last, Sibyl.'

The words fell into Sibyl's heart with a great heavy thud. And she didn't know why. Yes, at last she was rid of him. And yet…

She and Elena exchanged a glance.

'If he is gone then I suppose I'll be recalled,' said Elena. 'Sibyl can't exactly extract secrets from a dead man.'

'Anyway, unnecessary now because Alsace is free,' Margaux said. 'Your job is done. Yours too, Sibyl. No more spying! No more Marlene Schuster!'

'But Colmar is still overrun with Germans,' said *Oncle* Yves. 'Alsace will not be free until Colmar is free.'

'Pah! That is just a question of days now. Strasbourg has fallen and that is the main thing. If Strasbourg is free then all Alsace is free.'

'I wouldn't be so sure,' said *Oncle* Yves, but he was disinclined to argue. He refilled his wine glass.

Sibyl looked at Elena. 'We'll have to wait for instructions. They'll let us know if our job is done.'

'And did you hear that bit about the Free French? It was they who captured the Germans! That's our Jacques, Sibyl. Jacques is the hero of the day. Let us drink to Jacques!'

She grabbed the bottle from *Oncle* Yves and refilled everyone's glasses.

'To Jacques, our local hero! To France! To Alsace! To Strasbourg! To Liberty!'

The cheers went up one by one.

The last cheer was given by *Oncle* Yves: 'To Colmar! May you soon be free as well!'

# Chapter Forty

The fall of Strasbourg was a perfect disaster for Germany – from a military viewpoint, but mostly psychologically. After Paris, no other French city was a source of such symbolic meaning, such national pride, as Strasbourg. Hitler craved Strasbourg. And now it was gone, the swastikas removed from the cathedral towers and replaced with the Tricolore. The humiliation gave rise to a huge wave of renewed energy and determination; but the situation, for Germany, was bleak.

The US Seventh Army, led by General Alexander Patch, had struggled through difficult winter conditions during the Vosges mountains campaign, clearing strong and entrenched German forces from the west bank of the Rhine. By the end of November German forces had been driven back to the Rhine on the northern and southern edges of the Allied advance; Alsace was almost completely in Allied hands.

*Almost.*

The German Nineteenth Army, led by Infantry General Siegfried Rasp, still held Colmar and its environs.

And was not about to give those up so quickly.

Under direct orders from Himmler, who in turn received direct orders from Hitler himself, they fought with a ferocity almost unequalled throughout the war, and with this renewed tenacity managed to hold onto a bridgehead forty miles wide and thirty miles deep on the west bank of the river Rhein.

The centre of this bridgehead was Colmar. It was a deep pocket of Germany in the midst of ground the Allies had won, at the very eastern edge of France. The very last speck of France still in German hands.

The battle for France would not be over until the Colmar Pocket was emptied.

But the Allies were weary from six months of fighting. Their logistics were stretched thin. They lacked fresh troops and supplies needed to push hard. The terrain was unfamiliar, the winter harsh – the worst winter of the century, in fact, with a metre of snow and temperatures as low as minus four degrees centigrade. The Germans were entrenched in small villages of sturdy stone construction: strong defensive positions.

French forces, under the command of General Jean de Lattre were strained. African troops, experienced from fighting in Italy, had been replaced with French Forces of the Interior, troops of limited quality and experience. These troops might well be capable of defensive fighting, but when it came to offensive operations, and especially complex activities, they were, basically, greenhorns.

In other words, the French troops were weak, fighting against a highly motivated Third Reich army consisting of Hitler's elite. What chance did they have? And so the Germans held on to the Colmar Pocket as a tiger holds on to its prey.

After celebrating Strasbourg's liberation, *Oncle* Yves and Sibyl returned to Colmar and life went on as before. As *Oncle* Yves had noted, nothing had changed in the town. The same German soldiers dominated the streets; more soldiers than civilians, as usual, some with, some without, the Nazi armbands. It was as if Strasbourg had not fallen; as if nobody had heard the news. After the euphoria of November 23rd it was a let-down, a fall to earth. Nothing had changed. Colmar was as captured as ever, in the palm of the Boche, as *Oncle* Yves put it.

Sibyl was aware of a heaviness of heart that lingered in spite of all attempts to shake it off. The war was nearing its end; Alsace was partly free, and if Colmar wasn't free yet it was only a question of time. The Allies were making their way south from Strasbourg, no doubt. And Jacques, with the Free French forces. The Americans.

The French army. They were on their way. It was just a matter of time before they'd drive the Germans from Colmar's streets.

She would never again have to put up with Colonel Wolfgang von Haagen and his misplaced courtship. Never again need to pretend a closeness she did not feel, never again have to lie, never again have to betray. And yet...

And yet, his confession preyed on her mind; his meltdown in the restaurant. And despite all reasoning, all self-reprimands, all the stern pull-yourself-together scolding she gave herself, she could not but feel pain – on his behalf. And she couldn't help wondering, was he dead? Captured? She'd never know, now, and that lack of an ending nagged at her, like having an exciting novel torn from her hands a chapter before the climax. It left a frayed residue. Well, perhaps she could find out, when this was all over. There'd be records, surely, and once relieved of her agent role she could enquire. For her own satisfaction. Just to end the uneasiness, put an end to the story.

At least she didn't have to marry the creature; but even relief was no adequate conclusion.

She acknowledged that he was a man who had made a terrible mistake and had paid for it. No need to feel sorry for him. And yet, she did. And in a way she hoped he was dead. Better to be dead than captured and live with the agony he'd expressed for the rest of one's life.

Worse yet, possibly, for him: if captured he'd eventually know that Marlene Schuster was a myth, an actress, a spy; he would have to live with that betrayal for the rest of his life. No, let him be dead. Far kinder to wish him dead than to wish him captured.

A week passed. No news from Baker Street, no recall from duties, no instructions at all. Just life as cobbler's assistant Marlene Schuster, also known as Jeanne Dauguet, also known, in the far distant past, as Sibyl Lake.

*

The doorbell jangled. She did not turn around; she was fiddling with a thick shoelace, trying to thread it into a too-small eyelet. 'Just a moment!' she called.

'Marlene. It's me.' The voice was low, without any inflection whatsoever. And unmistakeable. She whipped around.

'Wolfgang!' Indeed. It was him; or rather, an apparition bearing a slight resemblance to the man she had known. His face was drained, his eyes sunken, his cheeks hollow, the cheekbones and chin sharp and prominent, the skin itself sallow. He wore a greatcoat, which hung from his shoulders which, unbelievably, seemed rounded, hunched, rather than sharply pulled back as usual. The whole figure was that not of a confident Wehrmacht officer at the height of his career, but of a man defeated, lost, who had tried on a military uniform for the sake of image.

She jumped to her feet, dropping the shoe and for a short moment simply stood there, stiff with shock; the dead man of her imagination risen. Shock, guilt, confusion coursed through her, a tangle of reactions; and somehow, somewhere, even a tiny thread of – relief.

'Marlene. Marlene. I – come to me, my darling.'

Sibyl cast aside her confusion and, an actor leaping into character without missing a beat, she repeated, 'Wolfgang!' but this time in a voice infused with relief. 'I thought you were – I heard that Strasbourg had fallen and I thought…'

'That I was dead? Many of my comrades are dead. For some reason, they missed me; I was lucky. But they captured me, The Free French captured me. Don't just stand there: come to me!'

She raised the counter flap and passed through the gap. He pulled her to him, closed his arms around her and held her in silence for several moments. Her cheek against his chest, she could hear the thumping of his heart, and then the rasping of his sobs.

'Wolf – what's the matter?' She reached behind him and pulled the bolt on the door; this was not a scene for another customer to barge in on.

He managed to stutter, between sobs: 'They captured me and all the officers, Marlene. They mocked and taunted us and in that moment I only wanted to be dead, even though I knew now that I would die not a hero but a coward. And I thought of you and wanted only to take you in my arms once again. And now you are here.'

'Oh Wolf. Come, come through to my *Oncle* Yves – can I offer you a glass of water?'

'No – no. I must go now. The whole of the Colmar station is in turmoil – nobody knows what is happening. My comrades need leadership and I must go and lead them. But tonight, my love, tonight – may I pick you up at seven?'

She nodded. He buried his face in her hair, pressed her closer yet to him, sobbed again, then pulled himself together, gave a little bow, pulled back the bolt on the door, and was gone.

Sibyl locked the door again and ran through to *Oncle* Yves. She was trembling all over; she could hardly stand, so *Oncle* Yves stood up from his workbench, grabbed hold of her and led her to a chair. Slowly she regained her composure.

'*Oncle* Yves: you were right. It's not over. I think it's just about to begin.'


That evening, at the Rote Löwe, in their now-familiar cubicle, he told her the story.

'It was a complete disaster, Marlene. A catastrophe. The Wehrmacht's defence collapsed completely. All of us in the senior leadership, we panicked. Our morale was completely broken; I suppose we all know we have lost and knowing that – well, how can a man fight to the death knowing his death is in vain? We fled, Marlene! So many of us fled! I too fled; we fled even prior to the Allied push. All of us; we were completely demoralised, the army, the Waffen-SS, and the Luftwaffe ground forces. There was a complete breakdown in discipline such as I have never seen in

my entire life. It was abominable, atrocious. The SS had looted
Strasbourg even before fleeing. Soldiers ordered to fight to the last
round, fight to the death: they threw away most of their ammunition before the battle and then claimed that they had run out and
surrendered. If Hitler had seen that he would have hanged every
last one of us. Everyone ran away, district leaders, group leaders,
regiment leaders, the municipal authorities, the mayor and the
deputy mayor, government officials: they all took to their heels.
They all fled. Every last one. It was shameful, shocking – and in
retrospect I am ashamed and shocked by my own actions and I
wish they had killed me. The other officers – well, they were taken
prisoner, eventually marched off. We too, a small group of us, were
taken prisoner but they let us go and sent us away. I walked from
Strasbourg to Colmar. I ate only things I found along the way:
fallen apples, overripe grapes clinging to vines, plums from trees.
Luckily there was enough water, enough streams. I arrived back
at the officers' garrison late last night.'

'You said they captured you? The French?'

'Yes. The Free French captured us. They lined us up against the
wall, taunted us. We stood there with our hands up, prisoners. And
then a strange thing happened. They walked down the line, asking
all our names and ranks. And they picked out certain of us – about
ten of us, I think – and set us free.'

He spoke on and on, telling and retelling, relating his shame
and the disgrace that had befallen him and the entire army. His
death wish, and yet his relief at being alive, to once more hold
'Marlene' in his arms.

After several hours of lamentation, and a whole bottle of wine
emptied, almost entirely by him, he had calmed down considerably.
Far from acting drunk, he stopped the lamentations and seemed
almost to draw on last reserves of sobriety and reason.

'On my way here, dear Marlene, as I was tramping through
the mud and the cold wind was whipping at me, I had but one

thought: what if I had died? What would become of Marlene? And that is why I came to one conclusion: Marlene, we must marry as soon as possible. Before Christmas.'

'Get married, now? But, Wolf, that is impossible!'

'No, it is not impossible. Just a civil wedding, at the town hall. You have all your papers here, and I must only send for my birth certificate. It is easy. We must marry, Marlene, for several reasons. The first reason is of course selfish: I love you, I need you, I want you. I do not want to die in the next battle – oh yes, there will be another battle, my dear! – without having loved you entirely, body and soul. Marrying you will bring so much comfort to me, give me so much strength!

'But that is only the selfish reason. For your sake, too, it is better we marry now. This is for your own future. Look at you, a poor cobbler's girl. But when I die, Marlene: as my widow you will inherit my entire property, automatically, and no one can contest it. That is actually quite a significant inheritance. I own a villa in Munich, which was left to me by my grandparents. And quite a substantial amount of capital, and shares in some businesses. And of course you will also receive a widow's pension. Your life will be quite a different one. I would leave this to you with a big heart and all my love – I would not begrudge you marrying again, my beloved. I want you to be happy.'

'But why are you so sure that you will die?'

'Because I can no longer fight this war for Germany, knowing what I now know, Marlene, knowing the evil behind my forces. I just cannot. And now most of the other men know it too. Their spines are as limp as vines. Mine too. I should have died. And in the next battle it is very likely that I will die. Because, Marlene, this will not happen again. I cannot live with such ignominy; I must fight the next battle like a man, a soldier, to the death. I cannot live on knowing I was a coward. My death is very likely considering what happened in Strasbourg – I am determined not to let that be my last fight. I am not a coward and the next time I will fight bravely to the death, not because Hitler ordered it, not for the Third Reich, but for my own honour, to clean my slate of disgrace.'

'But – if Strasbourg has fallen surely it means that all of Alsace is now French? That the Wehrmacht will retreat from Colmar as well?'

'Not a bit of it! Who told you such nonsense! We are going to fight on – this time, really to the death. Hitler will not surrender Colmar. He has ordered a fight to the death, which means my death as well. We will not flee again. But I want you well taken care of, as my widow. And, Marlene, before I die, I want to hold you, feel you, love you. Surely you can do this one thing for me? Marry me now?'

She heard the words, but as if from far away. Louder, to her, was the insistent thudding of her heart, the cry of her own inner resistance: *no, no, I cannot!*

And then, another cry: *For France, For Alsace!*

'You have nothing to say? You cannot say yes? That is all I want. So with that in mind, I propose that tomorrow we go to the town hall and apply to marry as soon as it is feasible. What do you say to that?'

Stunned into speechlessness, Sibyl groped for an adequate excuse.

'Wolf, I understand,' she said, struggling to keep her speech steady. 'I do; and it is a good idea for all your reasons. But – but what I would be afraid of…'

He took her hand. 'What would you be afraid of, my darling? There is nothing to fear.'

'What if – what if you fell, if you really died – I really hope not, but what if – you died in battle and then I found I was going to have a baby?'

Instead of sharing her distress at such a thought, his eyes actually lit up.

'But that would be the grandest thing, my dear! I would love nothing more than to leave a son – or even a daughter – when I die. This possibility had not even occurred to me –of course, if I survive, that is my dream, but to leave a child behind when I die – Marlene, there is nothing to fear. There is enough money. You would have a home. My parents would help, they would take you in, they would love you. I already told them all about you and my intention of marrying you. This engagement ring' – he raised her hand to his lips – 'this ring is an heirloom; it was my grandmother's. You would be part of my family. Even if Germany loses the war, you would be cared for. You would have a home in a beautiful part of Germany. You would raise my child in comfortable circumstances. You would…'

She had to stop him; he was getting carried away by a dream of posthumous glory.

'No, Wolf, no. I do not want to raise a child without a father. I refuse to even contemplate it.'

His smile faded, his shoulders slumped.

'Well, then, maybe not. Maybe no child for now, and maybe, just maybe, there is a small chance I might survive. But we still must marry. There are ways and means of preventing conception. We will find out what can be done. But we must definitely marry soon. Please say yes, Marlene. Please do it: for me, but also for you. I know you don't love me fully yet but surely what I have said, is incentive enough?'

'I will think about it. Give me a few days.'

'A few days is too long, my darling – it is already December! We must act quickly!'

'Then give me two days. I must discuss it with *Oncle* Yves. I must be sure. Give me two days.'

He nodded. 'Very well. I will return the day after tomorrow. And hopefully, there will be good news.'

# Chapter Forty-One

Her message to Acrobat the next day was succinct. And, she thought, most probably redundant since she knew the answer.

'Percy proposes wedding before Christmas. Advice required.'

Indeed, redundant. The reply was even more succinct:

'Congratulations.'

'What a girl won't do for her country,' said Sibyl.

'It's not even technically your country,' said Elena. 'You're actually English. Which makes it all the more heroic.'

'I might have a British passport, but France is the country of my heart. It's always been that way.'

'Well, I know I couldn't marry a German! Share his bed! Oh, even the thought makes me puke.'

Margaux shook her head in disbelief.

'You English are such prudes! What's so heroic about it? You get a handsome officer who adores you, and when he dies – hopefully soon, seeing as he's the enemy – you get to inherit a small fortune.'

'No, I don't. You forget that the wedding is a sham. Marlene Schuster does not exist. She's a myth; or rather, she's actually Jeanne Dauguet, who is actually dead. It's all make-believe.'

'What a pity! Think of that villa in Munich. You could move there after the war!'

'Who said I want to live in Munich! And I wish you'd all stop being so flippant about it. This is serious… how can I possibly?'

'Oh, Sibyl, don't be melodramatic. It's just a piece of paper. It's your job. Marry him, play the part, be nice to him, and you could very well win us the war in a day or two. Think of all the pillow talk! If he's been so generous with secrets before marriage, think of what you'll get out of him after a few sweet kisses!'

'Margaux, just shut up, all right? And take me home.'

# Chapter Forty-Two

'We need a home, my darling. We need a place of our own, and I have thought of just the thing.'

'Really? Where?'

Sibyl's consent to an early wedding had pitched von Haagen into a flurry of activity. It had cast away his gloom, straightened his back. Immediately he had sent for his birth certificate and other documents; the wedding date had been set for December 12th.

It was all happening far too fast for Sibyl's liking; an express train hurtling into a great blackness, a train she could not get off, try as she might; for it was necessary. She was just a cog in a greater wheel, a wheel in which personal feelings played no role whatsoever. And she was trying. Trying to play the part. Again and again she recalled her training, the psychological part of it. She was playing a part; the part of dedicated fiancée. She had to fling herself into the role, suppress the natural emotions of resistance and rebellion; pretend to love him, pretend to care, because that was what the role demanded. She was slowly getting better at it. If she could just forget, put aside for the moment, this man's connection to the world's most dangerous tyrant, the monster who would destroy the world, and see him simply as a man; a man who genuinely loved her. If she could just peel away the hostility towards what he represented and remember, bring to mind, that behind his outward manifestation of a German officer, her enemy, stood just that, a man. If she could forget his nationality, his status, his function, and see him for who he was. What if the same man had been English? Would it have been easier?

*No, because I love Jacques.*

But if there were no Jacques. And von Haagen were English. What then?

*No, because I love Jacques.*

But what if. What if he were just a man who loved you, without all these pesky attributes? Just a loving man with a need to open his heart to you, confide in you, put all his trust in your hands. Would marrying him still be such a terrible thing?

*Yes, because it is Jacques that I love.*

But she was an agent, playing a part, and this was what she had to do.

'It is just a few doors away from you: an empty house; it once belonged to a violin-maker, I believe.'

'Yes, I know the house. It is boarded up.'

'That does not matter. The boards are rather ugly, but they will be removed. It's quite a pretty house. I shall arrange to be billeted there and then we can live together. This can happen very soon. I will inspect the house and make sure it is habitable. Or else, we can look for a place together, a villa perhaps, in another part of town. Unfortunately, I don't have much time for house-hunting right now. We are all busy planning the next offensive.'

'Really? So soon?'

'Of course. We cannot waste time; Hitler is furious at losing Strasbourg. He's absolutely incensed; no, apoplectic with rage. I can just imagine it; I've seen his tantrums. Not a pretty sight at all. I have to admit to a certain amount of *Schadenfreude!*' He grinned at her.

'He won't stand for it; he insists that we cannot *at any cost* lose Colmar as well; in fact, he wants us to regain Strasbourg so that even if Germany loses the war, which is a foregone conclusion, Alsace will remain German territory. He is so determined – well, I should not be telling you this, but you are my fiancée, after all…'

He stopped, held her gaze, begging for confirmation. She smiled in reassurance, taking both her hands in hers.

'Yes… of course. You can tell me anything. You know it.'

'That's such a help to me. I carry around all this stress and just having an outlet, a sounding board: it takes a burden off my shoulders. I cannot talk to the other men as they are carrying burdens of their own. We are all under such pressure. Talking helps so much – I am but human, beneath it all. The image of a dispassionate soldier, just following orders – well, it's all just that, an image, isn't it? Created to impress others, to convey the illusion of indestructible power. But you know, Marlene: we are still human. We have families, wives, children; every soldier is also human. Hitler's rage shows that he too is human, not the all-powerful God he paints himself as. Hitler too has a woman, Eva Braun. You did not know that, did you? It is kept a secret from the public so that they believe he is above human passions. He is not.

'And, you know, even Goebbels – you know of Goebbels? Minster of Propaganda? Of course you do. Everyone has heard of Joseph Goebbels – that tough, powerful henchman of Hitler? Evil, like Himmler, like Hitler himself. You think he is above everything? That he has no feelings? That he is made of stone?

'Wrong! He too fell for a woman, a Czech film star. He was besotted with her, wanted to give up his family, even his career. Hitler ordered him to drop her but he could not. He resigned his post, a position at the very top of the Nazi hierarchy! So much he loved this woman. But Hitler did not accept his resignation. He forced Goebbels to give her up. Such is the power of love! It can defeat even the staunchest Nazi, because they too are human behind it all, they too have needs – a need to share their burdens, their pains. A man's wife is his other half, the confidante of his heart. He can be truly himself with his wife. She alone can see beyond the illusion, see the real man, know his weaknesses and not judge him for them, because she loves him. Is that not so, my darling? That is how I regard marriage. That is how our marriage will be, even if it is but short. Although…'

He paused, which gave her the opportunity of bringing him back to the topic; to whatever burden it was he wanted to share with her. She had to cut short what promised to be a rumination on the respective roles and psychology of husband and wife, soldier and confidante.

'Of course, Wolf! You can tell me anything. That's what I'm here for: to help you with your burdens. You can tell me whatever is in your heart.'

'This is not so much a burden, though, as a military secret of momentous significance. Very few officers know of it; basically, just the generals and a few other senior officers. And it means, it could mean – that we have a slight hope of a recovery in Alsace. That we could, possibly, hold Alsace, win back Strasbourg and keep Alsace after the Allies have withdrawn. It's been said that General Eisenhower is not at all interested in holding on to Alsace, that he could withdraw the American troops, and the French army could not hold on to it. The Americans are keen to cross the Rhine into Germany and let go of Alsace. This is what our spies have discovered. But that's not the main thing that gives me hope.'

She squeezed his hands, leaned into him, rested her head on his shoulder.

'What is it, *mein Schatz*? Don't keep me in suspense like this…'

It was the first time she had used a pet name with him. It seemed necessary, considering the delicacy of the situation. Instinct told her he was holding back, talking, chattering even, to delay a revelation, resisting disclosure as a good officer should. Which meant, perhaps, that what he had to say was, indeed, significant. In his next breath she was rewarded. It burst from him.

'Heinrich Himmler has been placed in charge of the operation!'

'What? You mean…'

'Yes! Himmler himself! Hitler himself has given him command of the Army Group Upper Rhine, therefore of all Alsace – and he reports directly to Hitler himself, unlike all other commanders.

This shows just how vital Alsace is to Hitler, which will mean that the troops will find enormous motivation; this, my darling, is why I am so confident we can win back Strasbourg and keep Alsace; especially in the light of Eisenhower's disinterest. Do you understand, my darling, how important this is? It could very well mean that we shall indeed remain the victors in Alsace after the Americans withdraw; which means: perhaps I will not die, and we will, after all, have a life together. Right now, Himmler is on his way to Colmar. We are having a crisis meeting on Monday morning: all the generals and senior officers, and Himmler. And I am thrilled beyond measure.'

Sibyl forced her voice to remain steady.

'I thought you detested Himmler? I thought he was the most vile, dangerous, brutal man in Hitler's inner circle? I thought he...'

'Don't you see, my dear, the one has nothing to do with the other. Indeed. Himmler is responsible for the most atrocious crimes against the Jews, and there can be no forgiveness for the death camps. After the war is over I am sure he will be brought to trial for his crimes. But this is a military operation: a different matter altogether. It's about us holding on to the Alsace, come what may, and only a man of Himmler's stature can inject the Wehrmacht with fresh energy. The SS Stormtroopers – they will do exactly as he says; he is after all head of the SS. And as much as I despise the man, I have hope again.

'I am at that stage, Marlene, in which I don't care about anything but making the best out of the disaster of this terrible war. I loathe them all: Hitler, Himmler, the whole pack of them. They whipped us into this catastrophe which has cost so many lives. I don't care that Germany will lose the war – Germany deserves to lose! All I care about now is my personal future, and I can only secure that by helping us to win the next battle, win back Alsace. And so, Himmler gives me hope, though I detest him. He gives me hope for Alsace – a province I have learnt to love – and hope that I may have a life with the woman that I love. And I want you to join me in that hope. Pray for me, Marlene: pray that I survive the next chapter of this war, and may live to realise my dream – our dream.'

She struggled to swallow the lump of bile that suddenly rose in her throat; struggled to breathe, to remain calm, not to leap to her feet and race off to get an emergency message off to Acrobat.

'So – now you think Alsace will remain German? That the Americans will back out of the defence?'

'Exactly. I concede – we all do, Hitler included – that Germany has lost the war. But Alsace will remain German territory. It's not worth it for Eisenhower to keep up the defence with the subsequent loss of American lives, and France cannot defend it without the Americans. So Alsace will remain part of Germany, a part of the state of Baden across the Rhine. This is wonderful news. It means that I can remain here. How would you like it, my dear, if we made Alsace our permanent home? I could sell the Munich house and we could purchase a villa near one of the villages – near Riquewihr, for instance. I would eventually retire from the military; I'd like to try my hand at managing a small vineyard. Maybe we can buy someone out, live here, raise our children here. How does that sound to you?'

Hopefully he didn't notice her hesitation. It was becoming increasingly difficult to create appropriate responses to his ever more outlandish suggestions.

'Well, that sounds marvellous! You know I'd love to stay here. Alsace is my real home. I'd love to put down permanent roots.'

'Well then – now you too can hope for a German victory in Alsace. Yes, Colmar will be involved in the war and it will be unpleasant for you, but you'll be out of danger, as will the citizens. We all want to keep the town intact with as few civilian casualties as possible. It will only be for a short while. Himmler may not have much military experience but his very presence here will motivate the soldiers and they'll renew their pledge to fight for victory. We shall overcome. This one last piece of territory shall remain in German hands.'

'You said, Himmler is actually coming to Alsace? To Colmar?'

'He's on his way right now. We're going to have a celebratory dinner at the Villa Schönblick on Saturday night; he'll be there. I would like you to attend. Many of the officers are bringing their girls; respectable girls, I mean, if they have one. Very few do – I'm one of the lucky ones. I have you.' He squeezed her hand. She squeezed his back, ran her thumb over the back of his.

'So I will get to meet Mr Himmler?'

'You will! I admit, he's a despicable person but he has a lot of influence and it's an opportunity for us to get in his good books. I'm sure he'll be charmed by you.'

'That should be… interesting, I suppose. And a bit frightening.'

'No need at all to be frightened, my dear. I'm sure you'll charm him. It's just a pleasant social evening before the planning starts in earnest on Monday.'

'Is Himmler staying at the Villa Schönblick?'

Was that a little too probing a question? Was it something an innocent Marlene Schuster would ask? Von Haagen seemed to think so.

'No – he will have a suite of his own at the Rote Löwe, along with some of the generals. The dinner, though, will be at the Villa, and the talks as well. The Rote Löwe does not unfortunately have a conference room. But you needn't worry your pretty little head about that; we military people will make sure you're safe.'

She'd probed enough; it was time to be sweet bland Marlene Schuster again.

'Well, I know nothing of politics and all I care about, really, is leading a good, quiet life and raising my family, if I am granted one, in peace. I just want you to stay safe, Wolf. I don't like the idea of you going to battle again.'

'That's a soldier's life, my dear; that's the risk, and the risk his family must take. But hopefully this will be the last time, for me at least. I just want this damned war over and done with, so that we can start rebuilding; rebuilding our country, our lives.'

She sighed. 'Don't we all.'

# Chapter Forty-Three

'Herr Himmler, I'd like you to meet my fiancée, Marlene Schuster.'

Heinrich Himmler, *Reichsführer* of the *Schutzstaffel* – the dreaded SS, the most horrifying branch of the Nazi Party. Himmler, head of the Gestapo, the brains and the brawn behind the terror that held most of Europe in thrall. Heinrich Himmler, quiet and deadly. He stood before Sibyl and smiled, giving a slight bow as he shook her hand.

He was as immaculately dressed as she had come to expect from her contact with German high-ranking officers: not a speck of dust on his uniform, not a smudge on the shine of his knee-high black boots, the red, black and white swastika armband neatly fixed around his upper arm. Not a hair out of place; not that he had much hair, as it was cropped impossibly short beneath his insignia-emblazoned cap. He wore round rimless spectacles and had rather the appearance, Sibyl thought, of a harmless, chinless academic rather than a ruthless tyrant.

Knowing the truth behind the deceptive appearance, Sibyl was chilled to the bone and it took all her strength to keep her hand from trembling as she reached out to take his. His too was cold.

'Very pleased to meet you, *Fräulein* Schuster!'

'She's a born Alsatian. We are to be married this month!' Sibyl was relieved by von Haagen's interruption; it meant she did not have to speak. Not yet.

'Well, I congratulate you both! May your married life be blessed and happy! Heil Hitler!'

Already he had moved on to the next sycophantic officer, a major she had met briefly on a previous occasion, who had also brought his girl to be introduced. The heavy thudding of her heart slowed down by the time von Haagen had led her to their table.

'Awful man. Terrible man,' he whispered in her ear as he pulled out a chair for her.

It was after the main course that Sibyl asked to be excused; she needed *die Toilette*. She had used this a few times in the past; it was downstairs, in the basement. In former times, in the days when she was still Sibyl Lake, the basement had been a place for the boiler room and a laundry, lines strung across a large room where the family had hung their wet sheets and clothing on rainy days. When the children played outside – in the garden, in the lane behind the garden, in the stream beyond the lane – they had returned to the house through that back door, leaving their muddy boots in the basement. There had also been a cloakroom for raincoats and boots, a storeroom for garden tools, and one for trunks and boxes and suitcases belonging to the family. That had all been cleared away for the billeting of German officers, replaced with military paraphernalia of a generic kind. A large cloakroom took up the bulk of the space, with rows of metal lockers, shelves for boots.

And, at the very back, there was a door. And a window.

She had discussed it all with Jacques and Margaux the day before. 'There's a back entrance to the property,' she said. 'A metal gate, in a high hedge, leading to a narrow lane, leading to fields, woods, a stream, a ruined cottage. We children used to play there. I remember it well. There's a steep staircase leading to the basement, and a door. We can get in that way. Well, one of us. The other has to stand guard.'

'Are you sure there's no watchman out the back?'

'I'm fairly sure. There are two sentries at the main gate; probably they do occasional patrols around the back. We'll have to check.

You can check that on Saturday night while I check the door from the inside. And the window.'

Now, she tried the door. It was, as to be expected, locked, with a key that was missing. Not a problem; her training had included the picking of locks. Three bolts, top, bottom and to the side, reinforced the lock. She pulled them all back, with some effort, as they were rusty, and stuck, which was a good sign. It meant the back door was never used and most probably never checked.

Now for the window. It was a small one, high up on the wall. Big enough for her to crawl through, if need be, but too high to reach now, too high to unlock. It would have to be the door.

She returned to the dining hall. On the way she tried the door to the conference room, next to the dining room. It, too, was locked. Not a problem.

She walked across to her table, sat down, and spent the rest of the evening making small talk with their table companions; as usual, a group of rather uncouth Wehrmacht officers, many of whom she had met before. Some of them had women, girls, with them. As von Haagen had promised, respectable girls. Alsatian girls. Collaborators. The women all eyed each other up suspiciously, and spoke only to their men, in guarded whispers, rubbing their arms, batting their eyelashes, twirling tendrils of their hair.

Heinrich Himmler sat at a table prominently located in the bay window, together with several SS generals. There were no women at his table.

'Those are some of Hitler's best generals,' von Haagen whispered to her. 'All sent here specifically for Operation Nordwind.'

Operation Nordwind. So that was it. Hitler's last stand in France. But not if she could help it.

# Chapter Forty-Four

'Are you sure the talks start on Monday?'

'Absolutely. Once Wolfgang started talking he couldn't stop. It was like a broken dam. Three days of strategy talks, starting on Monday, in the conference room.'

'And Acrobat has given the green light?'

She nodded.

'Assassination is not really in my remit. Even Intelligence is not in my remit; Special Operations is mostly about sabotage. But there's this rivalry with MI6, who kind of look down on us. SOE's keen to show we can do more than just blow up bridges. It's not terribly complicated. All I have to do is find a place for the PE.'

'Doesn't he have bodyguards? Such a high-ranking dignitary?'

She shook her head. 'Himmler created the Schutzstaffel, the protective guard, but it was all for Hitler's benefit. To protect the Führer. Even then, the two attempts on Hitler's life only failed by accident – in both cases, it was a lucky escape and the SS had nothing to do with protecting him. It all seems terribly lax, considering. Himmler doesn't have a bodyguard.'

'So it's just a matter of placing the PE, and then – boom.'

'That's about it.'

'And your Wolfgang will go boom too.'

'Yes.'

'And after all the…' Margaux paused. 'All the intimacies you have exchanged, you can just blow him up, just like that?' She clicked her fingers.

'It's my job. It's what I was trained for. Listening to him tell all was just my job.'

Margaux shook her head slowly.

'You *Anglaises*… talk about *sangfroid!*'

Sibyl shrugged. 'It has to be done.'

'Well, anyway. Jacques will be there to back you up. And so will I.'


Margaux, true to her word, not only was there, she provided black clothes for both Sibyl and Jacques, a black cap for Sibyl. Black gloves. She dropped them both off near the lane that backed on to Villa Schönblick.

'Good luck. I'll be waiting.'

The night was appropriately, thankfully, dark; at 2 a.m. it was all black. Sibyl and Jacques were no more than shadows as they sprinted silently along the unpaved path that led to the villa. To their left were the high laurel hedges that protected the villa from prying eyes; the back gate was almost concealed in such a hedge, overgrown with ivy, and, like the bolts to the back door, rusted. Sibyl cut through the tangle of vines in no time and picked the lock. The gate creaked silently as she slipped through the opening. She nodded to Jacques in a signal to wait, and slunk over to the dark looming bulk of the building.

The outside steps leading down to the basement were steep and narrow and covered in moss. She moved soundlessly down to the back door and in a few seconds had picked the lock. Like the gate, the door creaked on its ancient rusty hinges. She stopped after slipping through it and listened.

The basement lay in darkness. Upstairs, on the ground level, a single light burned, casting a dim glow down the stairway. She wondered if she should turn it off; but no. The sentries outside at the front gate might come to investigate. Better to risk working in the glaring light, uncomfortable though it was. She felt naked, exposed; but there was no choice.

She walked silently upstairs and crossed the ground floor hall
to the conference room. This room had once been a library and
a downstairs guest room, which had been knocked into one; the
two doors were still in place, both locked. Sibyl guessed that the
door nearest to the front would be used, and so chose the far door
for her own entry. For the third time that night, she picked a lock.
This time, the door opened easily and without a squeak. She closed
the door behind her. The room immediately became pitch black;
and that was so much more comfortable than the glare outside in
the hall. She removed the torch from her pocket, switched it on,
cast it around the room.

At one end was a large fireplace, at the other a long sideboard
placed between windows; a small table sat near the door with a
tray of upturned glasses and an empty water jug. In the middle of
the room was a long, oval, magnificent conference table reaching
from one end of the room to the other.

Three possible hiding places at once leaped out at Sibyl: the
fireplace, the sideboard, the table itself. The decision was instant
and conclusive: the table. It was obvious, too, where Himmler,
as chairman of the meeting, would be sitting: at the head of the
table. Where would von Haagen sit? Somewhere along one of the
sides, no doubt. It didn't matter. Wherever he sat, he'd be toast.

She moved aside the chair at the table's head, removed her
backpack, dropped to all fours, crept under the table and shone
the light to its underside. The table was supported by two heavy,
ornately carved clawfoot pedestals at each end. A three-inch wooden
skirt ran all around the edge of the table, and at the backside of
this skirt was the stub of a ledge, that too running all around the
underside of the table. She shone the torch into her backpack,
removed the plastic explosive, yielding as a lump of putty. She
pressed it into the ledge beneath the table.

What was that? A floorboard above her head squeaked. And
another. Footsteps. She froze, her heart pounding so hard she felt

sure it must echo all through the house. The rest of her body was still, a statue, her hands still reaching up, her fingers still pressing the explosive. Listening, hardly breathing. Footsteps, definitely, but so soft their owner was most definitely barefoot. Or wearing socks. Did German officers sleep in their socks? In the December coldness, probably, yes. Silence. No steps on the staircase; a good sign. She breathed slowly, collectedly. In, out. Her heart seemed to have slowed as well. Still she did not move, her entire body on high alert, like a cat about to spring. A while of silence and then – the flushing of a toilet. The plumbing must be ancient: it roared through the building. She almost smiled to herself – did men really flush after a night-time pee? Apparently yes.

She was just about to return to the job at hand when a piercing male scream jolted her into a panic so intense she almost dropped everything to flee. Another scream and then a scream that took voice, and the voice was calling, calling her name: *Marlene! Marlene! MARLENE! Hilf mir, hilf mir! Marlene! Help me, help me!*

Without a second thought she sprang to her feet with the silence of a cat, drew the gun from her belt, slipped the L-capsule from her pocket and into her mouth, between her gum and her lip. Did Wolf somehow sense her presence in the house? Would they all come storming down? An unlikely, irrational, panicked idea but this was not the time to weigh the rationality of an outcome. She cocked the pistol and hid behind the door, even as other voices, shouts, echoed through the house: *Halt die Klappe, Wolf! Schlaf wieder! Halts Maul! Ruhe!* Shut your gob, Wolf! Go back to sleep! Quiet!

The screams stopped as suddenly as they had started; there was motion upstairs, as if men were moving around, going from bed to bed; and then, at last, silence once more.

It was over. The terror, the dread, the panic. The pounding of her heart. The nightmare. She removed the L-pill from her mouth, put it in her pocket.

She returned to the table, crouched to the floor, set the timer.

It would go off at ten the next morning. The strategy talks would be in full swing by then. Everyone would be there. The entire Colmar high command. Heinrich Himmler. Commander of the forces in Alsace.

She crept out the way she had come, closing all doors as she left. Flitted across the back lawn, out the back gate. Jacques was waiting in the lane. They sprinted off into the night, down into the street where Margaux waited, not in the van, this time, but in the inconspicuous black Renault.

'Let's go home now,' she said. 'And back at nine. We need to witness this.'


As promised, they were back soon after nine, again in the Renault. Margaux did not drive past the villa; instead, she looked for a spot quite far down the street and parked on the roadside, behind another car. The villa was not visible from here. The explosion would be.

They waited. Sibyl checked her watch every few minutes. They did not speak. The insides of her mouth felt dry, her saliva tasted bitter. Inside her, something was building, swelling, a nameless lump of – something. Something bad. Something big: enormous, heavy, monstrous. Vile.

The second hand on her watch jerked forward bit by bit, dividing the free flow of time into increments. Ten minutes to go. They should not have come so early. Waiting here for so long – a waiting car was suspicious. There was little traffic and fewer passers-by, but still. Three people waiting in a car? It's something a passer-by would surely notice, remember, once an investigation started. A silly mistake. On the other hand…

'One minute to go,' whispered Margaux. Sibyl took the deepest breath in her life, held it, and – a blast tore the air, literally ear-splitting, in that afterwards she was momentarily deaf. Ahead, a giant ball of fire and smoke rose from between the stately buildings lining the road.

'Got 'em!' cried Margaux, exultation in her voice, and in that moment switched on the ignition and the car plunged away, not towards the explosion but away from it, far away from it, through the town and out into the country and Sibyl's hearing returned and what she heard was laughing, loud, raucous laughing and triumphant yells of *We did it! We got 'em!* from Margaux and Jacques. She herself said nothing. The lump of whatever it was in her innards had grown to bursting point, filling her, strangling her throat, erupting.

She was crying. Not just crying, bawling. Ugly, violent, virulent weeping racked her body. She couldn't help it, couldn't stop it. She wailed in the agony of that weeping, bawled at the top of her blubbering voice, bellowed with anguish, howled and roared. Noises exploded from her that weren't even human, the lamenting of a beast, and it was her.

She felt nothing, saw nothing, heard nothing in that first eruption of anguish but then the noises slowed down to a wail and then into quiet weeping and she felt Jacques' hand on her back, Jacques leaning forward from the back seat, and she heard Jacques' voice trying to comfort her, and then Jacques and Margaux talking about her as if she weren't present, as if she was a patient in a mental hospital.

'It's all the pressure of the last few weeks,' Margaux said in a hushed voice as she drove. She was nodding her head, agreeing with her own diagnosis. Sibyl saw her through the tears.

'The first time you actually kill people, I mean, directly, deliberately, it's a big thing. I remember myself,' Jacques agreed. 'I had a meltdown too.'

'It's good she can release the tension this way,' said Margaux. 'She'll be fine by the time we get home.' And, in a louder voice, 'That's right isn't it, Sibyl? You'll be fine. Let the tears come. It's a good release.'

'It's all right. You did right. They're all gone, the bastards. It's for France. For freedom.' He handed her a handkerchief; a dirty one, and a little late, since the tears no longer flowed. She turned her head away from them and gazed out of the window at the vineyards fleeting past, dry-eyed now, but her nose full of snot. She took the handkerchief and blew into it.

*They don't understand. They never will. He put his life, his heart in my hands. He trusted me. He loved me. I betrayed him. I killed him. He's dead, and I killed him, and it was an act of betrayal. My job, indeed. But on a human level, an act of betrayal.*

They would never get it. She could never say it out loud.

Later, they all celebrated; Sibyl, quiet now and dry-eyed, tried to smile and be part of the general jollity, tried to take part. Victoire was there, and Pierre, and *Oncle* Yves, and Elena, all excited and delighted, patting her on the back, congratulating her. Margaux popped a bottle of her best crémant; it frothed up over her hand and onto the kitchen floor. '*Vive la France! Vive L'Alsace! Vive la Liberté!*' they all cried, but she had heard it all before, at the fall of Strasbourg. But this, apparently, was bigger, because with Heinrich Himmler and all the generals in the plan for Operation Nordwind dead, the German forces in Alsace would be leaderless, a headless animal. There was no other option, now, but retreat, as Margaux explained again and again. That was why this was, in effect, the very last stroke for a free France, and she, Sibyl, had dealt that stroke. The honour was all hers. She'd probably get a medal.

The telephone rang.

'I'll get it,' said Margaux, and walked into the hall.

*Oncle* Yves began to sing the 'The Marseillaise' in a shaky old-man voice, and everyone joined in, and Sibyl tried to join in but her heart was heavy, aching, actually, but it didn't show and she had to hide it. It was unpatriotic. Treasonous, even. *Himmler is dead!* She scolded herself. *It's a day of great rejoicing! The monster of the Nazis is dead and now it will all collapse, and it's all thanks to you.* She should be proud of herself. But all she could think of was Wolf: Wolf's trusting eyes, Wolf saying, *you are the confidante of my heart.*

The kitchen door opened as Margaux returned. But she didn't enter the room. She stood in the doorway. They sang, waving the French flag; they rejoiced, raised glasses on high, grinned at each other, hearts filled with the stirring, bloodthirsty lyrics of the Marseillaise:

> *Grab your weapons, citizens!*
> *Form your battalions!*
> *Let us march! Let us march!*
> *May impure blood*
> *Water our fields!*

Jacques noticed Margaux, standing in the doorway. Sibyl had seen her long ago, locked eyes with her, read the rigid lines of her now unsmiling face. Jacques stopped singing.

'Come on in, Margaux. What's the matter?'

Margaux did not move. Now everyone stopped singing. Everyone stared. Somehow, they understood, without words. But finally, Margaux spoke, in a strangled stuttering voice.

'The meeting was postponed. The bombed room? It was empty. Himmler is alive.'

# Chapter Forty-Five

Jacques spirited Sibyl back to Colmar within the hour. She could not risk a Château Gauthier vehicle; one had to assume the SS would be swarming everywhere; and they were. They went by foot, on bicycle, by horse carriage and delivery van, from village to village, friendly farm to friendly farm. Not that Sibyl considered herself a prime suspect, but she was the perpetrator, and her heart was galloping, and not until she was safely behind her counter at the cobbler's did her breath flow comfortably again. And not even then.

News of the bomb attack was all over town, said *Oncle* Yves, who had gone to the market to hear the gossip. Everyone knew. Everyone knew it had failed. No-one knew the details.

What had gone wrong? There was no way of knowing. Had the room been checked for explosives, and evacuated at the last moment? Had the conference been postponed for other reasons? Where was Himmler now? Where was von Haagen?

Did he suspect her?

That was the question hammering at the back of Sibyl's mind, for a guilty mind is a restless mind, perception biased to the point of paranoia.

He *had* told her. He *must* suspect her. They *would* come after her…

But perhaps not. She should have stayed away from Colmar. No. It was right to return. Suicide pills, hidden in shirt pockets and lingerie – just in case. Brazen it out. If they came for her: deny, deny, deny. Or did they have proof? Had von Haagen confessed to indiscretions? To pillow talk, even without a pillow? What did they know? What did he think? Would he be back?

Sibyl sat in the cobbler's shop behind the counter, reading Rilke poetry, or trying to read, as her mind was chaos.

The window was still boarded up; she could not see the street, which made it all so much worse. If the Gestapo came it would be without warning, bursting through the door; no jangle of bells to announce them. No polite small talk. No *Guten Tag, Frau Schuster*. They'd charge in with pointing pistols, frogmarch her away.

But maybe not.

It was, she realised, the ultimate test for von Haagen. Trust no-one: it was the fundamental warning given to all wartime players. Trust no-one. As a good German he should turn himself in, turn her in. *Yes: I told my fiancée. She knew. I am the leak. She is the leak.*

And yet. Von Haagen's face hovered before her mind's eye, and in it was a trust so inviolable, so intimately fused with his very sense of survival, his need to survive this war and live on with her at his side: it generated a reciprocal trust, trust in him. That he would not betray her.

*You are the other half of my soul,* he had said at their last meeting. *My better half.*

He clung to that belief as a drowning man to a lifebelt. She knew he would never let go, never betray her. Betrayal was *her* game, not his. And it would continue. Her job was not yet over.

And yet: she had wept for him, believing him dead, believing she had killed him. She had not only wept for him: it had been a complete breakdown, a crumbling of self, faced with the magnitude of her betrayal, faced with the knowledge that she had done the unthinkable, betrayed love that was true and genuine.

In a matter of hours she had regained her professional identity, put such sentimental notions behind her. She had done her job, and that was all. She would continue to do it; she would wear the mask she had been contracted to wear, and life as Marlene Schuster, cobbler's assistant, would continue. Von Haagen would return. She would betray him again and again; for the duration.

\*

They came that evening. They did not burst through the door in the scenario of her imagination and her fears. They came, indeed, to the familiar jangling of bells, and they greeted her by name. Again, it was two of them; but not the same two.

'*Sicherheitspolizei. Sturmbannführer* Weber. This is *Obersturmführer* Müller. Good evening, *Fräulein* Schuster. Please be so kind as to show us your identity papers.'

Sibyl did as asked. Her identity card was passed between them, inspected and handed back. *Sturmbannführer* Weber nodded. *Obersturmführer* Müller took a notebook out of his uniform pocket and held it with a pencil poised above it. *Sturmbannführer* Weber nodded at his colleague.

'*In Ordnung*. Now, *Fräulein* Schuster, if you don't mind, we have a few questions regarding some of your personal relationships. We believe you are the niece of Herr Schuster. Is that correct?'

Sibyl nodded. 'Yes. That's true.'

*Obersturmführer* Müller scribbled in his notebook.

'But you did not grow up in Colmar. You came from Paris, recently. Is that also true?'

'Yes. But I was born in Colmar and my parents are both Alsatians. Were. My father died when I was a child.'

That was a mistake. Answer questions, but only what was asked. Don't offer them more.

*Sturmbannführer* Weber nodded again, as if to agree with her. 'Now, *Fräulein* Schuster, we are interested in your more personal relationships. Your friends and – ah – lovers. We believe you are the mistress of *Oberst* Wolfgang von Haagen?'

She shook her head. 'I am not his mistress. I am his fiancée.'

*Sturmbannführer* Weber smirked. 'Often those two are one and the same. But we will accept your terminology. Our next question is, how long have you been intimate with the Herr *Oberst* – though I believe he was a Major back then?'

'We met in July.'

'We would like details of that first meeting. How did you approach the Herr *Oberst*? And why?'

'I did not approach him. He approached me.'

'Go on – tell us how this encounter took place.'

'I was walking from the station with a heavy suitcase. Major von Haagen very kindly offered to carry the suitcase for me.'

'You did not approach him, ask for help?'

'No.'

They both nodded, as if Sibyl's denial confirmed information they already had. *Obersturmführer* Müller scribbled furiously.

'Now, we would like to know more about the details of your relationship. I assume the two of you have many intimate conversations?'

'Well, we have conversations. I don't know what you mean by intimate.'

'Well – of an intimate nature. Lovers are after all inclined to share the details of their lives, their hopes and fears, their – ah – most intimate secrets. Do you have this kind of conversation with the Herr Oberst? What do you discuss?'

'We talk about culture, books, music, art. We like the same things. And we talk about our future together. We plan to marry soon.'

'When a man has met the woman he plans to share his life with, sometimes he is inclined to discuss matters that – ah – are better kept to himself. Did Herr Oberst speak to you of military matters?'

'No. Of course not. Only things that are generally known.'

'But how do you know what is generally known and what is not?'

'Because they are in the newspapers. My uncle buys a newspaper sometimes and I read it.'

'Did you know of any visiting dignitaries in Colmar?'

'No.'

'Did you know of any planned conferences? The dates and times?'

She held his gaze. Steady. In spite of a heart thumping so loud she was sure he could hear it.

'No.'

'*Fräulein* Schuster – did you hear of a somewhat large explosion in Colmar this morning?'

'I heard of it, yes. People were speaking of it in the market.'

'Where were you, *Fräulein* Schuster, last night?'

'I was in bed.'

'You did not go out?'

'No.'

'Where were you at about nine thirty this morning?'

'I was working. Here.'

'You were not in a black Renault, which was seen in the vicinity of the explosion?'

'No.'

'When did you go to the market?'

'I don't know the exact time. Around lunchtime.'

'Can you recall anyone you spoke to at the market? Do you have witnesses, for your whereabouts last night and this morning?'

'Well, my uncle, for one. I spoke to a few people at the market. I don't know if they will remember me.'

*Sturmbannführer* Weber looked at *Obersturmführer* Müller. 'Have you got that, Herr *Kollege*? Good. *Fräulein* Schuster, we thank you for your cooperation. We will check the details of what you have told us and if necessary get back to you. In the meantime, we would like to speak to your uncle. Please could you…'

# Part Four

## The Colmar Pocket

*'We can still lose this war.'*

>                           *General George Patton, 4 January 1945*

*'Whatever you do, don't crush the vines.'*

>            *Jean Joseph Marie Gabriel de Lattre de Tassigny*

# Chapter Forty-Six

On the third day, he came.

Smart as ever, buttons gleaming, cap straight, he burst into the shop with a jangling of bells and a bounce, almost a swagger, to his step; gone was the solemn intensity, the gravitas of their last encounter. 'Wolfg—'

But he was already mid-speech, beaming, as he reached across the counter and took her hands in his. He radiated confidence, his demeanour not that of a man in the aftermath of a bomb attack. In the reversed world of values that was her work, that meant bad news.

'I've so much to tell you, but no time now. I just dropped in to say I'll pick you up tonight at seven, for dinner – if you're free?' Always that polite addendum; surely he knew, by now, that she was always free, that she had no social life besides him.

'Yes, yes, of course. Are you all right? I heard…'

'Yes, yes, the explosion.' He brushed it away with his hands. 'An amateur bomb attack. Nobody killed, though they did make the villa unliveable – we all have to move out, which is part of the reason I haven't been able to come earlier. I hope you weren't worried –oh!' he exclaimed, interrupting her again, 'You were, weren't you! Of course you were! Well, as you see, I'm alive and well and full of good news. But I have to go. I'll see you tonight.'

'I thought you were dead,' she had started to say, but he'd pre-empted her and the words died on her lips.

And he was gone. She shrugged, and continued the work she'd been doing, threading laces through a farmer's ancient pair of leather boots.

He was back promptly at seven, whisking her out of the door in a flurry of compliments (*You are more beautiful by the day! How do you do it?*) and admiring glances. In the lane waited a new vehicle: not the motorcycle – the last few weeks had been bitterly cold, ruling out motorcycles with sidecars – and not the Mercedes-Benz, but a small black round-topped automobile.

'A Beetle!' he said. 'Volkswagen; see, Hitler did do some good; it's a people's car, small and inexpensive, a car the ordinary man can afford. Not that I am ordinary, or you – but the Benz wasn't available and one of my colleagues lent me this. What do you think?'

'It's adorable!' said Sibyl as she slid into the passenger seat. Von Haagen shut the passenger door and sprinted around to the driver's door, climbed in and drove off.

Again he beamed at her. 'So, how have you been?'

'Well, I was worried! I knew you had that conference, so…'

'Yes, yes. Fortunately, the conference was postponed. General Wiese had an upset stomach and as he's the most experienced Wehrmacht general we couldn't start without him, not even with Herr Himmler. So… the bomb misfired. So much for British terrorists!' he laughed.

'Why do you think they were British?'

'Plastic explosive. Where would French terrorists get it from, if not from the British? As I said, an amateur attempt.'

'But if the conference had taken place as planned…' she pulled herself together. No room here for taking offence. 'Wolfgang, you could have been killed! I was distraught! And no word from you!'

'I'm sorry, darling; I just didn't have the time to come by and reassure you. But I knew it would be in the next day's news – your uncle reads the news, doesn't he? So I was sure you'd be informed. But – and this is what I came to tell you – there's good news in the bad. We have all had to be rehoused – even though only half the house was destroyed, it's unsafe. And anyway, the staircase was hit.

So all the officers have been billeted elsewhere. And guess where I've been billeted? At my request?'

She shook her head, even though she had guessed it right away.

'The violin-makers! At the moment we're all cramped in various hotels but as soon as the house has been fixed up a little I'll move in. I'll be a few doors away from you! Isn't that wonderful!'

'Wonderful!'

'But there's also some bad news. And more good news. And bad news. But the general outcome is – well, you'll hear it all tonight. I have so much to tell.'

Once they were seated in their cubicle at the Rote Löwe, and once he had ordered –lamb chops for both of them, and gewürz-traminer – he plunged right into the volley of news.

'… as I was saying. I'll be moving into the very house I had picked out as our first marital home. But – well, I'm sorry, darling. I know I promised an early wedding but it just isn't to be. Not even with pulling strings from above; it takes time to get all the papers together – I need an *Eheunbedenklichkeitsbescheinigung* from Munich – damn German bureaucracy!'

'What on earth is that?'

'*Eheunbedenklichkeitsbescheinigung?* Proof that a person is not already married. You will need one too, from Paris. That will take months. And the civil offices here also need months, to arrange everything, and no amount of pressure will speed them up. Unfortunately. So that's the bad news.'

'Oh, what a pity!' she said, even as a hundredweight fell from her shoulders, even as she cursed herself, and the silent word *hypocrite!* drifted across her mind.

'But I've put in the all the applications and we'll be married as soon as we can, and the way things are going, the war will be over by then and Alsace will be German.'

'What! Really? You said…'

'I said we would all fight to the death, so that Germany will at least go down with honour, and not in cowardice, fleeing from the enemy with our tail between our legs. I have to admit, it didn't look good, the last time we met. I really didn't think I'd survive the next phase of the war. That's why I wanted to marry so early but now…'

There was a long pause; Sibyl realised she was holding her breath and had to make a conscious effort to relax, to breathe, to sound intrigued and not anxious.

'Go on! Don't keep me in suspense!'

He laughed, and filled her glass. 'We must drink to this!' he exclaimed. 'Marlene! I have been withdrawn from field duty! As I've been the Commandant of High Alsace for the last three years, there's no-one who knows this area better than me. So I am to stay in Colmar and work with the generals on strategy. A desk job! I'll be safe! And I know I said I want to regain my own honour and die fighting, but I don't. It may be selfish, and personal, but I want you. I want a home with you, and if a safe desk job is the price I have to pay in order to survive these terrible times and be with you – I will happily pay that price. My honour will be vicarious, through the German army, which will be victorious in this one small way: my dear, we are going to win Alsace! With absolute certainty! Honour will be restored!'

She tried to keep her voice steady.

'How – how do you know that?'

'Just a minute.' He stood up, left his full glass on the table, edged out of the cubicle, and strode towards the door leading to the toilets, beside the bar. Sibyl was left to stew in suspense. She sipped at her wine, topped up her glass. But von Haagen did not take long. A minute later he was sliding back into his seat at the back of the cubicle, reaching for her to edge nearer. She did. He lowered his voice.

'The coast is clear. Now, what I am about to tell you is absolutely confidential. I shouldn't even be telling you – but you know that and

I know your lips will be sealed tightly. Not even your uncle must know this. But,first of all, there is news that General Eisenhower plans to remove the Amis out of Strasbourg. Strasbourg will be left without a strong defence; the French armies cannot hold her. We will take her back. Eisenhower isn't interested in Alsace. He wants his best men to fight in the Ardennes, a battle which is still raging with our army winning. This is Hitler's last stand, my darling, and it is a furious, powerful one.

'But that is not all, and not the main thing. New Year's Day 1945: that is the day of the German resurrection in Alsace. We have planned a tremendous attack, midnight on the 31st December. It's a secret attack. The Amis will be totally unprepared; they have their weakest men, greenhorns who've never fought a real battle. Much less in a cruel French winter. Whereas Hitler has sent his strongest troops, his best generals, to win this last stand. This will be the most significant battle of the entire war – guaranteed. I won't go into details, I'm sure they'd bore you. But I want to put hope in your heart. We will win. I promise. We will be together. Alsace will be German, we can make it our home. I shall retire from the army; as I told you before, I'd like to get into wine-growing, a nice safe peacetime occupation, and lucrative as well. I'm sure there are one or two vineyards whose owners will decide to cut their losses and move to France rather than stay in Alsace once it is finally German in a time of peace. Because yes, peace is coming; but in that peace the question of Alsace will be settled once and for all, as German.'

'You are sure about that?'

'Positive. There will be fierce fighting, and the war will come to Colmar – don't worry, you'll be safe. Neither Germany nor France wants to see Colmar destroyed; it won't be bombed, and civilians will be safe. So it's not over yet. But Germany is on a path of victory. New Year marks a new beginning. Operation Northwind will change everything. And that is the reason, my dear, why you see me so confident today. I am fired by hope and courage, a knowledge of victory to come, and peace, and a lifetime with you as my wife, as my life. And now, my dear, let us drink to that!'

He raised his glass. So did she, smiling, her eyes locked with his. The glasses chinked; they drank to their future.

And all the while Sibyl's only thought was, *how do I get hold of Jacques? Of Margaux? How do I pass this on?*

# Chapter Forty-Seven

Fired by hope and courage, indeed he was. A second glass, and a third, loosened his tongue yet more; von Haagen grew sentimental, garrulous. He took her hand, stroked the back of it with his thumb, touched her face, tucked a stray curl of hers behind her ear, and Sibyl grew more and more silent, punctuating his talk only occasionally with a non-committal grunt or appeasing nod. In the end he noticed.

'You're so quiet, darling. Aren't you just as excited as I am? It's almost over, I promise you. We can start to look forward now, plan our lives – oh, darling, what's the matter?'

For Sibyl had pulled her hand from his, tucked it under her armpit, and even through his excitement he noticed her agitation.

'My dear, what's the matter? You're upset? Have I said something wrong?'

'No – yes – I don't know. I just know it's not going to be that easy. What if – what if…'

'What if – what?'

'You shouldn't be telling me these things, Wolf. Really not. They're highly confidential. Even I know that and I'm not in the military. They're top secret!'

It was a risk, reprimanding him. But a risk she had to take. The more innocent and genuine she appeared to him, the more secrets he would share. And she had to warn him: that the Gestapo might suspect them both.

'Yes, but—'

'But nothing! It's just wrong! You could get me into trouble! I've already had to lie about it and I'm not good at lying.'

'Lie about it? How? When? – Oh!'

Realisation struck him and he struck his own forehead.

'Don't tell me they've come to question you?'

'Yes, they have! Of course they have and I had to lie, tell them you had told me nothing, and it scared me to death! I could swear they knew I was lying. They said they'd be back! You could get me into deep trouble by telling me these things!'

'Oh my dear. I'm sorry, so sorry. I should have realised – warned you somehow. I didn't think – you see, I thought I'd convinced them.'

'Convinced them of what?'

'Well, of course, after a major assassination attempt like that, everyone is under suspicion, even the highest officers, even the generals. So we were all subject to visits by the Gestapo – and some quite rigorous questioning. The Gestapo, after all, is directly answerable to Himmler, so an attempt on Himmler's life, well, of course they had to probe. There's a leak somewhere – most probably an innocent leak on the part of the soldier. Some officer telling his girlfriend too much, the girl being in the pay of the enemy. But, my dear, it's not you they're after. I could prove your innocence. The main thing is that it was I who approached you, not the other way around. You can't imagine the way some of these French hussies flirt with German officers; you can't blame them, perhaps, because all they want are a few favours, food, money, support. Many officers have their girls, their whores. And I assure you, not all of them have sealed lips! A man needs to let off steam after hours, and if he's had a drink or two – well. So I'm sure that's what happened. An officer leaked, the girl told the enemy. That's the general conclusion. It could be anyone.

'But not you, my dear. You're my fiancée, not some loose girl from the streets! I made sure that you are cleared of suspicion – of course I stood up for you! You're on our side – you even look innocent, which is more than I can say of some of those floozies. But they had a job to do. They had to interview you, my dear;

it's just German efficiency. You don't really think you're a suspect? Why, that would be laughable!'

'I *am* a suspect, Wolf – they made it quite clear, and it's frightening! Everyone knows what the Gestapo does to people they don't like!'

'No, darling. Please don't be scared. It was just a routine interview. They spoke to *all* the officers, *all* the girls. The leak could be anyone, but nobody really suspects you. Rest assured, that was your first and last encounter with the Gestapo. I know it can be nerve-wracking. But I will protect you.'

'They're all over the place, now. Even *Oncle* Yves was interviewed! They never used to come down this road before – now they march down twice a day. It's terrifying!'

'They have to be alert, my dear. That was a serious attack and could have had dire consequences. Of course, they have increased security. But I always say – the innocent have nothing to fear. Come, now, give me back your hand.'

She laid her hand on the table; he took it, squeezed it, stroked it.

'See. Don't be afraid, my darling. You can rely on me, lean on me for strength. All will be well. They'll find the leak. In fact, I think I know who it is; I passed on the word.'

'You do? Who?'

'Oh, what does it matter? One of the loose girls. She's well known among the officers. She made a play for every one of us, and some of us succumbed over the years. She's quite pretty you know, and obviously the men aren't saints. They have their needs. Her name is Grete. I'm convinced she got one of the officers to talk. Anyway, I passed her name on to the Gestapo. I'm sure I'm not the only one who mentioned her name; they'll probably arrest her before long.'

'Really! And then?'

'They'll get her to talk. Trust me, the Gestapo have their methods. No-one can resist them, much less a cheap little French slut.'

'But – what if it's not her? What if it's someone else?'

SHARON MAAS

He reached out, stroked her face.

'Darling – it's nothing to worry your little head about. Someone did it, and the Gestapo will find out who and eliminate them. Don't fret about it. The main thing is, you're above suspicion. It's over. They will probably find the leak, patch it up, and that's that.'

And so, as if Sibyl didn't already have enough to agonise about, the innocent girl Grete joined the legion of her cares, and her responsibilities. Another sleepless night lay ahead.

# Chapter Forty-Eight

It was sometime in the middle of the night. She lay awake, going over the conversation again and again, agonising over the possible outcome and her own inability to raise the alarm; any contact with Margaux or Jacques now would be almost suicidal. The seconds ticked by silently. Her windowless room was pitch black, and so silent she could hear her own breathing in the darkness. A vague creak seemed to come from far away. Immediately she was on the alert, holding her breath, waiting for a repeat that did not come. The dark silence seemed everlasting, and thick, and now she could hear the rapid beating of her own heart, but nothing else, and yet… she sensed a presence. She tensed. Her hand slipped under her pillow, where a knife lay hidden. And then, another almost imperceptible creak, a sliver of greyness where the door should be, and then, as she noise-lessly moved into sitting position, knife at the ready, prepared to pounce, a whisper:

'Sibi!'

'Jacques!' she gasped, and in a trice, as smoothly and silently as a cat, he had pounced across the narrow space between door and bed and was beside her, in her arms, the knife's clatter as it hit the floor so loud they both drew in their breath and held still before they remembered that there was only *Oncle* Yves in the house beside them, and he was not the enemy, and they breathed again.

'Ssshh! Come here, you!' whispered Sibyl. 'What are you doing here? How did you get in?' She pulled him down to the bed. They huddled together, leaning against the back wall, the eiderdown pulled up around their shoulders.

'I have a back-door key now. *Oncle* Yves gave me one. So I can surprise you in the night!'

'It's dangerous for you to have a key!' she admonished.

'I knew you'd say that so I didn't tell you. It's for emergencies. Like now.'

'What emergency – Oh! Jacques! I have such things to tell you!'

'And so do I – that's why I came. Sibi – you won't believe it. Alsace, my beautiful Alsace, is a warzone. In ruins. It's beyond belief. I've managed to get around in spite of the snow and what I've seen, what I've heard, Sibi – it is – just devastating. I can't even begin to describe it.'

'Tell me, Jacques, tell me. Get it out. Share it with me.'

'I went with one of the generals to some of the outlying villages, Sibi. A reconnaissance tour. I can't even begin to tell you what we saw. Devastation, pure devastation. Not even twenty miles from Colmar. Kientzheim! Ammerschwihr! Ruins! The countryside, the villages: devastated. Everywhere, shouting and stifled screams and the guns of the Boche, the steady staccato snapping of machine guns. The Boche are hidden away in buildings and they fire from windows and crevices and doorways and church steeples. Tanks rumbling and churning through cobbled village streets lined by those charming half-timbered houses.

'Abandoned tanks, black hulks among the charred ruins of homes. In the streets, white phosphorous shells bursting every-where. Yellow flames pouring from windows and open doorways. Buildings belching smoke because there's nothing more to burn in them. Abandoned villages like ghost towns; snipers lurking in shadows, creeping through ruins and rubble. Mortars exploding without warning, scattering rubble everywhere. Every now and then, wherever there's life, a voice screaming "Medic! Medic!" We picked up quite a few wounded, took them to a field hospital.

'But the countryside, Sibi, the surrounding fields, once covered in a peaceful mantle of beautiful white snow; now, all gone, the snow a churned-up mess, pockmarked by craters, stained black from soot and scarlet from blood.

'Jebsheim! Sibi, Jebsheim is a slaughterhouse. Indescribable. *Incroyable.* Dead bodies abandoned, lying everywhere. You have to step over them, step *on* them, even. I can't even…'

By now he was sobbing and she wept with him. They clung together, weeping for the pillage of Alsace. And then Jacques pulled away and dried her tears with a corner of a sheet and his own tears, and continued, his voice now collected, yet breathlessly, sentences running into each other.

'Eisenhower wants to withdraw from Strasbourg, from Alsace-Lorraine – he needs his troops for the Ardennes; he's in a hurry to enter Germany and move eastwards. Alsace is not a priority for him and that would mean we – the French army, the Free French – cannot keep off the Germans. General Devers is against it – he wants to stay in Alsace, hold on to Strasbourg but he and Eisenhower are at loggerheads and guess who has the last word. It's a disaster! I came to warn you. Colmar itself might be next. I want you to leave, with me, tonight.'

At this point Sibyl interrupted.

'You mean, give up? No, Jacques, no! Never! I'm staying here. I need to be here. We can win this yet. I only wish – I could do something. I'm a nurse. I should be out there in a field hospital, helping – I wish I could! That's my real job. But – listen. I can still be of use exactly where I am. I know so much, so much more; I'm so glad you came. There's so much to tell you…I know it looks bad but maybe, just maybe…'

She told him then about the surprise attack planned for the New Year.

'You must pass this on! The Allies can still win, if they know of the attack!'

Jacques' reaction was disappointing.

'And he really didn't tell you exactly where they were going to attack? That's the most important thing, Sibi. We have to know that. You should have wriggled that out of him.'

'How could I, without appearing too interested? Already they're all on the alert for a spy, already they all think it's a woman. He doesn't suspect me at all, but if I ask too many pertinent questions…'

'Ok. I understand. But you must keep talking to him, keep him talking. Find out as much as you can. I can't come back to Colmar for a while. And for you, the connection to Margaux – well, it's no more. Ribeauvillé is safe now, outside the Colmar Pocket, in French hands. Elena is still there but you can't contact her. She is getting news through me, through the Free French…'

He told her of a net of couriers, starting with Madame Guyon, the cleaner. 'I now work with the *Bureau central de renseignements et d'action.* I'm more of a scout than a courier due to my local knowledge.'

'So – you're not actually fighting any more?'

'No. I'm helping with strategy.'

'Just like von Haagen, for the enemy. Oh, the irony!'

'And you are not falling in love with him? He's very handsome.'

'How do you know that? Who told you?'

'Nobody told me. I saw him when we captured those officers at Strasbourg…'

'You? *You* took him prisoner?'

'Well, not me alone. I said *we.* I was sorry we had to let him go. I'd have loved to keep him – pack him off to a prisoner of war camp…but orders are orders, and, there was you, waiting. The sacrifices we have to make sometimes!'

'I didn't know that.'

'You could have guessed. He was more important to us free, because of you. But now, I don't know. He can offer you so much more than I can.'

'Jealousy doesn't become you, Jacques!'

'Still it is not easy.'

'It's not easy for me, either. It'd be easier if he was a bad man, evil. I could handle that. But he isn't.'

'So you like him, a little? You know that *like* can turn to love?'

'It won't, in this case.'

He sighed. 'I will try not to feel jealous. I know it is just your job. I know it is for France. I know you must do – whatever you must. But still…I am only a man. Only human.'

'I love *you,* Jacques. Remember that. That's all that matters.'

'I can't offer you much, after the war; I won't be a valiant *maquisard* anymore, a hero; just a humble winegrower in the employ of Château Laroche-Gauthier.'

'The best winegrower in Alsace. A winegrower who loves me. Sounds good to me.'

He nuzzled her neck. 'And you really prefer French love to German?'

'Any day or night. But it's so cold…my cheeks are freezing! Come, snuggle down under the blankets.' She pulled him down; they lay beneath the blanket, clasped together, sharing their warmth, their despair, their hope.

'What will we do, when it's over? Where will you go, chérie? Back to England?'

'Alsace is my hope. I belong here, whatever happens. But…'

She told him then of von Haagen; his proposal, his plan.


Later, she said, 'Jacques – listen. There's another thing I'm worried sick about. There's a woman, Grete. They might arrest her: von Haagen says she's the main suspect for the Himmler bomb attack. I want to help her, hide her somehow, but Colmar is swarming with Gestapo. I've been lying here trying to figure out ways to rescue her – she's got a child!'

'Do you know where she lives?'

'She told me once. I know the street, not the house number.'

'*D'accord.* I'll find out somehow. We'll figure out a way.'

She woke late the next morning. Jacques was gone.

Two days later, von Haagen moved in to the violin-maker's house. There had been activity around the property the day before; tradesmen came, a plumber, a carpenter. Germans, it seemed, men who had been imported from Germany to help settle the Alsace. The house had been made habitable for the winter; coal delivered for the stove, electric current reconnected, an armchair, a carpet, even. Von Haagen invited her over to inspect and approve.

He led her into the tiny salon, cosy now with the floorboards carpeted and the little black cast-iron stove in the corner giving off a pleasant warmth that seemed to sink right through to the bones. A small glass window in the front door of the stove revealed golden dancing flames. Beside the stove, a basket of coal lay ready to keep the fire burning. It was the warmest Sibyl had been for weeks. She stood before the stove, palms held out, as if to soak in the warmth, to store it for later.

Von Haagen put down his briefcase beside the armchair and came to stand beside her. He placed an arm around her waist.

'Think of this as your home, too, my dear. Though we shall not be living together, I want, I hope…I don't expect you to cook for me – I'll be eating with the other officers at the Rote Löwe. But for you to be here, when I come home at night…for you to be waiting for me…the fire lit, your arms…'

'Wolf, we need to talk about that. Everything's moving so quickly, and since we won't be married yet…'

'I know what you're worried about. But, you know, from the start I told you that my intentions are honourable and I promise again not to compromise you in any way; I promise to wait. But oh, my dear…if you knew. If you only knew.'

Gently he turned her around so that she faced him. He clasped her even closer, nuzzled her hair, her neck. A shudder went through him; a shivering of his whole body, but it was not from cold. It couldn't be; not with that stove before them.

'Come,' he said, and led her to the armchair. He sat down, pulled her to his lap. Held her close. She let him, but did nothing to encourage him. He moaned.

'At last – we are alone together, completely alone. And I – oh, my darling. You cannot imagine, what it is like; for a man to spend his days surrounded only by soldiers and war and plans for more war and violence, by roughness and primitive maleness and – and then to come home to this. To you. You are so soft. So feminine. You smell so good. Just to touch you. Your hair. Your cheeks. Your lips.'

He kissed her, gently, just a touch of the lips, and pulled away.

'You bring healing to me. All the ragged edges of my soul, they fall away when I am with you. How I long – oh, how I long…'

And then, abruptly, he pushed her away. 'I cannot – I must not. I am so sorry, my dear. I must ask you to leave. Please, leave. Now.'

'Wolf – it's all right. You don't need to…'

'Oh Marlene, my love – if only – but until we are wed I must learn to control myself. Forgive me. I will try harder next time. But this place, and you – it is like a foretaste of home, of all I yearn for. This blasted war! But I will lose my mind if you stay longer. So – go, please go. Don't worry about me. I can take care of myself.'

She nodded and stood up. He too stood up. They walked to the door, silently. He reached for her coat, helped her into it.

'I'll see you tomorrow, if I may,' he said. 'I promise to be better behaved.'

She nodded, stood on her toes, reached up her face to kiss him on the cheek. He turned his face away, so that she kissed air, and reached up to unhook his own greatcoat from the coatstand. He said nothing, but a vein in his neck throbbed, as if under great tension, and the smile he gave her was strained.

'Are you going out? I though you were finished for the day?'

'I – I just have to talk to someone; a – a colleague.'

'I see.'

They walked down the stairs together; she took hold of his hand, but it was stiff and unresponsive, and the moment they walked out of the door he retrieved it to pull on his gloves. Sibyl shoved her own hands into her coat pocket. It was a thankfully very warm sheepskin which *Oncle* Yves had rescued from the attic, with a woolly hood.

'Well, goodbye then,' she said; but he barely nodded and walked away in the opposite direction. She stood and stared after him; why had he not walked her home? Then she shrugged and walked the few paces home herself.

*Oncle* Yves noticed at once that something was wrong. 'Back already? And why the frown? Lover's tiff?'

'I don't know; I mean, I do know but…' She told him what had happened. Failing a best female friend, or a sister nearby, he had become something of a confidant over the last few weeks. She desperately missed Margaux and Elena; but here she was, stuck in the Colmar pocket, war raging all over the countryside. Cynical as *Oncle* Yves was and mocking of her relationship, he nevertheless sometimes offered little jewels of wisdom, titbits of advice which she took to heart and acted on.

Now, he roared with laughter. 'And you really don't know where he rushed off to?'

'No – it was so sudden!'

'You must be the most naïve female this side of the English Channel! Any Frenchwoman would have known his problem immediately; and would have prevented it. You women are such prudes, too ladylike for your own good! You should have helped him out.'

'What do you mean?'

He told her. She blushed.

'You really don't know much about men, do you?'

'Of course I know about men! I worked for years in a men's ward; they told me all their problems!'

'Ah, but this is different. You did not have to seduce your patients. Didn't they tell you all this in agent training? What to do in such a situation? How to seduce a man?'

'He doesn't *need* seducing! He's doing his best not to seduce *me* and I don't know how to handle it! He's put me on a pedestal – and anyway, I can't, *Oncle* Yves. I just can't. Jacques…'

*Oncle* Yves snorted. 'Forget Jacques for the time being. This is work. It's what they employed you for. You're doing a job. You'll do a much better job, trust me, if you let go of this prudish nonsense. You can't take him this far and leave him hanging. Do what you have to do, *ma chère,* give him what he needs, and he'll rain you with diamonds – of the sort you need to win the war. It's easy.'

'Maybe for you. Goodnight, *Oncle* Yves.' She wrapped her coat tightly around her and walked out the door into the freezing stairwell.

'Think about what I said!' he roared after her.

# Chapter Forty-Nine

The cold was so bitter it cut through to the bone, chilled the blood. There was no relief, but for the little cast-iron stove in *Oncle* Yves' workshop. During the day he left the connecting door open so that a little warmth came through to the shop but it wasn't enough; she wore her coat and cap and even gloves while sitting behind the counter.

The Germans had arranged for coal to be delivered from the 'coal pot' of Essen in northern Germany but it was strictly rationed and it was going far too quickly; and it wasn't even January yet. The pile of coal nuggets in the coal-room down in the cellar was diminishing at an alarming rate. If the temperature dropped further, and if the winter dragged on, *Oncle* Yves said, they would have to axe the wooden furniture up in the attic. Unless the Germans brought in more coal. Unless the war ended suddenly, and it rained coal nuggets. But no-one believed it.

Outside, *Gerechtigkeitsgasse* was a white alleyway, half a metre deep in snow, with narrow channels on both sides where residents had dug pathways of access to the main streets, and sprinkled them with ash to prevent slipping. Each house was required to have cleared their own space by seven each morning, and this job fell to Sibyl, not only for the cobbler's shop but for her second home, the violin-maker's. It was the worst part of the day.

But, she reminded herself, she still had the better part. The soldiers out there fighting for their lives, for the life of France – they were living a hell. Some of them, she learned, were from Africa; they had never even seen snow before, had never had to cope with a European winter. What must they be going through? Rumours and reports of the fighting trickled through the grapevine. Alsace, the plains and forests and fields, had turned into a slaughterhouse. Dead bodies lay buried in snow, frozen and discarded. French bodies, German bodies, American bodies. They lay abandoned and more snow fell and more bodies. Alsace ran with blood.

Except for the vineyards.

Sibyl had another source of warmth: the second home she shared with von Haagen. Every evening at seven she went over to the violin-maker's house. She fetched coal from the cellar –no rationing here; von Haagen's coal would never run out – and got the fire going and soon the little parlour glowed with warmth, and she would snuggle into the armchair and draw it near to the stove and cuddle with a book, and wait for him.

She found herself looking forward to the evenings. Sometimes he came, sometimes he didn't. When he came it was somehow different, since that last evening when she had sat on his lap.

He had had a second armchair delivered, and now they sat apart, each in their own chair; von Haagen carefully steering the conversation into safe topics such as literature and music; she trying to find an opening, a crack of intimacy, in which she could apply *Oncle* Yves' advice. But no such crack appeared. Von Haagen had reverted into a stiff, formal, courteous version of himself; he no longer spoke of marriage, he no longer bared his soul to her. It was worrying.

One day he brought a radio. Radios, of course, were forbidden for Alsatians and since that one day after the fall of Strasbourg, Sibyl had never listened again. But now: here was a radio. When she was alone she listened, and occasionally managed to tune into the BBC. How different those reports were to the heavily censored ones delivered by Goebbels' propaganda machine! Whenever she heard von Haagen's step on the wooden stairs she quickly changed

channel. She would jump up and open the door and welcome him
with open arms, leading him into the comforting warmth of the
little room where she would sit him down in his armchair, pour
him a glass of wine, welcome him with cheery chatter.

But, she found, she was no good at the art of seduction. Von
Haagen continued to hold her at arms' length, even push her away
if she came too close, his demeanour controlled, reserved.

Shortly before ten he would get up and fiddle with the radio
controls. He would find Radio Belgrade, and at ten when 'Lili
Marlene' came on he would sink into his armchair and weep. She
would follow him there and wipe his tears away; but always he
pushed her away.

'I must face this alone!' he told her. 'Just be near me; it is all I ask.'

Christmas was fast approaching; there was going to be Christmas
party at the Rote Löwe the night before Christmas Eve. She dreaded
it – a room full of drunken German officers! And it was every bit
as dreadful as she had anticipated.

Then it was Christmas Eve. She had made him a present; knitted
him a long, multicoloured scarf out of a myriad bits and pieces of
wool she had found in the attic or manged to buy from one of the
market stalls. It had turned out quite pretty, finally; simple but the
colours somehow evoked joy in the bleakness of wartime winter.

'One day you will wear it, when all this is over,' she said, and
hated herself as she knew he never would – but she could not
think that far. This was Marlene speaking, because Marlene was
all she could be; there was no future except the one he planned,
and she, as Marlene, had to live for that future. The other half of
her being: it was submerged deep within her. She could not allow
the two selves to mix.

He had brought her a wrapped present, a large box, tied up
even with a bow.

'This is for you, my love. But hopefully we can share it for now.'

She cried out in delight, clapped her hands. 'What is it? What is it, Wolf?'

'Open it and see!'

She peeled away the paper – carefully, for though the war might indeed be near the end, the 'waste nothing' creed was deeply ingrained in her mind. So she folded every scrap of paper, rolled up the ribbon until, finally, a box, more a kind of a suitcase, lay exposed, with a picture on it, and writing. She actually screamed in glee.

'Telefunken', it said on the box. Beneath that was a small picture of a gramophone. A gramophone in a wooden box styled as a small suitcase.

'Oh Wolf, Wolf, Wolf, I can't believe it! Oh, this is too good to be true!' She flung her arms around him. His smile was shy, pleased at her joy.

'There's more,' he said, and produced a second, much smaller parcel. When she unpacked that she found it was a pile of records.

'I can't believe it! This is just – too good to be true!'

'Well, it's true,' he said. 'The records – well, it's some classical music, Beethoven, Mozart – but also some popular tunes from pre-war Berlin. *The Threepenny Opera*, of course. But – and you must keep this a secret – even some American records. And French – I thought you'd like that! Edith Piaf. I used to listen to all this before we were at war and I kept them. This is my own personal collection. My parents sent it.'

'I can't believe you like this sort of music. I though you only listened to Bach and Brahms!'

He chuckled 'Oh, that nonsense! And the Rilke poems… see, I was under the impression that a man has to impress a woman. With his refined culture. Especially a chic Parisian woman.'

'It had the opposite effect. I thought you were a pretentious jackass. You were obnoxious, Wolf.'

He had the grace to blush. 'I suppose we men know very little about women, and what makes them tick. We don't understand you.'

'That's true. We can be very complicated. Even some women don't understand themselves. I for one – sometimes I think I know nothing at all about myself. I…'

She stopped speaking abruptly.

'What were you going to say?'

'Nothing. Just that I'm very, very moved. Thank you, Wolf.'

She touched his arm. Again, that almost shy smile.

'Let's try it out, shall we? You choose a record.'

'No, you.'

He set the gramophone on the table, connected the cable to the mains, searched through the records until he found the one he was looking for.

'Hitler would say this is *verboten,'* he said. 'But you know what? Screw Hitler.'

He placed the record on the turntable and turned the gramophone on. Carefully, he raised the needle arm and placed it on the record. It began to spin.

'Do you know this one?' he said. The first bars of something very familiar indeed filled the room. Her heart gave a little leap as a wave of nostalgia broke over her. It was 'Cheek to Cheek', from the film *Top Hat* – she had seen it in the cinema with Elena, swooned to it, longed to be in love, to dance to it, a giddy teenager.

'Oh Wolf! It's the best present I've ever had! Come – let's dance?'

She jumped up and pulled him to his feet.

'Really?' He seemed reluctant, but it was a hopeful reluctance, the reluctance of a man who can't believe his luck, for whom Christmas has come early.

'Yes! Really!'

He lost no time. His arms closed around her; they danced, pressed together, their bodies closer than ever before. He was almost a head taller than her; his cheek rested against her forehead.

Emotion swelled within her; evoked by the song, the dance, his closeness, and, despite herself, by him.

'I love you,' he whispered. 'I love you so much.'

'Hmmmm,' she murmured.

He pulled a little way apart from her, looked down at her.

'Marlene – are you beginning to have feelings for me? Just a little bit? I know I promised you that love would grow, once we are married – but has it begun to sprout, just a little?'

'Just a little,' she whispered. The odd thing was – it was true.

They danced some more, to other songs, von Haagen carefully selecting each record and placing it on the turntable.

Later, he sat down on the armchair and pulled her down to sit, not on his lap as before, but on the armrest. But his arm was around her, and hers around him, and she leaned into him.

'That's such a lovely present,' she said. 'My silly scarf – it seems so inadequate.'

'I love your scarf. I will wear it every day once I am in civilian clothes.'

'What, even in summer!' she laughed.

'Even in summer.'

He was silent then, as if contemplating something. Then he said, hesitantly:

'Marlene, my darling, I was wondering if I could – just this once – because it is Christmas…'

'What would you like, my dear?'

'Just to touch your breast – without clothes – feel your skin?'

'Oh, you dear, dear man!'

She immediately stood up, removed first her cardigan, then unbuttoned her blouse and removed it, then her brassiere. Only then did she down again; this time on his lap. He gasped; his hand hovered above the swell of her breast, hesitant.

'Go on!' she said, and placed her hand on his, gently pressing it down. And then he cupped her breast, fondled it, gently. She leant in, kissed him. On the lips.

'You may,' she whispered. 'You may. *Komm zu mir.* Come to me.'

They were silent for several minutes. Then he gently pushed her off his lap, stood up, reached out his hand for hers. She gave him it. He pulled her to her feet. They looked into each other's eyes, his gaze questioning, hers affirming. She nodded slightly. He led her into the bedroom.

# Chapter Fifty

The war stopped for Christmas Day. Sibyl spent the day with von Haagen, wrapped in his arms, cuddled in his bed, enclosed in a membrane of his love, a love so tender she imagined herself in heaven, shielded from the horrors of war, enfolded in the warmth given off by the little stove and by the fluffy eiderdowns and bare skin, enclosed in a cocoon of gladness and protected from the bitterness of winter and war outside the walls of crooked little home.

Now and again von Haagen left the building, sallied out into the cold whiteness of winter and returned with food prepared and packed by the Rote Löwe, offering it to her as to a goddess; which, in his eyes, she was, as he told her again and again, for surely such healing was divine?

He suggested attending a carol service at church that afternoon. She declined; fearful of the guilt such an event might expose. Instead, they listened to German carols on the radio: *O Du Fröhliche*, and *Alle Jahre Wieder*, and, of course, *Stille Nacht, Heilige Nacht*. They all imparted a certain unique sense of Christmas, of peace, and healing, and nostalgia; and strangely, for her no guilt, but only warmth and closeness. He spoke of Christmasses to come, when they'd have their own home, perhaps here in Alsace, surrounded by their future children. And even then she felt not guilt, but peace. As if that impossible dream could ever come true.

She finally returned home on Boxing Day, when war resumed and von Haagen returned to work. She had hoped to avoid *Oncle* Yves; but there he was, coming up the stairs from the cellar, a bucket of coal in his hands.

'Well,' he said, 'you look like the cat who got the cream!'

'Yes, well…' she muttered, and ran up the stairs to her room. Crawling into bed, she wrapped the duvet around her shivering body, and curled into a foetal position. She could not face *Oncle* Yves' prying questions today; she had to think. And as the glitter from the last two nights and the day between them fell away from her she began to make logical sense of her new status.

The hours stolen from war and mayhem, the hours given to love, had thrown her completely off her previously so steady feet. And yet, now, regarding it all in the clear light of day and without the beguiling distraction of von Haagen's presence, von Haagen's hands, his lips, his body next to hers, his voice, his loving words, she found there was no regret, no sense of shame or guilt. But emotions tumbled within her, and she struggled to understand.

As the morning slipped by the inner turbulence receded and an inkling of comprehension settled within her. What she had done in that stolen interlude, the persona she had been: that was Marlene Schuster, von Haagen's Frau. The word *Frau* in German has a double meaning; woman as well as wife. She was both. His woman and, as Marlene, his future wife.

He had said so himself. 'You are my *Frau*. I don't need papers to prove it, to justify it. *Meine Frau.*'

It was an identity she had, as Marlene, embraced, agreed to embrace. She had fallen naturally into it without planning to, without scheduling it, without discussing it with Acrobat. And now it had happened there was no going back. It was up to her to live that role completely, as thoroughly as if she really *was* Marlene Schuster, an innocent citizen of Colmar wooed and won by von Haagen, a woman who had agreed to become his wife. She was playing a part and playing it thoroughly. It was just a role. She told herself that again and again. Just a role. And yet: a role she embodied so completely, so thoroughly, it was impossible to tell where the role began and she, the part of her that was not Marlene Schuster, ended.

Because Jeanne Dauguet was also a role. Jeanne was an SOE agent, sent to France to help defeat the Boche, to win the war. Jeanne Dauguet was constantly on the alert; bland, watchful, competent. Jeanne was a skilled operator who considered options and acted accordingly. Jeanne Dauguet had taken the decision to let herself be usurped by Marlene Schuster. Jeanne Dauguet had gone into hiding; but she was still there, lurking in the background, awaiting her chance. She was an identity, no more than a skin to slip into and out of at will. A sly, ugly identity, one that would betray Marlene in a trice, and von Haagen. Stab them both in the back.

And somewhere, far, far away, hidden in the depths of her subconscious, lay a third identity, bearing the label Sibyl Lake. Sibyl, over the last few months, had only seldom put in an appearance; basically, only Jacques could summon her, she came alive only for Jacques. But Sibyl, and Jacques, were right now so far away as to be nothing but a vague memory.

Three identities, three roles. As the hours slipped by even Marlene, she who had surged to the forefront and taken over Christmas in a whirlwind of delight, receded. Not one of her three roles, she realised, had any real substance; not one of them was concrete not even Sibyl, her original identity. Each identity was really just a collection of attributes: characteristics, personal traits, flaws, virtues. Over the last few months she had learnt to slip in and out of each of them at ease; until Marlene had taken over.

Did that make her, somehow, a hypocrite, a fraud, a *Tartuffe*, as in Moliere's play? A despicable person who actually should be ashamed to show her face in a church? Von Haagen, if he knew the truth, would certainly think so. But he did not know. Only she knew the deeper truth: behind and beyond all of these single and separate identities, yes, even including the original one of Sibyl Lake, was a true one, a single one, a deeper one; an identity that could truly care and love, could feel love and revulsion and even hate – hate for the likes of Hitler and Himmler – an identity that was separate from each of those roles and yet gave substance to each of them.

Right now, this real *self* carried the role and wore the label of Marlene Schuster. But behind that role and that label was this: a real and throbbing heart. A heart filled with genuine love, genuine caring; and now it was all directed at this so-called enemy, this man she had been sent to deceive and, one day, destroy. She had learned to meet him in a place of love; and love, if pure, if unselfish, is never deceitful. That was the truth.

And then, from somewhere deep inside her, a voice rose up, stern, loud, dismissing all other voices: *Shut up. Stop overthinking it all. Stop rationalising it all, stop analysing it all. You, Marlene, are in love. Give yourself up to that; live it as best you may and cross each bridge as you come to it.*

She rose from her bed, washed and dressed herself, stomped out the back door into the courtyard and back to the violin-maker's house. She lit the fire, made herself some food and listened to records the rest of the day and into the night, and waited for von Haagen to come home.

It was less than twenty minutes to midnight on New Year's Eve. Across the snowdrifts on the open rolling fields of Alsace, right across to the white snows of the Vosges foothills, figures clad in white crept south in stealth. It was the women who first heard the renewed rumble of war. Wary, they exchanged looks: was that American artillery, or French – or, God forbid –German? By now, after four years of annexation, their ears were keenly tuned to the differences, and fear clouded their glances. They knew; they had heard the rumours. It was time for the citizens of Alsace, once again, to hide in cellars, to pack their carts, once again to flee into the snow-covered mountains, to empty the streets of their towns and villages. The Boche was on the attack. Operation Nordwind had descended upon Alsace.

The men of General Devers' 7th army were still celebrating. Though General Patch had warned them that a German attack could be expected on New Year's Day, the GIs were confident that the war would soon be over. After all, amost all of France had been restored to France, and all that was left was that small but pesky Colmar pocket. Russia was at Berlin's door. Hitler must be frantic! Humiliating defeat would soon be his! The men laughed and celebrated the turn of the year. The American role in Europe would be that of an occupying force, restoring peace to a ravished Germany. Some of them might be sent off to Asia, to fight another day, but this chapter of war, Europe, was over. The Third Reich was in its death throes.

But then, across the snowy fields, they came: men in white, camouflaged against the snow. The German onslaught was as terrible as it was swift. Tanks rolled through charming little villages, through the ravines of the Vosges, across the plains. Guns roared, bombs exploded. Just before midnight, American guns boomed in response to frantic calls: units in the mountains had been infiltrated and surrounded, and the eerie white-clad Boche was everywhere.

On the dot of midnight, German radio sent out a personal broadcast by Hitler, who had not addressed his people since July 1944. *Germany would never surrender!* he proclaimed. It was a war unto death. Germany was on a God-given mission; this would be war without mercy. It might be the eleventh hour; but with the Almighty behind them, German triumph was assured.

Close to the German border one patrol sergeant looked down from a small hill and saw the biggest swarm of Krauts he had seen in his life; all in white, in triangle formation, with the base of the triangle heading straight for his company.

Soon the Americans were surrounded by the enemy; the GIs opened fire as the Germans charged, screaming *Happy New Year, Yankee bastards! Happy New Year, sons of bitches!*

The attackers yelled and howled as they stormed the hill, cursing and behaving like drunken maniacs; the Americans poured fire on them, and in time the yelling gave in to the agonised screams of the wounded. It was a massacre; a massacre of Germans, the snow turned pink from German blood, the ground littered with the dead and dying. It was just one of many such attacks across Alsace.

Sibyl became his *Frau*, his woman, his wife; warming his home, his bed. She provided him comfort when he came home, his spirit shattered and tattered from the living nightmare that was his daily fare, flinging his briefcase into a corner as if he could no longer bear the sight of it. The war was vicious, more vicious, perhaps, than in all the preceding years of Germany's occupation of France. The death toll mounted, on every side; Americans, Frenchmen, Germans – their bodies lay scattered and bleeding in the forests of the Vosges and the ruined villages and the plains; their blood stained the once pristine snow and made of the province a slaughterhouse. Neither side seemed to be winning; but Colmar, at the centre of its pocket, held fast. Von Haagen came home sometimes late at night, and his Frau, his Marlene, would be waiting for him, soothing his soul, healing his inner wounds.

'You are my salvation!' he said to her, and sometimes he wept. She wept too. She wept for all the blood spent, all the wounds left gaping, the pain and the torture of war. She wanted to do more than soothe a single soul, heal a single heart that bled only in metaphor. The nationality of the wounded did not matter to her; she was as prepared to nurse Germans as she was to nurse a Frenchman or an American.

'There must be a field hospital I can join, Wolf! I want to help, I want to work. I'm sitting uselessly in that cobbler shop all day, twiddling my thumbs. We have hardly any customers now. Surely there is something I can do to help? Surely the field hospitals accept volunteers, even if they are untrained? Can't you enquire for me?'

The lie, that she was untrained, slipped lightly through her lips. Marlene Schuster was untrained. Jeanne Dauguet had, it seemed, done some unskilled work in hospital and she had studied biology, after all; surely that experience could be of use in a field hospital? Von Haagen looked doubtful but promised to enquire.

The reply, when it came, was negative. He gave no explanation. She suspected he had not enquired at all; for he wanted her all for himself. If she too came home shattered and tattered, who would rescue them both? She accepted his decision with a shrug and a sigh; as Marlene Schuster would.

But every night, for just an hour, the hour when von Haagen slept deep and sound, Marlene Schuster became Jeanne Dauguet. In the silence and blackness of night Jeanne Dauguet would steal from their bed, from their room, and creep into the parlour, now already cold as the stove was dead. Jeanne Dauguet would sink to the floor in the corner where he had flung his briefcase in disgust. She would remove the latest papers, and with the help of the kitchen torch, inspect the notes von Haagen had made the day before. She would read the maps and try to make sense of them, as she had been taught in training. She would commit it all to memory. The first time she had done this she had gasped in shock: in a side pocket of the briefcase lay a Luger.

But of course von Haagen carried a gun. He was a soldier. Soldiers carried weapons. As did agents. But her own gun, a Sten, was nowhere nearby, for Marlene Schuster did not need a gun. The Sten was hidden away in Margaux's attic. There it was safe; and she was safe. As long as she was Marlene Schuster she was safe. At the end of each night's briefcase inspection Jeanne Dauguet returned to their bed and became Marlene Schuster.

Every day, for a few minutes, she also became Jeanne Dauguet when she made her notes in tiny writing on scraps of paper; and later again, when Madame Guyon came by to cook a simple midday meal for her and *Oncle* Yves, and she slipped that piece of paper into a slot in her shoe.

For the rest of her time she was Marlene Schuster, von Haagen's *Frau*. How proudly he used that word now, the word with the double meaning! *Meine Frau*. My woman, my wife. Just as she could, if she so wished, refer to him as *Mein Mann*. My man, my husband. They were no longer boyfriend and girlfriend; more than merely lovers. *Mann* and *Frau*.

And then came the night that everything changed. Leafing through the pile of papers on the floor next to the briefcase, she came across a new document. It was different from the others, which were mostly scribbled notes and sketches, maps, thumb-marked protocols of meetings. What she found was a stiff, shiny new document bearing the red official seal of a public notary, one based in Freiburg, across the Rhine. She remembered he had had to go to Freiburg a few days ago, for military reasons; he must have done this then.

On the cover page was written, in the spiky Fraktur typeface of the Third Reich, in thick black letters, the word 'Testament'. Her hand shook as she turned the page; her eyes misted over as she read the second page. Von Haagen's will was simple. He had left all his worldly possessions, including his villa in Munich, to his Frau Marlene Schuster.

That was the moment that Jeanne Dauguet died. It was a gentle death, a simple fading away into nothing, a dissolution into the entity that was Marlene Schuster. She placed all the documents back into the briefcase, clicked its lock, crept back to bed, wrapped her arms around von Haagen, and wept silently into the dawn.

Meanwhile, trouble was brewing. On January 1st General Eisenhower instructed General Devers – responsible for the defence of Alsace – to retreat. American troops were sorely needed in the Ardennes; Alsace was not worth saving, at least, not worth saving to the Americans. Hearing the news, General de Gaulle was incensed; he ordered his Defence Chief of Staff to return to

Eisenhower and 'shake him up'. De Gaulle had taken the decision to defend Alsace, with the aid of Allied forces; but, if necessary, France would defend Alsace on its own. Strasbourg, said de Gaulle, must be defended toward and against everyone; if required, house to house. If necessary, Strasbourg would become a French Stalingrad. De Gaulle gave orders to General de Lattre de Tassigy of the Free French army to assure the defence of Strasbourg, with or without the Americans. Telegrams whizzed back and forth, to US President Roosevelt, and to Winston Churchill; Roosevelt was informed that the French could not accept the withdrawal of American troops, and a copy was sent to Chuchill, with the request to support the French. Roosevelt replied that he would defer to Eisenhower on the decision. But Churchill left at once for Versailles.

On January 3rd Eisenhower, de Gaulle and Churchill gathered for a crisis meeting; Eisenhower and de Gaulle both argued their sides, while Churchill adjudicated. Eisenhower accused the French leader of too much emotion and declared his order would stand. De Gaulle's response was that the decision would rupture the Allied command and that he would withdraw the French armed forces from the Supreme Headquarters Allied Expeditionary Force. Eisenhower flew into a rage; if the French pulled out of SHAEF, he said, they would receive no further petrol, ammunition or logistical support from the Americans. De Gaulle said that if America deprived the French of war supplies he would deprive the Allies of the use of the French railway system and communication facilities. If America withdrew from Strasbourg, he said, he would give the order to a French division to barricade itself inside Strasbourg. 'Before the scandalised world, you will be obliged to go in and free it.' It was a verbal battle of one-upmanship; and to everyone's relief at this point Eisenhower gave in; he modified his orders, and instructed General Devers to hold Strasbourg firmly. As he left the meeting, Churchill remarked to Eisenhower: 'I think you've done the wise and proper thing.'

# Chapter Fifty-One

It was the following evening that Sibyl finally found the solution to her crisis of truth. It was so very simple – why hadn't she thought of it weeks ago? Now, the idea came to her as von Haagen came back early from a frustrating day on the field. They had not been able to get very far, he complained; the bloodstained snow was too thick, too strewn with bodies that there had been no passage. And Germany was losing.

'I am sick to my stomach of this war,' he said. 'I just want it over and done with. I don't care any more who wins. I don't care about honour and pride. Damn Hitler for putting us through this ordeal! The man is mad, stark raving mad.'

He had often made such utterances, and since the start of January and the launch of Operation Northwind they were becoming ever more traitorous to his own side. Now, he fiddled with the radio and found the BBC. The five pips sounded, and then the news. So different to the furious propaganda spouted by Goebbels on *Deutschlandfunk,* the rabid rants proclaiming an imminent triumph for the invincible God-ordained German troops. In calm, cut-glass English, the newsreader described the good news of Allied progress in Alsace; the Colmar Pocket would soon be cleared, he prophesised, after which the Allies would cross the Rhine and proceed into Germany. It all seemed so obvious, so predestined, so peaceful. Who would not be convinced?

And suddenly it came to her. The brilliant solution to all her problems. The easy, obvious way to win this war.

So obvious. Yes, it had been obvious for a long time but she had been blind; blinded, perhaps by her own shame, her own guilt; the knowledge of the uproar the step she must take would cause; anger on von Haagen's part, no doubt, fury even. But then she would take him in her arms, soothe him, calm his anger, explain to him, apologise, show him that she'd had no choice, really; let him know the truth of her slow but gradual and unrelenting growth into love.

She must turn him. Recruit him. She must confess.

Then *he* would be the spy, not her.

It was so very simple.

Turning a German: surely the highest service a British agent could provide! Then there would be no more subterfuge. No more lies. No more sneaking around in the dark. Nothing more behind his back. Everything would be out in the open because now he would be working for her, delivering German secrets, German plans into her hands. The war would be over in a matter of days. Surely.

All she had to do was confess.

But how would he take it? How would he react to the knowledge that she had tricked him, led him on in the beginning, practically made a fool of him? That was the part that worried her. She left him listening to the BBC and kneeled before the stove while considering the best way to break her confession. It had to be done subtly, wisely, taking his feelings, his reactions, his pride into consideration and choosing her words carefully. She would need to guide him into understanding, give him something to hope for, live for. She rattled the grid, so that ash fell into the container tray below. It was quite full, needed emptying. She removed it from the stove, swept up the ashes that had fallen to the floor tiles surrounding the stove, added them to the tray and stood up.

'I'm just going down to the cellar to empty this and get some more coal,' she said as she passed him.

'Don't bother – it's so dark down there. I'll do it in a minute – this is interesting,' he said.

'It's all right, I can do it.' She walked past him with the tray, out the door and into the cold stairwell. She switched on the light and made her way down into the cellar. There, she emptied the ash tray and filled a bucket with coal nuggets, made her way back upstairs. She replaced the tray in the stove and poured more coal onto the glowing embers.

The BBC report was over. Von Haagen stood up, walked to the table and poured them both a glass of gewürztraminer. He set the glasses down on the side table beside the bigger armchair.

'I got some ham today,' he said, walking towards the kitchen. He returned with a plate on which was a sizeable side of ham, and a knife. 'Sorry, no bread available. But I did find some crackers. They'll do.' He placed the plate on the table next to the wine.

'Time to get cozy,' he said, and walked over to the gramophone. He lifted his briefcase from the floor to the dining table, rummaged in it and removed an item. His back was to Sibyl; she could not see what it was.

'What have you got there?'

'A surprise,' he said. He waved a square of cardboard at her; the jacket of a record. He removed the record from its jacket and put it on the turntable. Soon deep crooning, almost guttural and deeply sensual tones filled the room: 'Lili Marlene'. Sibyl closed the stove door and looked up in astonishment.

'You have a *record* of it?'

'That's right. I got it in Freiburg the other day. It's sung by Marlene Dietrich. Marlene, singing about Marlene, for my Marlene. What could be more fitting? Come here, you.'

He stretched out his hand; she took it, and he pulled her to her feet; he waltzed her to the armchair, plonked himself down and pulled her down to his lap.

'Did you know that Marlene Dietrich moved to America? Gave up her German citizenship? Changed sides? There's even an English version of 'Lili Marlene'. All the soldiers listen to Radio Belgrade, on all sides.'

'I didn't know that,' said Sibyl.

'Probably a good decision on her part. History will adore her for it, and hate Germans. We will be the scum of the earth. When they find out what Himmler has done…'

He shook his head; but he had provided the perfect opening for her proposal. She stroked his hand.

'Wolf. Why don't you do that too?'

His head jerked away. His voice was stern.

'Do what?'

'Change sides.'

'You mean, defect? Join the Allies? Commit treason?'

She detected a note of outrage; it wasn't working. His *Soldatenstolz,* his soldier's pride and sense of loyalty, his very Germanness was too deep. She'd have to backtrack, approach this from a different angle. He was not to be turned…at least, not yet. She had planted a seed; she must let it grow. Soon he would understand that after the war, being German would be a shameful thing. History would condemn his Fatherland for plunging the world into such horrors. And if it was true, what he had told her about concentration camps – well, surely that was even more reason to defect, to stand on the side of the victorious Allies; the side of righteousness! It would take time, but she would convince him. Slowly, steadily, she would bring him to her side, coax him into treachery. Make of him an ally. She knew exactly how. She stroked his cheek, kissed his forehead, then his lips. She spoke softly, winningly.

'I meant, join the winning side; it seems the Allies are going to win. The Russians are two steps from Berlin: you heard it on the BBC! What then, Wolf? I mean, with us? Surely it would be a good idea for you to reconcile with the idea of Alsace being French again? Think of it. What does it matter, if Alsace is French or German? We can still live here together. We can still make it our home. It doesn't have to be German, does it?'

He was silent for while. Took a sip of his wine. She waited.

'I suppose not. But we would be ostracised. You would be hated as a collaborator. Our children would be outcasts.'

'I think people would get used to us. And we would just teach our children to be strong, even as outcasts. If the parents are strong, the children are strong. I think we should start planning ahead.'

'It's is all I dream of. Making a home with you…living in peace. Starting a family.'

'Me too. And I do want to stay here, in Alsace. Alsace is my home; my birthright.'

'Alsace is a bloodbath right now.'

'But after the war it will be cleaned up. We can do as you said: buy a house here, settle in. Build a life of peace.'

He sighed in ecstasy. 'Children. I want children. Lots of them. Six or seven.'

She chuckled. 'Six or seven? That's too many, Wolf!'

'I was an only child – I longed for brothers and sisters!'

'We can have a *few* children, just not six or seven!'

She held up three fingers. 'Three! That's how many. One of each, and then one of either. Two boys and a girl or two girls and a boy. Oh Wolf!'

But his body had stiffened. He did not smile, nor even meet her eyes. In fact, he was pushing her away, and his face was grim, scowling.

'Wolf? What's the matter, Wolf?'

He pushed her to her feet; she stumbled. He did not help her find her balance. He strode across the room to the table. And in that moment realisation dawned.

Three. The number three. Thee fingers.

She had held up three fingers, like the English.

The Germans, when counting on their fingers, started with the thumb. So did the French. They had taught her this in training. She had completely forgotten.

He had seen it immediately. Seen her for what she was: a spy. In an instant, Marlene collapsed and all there was left was Jeanne. She knew what he was doing, there at the table, at the briefcase.

In a trice she had grabbed the knife resting on the plate next to the ham. Grabbed it and lunged across the room, knife in hand. His back was still turned to her: he seemed to be hesitating; was that a shudder? That little jolt of his shoulder – was it a sob? But *she* could not afford to hesitate. His back was turned; it was a cowardly thing but there was no time for scruples now. She had to do it. She had no choice. Plunging it into his back would not kill him but it would wound him, wound him enough to, to perhaps, talk? Explain? Kill? Could she do it? Would he listen, once wounded? Could she save it all? A cry, a stifled sob, escaped her lips as she rushed to him, arm raised, knife poised to attack.

But in that moment he swung around and grabbed her wrist, twisted it, forced it open. She cried out in pain, and the knife dropped from her fingers.

'Cheat! Hypocrite! Liar,' he snarled.

'No, no, Wolf, it's not true! I love you! I was going to tell you everything! I was going to…'

But he had let go of her hand and in his he held his Luger, aimed at her.

Her hands flew up above her head. He cocked the pistol. It clicked as he released the safety catch.

'Please. Wolf, Wolf, listen to me. Don't do this. Please understand. I changed. I was going to…'

'How could you? I loved you. I love you.'

And with those words his hand whipped backwards, the barrel aimed at his own head and a split second later, that head, that beloved head – which just minutes ago she had clasped to her breast and stroked and kissed – exploded, erupted into a red burst of blood and brains and bone and the body beneath it collapsed to the floor, and all that was left was the piercing scream splitting her throat. A scream that seemed to go on forever until at last, exhausted, it spluttered into a low moan of agony.

Covered in blood herself, slivers of brain and splinters of bone all over her clothes, Sibyl finally stood up and stumbled her way down the stairs, out the back door, across the courtyard and over to her own home. The home that had never been a home.

# Chapter Fifty-Two

The *Kripo* came later that day. Sibyl was in no state to be interviewed but her grief was so palpable, her devastation so complete, they did not stay long; the coroner's verdict of suicide would not be contested. It was obvious.

*Oncle* Yves supplied the missing information: yes, his niece Marlene Schuster, von Haagen's dearly beloved fiancée, had been with him when he had turned the gun on himself. He had been severely depressed due to the inevitability of German defeat. *Fräulein* Schuster could not have prevented it; it all happened too quickly and she was plainly shattered by the event. He himself had gone across to ascertain what had happened after her arrival home; he had then reported the death to police headquarters. That was all.

On further questioning he admitted to removing a side of ham and a half-full bottle of gewürztraminer from the scene; charges of theft were made and later dropped.

Sibyl went into hibernation, refusing to leave her room for any reason but the bathroom and toilet. She sobbed beneath the eiderdown, her head usually buried in a pillow, or else she slept, falling into coma-like slumber that could last all day or all night. Margaux came once the snow was adequately cleared. Jacques was with her. She did not respond to either. A week passed, and another and another.

And then came the day that *Oncle* Yves refused to indulge her a moment longer.

'You are getting out of bed today!' he scolded. 'You are getting dressed and coming with me!'

He forced her out of bed. He pulled clothes on to her, even while she protested. He dragged her down the stairs, pushed her arms into the sleeves of her sheepskin jacket and her feet into her boots. He hauled her out of the front door and along the streets to the main square of Colmar. It was crowded: filled with laughing citizens, cheering and singing the Marsellaise, rejoicing, dancing citizens crying *France is free! Alsace is free!*

Earlier that day army tanks once more had rolled through the streets of Colmar; the citizens, peering from their windows, had at first doubted what they saw. Had the Boche returned? Whose tanks were these? But slowly the news spread and they emerged from their cellars and poured into the streets, singing and cheering. The tanks were French!

Sibyl watched as the overjoyed people ripped banners and flags bearing the swastika from the town hall and all the buildings; she smiled to see them trampling over discarded swastika flags, hundreds and thousands of them. Soldiers of the Free French marched by, now and then grabbing a girl and hugging her and dancing with her, and singing, and cheering, and more singing; bottles of Alsatian wine passed from hand to hand, lips to lips. Bells from all the churches rang out in joy; people, strangers, clutched each other, danced. Someone grabbed Sibyl and swung her around. She smiled; at last, she laughed.

Later, they watched as a group of citizens walked the streets and wrenched the German road signs from the walls; and nailed new French signs at every street corner; obviously improvised, painted on wooden slats until proper signs could be made. She watched as the hated *Gerechtigkeitsgasse* sign was torn from the wall of her own lane, and the new sign *Rue des Géraniums* nailed on in its stead.

On February 5th the last of Colmar's German troops retreated over the Neuf-Brisach bridge, the bridge Jacques had tried and failed to demolish. Once the Boche reached the other side they blew up the bridge themselves.

On February 9th, further north from Colmar, the last German forces retreated over the Chalampé bridge. That bridge, too, they bombed behind them. It was the final act in the drama of the annexation of Alsace.

The Allies crossed the Rhine anyway. On March 7, 1945, US forces captured the railway bridge at Remagen, which German troops had tried, but failed to destroy, one of very few bridges across the Rhine still standing. And it enabled thousands of Allied troops to cross the river and make their way east, to the discovery of horrors that equalled those of war.

'My darling,' said Margaux when Sibyl finally turned up on her doorstep. 'What took you so long?'

She released the woman she regarded as a daughter. Sibyl shrugged, smiled; she still struggled with words. But then Margaux was Margaux again, talking nineteen to the dozen and rustling up a hearty stew.

'The last of the rabbits,' she said. 'It's a good thing the war is over. Excellent timing.'

She glanced up at the clock.

'They will be in soon, and starving,' she said. 'They are all clearing the snow over at Madame Boucher's. They can't wait to see you.'

'Who are *they?*' asked Sibyl, already weary – and wary. 'Is Jacques among them? Is he coming?' She couldn't face Jacques. Not yet, and not now, with others around. Maybe never. Margaux made it sound as if an entire village was about to descend on them.

'No, not Jacques. Jacques is very busy these days. But – well, you'll see!'

She saw. They came, and among them were three unexpected faces, two familiar, one quite new.

'Maxence!' cried Sibyl, throwing her arms around Jacques' father, but then, 'Marie-Claire! Oh Marie-Claire! How wonderful to see you!'

Marie-Claire came forward and hugged her.

'I am a widow now. And my mother has finally forgiven me.'

'Yes. She has paid penance enough. A daughter is always a daughter,' said Margaux.

A stranger came forward, holding out his hand in greeting, a man of unbearable thinness, his eyes sunken into the hollows of skeletal cheeks, clothes hanging on to a basic framework of bones.

'Meet Hanner,' said Margaux. 'Hanner Koch. He is Victoire's protégé, one of the waifs and strays she is always collecting – she takes after me in that. But this one is German.'

'I have heard all about you,' said Hanner in broken French, 'and I could not wait to meet you. I was hiding in the forests and this kind girl found me.'

'Hiding in the forests? In this weather?' She spoke German; his French was terrible.

'Well – someone helped me. He refused to speak German even though I think he understood me. He only spoke French. He hid me in a castle and then led me through the forest to a kind of wooden hut. There was a little stove, and logs. And dried fish. And then Victoire here found me. The man brought her. She is his sister.'

He placed an arm around Victoire and pulled her forward.

'*Il est beau, n'est pas?*' said Victoire, planting a kiss on his stubbly cheek, and indeed, the deserter, for that was what he was, showed signs of rugged handsomeness once he was fed back to health. Hanner obviously had a story to tell, one of survival and rebellion. She would hear all these stories – in time.

'Lucien is alive,' said Margaux then. 'He is in a prisoner of war camp in Germany but will soon be released. And Maxence and I are to be married. Jean-Pierre has finally filed for divorce – he wants to marry his mistress, who is now a rich widow. It is complicated but we will get there in the end. And then Maxence will recover the vineyard he once lost, and we will run the vineyard as partners.'

Hiding behind Maxence was a diminutive person Sibyl had not noticed at first; a woman. She came forward, holding out her hand; in her other hand was that of a child.

'I want to thank you,' said Grete, 'for arranging for my rescue. Yvonne and I are now safe but we were in grave danger. We had nothing to do with that bombing, nothing!'

'I know that,' said Sibyl, as she hugged her. 'But it was not me who arranged your rescue. It must have been Jacques.'

'I have heard of this Jacques,' said Grete, 'But I have not met him yet. I look forward to doing so. He is quite famous now – a hero of France.'

'I know.'

There was one more person to greet. Elena, who had kept to the back of the room as Sibyl was welcomed. Finally she came forward, arms held out, and Sibyl fell against her with a sigh of deep satisfaction.

'We must talk later,' Elena whispered into her ear.

After dinner they talked, just the three of them, Sibyl, Elena and Margaux.

'Acrobat says we must return as soon as possible,' said Elena. 'He will send a plane for us. The trouble is the landing field is deep in snow. As soon as we have cleared it we must get ready to be picked up.'

'But I don't want to go back!' cried Sibyl, 'I need to stay here!'

'You must, we must. It's a matter of demobilisation. Our job is over; we need to be officially signed off. Official Secrets Act, thanks for your sacrifice, and all that. Our work is done.'

'Then I will go and come back. It's not nearly done for me!'

'You mean…Jacques?'

'Among other things. But Jacques – Margaux, it will take time before I can face Jacques again and we can both digest what has happened, and talk. It's not easy. I would prefer – to wait.'

'Wait for what? The sooner you put the past behind you the better, Sibyl. That episode with your German soldier – it was an aberration. It was not real.'

'It was very real, for me.'

'I'm not going to argue with you, Sibyl. You are adult and must know what you are doing.'

'I do. I've already spoken to someone from the Red Cross. I am going to volunteer with them, as a nurse. Go with them into Germany. The war is not yet over. There is work to be done.'

'Ah, that's a good idea. It will help you to help others, I think. Very good…and…oh! But I heard there was a will? He left you everything? Is that the real reason you want to return? Are you going to claim your inheritance? Will his parents contest it?'

'I am not that mercenary.' Sibyl looked straight into Margaux's eyes. 'I told you this before, Margaux. I have no legal right to anything he might leave me. His will – well, he left it all to Marlene Schuster, as I told you, who does not exist, for she is an alias of Jeanne Dauguet, who is dead. I am not going to take what is not rightly mine.'

'Nobody need know that you are not Jeanne Dauguet. And besides…I'm sure a good lawyer could make the argument that it is YOU he loved and left everything to, not some ghost.'

'It's possible. But I would never make such a claim, or fight such a battle. It wouldn't be right.'

Margaux shrugged. 'If you say so.'

An awkward silence fell between them, filled by a name they all seemed reluctant to mention; a name that kept cropping up only to be dismissed again. As if it didn't matter. Though they all knew it did. Finally Sibyl found the courage to speak it.

'So – Jacques? You said he's busy? Busy doing what?'

The back door blew open with a gust of cold air. And there he stood.

'Speak of the devil,' said Jacques, and swept Sibyl into his arms.

Margaux and Elena melted discreetly into the parlour. Jacques rubbed his hands together, blew on them to warm them. 'It is freezing outside,' he said.

'Shall I make you a tisane? It will warm you.'

'You will warm me,' said Jacques. He sat down at a kitchen chair and pulled Sibyl onto his lap. A ridiculous shyness overcame her. She had no words, could not look at him.

'Look at me!'

She did. But then she stood up and put a kettle on the stove to boil water for his tisane.

'It's all right, Sibi. I know. You did a job. Everything you did was right.'

'You don't know,' she whispered as she opened a cupboard for a mug. 'It's not fair. Jacques, not fair to you. Everything has changed. Our hopes, our promises – I have betrayed everything. I am going to volunteer with the Red Cross. I am going to work in Germany.'

'Ha! Since when do you owe the Germans your allegiance?'

'Because I – because…'

'It is over, Sibi. The war is over. Last year we promised each other that when the war was over, our life would begin.'

'Everything has changed. I have changed. You have changed. I must find a different future. There is so much work to be done. There are tasks to be done. The concentration camps in Germany…'

'Sibi, there is work to be done *everywhere*. Alsace is in ruins. I am helping to build it up again. People are desperate, homeless, starving, sick. Why would you run off to work in Germany, when Alsace is bleeding?'

*Guilt,* she wanted to say. *Because I misled a good German and I am responsible for his death.* But she could not say it. Not to Jacques. Instead, she said:

'It's a long story, Jacques, and I will tell you one day. But not today.'

She placed herbs in Margaux's old cracked teapot. She filled it with hot water.

'I don't want to hear your story. Ever. It is over. It has all been
a terrible nightmare and we all did things that we'd never have
done if not for one insane tyrant. He has destroyed Europe, Sibi.
Will you let him destroy your life as well? I remember so well that
day when you dropped from the sky. I remember the almost full
moon, the whiteness of your parachute, and then the joy that lit
your eyes when you recognised me. You brought goodness with
you; I felt it, I knew it, that night. Will you let that tyrant destroy
that goodness? We must move on, Sibi, away from destruction. We
must heal what has been destroyed. You and me. We must stand
up in the middle of these ruins and find healing – for ourselves
and for the world around us.'

'Here is your tisane.' She placed a steaming cup on the table
before him. He cupped it with his hands. Then he let go, pulled
her to his lap, placed her hands around the cup, and his around
hers. He held her close. Spoke so softly she could hardly hear his
voice. Slowly, gently, hesitantly and at first his voice cracked as he
spoke, as if he himself was cracked, deep inside; but with every
word strength gathered and filled the words, until at last they
became triumphant.

'We Alsatian winemakers have a saying. In a year when a war
begins, the wine is bad. It is a reflection of the life outside, Sibi, a
mirror of the evil in the world. The wine is bad and our hearts are
filled with fear and loathing. But in a year when a war ends, the
wine is good, and our hearts are filled with goodness. This will be
a good year.'

# A Letter from Sharon Maas

Dear Readers,

I do hope that you enjoyed reading *The Soldier's Girl* as much as I enjoyed writing it, and that as you turned the last pages you felt something of the satisfaction I felt at writing the last words; that sense of arriving at a journey's end. If you did enjoy it, and want to keep up-to-date with all my latest releases, just sign up at the following link. Your email address will never be shared and you can unsubscribe at any time.

*www.bookouture.com/sharon-maas*

And what a trip it's been. It really began many decades ago, when I was a student in the wonderful South Germany town of Freiburg, just across the Rhine from Colmar. Every summer I would visit my dear friend Trudel, an extraordinary woman who in those years had become something of an Ersatz-mother to me. I first met Trudel in 1974, in India; she took me under her wing, rather in the way Margaux, in *The Soldier's Girl*, takes young people, waifs and strays, under her wing. After all, I was more or less on my own in Germany, finding my legs and my independence after a failed marriage.

Trudel was born in Ribeauvillé and considered herself an Alsatian; but she told me very little about Alsace during the summers I spent with her. Her stories were of Berlin during the war years, and of the incredible island on the Seddiner See where she met her future husband, unforgettable stories of unforgettable people. Her home near Colmar, nestled in the garden she so loved, was a magnet for young people like me; I will never forget the 80th birthday party her children Regine and Thomas threw for her, when the older 'Berliner' crowd met with the younger generation. She was truly a stalwart; one of those marvellous women who, just by being who they are, bring strength and inspiration to others. Trudel passed away at the ripe old age of 102, physically frail as one would expect of a woman of her age, but mentally as astute and wise as ever. She had been living alone in that Alsatian house, winter and summer, for many years at the time.

So when my publishers suggested that I might like to try my hand at a World War II novel, the setting was as clear as day. Where else but Alsace?

It seemed the perfect place: not only one of the most picturesque regions of France, but a place I already loved, balanced as it was between the two European countries I knew the best. But that was just the beginning...

The story of Alsace, I discovered, is a captivating chapter the history books almost forgot to tell. It gave me great joy to discover that chapter for myself, and now to tell that tale as a backdrop to Sibyl's story. Somehow, I felt that it was Trudel guiding my hand as I wrote it.

I hope you loved *The Soldier's Girl* and if you did I would be very grateful if you could write a review. I'd love to hear what you think, and it makes such a difference helping new readers to discover one of my books for the first time.

I love hearing from my readers – you can get in touch on my Facebook page, through Twitter, Goodreads or my website.

Thanks,
Sharon Maas

sharonmaasauthor

@sharon_maas

www.sharonmaas.com

# Historical Notes

This is a work of fiction, but the historical background – the annexation and liberation of Alsace – is true. I have added a detail to the known history: a Resistance movement. An Alsatian living today might inform you that there was no Resistance in Alsace because it was annexed, not occupied. But fiction is all about 'what if' and I am sure there were people such as Jacques and the other *maquisards*, young men and even women who loathed the situation so much that they tried to do something about it. Marcel Weinum was one of these; he lived, resisted, and was executed for his troubles, aged only 18. Had he not been executed no-one would have heard of him. Let us remember him and others like him who resisted anonymously, forgotten by history.

There was no Special Operations Executive agent sent to Alsace. There were, indeed, only 39 female SOE agents. Sibyl is a fictitious 40th female agent.

Heinrich Himmler was indeed appointed Commander of the Alsace action, Operation Northwind, reporting directly to Hitler; he did go to Alsace. However, as far as I know, there was no assassination attempt against him. More's the pity!

# Acknowledgements

Thanks to my super editor Lydia Vassar-Smith for her enthusiasm for this story and her help in sending it out into the world and into the hands of my readers. Also huge thanks to Claire Bord, Jacqui Lewis, Lauren Finger, Kim Nash, Ellen Gleeson and to everyone else on the Bookouture team – last but not least, of course, Oliver Rhodes!

Thanks of course to my children, Saskia and Miro. It's so easy to fly off into a fictional world and never return; thanks to you all for helping to keep me grounded!

76313198R10228

Made in the USA
Columbia, SC
23 September 2019